Ed McBain is one of the most illustrious names in crime fiction. In 1998, he was the first non-British author to be awarded the Crime Writers' Association Cartier Diamond Dagger Award and he is also a holder of the Mystery Writers of America's coveted Grand Master Award. Ed McBain died in 2005. Visit his website at www.edmcbain.com.

TRANSGRESSIONS

Three brand new novellas

JEFFERY DEAVER
ED McBAIN
JOYCE CAROL OATES

Edited by Ed McBain

An Orion paperback

First published in Great Britain in 2005
by Orion
This paperback edition published in 2006
by Orion Books Ltd,
Orion House, 5 Upper St Martin's Lane,
London WC2H 9EA

1 3 5 7 9 10 8 6 4 2

A CIP catalogue record for this book
is available from the British Library.

ISBN 13: 978-0-7528-7947-5
ISBN 10: 0-7528-7947-2

Printed in Great Britain by Clays Ltd, St Ives plc

The Orion Publishing Group's policy is to use papers that
are natural, renewable and recyclable products and made
from wood grown in sustainable forests. The logging and
manufacturing processes are expected to conform to the
environmental regulations of the country of origin.

www.orionbooks.co.uk

Contents

Introduction

When I was writing novellas for the pulp magazines back in the 1950s, we still called them "novelettes," and all I knew about the form was that it was long and it paid half a cent a word. This meant that if I wrote 10,000 words, the average length of a novelette back then, I would sooner or later get a check for five hundred dollars. This was not bad pay for a struggling young writer.

A novella today can run anywhere from 10,000 to 40,000 words. Longer than a short story (5,000 words) but much shorter than a novel (at least 60,000 words) it combines the immediacy of the former with the depth of the latter, and it ain't easy to write. In fact, given the difficulty of the form, and the scarcity of markets for novellas, it is surprising that any writers today are writing them at all.

But here was the brilliant idea.

Round up the best writers of mystery, crime, and suspense novels, and ask them to write a brand-new novella for a collection of similarly superb novellas to be published anywhere in the world for the very first time. Does that sound keen, or what? In a perfect world, *yes*, it *is* a wonderful idea, and here is your novella, sir, thank you very much for asking me to contribute.

But many of the bestselling novelists I approached had never written a novella in their lives. (Some of them had never even written a short story!) Up went the hands in mock horror. "What! A novella? I wouldn't even know how to *begin* one." Others thought that writing a novella ("*How* long did you say it had to be?") would constitute a wonderful challenge, but bestselling novelists are busy people with publishing contracts to fulfill and deadlines to meet, and however intriguing the invitation may have seemed at first, stark reality reared its ugly head, and so . . .

"Gee, thanks for thinking of me, but I'm already three months behind deadline," or . . .

"My publisher would *kill* me if I even dreamed of writing something for another house," or . . .

"Try me again a year from now," or . . .

"Have you asked X? Or Y? Or Z?"

What it got down to in the end was a matter of timing and luck. In some cases, a writer I desperately wanted was happily between novels and just happened to have some free time on his/her hands. In other cases, a writer had an idea that was too short for a novel but too long for a short story, so yes, what a wonderful opportunity! In yet other cases, a writer wanted to introduce a new character he or she had been thinking about for some time. In each and every case, the formidable task of writing fiction that fell somewhere between 10,000 and 40,000 words seemed an exciting challenge, and the response was enthusiastic.

Except for length and a loose adherence to crime, mystery, or suspense, I placed no restrictions upon the writers who agreed to contribute. The results are as astonishing as they are brilliant. The ten novellas that follow are as varied as the men and women who concocted them, but they all exhibit the same devoted passion and the same extraordinary writing. More than that, there is an underlying sense here that the writer is attempting something new and unexpected, and willing to share his or her own surprises with us. Just as their names are in alphabetical order on the book jacket, so do their stories follow in reverse alphabetical order: I have no favorites among them. I love them all equally.

Enjoy!

ED MCBAIN
Weston, Connecticut
August 2004

TRANSGRESSIONS

JEFFERY DEAVER

Jeffery Deaver has had a rapid and much-deserved rise to the top of the bestseller lists. His novels have always been riveting reads, especially those he wrote about Rune, a woman living and working in New York City. Seen through her eyes, the urban landscape is a wondrous—and sometimes frightening—place indeed. Fans of his work know that this is to be expected, or he can take the most commonplace career or event—news reporting, marriage—and turn it upside down with one of the surprising plot twists that have become his trademark. These days, he writes such bestsellers as *Praying for Sleep*, *A Maiden's Grave*, *Hard News*, and *The Bone Collector*, featuring the brilliant quadriplegic detective Lincoln Rhyme and his assistant Amelia Sachs. *The Bone Collector* was the basis for the successful movie of the same name starring Denzel Washington and Angelina Jolie. His readership expands with each new novel, and with each new short story he writes. His most recent novel is *The Twelfth Card*, and a collection of short stories, *Twisted*, came out in November 2004.

FOREVER

Jeffery Deaver

Mathematics is not a careful march down a well-cleared highway,
but a journey into a strange wilderness, where the explorers often
get lost.

—W. S. ANGLIN, "Mathematics and History"

∞

An old couple like that, the man thought, acting like kids.

Didn't have a clue how crazy they looked.

Peering over the boxwood hedge he was trimming, the gardener
was looking at Sy and Donald Benson on the wide, back deck of
their house, sitting in a rocking love seat and drinking champagne.
Which they'd had plenty of. That was for sure.

Giggling, laughing, loud.

Like kids, he thought contemptuously.

But enviously too a little. Not at their wealth—oh, he didn't re-
sent that; he made a good living tending the grounds of the Bensons'
neighbors, who were just as rich.

No, the envy was simply that even at this age they looked like
they were way in love and happy.

The gardener tried to remember when he'd laughed like that
with his wife. Must've been ten years. And holding hands like the
Bensons were doing? Hardly ever since their first year together.

The electric hedge trimmer beckoned but the man lit a cigarette
and continued to watch them. They poured the last of the champagne into their glasses and finished it. Then Donald leaned for-

ward, whispering something in the woman's ear and she laughed again. She said something back and kissed his cheek.

Gross. And here they were, totally ancient. Sixties, probably. It was like seeing his own parents making out. Christ . . .

They stood up and walked to a metal table on the edge of the patio and piled dishes from their lunch on a tray, still laughing, still talking. With the old guy carrying the tray, they both headed into the kitchen, the gardener wondering if he'd drop it, he was weaving so much. But, no, they made it inside all right and shut the door.

The man flicked the butt into the grass and turned back to examine the boxwood hedge.

A bird trilled nearby, a pretty whistle. The gardener knew a lot about plants but not so much about wildlife and he wasn't sure what kind of bird this was.

But there was no mistaking the sound that cut through the air a few seconds later and made the gardener freeze where he stood, between a crimson azalea and a purple. The gunshot, coming from inside the Bensons' house, was quite distinctive. Only a moment later he heard a second shot.

The gardener stared at the huge Tudor house for three heartbeats, then, as the bird resumed its song, he dropped the hedge trimmer and sprinted back to his truck where he'd left his cell phone.

The county of Westbrook, New York, is a large trapezoid of suburbs elegant and suburbs mean, parks, corporate headquarters and light industry—a place where the majority of residents earn their keep by commuting into Manhattan, some miles to the south.

Last year this generally benign-looking county of nearly 900,000 had been the site of 31 murders, 107 rapes, 1,423 robberies, 1,575 aggravated assaults, 4,360 burglaries, 16,955 larcenies, and 4,130 automobile thefts, resulting in a crime rate of 3,223.3 per 100,000 population, or 3.22 percent for these so-called "index crimes," a standardized list of offenses used nationwide by statisticians to compare one community to another, and each community to its own past. This year Westbrook County was faring poorly compared with last. Its year-to-date index crime rate was already hovering near 4.5 percent and the temper-inflaming months of summer were still to come.

These facts—and thousands of others about the pulse of the

county—were readily available to whoever might want them, thanks largely to a slim young man, eyes as dark as his neatly cut and combed hair, who was presently sitting in a small office on the third floor of the Westbrook County Sheriff's Department, the Detective Division. On his door were two signs. One said, DET. TALBOT SIMMS. The other read, FINANCIAL CRIMES/STATISTICAL SERVICES.

The Detective Division was a large open space, surrounded by a U of offices. Tal and the support services were on one ascending stroke of the letter, dubbed the "Unreal Crimes Department" by everybody on the other arm (yes, the "Real Crimes Department," though the latter was officially labeled Major Crimes and Tactical Services).

This April morning Tal Simms sat in his immaculate office, studying one of the few items spoiling the smooth landscape of his desktop: a spreadsheet—evidence in a stock scam perpetrated in Manhattan. The Justice Department and the SEC were jointly running the case but there was a small local angle that required Tal's attention.

Absently adjusting his burgundy-and-black striped tie, Tal jotted some notes in his minuscule, precise handwriting as he observed a few inconsistencies in the numbers on the spreadsheet. Hmm, he was thinking, a .588 that should've been a .743. Small but extremely incriminating. He'd have to—

His hand jerked suddenly as a deep voice boomed outside his door, "It was a goddamn suicide. Waste of time."

Erasing the errant pencil tail from the margins of the spreadsheet, Tal saw the bulky form of the head of Homicide—Detective Greg LaTour—stride through the middle of the pen, past secretaries and communications techs, and push into his own office, directly across from Tal's. With a loud clunk the detective dropped a backpack on his desk.

"What?" somebody called. "The Bensons?"

"Yeah, that was them," LaTour called. "On Meadowridge in Greeley."

"Came in as a homicide."

"Well, it fucking wasn't."

Technically, it *was* a homicide—all non-accidental deaths were, even suicides, reflected Tal Simms, whose life was devoted to making the finest of distinctions. But to correct the temperamental Greg LaTour you had to either be a good friend or have a good reason and Tal fell into none of these categories.

"Gardener working next door heard a coupla shots, called it in," LaTour grumbled. "Some blind rookie from Greeley P.D. responded."

"Blind?"

"Had to be. Looked at the scene and thought they'd been murdered. Why don't the local boys stick to traffic?"

Like everyone else in the department Tal had been curious about the twin deaths. Greeley was an exclusive enclave in Westbrook and—Tal had looked it up—had never been the scene of a double murder. He wondered if the fact that the incident was a double *suicide* would bring the event slightly back toward the statistical norm.

Tal straightened the spreadsheet and his notepad, set his pencil in its holder, then walked over to the Real Crimes portion of the room. He stepped through LaTour's doorway.

"So, suicide?" Tal asked.

The hulking homicide detective, sporting a goatee and weighing nearly twice what Tal did, said, "Yeah. It was so fucking obvious to me. . . . But we got the crime scene boys in to make sure. They found GSR on—"

"Global—?" Tal interrupted.

"GSR. Gunshot residue. On both their hands. Her first, then him."

"How do you know?"

LaTour looked at Tal with a well, duh blink. "He was lying on top of her."

"Oh. Sure."

LaTour continued. "There was a note too. And the gardener said they were acting like teenagers—drunk on their asses, staggering around."

"Staggering."

"Old folks. Geezers, he said. Acting like kids."

Tal nodded. "Say, I was wondering. You happen to do a questionnaire?"

"Questionnaire?" he asked. "Oh, your questionnaire. Right. You know, Tal, it was just a suicide."

Tal nodded. "Still, I'd like to get that data."

"Data plural," LaTour said, pointing a finger at him and flashing a big, phony grin. Tal had once sent around a memo that included the sentence "The data were very helpful." When another cop corrected him Tal had said, "Oh, *data*'s plural; *datum*'s singular." The ensuing ragging taught him a pointed lesson about correcting fellow cops' grammar.

"Right," Tal said wearily. "Plural. It'd—"

LaTour's phone rang and he grabbed it. " 'Lo? . . . I don't know, couple days we'll have the location . . . Naw, I'll go in with SWAT. I wanta piece of him personal. . . ."

Tal looked around the office. A Harley poster. Another, of a rearing grizzly—"Bear" was LaTour's nickname. A couple of flyblown certificates from continuing education courses. No other decorations. The desk, credenza, and chairs were filled with an irritating mass of papers, dirty coffee cups, magazines, boxes of ammunition, bullet-riddled targets, depositions, crime lab reports, a scabby billy club. The big detective continued into the phone, "When? . . . Yeah, I'll let you know." He slammed the phone down and glanced back at Tal. "Anyway. I didn't think you'd want it, being a suicide. The questionnaire, you know. Not like a murder."

"Well, it'd still be pretty helpful."

LaTour was wearing what he usually did, a black leather jacket cut like a sport coat and blue jeans. He patted the many pockets involved in the outfit. "Shit, Tal. Think I lost it. The questionnaire, I mean. Sorry. You have another one?" He grabbed the phone, made another call.

"I'll get you one," Tal said. He returned to his office, picked up a questionnaire from a neat pile on his credenza and returned to LaTour. The cop was still on the phone, speaking in muted but gruff tones. He glanced up and nodded at Tal, who set the sheet on his desk.

LaTour mouthed, Thank you.

Tal waited a moment and asked, "Who else was there?"

"What?" LaTour frowned, irritated at being interrupted. He clapped his hand over the mouthpiece.

"Who else was at the scene?"

"Where the Bensons offed themselves? Fuck, I don't know. Fire and Rescue. That Greeley P.D. kid." A look of concentration that Tal didn't believe. "A few other guys. Can't remember." The detective returned to his conversation.

Tal walked back to his office, certain that the questionnaire was presently being slam-dunked into LaTour's wastebasket.

He called the Fire and Rescue Department but couldn't track down anybody who'd responded to the suicide. He gave up for the time being and continued working on the spreadsheet.

After a half hour he paused and stretched. His eyes slipped from the spreadsheet to the pile of blank questionnaires. A Xeroxed note was stapled neatly to each one, asking the responding or case officer to fill it out in full and explaining how helpful the information would be. He'd agonized over writing that letter (numbers came easy to Talbot Simms, words hard). Still, he knew the officers didn't take the questionnaire seriously. They joked about it. They joked about *him* too, calling him "Einstein" or "Mr. Wizard" behind his back.

1. Please state nature of incident:

He found himself agitated, then angry, tapping his mechanical pencil on the spreadsheet like a drumstick. Anything not filled out properly rankled Talbot Simms; that was his nature. But an unanswered questionnaire was particularly irritating. The information the forms harvested was important. The art and science of statistics not only compiles existing information but is used to make vital decisions and predict trends. Maybe a questionnaire in this case would reveal some fact, some *datum*, that would help the county better understand elderly suicides and save lives.

4. Please indicate the sex, approximate age, and apparent nationality and/or race of each victim:

The empty lines on the questions were like an itch—aggravated by hot-shot LaTour's condescending attitude.

"Hey, there, Boss." Shellee, Tal's firecracker of a secretary, stepped into his office. "*Finally* got the Templeton files. Sent 'em by mule train from Albany's my guess." With massive blonde ringlets and the feistiness of a truck-stop waitress compressed into a five-foot, hundred-pound frame, Shellee looked as if she'd sling out words with a twangy Alabaman accent but her intonation was pure Hahvahd Square Bostonian.

"Thanks." He took the dozen folders she handed off, examined the numbers on the front of each and rearranged them in ascending order on the credenza behind his desk.

"Called the SEC again and they promise, promise, promise they'll have us the—Hey, you leaving early?" She was frowning, looking at her watch, as Tal stood, straightened his tie and pulled on the thin, navy-blue raincoat he wore to and from the office.

"Have an errand."

A frown of curiosity filled her round face, which was deceptively girlish (Tal knew she had a twenty-one year-old-daughter and a husband who'd just retired from the phone company). "Sure. You do? Didn't see anything on your calender."

The surprise was understandable. Tal had meetings out of the office once or twice a month at the most. He was virtually always at his desk, except when he went out for lunch, which he did at twelve-thirty every day, joining two or three friends from a local university at the Corner Tap Room up the street.

"Just came up."

"Be back?" Shellee asked.

He paused. "You know, I'm not really sure." He headed for the elevator.

The white-columned Colonial on Meadowridge had to be worth six, seven million. Tal pulled his Honda Accord into the circular drive, behind a black sedan, which he hoped belonged to a Greeley P.D. officer, somebody who might have the information he needed. Tal took the questionnaire and two pens from his briefcase, made sure the tips were retracted then slipped them into his shirt pocket. He walked up the flagstone path to the house, the door to which was unlocked. He stepped inside and identified himself to a man in jeans and work shirt, carrying a clipboard. It was his car in the drive, he explained. He was here to meet the Bensons' lawyer about liquidating their estate and knew nothing about the Bensons or their death, other than what he'd heard about the suicides.

He stepped outside, leaving Tal alone in the house.

As he walked through the entry foyer and into the spacious first floor a feeling of disquiet came over him. It wasn't the queasy sense that somebody'd just died here; it was that the house was such an unlikely setting for death. He looked over the yellow-and-pink floral upholstery, the boldly colorful abstracts on the walls, the gold-edged china and prismatic glasses awaiting parties, the collection of crystal animals, the Moroccan pottery, shelves of well-thumbed books, framed snapshots on the walls and mantle. Two pairs of well-worn slippers—a man's size and a woman's—sat poignantly together by the back door. Tal imagined the couple taking turns to be the first to rise, make coffee and brave the dewy cold to collect *The New York Times* or the Westbrook *Ledger*.

The word that came to him was "home." The idea of the owners here shooting themselves was not only disconcerting, it was down-right eerie.

Tal noticed a sheet of paper weighted down by a crystal vase and blinked in surprise as he read it.

> To our friends:
> We're making this decison with great contentment in
> hearts, joyous in the knowldge that we'll be together
> forever.

Both Sy and Don Benson had signed it. He stared at the words for a moment then wandered to the den, which was cordoned off with crime scene tape. He stopped cold, gasping faintly.

Blood.

On the couch, on the carpet, on the wall.

He could clearly see where the couple had been when they'd died; the blood explained the whole scenario to him. Brown, opaque, dull. He found himself breathing shallowly, as if the stains were giving off toxic fumes.

Tal stepped back into the living room and decided to fill out as much of the questionnaire as he could. Sitting on a couch he clicked a pen point out and picked up a book from the coffee table to use as a writing surface. He read the title: *Making the Final Journey: The Complete Guide to Suicide and Euthanasia*.

Okay . . . I don't think so. He replaced the book and made a less troubling lap desk from a pile of magazines. He filled out some of the details, then he paused, aware of the front door opening. Footsteps sounded on the foyer tile and a moment later a stocky man in an expensive suit walked into the den. He frowned.

"Sheriff's Department," Tal said and showed his ID, which the man looked at carefully.

"I'm their lawyer. George Metzer," he said slowly, visibly

shaken. "Oh, this is terrible. Just terrible. I got a call from some-body in your department. My secretary did, I mean. . . . You want to see some ID?"

Tal realized that a Real Cop would have asked for it right up front. "Please."

He looked over the driver's license and nodded, then gazed past the man's pudgy hand and looked again into the den. The blood stains were like brown laminate on cheap furniture.

"Was there a note?" the lawyer asked, putting his wallet away.

Tal walked into the dining room. He nodded toward the note. Together forever . . .

The lawyer looked it over, shook his head again. He glanced into the den and blinked, seeing the blood. Turned away.

Tal showed Metzer the questionnaire. "Can I ask you a few questions? For our statistics department? It's anonymous. We don't use names."

"Sure, I guess."

Tal began querying the man about the couple. He was surprised to learn they were only in their mid sixties, he'd assumed LaTour's assessment had been wrong and the Bensons were older.

"Any children?"

"No. No close relatives at all. A few cousins they never see. . . . Never *saw*, I mean. They had a lot of friends, though. They'll be devastated."

He got some more information, and finally felt he had nearly enough to process the data, but one more question needed an answer.

9. *Apparent motives for the incident:*

"You have any idea why they'd do this?" Tal asked.

"I know exactly," Metzer said. "Don was ill."

Tal glanced down at the note again and noticed that the writing was unsteady and a few of the words were misspelled. LaTour'd said something about them drinking but Tal remembered seeing a wicker basket full of medicine bottles sitting on the island in the kitchen. He mentioned this then asked, "Did one of them have some kind of palsy? Nerve disease?"

The lawyer said, "No, it was heart problems. Bad ones."

In space number nine Tal wrote: *Illness.* Then he asked, "And his wife?"

"No, Sy was in good health. But they were very devoted to each other. Totally in love. She must've decided she didn't want to go on without him."

"Was it terminal?"

"Not the way he described it to me," the lawyer said. "But he could've been bedridden for the rest of his life. I doubt Don could've handled that. He was so active, you know."

Tal signed the questionnaire, folded and slipped it into his pocket.

The round man gave a sigh. "I should've guessed something was up. They came to my office a couple of weeks ago and made a few changes to the will and they gave me instructions for their memorial service. I thought it was just because Don was going to have the surgery, you know, thinking about what would happen *if*. . . . But I should've read between the lines. They were planning it then, I'll bet."

He gave a sad laugh. "You know what they wanted for their memorial service? See, they weren't religious so they wanted to be cremated then have their friends throw a big party at their country club and scatter their ashes on the green at the eighteenth hole." He grew somber again. "It never occurred to me they had something like this in mind. They seemed so happy, you know? . . . Crazy fucked-up life sometimes, huh? Anyway, I've got to meet with this guy outside. Here's my card. Call me, you got any other questions, Detective."

Tal walked around the house one more time. He glanced at the calendar stuck to the refrigerator with two magnets in the shape of lobsters. *Newport Rhode Island* was written in white across the bright red tails. In the calendar box for yesterday there was a note to take the car in to have the oil changed. Two days before that Sy'd had a hair appointment.

Today's box was empty. And there was nothing in any of the future dates for the rest of April. Tal looked through the remaining months. No notations. He made a circuit of the first floor, finding nothing out of the ordinary.

Except, someone might suggest, maybe the troubled spirits left behind by two people alive that morning and now no longer so.

Tal Simms, mathematician, empirical scientist, statistician, couldn't accept any such presence. But he hardly needed to, in order to feel a churning disquiet. The stains of dark blood that had spoiled the reassuring comfort of this homey place were as chilling as any ghost could be.

When he was studying math at Cornell ten years earlier Talbot Simms dreamed of being a John Nash, a Pierre de Fermat, a Euler, a Bernoulli. By the time he hit grad school and looked around him, at the other students who wanted to be the same, he realized two things: one, that his love of the beauty of mathematics was no less than it had ever been but, two, he was utterly sick of academics.

What was the point? he wondered. Writing articles that a handful of people would read? Becoming a professor? He could have done so easily thanks to his virtually perfect test scores and grades but to him that life was like a Mobius strip—the twisted ribbon with a single surface that never ends. Teaching more teachers to teach . . .

No, he wanted a practical use for his skills and so he dropped out of graduate school. At the time there was a huge demand for statisticians and analysts on Wall Street, and Tal joined up. In theory the job seemed a perfect fit—numbers, numbers and more numbers, and a practical use for them. But he soon found something else: Wall Street mathematics was a fishy math. Tal felt pressured to skew his statistical analysis of certain companies to help his bank sell financial products to the clients. To Tal, 3 was no more nor less than 3. Yet his bosses sometimes wanted 3 to *appear* to be 2.9999 or 3.12111. There was nothing illegal about this—all the qualifications were disclosed to customers. But statistics, to Tal, helped us understand life; they weren't smoke screens to let predators sneak up on the unwary. Numbers were pure. And the glorious compensation he received didn't take the shame out of his prostitution.

On the very day he was going to quit, though, the FBI arrived in Tal's office—not for anything he or the bank had done—but to serve a warrant to examine the accounts of a client who'd been indicted in a stock scam. It turned out the agent looking over the figures was a mathematician and accountant. He and Tal had some fascinating discussions while the man pored over the records, armed with handcuffs, a large automatic pistol, and a Texas Instruments calculator.

Here at last was a logical outlet for his love of numbers. He'd always been interested in police work. As a slight, reclusive only child he'd read not only books on logarithms and trigonometry and Einstein's theories but murder mysteries as well, Agatha Christie and A. Conan Doyle. His analytical mind would often spot the surprise villain early in the story. After he'd met with the agent, he called the Bureau's personnel department. He was disappointed to learn that there was a federal government hiring freeze in effect. But, undeterred, he called the NYPD and other police departments in the metro area—including Westbrook County, where he'd lived with his family for several years before his widower father got a job teaching math at UCLA.

Westbrook, it turned out, needed someone to take over their financial crimes investigations. The only problem, the head of county personnel admitted, was that the officer would also have to be in charge of gathering and compiling statistics. But, to Tal Simms, numbers were numbers and he had no problem with the piggy-backed assignments.

One month later, Tal kissed Wall Street good-bye and moved into a tiny though pristine Tudor house in Bedford Plains, the county seat.

There was one other glitch, however, which the Westbrook County personnel office had neglected to mention, probably because it was so obvious: To be a member of the sheriff's department financial crimes unit he had to become a cop.

The four-month training was rough. Oh, the academic part about criminal law and procedure went fine. The challenge was the physical curriculum at the academy, which was a little like army basic training. Tal Simms, who was five-foot-nine and had hovered around 153 pounds since high school, had fiercely avoided all sports except volleyball, tennis, and the rifle team, none of which had buffed him up for the Suspect Takedown and Restraint course. Still, he got through it all and graduated in the top 1.4 percent of his class. The swearing-in ceremony was attended by a dozen friends from local colleges and Wall Street, as well as his father, who'd flown in from the Midwest where he was a professor of advanced mathematics at the University of Chicago. The stern man was unable to fathom why his son had taken this route but, having largely abandoned the boy for the world of numbers in his early years, Simms senior had forfeited all rights to nudge Tal's career in one direction or another.

As soon as he started work Tal learned that financial crimes were rare in Westbrook. Or, more accurately, they tended to be adjunct to federal prosecutions and Tal found himself sidelined as an investigator. He was, however, in great demand as a statistician.

Finding and analyzing data are more vital than the public thinks. Certainly crime statistics determine budget and staff hiring strategies. But, more than that, statistics can diagnose a community's ills. If the national monthly average for murders of teenagers by other teenagers in neighborhoods with a mean income of $26,000 annual is .03, and Kendall Heights in southern Westbrook was home to 1.1 such killings per month, why? And what could be done to fix the problem?

Hence, the infamous questionnaire.

Now, 6:30 P.M., armed with the one he'd just completed, Tal returned to his office from the Benson house. He inputted the information from the form into his database and placed the questionnaire itself into his to-be-filed basket. He stared at the information on the screen for a moment then began to log off. But he changed his mind and went online to the Internet and searched some databases. Then he read the brief official report on the Bensons' suicides.

He jumped when someone walked into his office. "Hey, Boss." Shellee blinked. "Thought you were gone."

"Just wanted to finish up a few things here."

"I've got that stuff you wanted."

He glanced at it. The title was, "Supplemental reports. SEC case 04-5432."

"Thanks," he said absently, staring at his printouts.

"Sure." She eyed him carefully. "You need anything else?"

"No, go on home. . . . 'Night." When she turned away, though, he glanced at the computer screen once more and said, "Wait, Shell. You ever work in Crime Scene?"

"Never did. Bill watches that TV show. It's icky."

"You know what I'd have to do to get Crime Scene to look over the house?"

"House?"

"Where the suicide happened. The Benson house in Greeley."

"The—"

"Suicides. I want Crime Scene to check it out. All they did was test for gunshot residue and take some pictures. I want a complete search. But I don't know what to do."

"Something funny about it?"

He explained, "Just looked up a few things. The incident profile was out of range. I think something weird was going on there."

"I'll make a call. Ingrid's still down there, I think."

She returned to her desk and Tal rocked back in his chair.

The low April sun shot bars of ruddy light into his office, hitting the large, blank wall and leaving a geometric pattern on the white paint. The image put in mind the blood on the walls and couch and carpet of the Bensons' house. He pictured too the shaky lettering of their note.

Together forever . . .

Shellee appeared in the doorway. "Sorry, Boss. They said it's too late to twenty-one-twenty-four it."

"To?—"

"That's what they said. They said you need to declare a twenty-one-twenty-four to get Crime Scene in. But you can't do it now."

"Oh. Why?"

"Something about it being too contaminated now. You have to do it right away or get some special order from the sheriff himself. Anyway, that's what they told me, Boss."

Even though Shellee worked for three other detectives Tal was the only one who received this title—a true endearment, coming from her. She was formal, or chill, with the other cops in direct proportion to the number of times they asked her to fetch coffee or snuck peeks at her ample breasts.

Outside, a voice from the Real Crimes side of the room called out, "Hey, Bear, you get your questionnaire done?" A chortle followed.

Greg LaTour called back, "Naw, I'm taking mine home. Had front-row Knicks tickets but I figured, fuck, it'd be more fun to fill out paperwork all night."

More laughter.

Shellee's face hardened into a furious mask. She started to turn but Tal motioned her to stop.

"Hey, guys, tone it down." The voice was Captain Dempsey's. "He'll hear you."

"Naw," LaTour called, "Einstein left already. He's probably home humping his calculator. Who's up for Sal's?"

"I'm for that, Bear."

"Let's do it. . . ."

Laughter and receding footsteps.

Shellee muttered, "It just frosts me when they talk like that. They're like kids in the schoolyard."

True, they were, Tal thought. Math whizzes know a lot about bullies on playgrounds.

But he said, "It's okay."

"No, Boss, it's *not* okay."

"They live in a different world," Tal said. "I understand."

"Understand how people can be cruel like that? Well, I surely don't."

"You know that thirty-four percent of homicide detectives suffer from depression? Sixty-four percent get divorced. Twenty-eight percent are substance abusers."

"You're using those numbers to excuse 'em, Boss. Don't do it. Don't let 'em get away with it." She slung her purse over her shoulder and started down the hall, calling "Have a nice weekend, Boss. See you Monday."

"And," Tal continued, "six point three percent kill themselves before retirement." Though he doubted she could hear.

The residents of Hamilton, New York, were educated, pleasant, reserved and active in politics and the arts. In business too; they'd chosen to live here because the enclave was the closest exclusive Westbrook community to Manhattan. Industrious bankers and lawyers could be at their desks easily by eight o'clock in the morning.

The cul-de-sac of Montgomery Way, one of the nicest streets in Hamilton, was in fact home to two bankers and one lawyer, as well as one retired couple. These older residents, at number 205, had lived in their house for twenty-four years. It was a six thousand-square-foot stone Tudor with leaded-glass windows and a shale roof, surrounded by five acres of clever landscaping.

Samuel Ellicott Whitley had attended law school while his wife worked in the advertising department of Gimbel's, the department store near the harrowing intersection of Broadway, Sixth Avenue, and Thirty-Fourth Street. He'd finished school in '57 and joined Brown, Lathrop & Soames on Broad Street. The week after he was named partner, Elizabeth gave birth to a daughter, and after a brief hiatus, resumed classes at Columbia's graduate business school. She later took a job at one of the country's largest cosmetics companies and rose to be a senior vice president.

But the lives of law and business were behind the Whitleys now and they'd moved into the life of retirement as gracefully and comfortably as she stepped into her Dior gowns and he into his Tripler's tux.

Tonight, a cool, beautiful April Sunday, Elizabeth hung up the phone after a conversation with her daughter, Sandra, and piled the dinner dishes in the sink. She poured herself another vodka and tonic. She stepped outside onto the back patio, looking out over the azure dusk crowning the hemlocks and pine. She stretched and sipped her drink, feeling tipsy and completely content.

She wondered what Sam was up to. Just after they'd finished dinner he'd said that he'd had to pick up something. Normally she would have gone with him. She worried because of his illness. Afraid not only that his undependable heart would give out but that he might faint at the wheel or drive off the road because of the medication. But he'd insisted that she stay home; he was only going a few miles.

Taking a long sip of her drink, she cocked her head, hearing an automobile engine and the hiss of tires on the asphalt. She looked toward the driveway. But she couldn't see anything. Was it Sam? The car, though, had not come up the main drive but had turned off the road at the service entrance and eased through the side yard, out of sight of the house. She squinted but with the foliage and the dim light of dusk she couldn't see who it was.

Logic told her she should be concerned. But Elizabeth was comfortable sitting here with her glass in hand, under a deep blue evening sky. Feeling the touch of cashmere on her skin, happy, warm . . . No, life was perfect. What could there possibly be to worry about?

Three nights of the week—or as Tal would sometimes phrase it, 42.8751 percent of his evenings—he'd go out. Maybe on a date, maybe to have drinks and dinner with friends, maybe to his regular poker game (the others in the quintet enjoyed his company, though they'd learned it could be disastrous to play with a man who could remember cards photographically and calculate the odds of drawing to a full house like a computer).

The remaining 57.1249 percent of his nights he'd stay home and lose himself in the world of mathematics.

This Sunday, nearly 7:00 P.M., Tal was in his small library, which was packed with books but was as ordered and neat as his office at work. He'd spent the weekend running errands, cleaning the house, washing the car, making the obligatory—and ever awkward—call to his father in Chicago, dining with a couple up the road who'd made good their threat to set him up with a cousin (e-mail addresses had been unenthusiastically exchanged over empty mousse dishes). Now, classical music playing on the radio, Tal had put the rest of the world aside and was working on a proof.

This is the gold ring that mathematicians constantly seek. One might have a brilliant insight about numbers but without completing the proof—the formal argument that verifies the premise—that insight remains merely a theorem; it's pure speculation.

The proof that had obsessed him for months involved perfect numbers. These are positive numbers whose divisors (excluding the number itself) add up to that number. The number 6, for instance, is perfect because it's divisible only by 1, 2, and 3 (not counting 6), and 1, 2, and 3 also add up to 6.

The questions Tal had been trying to answer: How many even perfect numbers are there? And, more intriguing, are there any *odd* perfect numbers? In the entire history of mathematics no one has been able to offer a proof that an odd perfect number exists (or that it can't exist).

Perfect numbers have always intrigued mathematicians— theologians too. St. Augustine felt that God intentionally chose a perfect number of days—six—to create the world. Rabbis attach great mystical significance to the number 28, the days in the moon's cycle. Tal didn't consider perfect numbers in such a spiritual or philosophical way. For him they were simply a curious mathematical construct. But this didn't minimize their importance to him; proving theorems about perfect numbers (or any other mathematical enigmas) might lead other insights about math and science . . . and perhaps life in general.

He now hunched over his pages of neat calculations, wondering if the odd perfect number was merely a myth or if it was real and waiting to be discovered, hiding somewhere in the dim distance of numbers approaching infinity.

Something about this thought troubled him and he leaned back in his chair. It took a moment to realize why. Thinking of infinity reminded him of the suicide note Don and Sy Benson had left.

Together forever . . .

He pictured the room where they'd died, the blood, the chilling sight of the grim how-to guide they'd bought. *Making the Final Journey.*

Tal stood and paced. Something definitely wasn't right. For the first time in years he decided to return to the office on a Sunday night. He wanted to look up some background on suicides of this sort.

A half hour later he was walking past the surprised desk sergeant who had to think for a moment or two before he recognized him.

"Officer . . ."

"Detective Simms."

"Right. Yessir."

Ten minutes later he was in his office, tapping on the keyboard, perusing information about suicides in Westbrook County. At first irritated that the curious events of today had taken him away from his mathematical evening, he soon found himself lost in a very different world of numbers—those that defined the loss of life by one's own hand in Westbrook County.

Sam Whitley emerged from the kitchen with a bottle of old Armagnac and joined his wife in the den.

It had been her husband arriving fifteen minutes ago, after all, driving up the back driveway for reasons he still hadn't explained.

Elizabeth now pulled her cashmere sweater around her shoulders and lit a vanilla-scented candle, which sat on the table in front of her. She glanced at the bottle in his hand and laughed.

"What?" her husband asked.

"I was reading some of the printouts your doctor gave you."

He nodded.

"And it said that some wine is good for you."

"I read that too." He wiped dust off the bottle, examined the label.

"That you should have a glass or two every day. But cognac wasn't on the list. I don't know how good *that* is for your health."

Sam laughed too. "I feel like living dangerously."

He expertly opened the bottle, whose cork stopper was close to disintegrating.

"You were always good at that," his wife said.

"I never had many talents—only the important skills." He handed her a glass of the honey-colored liquor and then he filled his. They downed the drink. He poured more.

"So what've you got there?" she asked, feeling even warmer now, giddier, happier. She was nodding toward a bulge in the side pocket of his camel-hair sport coat, the jacket he always wore on Sundays.

"A surprise."

"Really? What?"

He tapped her glass and they drank again. He said, "Close your eyes."

She did. "You're a tease, Samuel." She felt him sit next to her, sensed his body close. There was a click of metal.

"You know I love you." His tone overflowed with emotion. Sam occasionally got quite maudlin. Elizabeth had long ago learned, though, that among the long list of offenses in the catalog of masculine sins sentiment was the least troublesome.

"And I love you, dear," she said.

"Ready?"

"Yes, I'm ready."

"Okay. . . . Here."

Another click of metal . . .

Then Elizabeth felt something in her hand. She opened her eyes and laughed again.

"What . . . Oh, my God, is this—?" She examined the key ring he'd placed in her palm. It held two keys and bore the distinctive logo of a British MG sports car. "You . . . you found one?" she stammered. "Where?"

"That import dealer up the road, believe it or not. Two miles from here! It's a nineteen-fifty-four. He called a month ago but it needed some work to get in shape."

"So that's what those mysterious calls were about. I was beginning to suspect another woman," she joked.

"It's not the same color. It's more burgundy."

"As if that matters, honey."

The first car they'd bought as a married couple had been a red MG, which they'd driven for ten years until the poor thing had finally given out. While Liz's friends were buying Lexuses or Mercedes she refused to join the pack and continued to drive her ancient Cadillac, holding out for an old MG like their original car.

She flung her arms around his shoulders and leaned up to kiss him.

Lights from an approaching car flashed into the window, startling them.

"Caught," she whispered, "just like when my father came home early on our first date. Remember?" She laughed flirtatiously, feeling just like a carefree, rebellious Sarah Lawrence sophomore in a pleated skirt and Peter-Pan collared blouse—exactly who she'd been forty-two years ago when she met this man, the one she would share her life with.

Tal Simms was hunched forward, jotting notes, when the dispatcher's voice clattered thought the audio monitor, which was linked to the 911 system, in the darkened detective pen. "All units in the vicinity of Hamilton. Reports of a possible suicide in progress."

Tal froze. He pushed back from his computer monitor and rose to his feet, staring at the speaker, as the electronic voice continued. "Neighbor reports a car engine running in the closed garage at two-oh-five Montgomery Way. Any units in the vicinity, respond."

Tal Simms looked up at the speaker and hesitated only a moment. Soon, he was sprinting out of the building. He was halfway out of the parking lot, doing seventy in his Toyota, when he realized that he'd neglected to put his seat belt on. He reached for it but lost the car to a skid and gave up and sped toward the suburb of Hamilton on the Hudson, five miles away from the office.

You couldn't exactly call any of Westbrook County desolate but Hamilton and environs were surrounded by native-wood parks and the estates of very wealthy men and women who liked their privacy; most of the land here was zoned five or ten acres and some homes were on much larger tracts. The land Tal was now speeding past was a deserted mess of old forest, vines, brambles, jutting rocks. It was not far from here, he reflected, that Washington Irving had thought up the macabre tale of the Headless Horseman.

Normally a cautious, patient driver, Tal wove madly from lane to lane, laying on the horn often. But he didn't consider the illogic of what he was doing. He pictured chocolate-brown blood in the Bensons' den, pictured the unsteady handwriting of their last note.

We'll be together forever . . .

He raced through downtown Hamilton at nearly three times the speed limit. As if the Headless Horseman himself were galloping close behind.

∞

His gray sedan swerved down the long driveway leading to the Whitley house, bounding off the asphalt and taking out a bed of blooming white azaleas.

He grimaced at the damage as he skidded to a stop in front of the doorway.

Leaping from his car, he noticed a Hamilton Village police car and a boxy county ambulance pull up. Two officers and two medical technicians jogged to meet him and they all sprinted to the garage door. He smelled fumes and could hear the rattle of a car engine inside.

As a uniformed cop banged on the door, Tal noticed a handwritten note taped to the front.

> WARNING: The garage is filled with dangrous
> fumes. We've left the remote control on the groun in
> front of the flower pot. Please use it to the door and
> let it air out before entring.

"No!" Tal dropped the note and began tugging futilely at the door, which was locked from the inside. In the dark they couldn't immediately find the remote so a fireman with an axe ran to the side door and broke it open with one swing.

But they were too late.

To save either of them.

Once again it was a multiple suicide. Another husband and wife.

Samuel and Elizabeth Whitley were in the garage, reclining in an open convertible, a old-fashioned MG sports car. While one officer had shut off the engine and firemen rigged a vent fan, the medical

techs had pulled them out of the car and rested them on the driveway. They'd attempted to revive them but the efforts were futile.
The couple had been very efficient in their planning; they'd sealed
the doors, vents, and windows of the garage with duct tape. Shades
had been drawn, so no one could look inside and interrupt their
deaths. Only the unusual rattle of the engine had alerted a dog-
walking neighbor that something was wrong.

Talbot Simms stared at them, numb. No blood this time but the
deaths were just as horrible to him—seeing the bodies and noting
the detachment in their planning: the thoughtfulness of the warning
note, its cordial tone, the care in sealing the garage. And the underlying uneasiness; like the Bensons' note, this one was written in unsteady writing and there were misspellings—"dangrous"—and a
missing word or two: "use it to the door . . ."

The uniformed officers made a circuit of the house, to make certain nobody else was inside and had been affected by the carbon
monoxide. Tal too entered but hesitated at first when he smelled a
strong odor of fumes. But then he realized that the scent wasn't auto
exhaust but smoke from the fireplace. Brandy glasses and a dusty
bottle sat on the table in front of a small couch. They'd had a final romantic drink together in front of a fire—and then died.

"Anybody else here?" Tal asked the cops as they returned to the
main floor.

"No, it's clean. Neatest house I've ever seen. Looks like it was
just scrubbed. Weird, cleaning the house to kill yourself."

In the kitchen they found another note, the handwriting just as
unsteady as the warning about the gas.

> To our friends and family:
> We do this with great joy in hearts and with love for
> everone in our family and everyone we've known.
> Don't feel any sorrow; weve never been happier.

The letter ended with the name, address, and phone number of
their attorney. Tal lifted his mobile phone from his pocket and called
the number.

"Hello."

"Mr. Wells, please. This is Detective Simms with the county
police."

A hesitation. "Yes, sir?" the voice asked.

The pause was now on Tal's part. "Mr. Wells?"

"That's right."

"You're the Whitleys' attorney?"

"That's right. What's this about?"

Tal took a deep breath. "I'm sorry to tell you that they've . . . passed away. It was a suicide. We found your name in their note."

"My, God, no. . . . What happened?"

"How, you mean? In their garage. Their car exhaust."

"When?"

"Tonight. A little while ago."

"No! . . . Both of them? Not both of them?"

"I'm afraid so," Tal replied.

There was a long pause. Finally the lawyer, clearly shaken, whispered, "I should've guessed."

"How's that? Had they talked about it?"

"No, no. But Sam was sick."

"Sick?"

"His heart. It was pretty serious."

Just like Don Benson.

More common denominators.

"His wife? Was she sick too?"

"Oh, Elizabeth. No. She was in pretty good health. . . . Does the daughter know?"

"They have a daughter?" This news instantly made the deaths exponentially more tragic.

"She lives in the area. I'll call her." He sighed. "That's what they pay me for. . . . Well, thank you, Officer. . . . What was your name again?"

"Simms."

"Thank you."

Tal put his phone away and started slowly through the house. It reminded him of the Bensons'. Tastefully opulent. Only more so. The Whitleys were, he guessed, much richer.

Glancing at the pictures on the wall, many of which showed a cute little girl who'd grown into a beautiful young woman.

He was grateful that the lawyer would be making the call to their daughter.

Tal walked into the kitchen. No calendars here.

He looked again at the note.

Joy . . . Never been happier.

Nearby was another document. He looked it over and frowned. Curious. It was a receipt for the purchase of a restored MG automobile. Whitley'd paid for a deposit on the car earlier but had given the dealer the balance today.

Tal walked to the garage and hesitated before entering. But he steeled up his courage and stepped inside, glanced at the tarps covering the bodies. He located the vehicle identification number. Yes, this was the same car as on the receipt.

Whitley had bought an expensive restored antique vehicle today, driven it home and then killed himself and his wife.

Why?

There was motion in the driveway. Tal watched a long, dark-gray van pull up outside. LEIGHEY'S FUNERAL HOME was printed on the side. Already? Had the officers called or the lawyer? Two men got out of the hearse and walked up to a uniformed officer. They seemed to know each other.

Then Tal paused. He noticed something familiar. He picked up a book on a table in the den. *Making the Final Journey.*

The same book the Bensons had.

Too many common denominators. The suicide book, the heart diseases, spouses also dying.

Tal walked into the living room and found the older trooper filling out a form—not *his* questionnaire, Tal noticed. He asked one of the men from the funeral home, "What're you doing with the bodies?"

"Instructions were cremation as soon as possible."

"Can we hold off on that?"

"Hold off?" he asked and glanced at the Hamilton officer. "How do you mean, Detective?"

Tal said, "Get an autopsy?"

"Why?"

"Just wondering if we can."

"You're county," the heavy-set cop said. "You're the boss. Only, I mean, you know—you can't do it halfway. Either you declare a twenty-one-twenty-four or you don't."

Oh, *that*. He wondered what exactly it was.

A glance at the sports car. "Okay, I'll do that. I'm declaring a twenty-four-twenty-one."

"You mean twenty-one-twenty-four. . . . You sure about this?" the officer asked, looking uncertainly toward the funeral home assistant, who was frowning; even he apparently knew more about the mysterious 2124 than Tal did.

The statistician looked outside and saw the other man from the funeral home pull a stretcher out of the back of the hearse and walk toward the bodies.

"Yes," he said firmly. "I'm sure." And tapped loudly on the window, gesturing for the man to stop.

The next morning, Monday, Tal saw the head of the Crime Scene Unit walk into the Detective pen and head straight toward LaTour's office. He was carrying a half dozen folders.

He had a gut feeling that this was the Whitley scene report and was out of his office fast to intercept him. "Hey, how you doing? That about the Whitley case?"

"Yeah. It's just the preliminary. But there was an expedite on it. Is Greg in? LaTour?"

"I think it's for me."

"You're . . ."

"Simms."

"Oh, yeah," the man said, looking at the request attached to the report. "I didn't notice. I figured it was LaTour. Being head of Homicide, you know." He handed the files to Tal.

A 2124, it turned out, was a declaration that a death was suspicious. Like hitting a fire alarm button, it set all kinds of activities in motion—getting Crime Scene to search the house, collect evidence, record friction-ridge prints and extensively photograph and video the scene; scheduling autopsies, and alerting the prosecutor's office that a homicide investigation case file had been started. In his five years on the job Tal had never gotten so many calls before 10:00 as he had this morning.

Tal glanced into the captain's office then LaTour's. Nobody seemed to notice that a statistician who'd never issued a parking ticket in his life was clutching crime scene files.

Except Shellee, who subtly blessed herself and winked.

Tal asked the Crime Scene detective, "Preliminary, you said. What else're you waiting for?"

"Phone records, handwriting confirmation of the note and autopsy results. Hey, I'm really curious. What'd you find that made you think this was suspicious? Fits the classic profile of every suicide I've ever worked."

"Some things."

"Things," the seasoned cop said, nodding slowly. "Things. Ah. Got a suspect?"

"Not yet."

"Ah. Well, good luck. You'll need it."

Back in his office Tal carefully filed away the spreadsheet he'd been working on then opened the CSU files. He spread the contents out on his desk.

We begin with inspiration, a theorem, an untested idea: There is a perfect odd number. There is a point at which pi repeats. The universe is infinite.

A mathematician then attempts to construct a proof that shows irrefutably that his position either is correct or cannot be correct.

Tal Simms knew how to create such proofs with numbers. But to prove the theorem that there was something suspicious about the deaths of the Bensons and the Whitleys? He had no idea how to do this and stared at the hieroglyphics of the crime scene reports, increasingly discouraged. He had basic academy training, of course, but, beyond that, no investigation skills or experience.

But then he realized that perhaps this wasn't quite accurate. He did have one talent that might help: the cornerstone of his profession as a mathematician—logic.

He turned his analytical mind to the materials on his desk as he examined each item carefully. He first picked the photos of the Whitleys' bodies. All in graphic, colorful detail. They troubled him a great deal. Still, he forced himself to examine them carefully, every inch. After some time he concluded that nothing suggested that the Whitleys had been forced into the car or had struggled with any assailants.

He set the photos aside and read the documents in the reports themselves. There were no signs of any break-in, though the front and back doors weren't locked, so someone might have simply walked in. But with the absence of signs of physical assault an intrusion seemed unlikely. And their jewelry, cash, and other valuables were untouched.

One clue, though, suggested that all was not as it seemed. The Latents team found that both notes contained, in addition to Sam Whitley's, Tal's and the police officers' prints, smudges that were probably from gloved hands or fingers protected by a cloth or tissue. The team had also found glove prints in the den where the couple had had their last drink, in the room where the note had been found, and in the garage.

Gloves? Tal wondered. Curious.

The team had also found fresh tire prints on the driveway. The prints didn't match the MG, the other cars owned by the victims or the vehicles driven by the police, medical team, or the funeral home. The report concluded that the car had been there within the three hours prior to death. The tread marks were indistinct, so that the brand of tire couldn't be determined, but the wheelbase meant the vehicle was a small one.

A search of the trace evidence revealed several off-white cotton fibers—one on the body of Elizabeth Whitley and one on the living room couch—that didn't appear to match what the victims were wearing or any of the clothes in their closets. An inventory of drugs in the medicine cabinets and kitchen revealed no antidepressants, which suggested, even if tenuously, that mood problems and thoughts of suicide might not have occurred in the Whitley house recently.

He rose, walked to his doorway and called Shellee in.

"Hi, Boss. Havin' an exciting morning, are we?"

He rolled his eyes. "I need you to do something for me."

"Are you . . . ? I mean, you look tired."

"Yes, yes, I'm fine. It's just about this case."

"What case?"

"The suicide."

"Oh."

"I need to find out if anybody's bought a book called *Making the Final Journey*. Then a subhead—something about suicide and euthanasia."

"A book. Sure."

"I don't remember exactly. But *Making the Journey* or *Making the Final Journey* is the start of the title."

"Okay. And I'm supposed to check on—?"

"If anybody bought it."

"I mean, everywhere? There're probably a lot of—"

"For now, just in Westbrook County. In the last couple of weeks. Bookstores. And that online place, the big one, Booksource dot com."

"Hey, when I call, is it okay to play cop?"

Tal hesitated. But then he said, "Oh, hell, sure. You want, you can be a detective."

"Yippee," she said. "Detective Shellee Bingham."

"And if they *haven't* sold any, give them my name and tell them if they *do*, call us right away."

"We need a warrant or anything?" Detective Shellee asked, thoughtful now.

Did they? he wondered.

"Hmm. I don't know. Let's just try it without and see what they say."

Five minutes later Tal felt a shadow over him and he looked up to see Captain Ronald Dempsey's six-foot-three form fill the doorway in his ubiquitous striped shirt, his sleeves ubiquitously rolled up.

The man's round face smiled pleasantly. But Tal thought immediately: I'm busted.

"Captain."

"Hey, Tal." Dempsey leaned against the doorjamb, looking over the desktop. "Got a minute?"

"Sure do."

Tal had known that the brass would find out about the 2124, of course, and he'd planned to talk to Dempsey about it soon; but he'd hoped to wait until his proof about the suspicious suicide was somewhat further developed.

"Heard about the twenty-one-twenty-four at the Whitleys'."

"Sure."

"What's up with *that*?"

Tal explained about the two suicides, the common denominators.

Dempsey nodded. "Kind of a coincidence, sure. But you know, Tal, we don't have a lot of resources for full investigations. Like, we've only got one dedicated homicide crime scene unit."

"Didn't know that."

"And there was a shooting in Rolling Hills Estates last night. Two people shot up bad, one died. The unit was late running that scene 'cause you had them in Hamilton."

"I'm sorry about that, Captain."

"It's also expensive. Sending out CS."

"Expensive? I didn't think about that."

"Thousands, I'm talking. Crime scene bills everything back to us. Every time they go out. Then there're lab tests and autopsies and everything. The M.E. too. You know what an autopsy costs?"

"They *bill* us?" Tal asked.

"It's just the more we save for the county the better we look, you know."

"Right. I guess it would be expensive."

"You bet." No longer smiling, the captain adjusted his sleeves. "Other thing is, the way I found out: I heard from their daughter. Sandra Whitley. She was going to make funeral arrangements and then she hears about the M.E. autopsy. Phew . . . she's pissed off. Threatening to sue. . . . I'm going to have to answer questions. So. Now, what *exactly* made you twenty-one-twenty-four the scene, Tal?"

He scanned the papers on his desk, uneasy, wondering where to start. "Well, a couple of things. They'd just bought—"

"Hold on there a minute," the captain said, holding up a finger.

Dempsey leaned out the door and shouted, "LaTour! . . . Hey, LaTour?"

"What?" came the grumbling baritone.

"Come over here. I'm with Simms."

Tal heard the big man make his way toward the Unreal Crimes side of the detective pen. The ruddy, goateed face appeared in the office. Ignoring Tal, he listened as the captain explained about the Whitleys' suicide.

"Another one, huh?"

"Tal declared a twenty-one-twenty-four."

The homicide cop nodded noncommitally. "Uh-huh. Why?"

The question was directed toward Dempsey, who turned toward Tal.

"Well, I was looking at the Bensons' deaths and I pulled up the standard statistical profile on suicides in Westbrook County. Now, when you look at all the attributes—"

"Attributes?" LaTour asked, frowning, as if tasting sand.

"Right. The attributes of the Bensons' death—and the Whitleys' too now—they're way out of the standard range. Their deaths are outliers."

"Out-liars? The fuck's that?"

Tal explained. In statistics an outlier was an event significantly different from a group of similar events. He gave a concrete example. "Say you're analyzing five murderers. Three perps killed a single victim each, one of them killed two victims, and the final man was a serial killer who'd murdered twenty people. To draw any meaningful conclusions from that, you need to treat the last one as an outlier and analyze him separately. Otherwise, your analysis'll be mathematically correct but misleading. Running the numbers, the mean—the average—number of victims killed by each suspect is five. But that exaggerates the homicidal nature of the first four men and underplays the last one. See what I mean?"

The frown on LaTour's face suggested he didn't. But he said, "So you're saying these two suicides're different from most of the others in Westbrook."

"*Significantly* different. Fewer than six percent of the population kill themselves when they're facing a possibly terminal illness. That number drops to two point six percent when the victim has medical insurance and down to point nine when the net worth of the victim is over one million dollars. It drops even further when the victims are married and are in the relatively young category of sixty-five to seventy-five, like these folks. And love-pact deaths are only two percent of suicides nationwide and ninety-one percent of those involve victims under the age of twenty-one. . . . Now, what do you think the odds are that two heart patients would take their own lives, and their wives', in the space of two days?"

"I don't really know, Tal," LaTour said, clearly uninterested. "What else you got? Suspicious, I mean."

"Okay, the Whitleys'd just bought a car earlier that day. Rare, antique MG. Why do that if you're going to kill yourself?"

LaTour offered, "They needed a murder weapon. Didn't want a gun. Probably there was something about the MG that meant something to them. From when they were younger, you know. They wanted to go out that way."

"Makes sense," Dempsey said, tugging at a sleeve.

"There's more," Tal said and explained about the gloves, the fiber, the smudges on the note. And the recent visitor's tire prints.

"Somebody else was there around the time they killed themselves. Or just after."

LaTour said, "Lemme take a look."

Tal pushed the reports toward him. The big cop examined everything closely. Then shook his head. "I just don't see it," he said to the captain. "No evidence of a break-in or struggle . . . The note?" He shrugged. "Looks authentic. I mean, Documents'll tell us for sure but look—" he held up the Whitleys' checkbook ledger and the suicide note, side by side. The script was virtually identical. "Smudges from gloves on paper? We see that on every piece of paper we find at a scene. Hell, half the pieces of paper *here* have smudges on them that look like smeared FRs—"

"FRs?"

"Friction ridges," LaTour muttered. "*Fingerprints.* Smudges— from the manufacturer, stockers, browsing customers."

"The fiber?" He leaned forward and lifted a tiny white strand off Tal's suit jacket. "This's the same type the Crime Scene found. Cotton worsted. See it all the time. The fibers at the Whitleys' could've come from anywhere. It might've come from you." Shuffling sloppily through the files with his massive paws. "Okay, the gloves and the tread marks? Those're Playtex kitchen gloves; I recognize the ridges. No perps ever use them because the wear patterns can be traced. . . ." He held up the checkbook ledger again. "Lookit the check the wife wrote today. To Esmerelda Constanzo 'For cleaning services.' The housekeeper was in yesterday, cleaned the house wearing the gloves—maybe she even straightened up the stack of paper they used later for the suicide note, left the smudges then. The tread marks? That's about the size of a small import. Just the sort that a cleaning woman'd be driving. They were hers. Bet you any money."

Though he didn't like the man's message, Tal was impressed at the way his mind worked. He'd made all those deductions—extremely *logical* deductions—based on a three-minute examination of the data.

"Got a case needs lookin' at," LaTour grumbled and tossed the report onto Tal's desk. He clomped back to his office.

Breaking the silence that followed, Dempsey said, "Hey, I know you don't get out into the field much. Must get frustrating to sit in the office all day long, not doing . . . you know . . ."

Real police work? Tal wondered if that's what the captain was hesitating to say.

"More active stuff" turned out to be the captain's euphemism. "You probably feel sometimes like you don't fit in."

He's probably home humping his calculator. . . .

"We've all felt that way sometimes. Honest. But being out in the field's not what it's cracked up to be. Not like TV, you know. And you're the best at what you do, Tal. Statistician. Man, that's a hard job. An *important* job. Let's face it—" Lowering his voice. "—guys like Greg wouldn't know a number if it jumped out and bit 'em on the ass. You've got a real special talent."

Tal weathered the condescension with a faint smile, which obscured the anger beneath his flushed face. The speech was clearly out of a personnel management training manual. Dempsey had just plugged in "statistician" for "traffic detail" or "receptionist."

"Okay, now, don't you have some numbers to crunch? We've got that midyear assignment meeting coming up and nobody can put together a report like you, my friend."

Monday evening's drive to the Whitleys' house took considerably longer than his Headless Horseman race night before, since he drove the way he usually did: within the speed limit and perfectly centered in his lane (and with the belt firmly clasped this time).

Noting with a grimace how completely he'd destroyed the shrubs last night, Tal parked in front of the door and ducked under the crime scene tape. He stepped inside, smelling again the sweet, poignant scent of the woodsmoke from the couple's last cocktail hour.

Inside their house, he pulled on latex gloves he'd bought at a drugstore on the way here (thinking only when he got to the checkout lane: Damn, they probably have hundreds of these back in the Detective pen). Then he began working his way though the house, picking up anything that Crime Scene had missed that might shed some light on the mystery of the Whitleys' deaths.

Greg LaTour's bluntness and Captain Dempsey's pep talk, in other words, had no effect on him. All intellectually honest mathematicians welcome the disproving of their theorems as much as the proving. But the more LaTour had laid out the evidence that the 2124 was wrong, the more Tal's resolve grew to get to the bottom of the deaths.

There *was* an odd perfect number out there, and there *was* something unusual about the deaths of the Bensons and the Whitleys; Tal was determined to write the proof.

Address books, DayTimers, receipts, letters, stacks of papers, piles of business cards for lawyers, repairmen, restaurants, investment advisors, accountants. He felt a chill as he read one for some new age organization, the Lotus Research Foundation for Alternative Treatment, tucked in with all the practical and mundane cards—evidence of the desperation of rational people frightened by impending death.

A snap of floorboard, a faint clunk. A metallic sound. It startled him and he felt uneasy—vulnerable. He'd parked in the front of the house; whoever'd arrived would know he was here. The police tape and crime scene notice were clear about forbidding entry; he doubted that the visitor was a cop.

And, alarmed, he realized that a corollary of his theorem that the Whitleys had been murdered was, of course, that there had to be a murderer.

He reached for his hip and realized, to his dismay, that he'd left his pistol in his desk at the office. The only suspects Tal had ever met face to face were benign accountants or investment bankers and even then the confrontation was usually in court. He never carried the gun—about the only regulation he ever broke. Palms sweating, Tal looked around for something he could use to protect himself. He was in the bedroom, surrounded by books, clothes, furniture. Nothing he could use as a weapon.

He looked out the window.

A twenty-foot drop to the flagstone patio.

Was he too proud to hide under the bed?

Footsteps sounded closer, walking up the stairs. The carpet muted them but the old floorboards creaked as the intruder got closer.

No, he decided, he wasn't too proud for the bed. But that didn't seem to be the wisest choice. Escape was better.

Out the window.

Tal opened it, swung the leaded-glass panes outward. No grass below; just a flagstone deck dotted with booby traps of patio furniture.

He heard the metallic click of a gun. The steps grew closer, making directly for the bedroom.

Okay, jump. He glanced down. Aim for the padded lawn divan. You'll sprain your ankle but you won't get shot.

He put his hand on the windowsill, was about to boost himself over when a voice filled the room, a woman's voice. "Who the hell're you?"

Tal turned fast, observing a slim blonde in her mid or late thirties, eyes narrow. She was smoking a cigarette and putting a gold lighter back into her purse—the metallic sound he'd assumed was a gun. There was something familiar—and troubling—about her and he realized that, yes, he'd seen her face—in the snapshots on the walls. "You're their daughter."

"Who are you?" she repeated in a gravelly voice.

"You shouldn't be in here. It's a crime scene."

"You're a cop? Let me see some ID." She glanced at his latex-gloved hand on the window, undoubtedly wondering what he'd been about to do.

He offered her the badge and identification card.

She glanced at them carefully. "You're the one who did it?"

"What?"

"You had them taken to the morgue? Had them goddamn *butchered*?"

"I had some questions about their deaths. I followed procedures." More or less.

"So you *were* the one. Detective Talbot Simms." She'd memorized his name from the brief look at his ID. "I'll want to be sure you're personally named in the suit."

"You're not supposed to be here," Tal repeated. "The scene hasn't been released yet."

He remembered this from a cop show on TV.

"Fuck your scene."

A different response than on the TV show.

"Let me see some ID," Tal said stepping forward, feeling more confident now.

The staring match began.

He added cheerfully, "I'm happy to call some officers to take you downtown." This—from another show—was a bit inaccurate; the Westbrook Sheriff's Department wasn't downtown at all. It was in a strip mall next to a large Stop 'N' Shop grocery.

She reluctantly showed him her driver's license. Sandra Kaye

Whitley, thirty-six. He recognized the address, a very exclusive part of the county.

"What was so fucking mysterious about their deaths? They killed themselves."

Tal observed something interesting about her. Yes, she was angry. But she wasn't sad.

"We can't talk about an open case."

"What *case?*" Sandra snapped. "You keep saying that."

"Well, it was a murder, you know."

Her hand paused then continued carrying her cigarette to her lips. She asked coolly, "Murder?"

Tal said, "Your father turned the car ignition on. Technically he murdered your mother."

"That's bullshit."

Probably it was. But he sidestepped the issue. "Had they ever had a history of depression?"

She debated for a moment then answered. "My father's disease was serious. And my mother didn't want to live without him."

"But his illness wasn't terminal, was it?"

"Not exactly. But he *was* going to die. And he wanted to do it with dignity."

Tal felt he was losing this contest; she kept him on the defensive. He tried to think more like Greg LaTour. "What exactly're you doing here?"

"It's my family's house," she snapped. "*My* house. I grew up here. I wanted to see it. They *were* my parents, you know."

He nodded. "Of course. . . . I'm sorry for your loss. I just want to make sure that everything's what it seems to be. Just doing my job."

She shrugged and stubbed the cigarette out in a heavy crystal ashtray on the dresser. She noticed, sitting next to it, a picture of her with her parents. For a long moment she stared at it then looked away, hiding tears from him. She wiped her face then turned back. "I'm an attorney, you know. I'm going to have one of my litigation partners look at this situation through a microscope, Detective."

"That's fine, Ms. Whitley," Tal said. "Can I ask what you put in your purse earlier?"

She blinked. "Purse?"

"When you were downstairs."

A hesitation. "It's nothing important."

"This is a crime scene. You can't take anything. That's a felony. Which I'm sure you knew. Being an attorney, as you say."

Was it a felony? he wondered.

At least Sandra didn't seem to know it *wasn't*.

"You can give it to me now and I'll forget about the incident. Or we can take that trip downtown."

She held his eye for a moment, slicing him into tiny pieces, as she debated. Then she opened her purse. She handed him a small stack of mail. "It was in the mailbox to be picked up. But with that yellow tape all over the place the mailman couldn't come by. I was just going to mail it."

"I'll take it."

She held the envelopes out to him with a hand that seemed to be quivering slightly. He took them in his gloved hands.

In fact, he'd had no idea that she'd put anything in her purse; he'd had a flash of intuition. Talbot Simms suddenly felt a rush of excitement; statisticians never bluff.

Sandra looked around the room and her eyes seemed mournful again. But he decided it was in fact anger. She said icily, "You *will* be hearing from my litigation partner, Detective Simms. Shut the lights out when you leave, unless the county's going to be paying the electric bill."

∞

"I'm getting coffee, Boss. You want some?"

"Sure, thanks," he told Shellee.

It was the next morning and Tal was continuing to pore over the material he'd collected. Some new information had just arrived: the Whitleys' phone records for the past month, the autopsy results, and the handwriting analysis of the suicide note.

He found nothing immediately helpful about the phone records and set them aside, grimacing as he looked for someplace to rest them. There wasn't any free space on his desk and so he stacked them, as orderly as he could, on top of another stack. It made him feel edgy, the mess, but there wasn't anything else he could do, short of moving a table or another desk into his office—and he could imagine the ribbing he'd take for that.

Data plural . . . humping his calculator . . .

Tal looked over the handwriting expert's report first. The woman said that she could state with 98 percent certainty that Sam Whitley had written the note, though the handwriting had been unsteady and the spelling flawed, which was unusual for a man of his education.

The garage is filled with dangrous fumes.

This suggested some impairment, possible severe, she concluded.

Tal turned to the autopsy results. Death was, as they'd thought, due to carbon monoxide poisoning. There were no contusions, tissue damage, or ligature marks to suggest they'd been forced into the car. There was alcohol in the blood, .010 percent in Sam's system, 0.019 in Elizabeth's, neither particularly high. But they both had medication in their bloodstreams too.

> Present in both victims were unusually large quantities of 9-fluoro, 7-chloro-1, 3-dihydro-1-methyl-5-phenyl-2H-1,4-benzodiazepin, 5-hydroxytryptamine and N-(1-phenethyl-4-piperidyl) propionanilide citrate.

This was, the M.E.'s report continued, an analgesic/anti-anxiety drug sold under the trade name Luminux. The amount in their blood meant that the couple had recently taken nearly three times the normally prescribed strength of the drug, though, it did not, the M.E. concluded, make them more susceptible to carbon monoxide poisoning or otherwise directly contribute to their deaths.

Looking over his desk—too goddamn many papers!—he finally found another document and carefully read the inventory of the house, which the Crime Scene Unit had prepared. The Whitleys had plenty of medicine—for Sam's heart problem, as well as for Elizabeth's arthritis and other maladies—but no Luminux.

Shellee brought him the coffee. Her eyes cautiously took in the cluttered desktop.

"Thanks," he muttered.

"Still lookin' tired, Boss."

"Didn't sleep well." Instinctively he pulled his striped tie straight, kneaded the knot to make sure it was tight.

"It's fine, Boss," she whispered, nodding at his shirt. Meaning: Quit fussing.

He winked at her.

Thinking about common denominators . . .

The Bensons' suicide note too had been sloppy, Tal recalled. He rummaged though the piles on his desk and found their lawyer's card then dialed the man's office and was put through to him.

"Mr. Metzer, this's Detective Simms. I met you at the Bensons' a few days ago."

"Right. I remember."

"This is a little unusual but I'd like permission to take a blood sample."

"From me?" he asked in a startled voice.

"No, no, from the Bensons."

"Why?"

He hesitated, then decided to go ahead with the lie. "I'd like to update our database about medicines and diseases of recent suicides. It'll be completely anonymous."

"Oh. Well, sorry, but they were cremated this morning."

"They were? That was fast."

"I don't know if it was fast or it was slow. But that's what they wanted. It was in their instructions to me. They wanted to be cremated as soon as possible and the contents of the house sold—"

"Wait. You're telling me—"

"—the contents of the house sold immediately."

"When's that going to happen?"

"It's probably already done. We've had dealers in the house since Sunday morning. I don't think there's much left."

Tal remembered the man at the Whitleys' house—there to arrange for the liquidation of the estate. He wished he'd known about declaring 2124s when he'd been to the Bensons' house.

Common denominators . . .

"Do you still have the suicide note?"

"I didn't take it. I imagine it was thrown out when the service cleaned the house."

This's all way too fast, Tal thought. He looked over the papers on his desk. "Do you know if either of them was taking a drug called Luminux?"

"I don't have a clue."

"Can you give me Mr. Benson's cardiologist's name?"

A pause then the lawyer said, "I suppose it's okay. Yeah. Dr. Peter Brody. Over in Glenstead."

Tal was about to hang up but then a thought occurred to him. "Mr. Metzer, when I met you on Friday, didn't you tell me the Bensons weren't religious?"

"That's right. They were atheists. . . . What's this all about, Detective?"

"Like I say—just getting some statistics together. That's all. Thanks for your time."

He got Dr. Brody's number and called the doctor's office. The man was on vacation and his head nurse was reluctant to talk about patients, even deceased ones. She did admit, though, that Brody had not prescribed Luminux for them.

Tal then called the head of Crime Scene and learned that the gun the Bensons had killed themselves with was in an evidence locker. He asked that Latents look it over for prints. "Can you do a rush on it?"

"Happy to. It's comin' outa your budget, Detective," the man said cheerfully. "Be about ten, fifteen minutes."

"Thanks."

As he waited for the results on the gun, Tal opened his briefcase and noticed the three letters Sandra Whitley had in her purse at her parents' house. Putting on a pair of latex gloves once again, he ripped open the three envelopes and examined the contents.

The first one contained a bill from their lawyer for four hours of legal work, performed that month. The project, the bill summarized, was for "estate planning services."

Did he mean redoing the will? Was this another common denominator? Metzer had said that the Bensons had just redone theirs.

The second letter was an insurance form destined for the Cardiac Support Center at Westbrook Hospital, where Sam had been a patient.

Nothing unusual here.

But then he opened the third letter.

He sat back in his chair, looking at the ceiling then down at the letter once more.

Debating.

Then deciding that he didn't have any choice. When you're writing a mathematical proof you go anywhere the numbers take you. Tal rose and walked across the office, to the Real Crimes side of the pen. He leaned into an open door and knocked on the jamb. Greg LaTour was sitting back in his chair, boots up. He was reading a document. "Fucking liar," he muttered and put a large check mark next to one of the paragraphs. Looking up, he cocked an eyebrow.

Humping his calculator . . .

Tal tried to be pleasant. "Greg. You got a minute?"

"Just."

"I want to talk to you about the case."

"Case?" The man frowned. "Which case?"

"The Whitleys."

"Who?"

"The suicides."

"From Sunday? Yeah, okay. Drew a blank. I don't think of suicides as cases." LaTour's meaty hand grabbed another piece of paper. He looked down at it.

"You said that the cleaning lady'd probably been there? She'd left the glove prints? And the tire treads."

It didn't seem that he remembered at first. Then he nodded. "And?"

"Look." He showed LaTour the third letter he'd found at the Whitleys. It was a note to Esmerelda Constanzo, the Whitleys' cleaning lady, thanking her for her years of help and saying they wouldn't be needing her services any longer. They'd enclosed the check that LaTour had spotted in the register.

"They'd put the check in the mail," Tal pointed out. "That means she wasn't there the day they died. Somebody else wore the gloves. And I got to thinking about it? Why would a cleaning lady wear kitchen gloves to clean the rest of the house? Doesn't make sense."

LaTour shrugged. His eyes dipped to the document on his desk and then returned once more to the letter Tal held.

The statistician added, "And that means the car wasn't hers either. The tread marks. Somebody else was there around the time they died."

"Well, Tal—"

"Couple other things," he said quickly. "Both the Whitleys had high amounts of a prescription drug in their bloodstream. Some kind of narcotic. Luminux. But there were no prescription bottles for it in their house. And their lawyer'd just done some estate work for them. Maybe revising their wills."

"You gonna kill yourself, you gonna revise your will. That ain't very suspicious."

"But then I met the daughter."

"Their daughter?"

"She broke into the house, looking for something. She'd pocketed the mail but she might've been looking for something else. Maybe she got scared when she heard we didn't buy the suicide—"

"*You*. Not we."

Tal continued, "And she wanted to get rid of any evidence about the Luminux. I didn't search her. I didn't think about it at the time."

"What's this with the drugs? They didn't OD."

"Well, maybe she got them doped up, had them change their will and talked them into killing themselves."

"Yeah, right," LaTour muttered. "That's outa some bad movie."

Tal shrugged. "When I mentioned murder she freaked out."

"Murder? Why'd you mention murder?" He scratched his huge belly, looking for the moment just like his nickname.

"I meant murder-suicide. The husband turning the engine on."

LaTour gave a grunt—Tal hadn't realized that you could make a sound like that condescending.

"And, you know, she had this attitude."

"Well, now, Tal, you *did* send her parents to the county morgue. You know what they do to you there, don'tcha? Knives and saws. That's gotta piss the kid off a little, you know."

"Yes, she was pissed. But mostly, I think, 'cause I was there, checking out what'd happened. And you know what she didn't seem upset about?"

"What's that?"

"Her parents. Them dying. She *seemed* to be crying. But I couldn't tell. It could've been an act."

"She was in shock. Skirts get that way."

Tal persisted, "Then I checked on the first couple. The Bensons? They were cremated right after they died and their estate liquidated in a day or two."

"Liquidated?" LaTour lifted an eyebrow and finally delivered a comment that was neither condescending nor sarcastic. "And cremated that fast, hm? Seems odd, yeah. I'll give you that."

"And the Bensons' lawyer told me something else. They were atheists, both of them. But their suicide note said they'd be together forever or something like that. Atheists aren't going to say that. I'm thinking maybe *they* might've been drugged too. With that Luminux."

"What does their doctor?—"

"No, he didn't prescribed it. But maybe somebody slipped it to them. Their suicide note was unsteady too, sloppy, just like the Whitleys'."

"What's the story on *their* doctor?"

"I haven't got that far yet."

"Maybe, maybe, maybe." LaTour squinted. "But that gardener we talked to at the Benson place? He said they'd been boozing it up. You did the blood work on the Whitleys. They been drinking?"

"Not too much. . . . Oh, one other thing. I called their cell phone company and checked the phone records—the Whitleys'. They received a call from a pay phone forty minutes before they died. Two minutes long. Just enough time to see if they're home and say you're going to stop by. And who calls from pay phones anymore? Everybody's got cells, right?"

Reluctantly LaTour agreed with this.

"Look at it, Greg: Two couples, both rich, live five miles from each other. Both of 'em in the country club set. Both husbands have heart disease. Two murder-suicides a few days apart. What do you think about that?"

In a weary voice LaTour asked, "Outliers, right?"

"Exactly.

"You're thinking the bitch—"

"Who?" Tal asked.

"The daughter."

"I didn't say that."

"I'm not gonna quote you in the press, Tal."

"Okay," he conceded, "she's a bitch."

"You're thinking she's got access to her folks, there's money involved. She's doing something funky with the will or insurance."

"It's a theorem."

"A what?" LaTour screwed up his face.

"It's a hunch is what I'm saying."

"Hunch. Okay. But you brought up the Bensons. The Whitley

daughter isn't going to off *them* now, is she? I mean, why would she?"

Tal shrugged. "I don't know. Maybe she's the Bensons' god-daughter and she was in their will too. Or maybe her father was going into some deal with Benson that'd tie up all the estate money so the daughter'd lose out and she had to kill them both."

"Maybe, maybe, maybe," LaTour repeated.

Shellee appeared in the doorway and, ignoring LaTour, said, "Latents called. They said the only prints on the gun were the Bensons' and a few smears from cloth or paper."

"What fucking gun?" he asked.

"I will thank you not to use that language to me," Shellee said icily.

"I was talking to *him*," LaTour snapped and cocked an eyebrow at Tal.

Tal said, "The gun the Bensons killed themselves with. Smears—like on the Whitleys' suicide note."

Shellee glanced at the wall poster behind the desk then back to the detective. Tal couldn't tell whether the distasteful look was directed at LaTour himself or the blonde in a red-white-and-blue bikini lying provocatively across the seat and teardrop gas tank of the Harley. She turned and walked back to her desk quickly, as if she'd been holding her breath while she was inside the cop's office.

"Okay. . . . This's getting marginally fucking interesting." La-Tour glanced at the huge gold watch on his wrist. "I gotta go. I got some time booked at the range. Come with me. Let's go waste some ammunition, talk about the case after."

"Think I'll stay here."

LaTour frowned, apparently unable to understand why somebody wouldn't jump at the chance to spend an hour punching holes in a piece of paper with a deadly weapon. "You don't shoot?"

"It's just I'd rather work on this."

Then enlightenment dawned. Tal's office was, after all on the Unreal Crimes side of the pen. He had no interest in cop toys.

You're the best at what you do, statistician. Man, that's a hard job. . . .

"Okay," LaTour said. "I'll check out the wills and the insurance policies. Gimme the name of the icees."

"The?—"

"The corpses, the stiffs . . . the losers who killed 'emselves, Tal. And their lawyers."

Tal wrote down the information and handed the neat note to La-Tour, who stuffed it into his plaid shirt pocket behind two large cigars. He ripped open a desk drawer and took out a big, chrome automatic pistol.

Tal asked, "What should I do?"

"Get a P-I-I team and—"

"A what?"

"You go to the same academy as me, Tal? Post-Incident Interviewing team," he said as if he was talking to a three-year-old. "Use my name and Doherty'll put one together for you. Have 'em talk to all the neighbors around the Bensons' and the Whitleys' houses. See if they saw anybody around just before or after the TOD. Oh, that's—"

"Time of death."

LaTour gave him a thumbs up. "We'll talk this afternoon. I'll see you back here, how's four?"

"Sure. Oh, and maybe we should find out what kind of car the Whitleys' daughter drove. See if the wheelbase data match."

"That's good thinking, Tal," he said, looking honestly impressed. Grabbing some boxes of 9mm cartridges, LaTour walked heavily out of the Detective Division.

Tal returned to his desk and arranged for the P-I-I team. Then he called DMV, requesting information on Sandra Whitley's car. He glanced at his watch. One P.M. He realized he was hungry; he'd missed his regular lunch with his buddies from the university. He walked down to the small canteen on the second floor, bought a cheese sandwich and a diet soda and returned to his desk. As he ate he continued to pore over the pages of the crime scene report and the documents and other evidence he himself had collected at the house.

Shellee walked past his office, then stopped fast and returned. She stared at him then barked a laugh.

"What?" he asked.

"This is too weird, you eating at your desk."

Hadn't he ever done that? he wondered. He asked her.

"No. Not once. Ever. . . . And here you are, going to crime scenes, cluttering up your desk. . . . Listen, Boss, on your way home?"

"Yes?"

"Watch out for flying pigs. The sky's gotta be full of 'em today."

"Hi," Tal said to the receptionist.

Offering her a big smile. Why not? She had sultry, doe eyes, a heart-shaped face and the slim, athletic figure of a Riverdance performer.

Margaret Ludlum—according to the name plate—glanced up and cocked a pale, red eyebrow. "Yes?"

"It's Maggie, right?"

"Can I help you?" she asked in a polite but detached tone. Tal offered a second assault of a smile then displayed his badge and ID, which resulted in a cautious frown on her freckled face.

"I'm here to see Dr. Sheldon." This was Sam Whitley's cardiologist, whose card he'd found in the couple's bedroom last night.

"It's . . ." She squinted at the ID card.

"Detective Simms."

"Sure. Just hold on. Do you have—"

"No. An appointment? No. But I need to talk to him. It's important. About a patient. A former patient. Sam Whitley."

She nodded knowingly and gave a slight wince. Word of the deaths would have spread fast, he assumed.

"Hold on, please."

She made a call and a few minutes later a balding man in his fifties stepped out into the waiting room and greeted him. Dr. Anthony Sheldon led Tal back into a large office, whose walls were filled with dozens of diplomas and citations. The office was large and beautifully decorated, as one would expect for a man who probably made a few thousand dollars an hour.

Gesturing for Tal to sit across the desk, Sheldon dropped into his own high-backed chair.

"We're looking into their deaths," Tal said. "I'd like to ask you a few questions if I could."

"Yeah, sure. Anything I can do. It was . . . I mean, we heard it was a suicide, is that right?"

"It appeared to be. We just have a few unanswered questions. How long had you treated them?"

"Well, first, not *them*. Only Sam Whitley. He'd been referred to me by his personal GP."

"That's Ronald Weinstein," Tal said. Another nugget from the boxes of evidence that'd kept him up until three A.M. "I just spoke to him."

Tal had learned a few facts from the doctor, though nothing particularly helpful, except that Weinstein had not prescribed Luminux to either of the Whitleys, nor had he ever met the Bensons. Tal continued to Sheldon, "How serious was Sam's cardiac condition?"

"Fairly serious. Hold on—let me make sure I don't misstate anything."

Sheldon pressed a buzzer on his phone.

"Yes, Doctor?"

"Margaret, bring me the Whitley file, please."

So, not Maggie.

"Right away."

A moment later the woman walked briskly into the room, coolly ignoring Tal.

He decided that he liked the Celtic dancer part. He liked "Margaret" better than "Maggie."

The tough-as-nails part gave him some pause.

"Thanks."

Sheldon looked over the file. "His heart was only working at about fifty per cent efficiency. He should've had a transplant but wasn't a good candidate for one. We were going to replace valves and several major vessels."

"Would he have survived?"

"You mean the procedures? Or afterward?"

"Both."

"The odds weren't good for either. The surgeries themselves were the riskiest. Sam wasn't a young man and he had severe deterioration in his blood vessels. If he'd survived that, he'd have a fifty-fifty chance for six months. After that, the odds would've improved somewhat."

"So it wasn't hopeless."

"Not necessarily. But, like I told him, there was also a very good chance that even if he survived he'd be bedridden for the rest of his life."

Tal said, "So you weren't surprised to hear that he'd killed himself?"

"Well, I'm a doctor. Suicide doesn't make sense to most of us. But he was facing a very risky procedure and a difficult, painful recovery with an uncertain outcome. When I heard that he'd died, naturally I was troubled, and guilty too—thinking maybe I didn't explain things properly to him. But I have to say that I wasn't utterly shocked."

"Did you know his wife?"

"She came to most of his appointments."

"But she was in good health?"

"I don't know. But she seemed healthy."

"They were close?"

"Oh, very devoted to each other."

Tal looked up. "Doctor, what's Luminux?"

"Luminux? A combination antidepressant, pain-killer and anti-anxiety medication. I'm not too familiar with it."

"Then you didn't prescribe it to Sam or his wife?"

"No—and I'd never prescribe anything to a spouse of a patient unless she was a patient of mine too. Why?"

"They both had unusually high levels of the drug in their bloodstreams when they died."

"Both of them?"

"Right."

Dr. Sheldon shook his head. "That's odd. . . . Was that the cause of death?"

"No, it was carbon monoxide."

"Oh. Their car?"

"In the garage, right."

The doctor shook his head. "Better way to go than some, I suppose. But still . . ."

Another look at the notes he'd made from his investigation. "At their house I found an insurance form for the Cardiac Support Center here at the hospital. What's that?"

"I suggested he and Liz see someone there. They work with terminal and high-risk patients, transplant candidates. Counseling and therapy mostly."

"Could they have prescribed the drug?"

"Maybe. They have MDs on staff."

"I'd like to talk to them. Who should I see?"

"Dr. Peter Dehoeven is the director. They're in building J. Go back to the main lobby, take the elevator to three, turn left and keep going."

He thanked the doctor and stepped back into the lobby. Cell phone calls weren't allowed in the hospital so he asked Margaret if he could use one of the phones on her desk. She gestured toward it distractedly and turned back to her computer. It was 3:45 and Tal had to meet Greg LaTour in fifteen minutes.

One of the Homicide Division secretaries came on the line and he asked her to tell LaTour that he'd be a little late.

But she said, "Oh, he's gone for the day."

"Gone? We had a meeting."

"Didn't say anything about it."

He hung up, angry. Had LaTour just been humoring him, agreeing to help with the case to get Tal out of his hair?

He made another call—to the Cardiac Support Center. Dr. Dehoeven was out but Tal made an appointment to see him at eight-thirty in the morning. He hung up and nearly asked Margaret to clarify the way to the Cardiac Support Center. But Sheldon's directions were solidly implanted in his memory and he'd only bring up the subject to give it one more shot with sweet Molly Malone. But why bother? He knew to a statistical certainty that he and this red-haired lass would never be step-dancing the night away then lying in bed till dawn discussing the finer point of perfect numbers.

"All the valves?" Seventy-two-year-old Robert Covey asked his cardiologist, who was sitting across from him. The name on the white jacket read *Dr. Lansdowne* in scripty stitching, but with her frosted blonde hair in a Gwyneth Paltrow bun and sly red lipstick, he thought of her only as "Dr. Jenny."

"That's right." She leaned forward. "And there's more."

For the next ten minutes she proceeded to give him the lowdown on the absurd medical extremes he'd have to endure to have a chance of seeing his seventy-third birthday.

Unfair, Covey thought. Goddamn unfair to've been singled out this way. His weight, on a six-foot-one frame, was around 180, had been all his adult life. He gave up smoking forty years ago. He'd taken weekend hikes every few months with Veronica until he lost her and then had joined a hiking club where he got even more exercise than he had with his wife, outdistancing the widows who'd try to keep up with him as they flirted relentlessly.

Dr. Jenny asked, "Are you married?"

"Widower."

"Children?"

"I have a son."

"He live nearby?"

"No, but we see a lot of each other."

"Anybody else in the area?" she asked.

"Not really, no."

The doctor regarded him carefully. "It's tough, hearing everything I've told you today. And it's going to get tougher. I'd like you to talk to somebody over at Westbrook Hospital. They have a social services department there just for heart patients. The Cardiac Support Center."

"Shrink?"

"Counselor/nurses, they're called."

"They wear short skirts?" Covey asked.

"The men don't," the doctor said, deadpan.

"Touché. Well, thanks, but I don't think that's for me."

"Take the number anyway. If nothing else, they're somebody to talk to."

She took out a card and set it on the desk. He noticed that she had perfect fingernails, opalescent pink, though they were very short—as befit someone who cracked open human chests on occasion.

Covey asked her a number of questions about the procedures and what he could expect, sizing up his odds. Initially she seemed reluctant to quantify his chances but she sensed finally that he could indeed handle the numbers and told him. "Sixty-forty against."

"Is that optimistic or pessimistic?"

"Neither. It's realistic."

He liked that.

There were more tests that needed to be done, the doctor explained, before any procedures could be scheduled. "You can make the appointment with Janice."

"Sooner rather than later?"

The doctor didn't smile when she said, "That would be the wise choice."

He rose. Then paused. "Does this mean I should stop having strenuous sex?"

Dr. Jenny blinked and a moment later they both laughed.

"Ain't it grand being old? All the crap you can get away with."

"Make that appointment, Mr. Covey."

He walked toward the door. She joined him. He thought she was seeing him out but she held out her hand; he'd neglected to take the card containing the name and number of the Cardiac Support Center at Westbrook Hospital.

"Can I blame my memory?"

"No way. You're sharper than me." The doctor winked and turned back to her desk.

He made the appointment with the receptionist and left the building. Outside, still clutching the Cardiac Support Center card, he noticed a trash container on the sidewalk. He veered toward it and lifted the card like a Frisbee, about to sail the tiny rectangle into the pile of soda empties and limp newspapers. But then he paused.

Up the street he found a pay phone. Worth more than fifty million dollars, Robert Covey believed that cell phones were unnecessary luxuries. He set the card on the ledge, donned his reading glasses and began fishing in his leather change pouch for some coins.

∞

Dr. Peter Dehoeven was a tall blond man who spoke with an accent that Tal couldn't quite place.

European—Scandinavian or German maybe. It was quite thick at times and that, coupled with his oddly barren office suggested that he'd come to the U.S. recently. Not only was it far sparser than the cardiologist Dr. Anthony Sheldon's but the walls featured not a single framed testament to his education and training.

It was early the next morning and Dehoeven was elaborating on the mission of his Cardiac Support Center. He told Tal that the CSC counselors helped seriously ill patients change their diets, create exercise regimens, understand the nature of heart disease, deal with depression and anxiety, find care-givers, and counsel family members. They also helped with death and dying issues—funeral plans, insurance, wills. "We live to be older nowadays, yes?" Dehoeven explained, drifting in and out of his accent. "So we are having longer to experience our bodies' failing than we used to. That means, yes, we must confront our mortality for a longer time too. That is a difficult thing to do. So we need to help our patients prepare for the end of life."

When the doctor was through explaining CSC's mission Tal told him that he'd come about the Whitleys. "Were you surprised when they killed themselves?" Tal found his hand at his collar, absently adjusting his tie knot; the doctor's hung down an irritating two inches from his buttoned collar.

"Surprised?" Dehoeven hesitated. Maybe the question confused him. "I didn't think about being surprised or not. I didn't know Sam personal, yes? So I can't say—"

"You never met him?" Tal was surprised.

"Oh, we're a very big organization. Our counselors work with the patients. Me?" He laughed sadly. "My life is budget and planning and building our new facility up the street. That is taking most of my time now. We're greatly expanding, yes? But I will find out who was assigned to Sam and his wife." He called his secretary for this information.

The counselor turned out to be Claire McCaffrey, who, Dehoeven explained, was both a registered nurse and a social worker/counselor. She'd been at the CSC for a little over a year. "She's good. One of the new generation of counselors, experts in aging, yes? She has her degree in that."

"I'd like to speak to her."

Another hesitation. "I suppose this is all right. Can I ask why?"

Tal pulled a questionnaire out of his briefcase and showed it to the doctor. "I'm the department statistician. I track all the deaths in the county and collect information about them. Just routine."

"Ah, routine, yes? And yet we get a personal visit." He lifted an eyebrow in curiosity.

"Details have to be attended to."

"Yes, of course." Though he didn't seem quite convinced that Tal's presence here was completely innocuous.

He called the nurse. It seemed that Claire McCaffrey was about to leave to meet a new patient but she could give him fifteen or twenty minutes.

Dehoeven explained where her office was. Tal asked, "Just a couple more questions."

"Yessir?"

"Do you prescribe Luminux here?"

"Yes, we do often."

"Did Sam have a prescription? We couldn't find a bottle at their house."

He typed on his computer. "Yes. Our doctors wrote several prescriptions for him. He started on it a month ago."

Tal then told Dehoeven how much drugs the Whitleys had in their blood. "What do you make of that?"

"Three times the usual dosage?" He shook his head. "I couldn't tell you."

"They'd also been drinking a little. But I'm told the drug didn't directly contribute to their death. Would you agree?"

"Yes, yes," he said quickly. "It's not dangerous. It makes you drowsy and giddy. That's all."

"Drowsy *and* giddy both?" Tal asked. "Is that unusual?" The only drugs he'd taken recently were aspirin and an antiseasickness medicine that didn't work for him, as a disastrous afternoon date on a tiny sailboat on Long Island Sound had proven.

"No, not unusual. Luminux is our anti-anxiety and mood-control drug of choice here at the Center. It was just approved by the FDA. We were very glad to learn that, yes? Cardiac patients can take it without fear of aggravating their heart problems."

"Who makes it?"

He pulled a thick book off his shelf and read through it. "Montrose Pharmaceuticals in Paramus, New Jersey."

Tal wrote this down. "Doctor," he asked, "did you have another patient here . . . Don Benson?"

"I'm not knowing the name but I know very little of the patients here, as I was saying to you, yes?" He nodded out the window through which they could hear the sound of construction—the new CSC facility that was taking all his time, Tal assumed. Dehoeven typed on the computer keyboard. "No, we are not having any patients named Benson."

"In the past?"

"This is for the year, going back." A nod at the screen. "Why is it you are asking?"

Tal tapped the questionnaire. "Statistics." He put the paper away, rose and shook the doctor's hand. He was directed to the nurse's office, four doors up the hall from Dehoeven's.

Claire McCaffrey was about his age, with wavy brunette hair pulled back in a ponytail. She had a freckled, pretty face—girl next door—but seemed haggard.

"You're the one Dr. Dehoeven called about? Officer—?"

"Simms. But call me Tal."

"I go by Mac," she said. She extended her hand and a charm bracelet jangled on her right wrist as he gripped her strong fingers. He noticed a small gold ring in the shape of an ancient coin on her right hand. There was no jewelry at all on her left, he observed. "Mac," he reflected. A Celtic theme today, recalling Margaret, Dr. Sheldon's somber step-dancer.

She motioned him to sit. Her office was spacious—a desk and a sitting area with a couch and two armchairs around a coffee table. It seemed more lived-in than her boss's, he noted, comfortable. The decor was soothing—crystals, glass globes, and reproductions of Native American artifacts, plants and fresh flowers, posters and paintings of seashores and deserts and forests.

"This is about Sam Whitley, right?" she asked in a troubled monotone.

"That's right. And his wife."

She nodded, distraught. "I was up all night about it. Oh, it's so sad. I couldn't believe it." Her voice faded.

"I just have a few questions. I hope you don't mind."

"No, go ahead."

"Did you see them the day they died?" Tal asked.

"Yes, I did. We had our regular appointment."

"What exactly did you do for them?"

"What we do with most patients. Making sure they're on a heart-friendly diet, helping with insurance forms, making sure their medication's working, arranging for help in doing heavy work around the house. . . . Is there some problem? I mean, official problem?"

Looking into her troubled eyes, he chose not to use the excuse of the questionnaire as a front. "It was unusual, their deaths. They didn't fit the standard profile of most suicides. Did they say anything that'd suggest they were thinking about killing themselves?"

"No, of course not," she said quickly. "I would've intervened. Naturally."

"But?" He sensed there was something more she wanted to say.

She looked down, organized some papers, closed a folder.

"It's just . . . See, there was one thing. I spent the last couple of days going over what they said to me, looking for clues. And I remember they said how much they'd enjoyed working with me."

"That was odd?"

"It was the way they put it. It was the past tense, you know. Not *enjoy* working with me. It was *enjoyed* working with me. It didn't strike me as odd or anything at the time. But now we know . . ." A sigh. "I should've listened to what they were saying."

Recrimination. Like the couples' lawyers, like the doctors, Nurse McCaffrey would probably live with these deaths for a long, long time.

Perhaps forever . . .

"Did you know," he asked, "they just bought a book about suicide? *Making the Final Journey*."

"No, I didn't know that," she said, frowning.

Behind her desk Nurse McCaffrey—Mac—had a picture of an older couple with their arms around each other, two snapshots of big, goofy black labs, and one picture of her with the dogs. No snaps of boyfriends or husbands—or girlfriends. In Westbrook County, married or cohabitating couples comprised 74 percent of the adult population, widows 7 percent, widowers 2 percent and unmarried/divorced/noncohabitating were 17 percent. Of that latter category only 4 percent were between the ages of twenty-eight and thirty-five.

He and Mac had at least one thing in common; they were both members of the Four Percent Club.

She glanced at her watch and he focused on her again. "They were taking Luminux, right?"

She nodded. "It's a good anti-anxiety drug. We make sure the patients have it available and take it if they have a panic attack or're depressed."

"Both Sam and his wife had an unusually large amount in their bloodstreams when they died."

"Really?"

"We're trying to find what happened to the prescription, the bottle. We couldn't find it at their house."

"They had it the other day, I know."

"Are you sure?"

"Pretty sure. I don't know how much they had left on the prescription. Maybe it was gone and they threw the bottle out."

Raw data, Tal thought. Wondering what to make of these facts. Was he asking the right questions? Greg LaTour would know.

But LaTour was not here. The mathematician was on his own. He asked, "Did the Whitleys ever mention Don and Sy Benson?"

"Benson?"

"In Greeley."

"Well, no. I've never heard of them."

Tal asked, "Had anybody else been to the house that day?"

"I don't know. We were alone when I was there."

"Did you happen to call them from a pay phone that afternoon?"

"No."

"Did they mention they were expecting anyone else?"

She shook her head.

"And you left when?"

"At four. A little before."

"You sure of the time?"

"Yep. I know because I was listening to my favorite radio program in the car on my way home. The Opera Hour on NPR." A sad laugh. "It was highlights from *Madame Butterfly*."

"Isn't that about the Japanese woman who . . ." His voice faded.

"Kills herself." Mac looked up at a poster of the Grand Tetons, then one of the surf in Hawaii. "My whole life's been devoted to prolonging people's lives. This just shattered me, hearing about Sam and Liz." She seemed close to tears then controlled herself. "I was talking to Dr. Dehoeven. He just came over here from Holland. They look at death differently over there. Euthanasia and suicide are a lot more acceptable. . . . He heard about their deaths and kind of shrugged. Like it wasn't any big deal. But I can't get them out of my mind."

Silence for a moment. Then she blinked and looked at her watch again. "I've got a new patient to meet. But if there's anything I can do to help, let me know." She rose, then paused. "Are you . . . what *are* you exactly? A homicide detective?"

He laughed. "Actually, I'm a mathematician."

"A—"

But before he could explain his curious pedigree his pager went off, a sound Tal was so unaccustomed to that he dropped his briefcase then knocked several files off the nurse's desk as he bent to retrieve it. Thinking: Good job, Simms, way to impress a fellow member of the Westbrook County Four Percent Club.

"He's in there and I couldn't get him out. I'm spitting nails, Boss."

In a flash of panic Tal thought that Shellee, fuming as she pointed at his office, was referring to the sheriff himself, who'd descended from the top floor of the county building to fire Tal personally for the 2124.

But, no, she was referring to someone else.

Tal stepped inside and lifted an eyebrow to Greg LaTour. "Thought we had an appointment yester—"

"So where you been?" LaTour grumbled. "Sleepin' in?" The huge man was finishing Tal's cheese sandwich from yesterday, sending a cascade of bread crumbs everywhere.

And resting his boots on Tal's desk.

It had been LaTour's page that caught him with Mac McCaffrey. The message: "Office twenty minutes. LaTour."

The slim cop looked unhappily at the scuff marks on the desktop.

LaTour noticed but ignored him. "Here's the thing. I got the information on the wills. And, yeah, they were both changed—"

"Okay, that's suspicious—"

"Lemme finish. No, it's *not* suspicious. The beneficiaries weren't any crazy housekeepers or Moonie guru assholes controlling their minds. The Bensons didn't have any kids so all they did was add a few charities and create a trust for some nieces and nephews—for college. A hundred thousand each. Small potatoes. The Whitley girl didn't get diddly-squat from them.

"Now, the Whitleys gave their daughter—bitch or not—a third of the estate in the first version of the will. She still gets the same for herself in the new version but she also gets a little more so she can set up a Whitley family library." LaTour looked up. "Now *there's* gonna be a fucking fun place to spend Sunday afternoons. . . . Then they added some new chartites too and got rid of some other ones. . . . Oh, and if you were going to ask, they were *different* charities from the ones in the Bensons' will."

"I wasn't."

"Well, you should have. Always look for connections, Tal. That's the key in homicide. Connections between facts."

"Just like—"

"—don't say fucking statistics."

"Mathematics. Common denominators."

"Whatever," LaTour muttered. "So, the wills're out as motives. Same with—"

"The insurance polices."

"I was going to say. Small policies and most of the Bensons' goes to paying off a few small debts and giving some bucks to retired employees of the husband's companies. It's like twenty, thirty grand. Nothing suspicious there . . . Now, what'd you find?"

Tal explained about Dr. Sheldon, the cardiologist, then about Dehoeven, Mac, and the Cardiac Support Center.

LaTour asked immediately, "Both Benson and Whitley, patients of Sheldon?"

"No, only Whitley. Same for the Cardiac Support Center."

"Fuck. We . . . what'sa matter?"

"You want to get your boots off my desk."

Irritated, LaTour swung his feet around to the floor. "We need a connection, I was saying. Something—"

"I might have one," Tal said quickly. "Drugs."

"What, the old folks were dealing?" The sarcasm had returned. He added, "You still harping on that Lumicrap?"

"Lumi*nux*." Makes you drowsy *and* happy. Could mess up your judgment. Make you susceptible to suggestions."

"That you blow your fucking brains out? One hell of a suggestion."

"Maybe not—if you were taking three times the normal dosage . . ."

"You think somebody slipped it to 'em?"

"Maybe." Tal nodded. "The counselor from the Cardiac Support unit left the Whitleys' at four. They died around eight. Plenty of time for somebody to stop by, put some stuff in their drinks. Whoever called them from that pay phone."

"Okay, the Whitleys were taking it. What about the Bensons?"

"They were cremated the day after they died, remember? We'll never know."

LaTour finished the sandwich. "You don't mind, do you? It was just sitting there."

He glanced at the desktop. "You got crumbs everywhere."

The cop leaned forward and blew them to the floor. He sipped coffee from a mug that'd left a sticky ring on an evidence report file. "Okay, your—what the fuck do you call it? Theory?"

"Theorem."

"Is that somebody slipped 'em that shit? But who? And why?"

"I don't know that part yet."

"Those *parts*," LaTour corrected. "Who and why. Parts plural."

Tal sighed.

"You think you could really give somebody a drug and tell 'em to kill themselves and they will?"

"Let's go find out," Tal said.

"Huh?"

The statistician flipped through his notes. "The company that makes the drug? It's over in Paramus. Off the Parkway. Let's go talk to 'em."

"Shit. All the way to Jersey."

"You have a better idea?"

"I don't need any fucking ideas. This's your case, remember?"

"Maybe *I* twenty-one-twenty-foured it. But it's *everybody's* case now. Let's go."

She would've looked pretty good in a short skirt, Robert Covey thought, but unfortunately she was wearing slacks.

"Mr. Covey, I'm from the Cardiac Support Center."

"Call me Bob. Or you'll make me feel as old as your older brother."

She was a little short for his taste but then he had to remind himself that she was here to help him get some pig parts stuck into his chest and rebuild a bunch of leaking veins and arteries—or else die with as little mess as he could. Besides, he claimed that he had a rule he'd never date a woman a third his age. (When the truth was that after Veronica maybe he joked and maybe he flirted but in his heart he was content never to date at all.)

He held the door for her and gestured her inside with a slight bow. He could see her defenses lower a bit. She was probably used to dealing with all sorts of pricks in this line of work and was wary during their initial meeting, but Covey limited his grousing to surly repairmen and clerks and waitresses who thought because he was old he was stupid.

There was, he felt, no need for impending death to skew his manners. He invited her in and directed her to the couch in his den.

"Welcome, Ms. McCaffrey—"

"How 'bout Mac? That's what my mother used to call me when I was good."

"What'd she call you when you were bad?"

"Mac then too. Though she managed to get two syllables out of it. So, go ahead."

He lifted an eyebrow. "With what?"

"With what you were going to tell me. That you don't need me here. That you don't need any help, that you're only seeing me to humor your cardiologist, that you don't want any hand-holding, that you don't want to be coddled, that you don't want to change your diet, you don't want to exercise, you don't want to give up smoking and you don't want to stop drinking your—" She glanced at the bar and eyed the bottles. "—your port. So here're the ground rules. Fair enough, no hand-holding, no coddling. That's my part of the deal. But, yes, you'll give up smoking—"

"Did before you were born, thank you very much."

"Good. And you will be exercising and eating a cardio-friendly diet. And about the port—"

"Hold on—"

"I think we'll limit you to three a night."

"Four," he said quickly.

"Three. And I suspect on most nights you only have two."

"I can live with three," he grumbled. She'd been right about the two (though, okay, sometimes a little bourbon joined the party).

Damn, he liked her. He always had liked strong women. Like Veronica.

Then she was on to other topics. Practical things about what the Cardiac Support Center did and what it didn't do, about care givers, about home care, about insurance.

"Now, I understand you're a widower. How long were you married?"

"Forty-nine years."

"Well, now, that's wonderful."

"Ver and I had a very nice life together. Pissed me off we missed the fiftieth. I had a party planned. Complete with a harpist and open bar." He raised an eyebrow. "Vintage port included."

"And you have a son?"

"That's right. Randall. He lives in California. Runs a computer company. But one that actually makes money. Imagine that! Wears his hair too long and lives with a woman—he oughta get married—but he's a good boy."

"You see him much?"

"All the time."

"When did you talk to him last?"

"The other day."

"And you've told him all about your condition?"

"You bet."

"Good. Is he going to get out here?"

"In a week or so. He's traveling. Got a big deal he's putting together."

She was taking something out of her purse. "Our doctor at the clinic prescribed this." She handed him a bottle. "Luminux. It's an anti-anxiety agent."

"I say no to drugs."

"This's a new generation. You're going through a lot of stuff right now. It'll make you feel better. Virtually no side effects—"

"You mean it won't take me back to my days as a beatnik in the Village?" She laughed and he added, "Actually, think I'll pass."

"It's good for you." She shook out two pills into a small cup and handed them to him. She walked to the bar and poured a glass of water.

Watching her, acting like she lived here, Covey scoffed, "You ever negotiate?"

"Not when I know I'm right."

"Tough lady." He glanced down at the pills in his hand. "I take these, that means I can't have my port, right?"

"Sure you can. You know, moderation's the key to everything."

"You don't seem like a moderate woman."

"Oh, hell no, I'm not. But I don't practice what I preach." And she passed him the glass of water.

Late afternoon, driving to Jersey.

Tal fiddled with the radio trying to find the Opera Hour program that Nurse Mac had mentioned.

LaTour looked at the dash as if he was surprised the car even had a radio.

Moving up and down the dial, through the several National Public Radio bands, he couldn't find the show. What time had she'd said it came on? He couldn't remember. He wondered why he cared what she listened to. He didn't even like opera that much. He gave up and settled on all news, all the time. LaTour stood that for five minutes then put the game on.

The homicide cop was either preoccupied or just a natural-born bad driver. Weaving, speeding well over the limit, then braking to a crawl. Occasionally he'd lift his middle finger to other drivers in a way that was almost endearing.

Probably happier on a motorcycle, Tal reflected.

LaTour tuned in the game on the radio. They listened for a while, neither speaking.

"So," Tal tried. "Where you live?"

"Near the station house."

Nothing more.

"Been on the force long?"

"A while."

New York seven, Boston three. . . .

"You married?" Tal had noticed that he wore no wedding band.

More silence.

Tal turned down the volume and repeated the question.

After a long moment LaTour grumbled, "That's something else."

"Oh." Having no idea what the cop meant.

He supposed there was a story here—a hard divorce, lost children. *And six point three percent kill themselves before retirement . . .*

But whatever the sad story might be, it was only for Bear's friends in the Department, those on the Real Crimes side of the pen.

Not for Einstein, the calculator humper.

They fell silent and drove on amid the white noise of the sportscasters.

Ten minutes later LaTour skidded off the parkway and turned down a winding side road.

Montrose Pharmaceuticals was a small series of glass and chrome buildings in a landscaped industrial park. Far smaller than Pfizer and the other major drug companies in the Garden State, it nonetheless must've done pretty well in sales—to judge from the number of Mercedes, Jaguars, and Porsches in the employee parking lot.

Inside the elegant reception area, Westbrook County Sheriff's Department badges raised some eyebrows. But, Tal concluded, it was LaTour's bulk and hostile gaze that cut through whatever barriers existed here to gaining access to the inner sanctum of the company's president.

In five minutes they were sitting in the office of Daniel Montrose, an earnest, balding man in his late forties. His eyes were as quick as his appearance was rumpled and Tal concluded that he was a kindred soul; a scientist, rather than a salesperson. The man rocked back and forth in his chair, peering at them through stylish glasses with a certain distraction. Uneasiness too.

Nobody said anything for a moment and Tal felt the tension in the office rise appreciably. He glanced at LaTour, who simply sat in the leather-and-chrome chair, looking around the opulent space. Maybe stonewalling was a technique that real cops used to get people to start talking.

"We've been getting ready for our sales conference," Montrose suddenly volunteered. "It's going to be a good one."

"Is it?" Tal asked.

"That's right. Our biggest. Las Vegas this year." Then he clammed up again.

Tal wanted to echo, "Vegas?" for some reason. But he didn't.

Finally LaTour said, "Tell us about Luminux."

"Luminux. Right, Luminux . . . I'd really like to know, I mean, if it's not against any rules or anything, what you want to know for. I mean, and what are you doing here? You haven't really said."

"We're investigating some suicides."

"Suicides?" he asked, frowning. "And Luminux is involved?"

"Yes indeedy," LaTour said with all the cheer that the word required.

"But . . . it's based on a mild diazepam derivative. It'd be very difficult to fatally overdose on it."

"No, they died from other causes. But we found—"

The door swung open and a strikingly beautiful woman walked into the office. She blinked at the visitors and said a very unsorrowful, "Sorry. Thought you were alone." She set a stack of folders on Montrose's desk.

"These are some police officers from Westbrook County," the president told her.

She looked at them more carefully. "Police. Is something wrong?"

Tal put her at forty. Long, serpentine face with cool eyes, very beautiful in a European fashion-model way. Slim legs with runner's calves. Tal decided that she was like Sheldon's Gaelic assistant, an example of some predatory genus very different from Mac McCaffrey's.

Neither Tal nor LaTour answered her question. Montrose introduced her—Karen Billings. Her title was a mouthful but it had something to do with product support and patient relations.

"They were just asking about Luminux. There've been some problems, they're claiming."

"Problems?"

"They were just saying . . ." Montrose pushed his glasses higher on his nose. "Well, what *were* you saying?"

Tal continued, "A couple of people who killed themselves had three times the normal amount of Luminux in their systems."

"But that can't kill them. It couldn't have. I don't see why . . ." Her voice faded and she looked toward Montrose. They eyed each other, poker-faced. She then said coolly to LaTour, "What exactly would you like to know?"

"First of all, how could they get it into their bloodstream?" La-Tour sat back, the chair creaking alarmingly. Tal wondered if he'd put his feet up on Montrose's desk.

"You mean how could it be administered?"

"Yeah."

"Orally's the only way. It's not available in an IV form yet."

"But could it be mixed in food or a drink?"

"You think somebody did that?" Montrose asked. Billings remained silent, looking from Tal to LaTour and back again with her cautious, swept-wing eyes.

"Could it be done?" Tal asked.

"Of course," the president said. "Sure. It's water soluble. The vehicle's bitter—"

"The—?"

"The inert base we mix it with. The drug itself is tasteless but we add a compound to make it bitter so kids'll spit it out if they eat it by mistake. But you can mask that with sugar or—"

"Alcohol?"

Billings snapped, "Drinking isn't recommended when taking—"

LaTour grumbled, "I'm not talking about the fucking fine print on the label. I'm talking about could you hide the flavor by mixing it in a drink?"

She hesitated. Then finally answered, "One could." She clicked her nails together in impatience or anger.

"So what's it do to you?"

Montrose said, "It's essentially an anti-anxiety and mood-elevating agent, not a sleeping pill. It makes you relaxed. You get happier."

"Does it mess with your thinking?"

"There's some cognitive dimunition."

"English?" LaTour grumbled.

"They'd feel slightly disoriented—but in a happy way."

Tal recalled the misspellings in the note. "Would it affect their handwriting and spelling?"

Dangrous . . .

"It could, yes."

Tal said. "Would their judgment be affected?"

"Judgment?" Billings asked harshly. "That's subjective."

"Whatta you mean?"

"There's no quantifiable measure for one's ability to judge something."

"No? How 'bout if *one* puts a gun to *one*'s head and pulls the trigger?" LaTour said. "I call that *bad* judgment. Any chance we agree on that?"

"What the fuck're you getting at?" Billings snapped.

"Karen," Montrose said, pulling off his designer glasses and rubbing his eyes.

She ignored her boss. "You think they took our drug and decided to kill themselves? You think we're to blame for that? This drug—"

"This drug that a couple of people popped—maybe *four* people—and then killed themselves. Whatta we say about that from a statistical point of view?" LaTour turned to Tal.

"Well within the percentile of probability for establishing a causal relationship between the two events."

"There you go. Science has spoken."

Tal wondered if they were playing the good-cop/bad-cop routine you see in movies. He tried again. "Could an overdose of Luminux have impaired their judgment?"

"Not enough so that they'd decide to kill themselves," she said firmly. Montrose said nothing.

"That your opinion too?" LaTour muttered to him.

The president said, "Yes, it is."

Tal persisted, "How about making them susceptible?"

Billings leapt in with, "I don't know what you mean. . . . This is all crazy."

Tal ignored her and said levelly to Montrose, "Could somebody persuade a person taking an overdose of Luminux to kill themselves?"

Silence filled the office.

Billings said, "I strongly doubt it."

"But you ain't saying no." LaTour grumbled.

A glance between Billings and Montrose. Finally he pulled his wire-rims back on, looked away and said, "We're not saying no."

∞

They next morning Tal and LaTour arrived at the station house at the same time, and the odd couple walked together through the Detective Division pen into Tal's office.

They looked over the case so far and found no firm leads.

"Still no who," LaTour grumbled. "Still no why."

"But we've got a how," Tal pointed out. Meaning the concession about Luminux making one suggestible.

"Fuck *how*. I want *who*."

At just that moment they received a possible answer.

Shellee stepped into Tal's office. Pointedly ignoring the homicide cop, she said, "You're back. Good. Got a call from the P-I-I team in Greeley. They said a neighbor saw a woman in a small, dark car arrive at the Bensons' house about an hour before they died. She was wearing sunglasses and a tan or beige baseball cap. The neighbor didn't recognize her."

"Car?" LaTour snapped.

It's hard to ignore an armed, 250-pound, goateed man named Bear but Shellee was just the woman for the job.

Continuing to speak to her boss, she said, "They weren't sure what time she got there but it was before lunch. She stayed maybe forty minutes then left. That'd be an hour or so before they killed themselves." A pause. "The car was a small sedan. The witness didn't remember the color."

"Did you ask about the—" LaTour began.

"They didn't see the tag number," she told Tal. "Now, that's not all. DMV finally calls back and tells me that Sandra Whitley drives a blue BMW 325."

"Small wheelbase," Tal said.

"And, getting better 'n' better, Boss. Guess who's leaving town before her parents' memorial service."

"Sandra?"

"How the hell d'you find that out?" LaTour asked.

She turned coldly to him. "Detective Simms asked to me organize all the evidence from the Whitley crime scene. Because, like he says, having facts and files out of order is as bad as not having them at all. I found a note in the Whitley evidence file with an airline locator number. It was for a flight from Newark today to San Francisco, continuing on to Hawaii. I called and they told me it was a confirmed ticket for Sandra Whitley. Return is open."

"Meaning the bitch might not be coming back at all," LaTour said. "Going on vacation without saying goodbye to the folks? That's fucking harsh."

"Good job," Tal told Shellee.

Eyes down, a faint smile of acknowledgment.

LaTour dropped into one of Tal's chairs, belched softly and said, "You're doing such a good job, Sherry, here, look up whatever you can about this shit." He offered her the notes on Luminux.

"It's Shellee," she snapped and glanced at Tal, who mouthed, "Please."

She snatched them from LaTour's hand and clattered down the hall on her dangerous heels.

LaTour looked over the handwritten notes she'd given them and growled, "So what about the why? A motive?"

Tal spread the files out of his desk—all the crime scene information, the photos, the notes he'd taken.

What were the common denominators? The deaths of two couples. Extremely wealthy. The husbands ill, yes, but not hopelessly so. Drugs that make you suggestible.

A giddy lunch then suicide, a drink beside a romantic fire then suicide . . .

Romantic . . .

"Hmm," Tal mused, thinking back to the Whitleys'.

"What hmm?"

"Let's think about the wills again."

"We tried that," LaTour said.

"But what if they were *about* to be changed?"

"Whatta you mean?"

"Try this for an assumption: Say the Whitleys and their daughter had some big fight in the past week. They were going to change their will again—this time to cut her out completely."

"Yeah, but their lawyer'd know that."

"Not if she killed them before they talked to him. I remember smelling smoke from the fire when I walked into the Whitley house. I thought they'd built this romantic fire just before they killed themselves. But maybe they hadn't. Maybe Sandra burned some evidence—something about changing the will, memos to the lawyer, estate planning stuff. Remember, she snatched the mail at the house. One was to the lawyer. Maybe that was why she came back— to make sure there was no evidence left. Hell, wished I'd searched her purse. I just didn't think about it."

"Yeah, but offing her own *parents*?" LaTour asked skeptically.

"Seventeen point two percent of murderers are related to their victims." Tal added pointedly, "I know that because of my questionnaires, by the way."

LaTour rolled his eyes. "What about the Bensons?"

"Maybe they met in some cardiac support group, maybe they were in the same country club. Whitley might've mentioned something about the will to them. Sandra found out and had to take them out too."

"Jesus, you say 'maybe' a lot."

"It's a theorem, I keep saying. Let's go prove it or disprove it. See if she's got an alibi. And we'll have forensics go through the fireplace."

"If the ash is intact," LaTour said, "they can image the printing on the sheet. Those techs're fucking geniuses."

Tal called Crime Scene again and arranged to have a team return to the Whitleys' house. Then he said, "Okay, let's go visit our suspect."

"Hold on there."

When Greg LaTour charged up to you, muttering the way he'd just done, you held on there.

Even tough Sandra Whitley.

She'd been about to climb into the BMW sitting outside her luxurious house. Suitcases sat next to her.

"Step away from the car," LaTour said, flashing his badge.

Tal said, "We'd like to ask you a few questions, ma'am."

"You again! What the hell're you talking about?" Her voice was angry but she did as she was told.

"You're on your way out of town?" LaTour took her purse off her shoulder. "Just keep your hands at your sides."

"I've got a meeting I can't miss."

"In Hawaii?"

Sandra was regaining the initiative. "I'm an attorney, like I told you. I *will* find out how you got that information and for your sake there better've been a warrant involved."

Did they *need* a warrant? Tal wondered.

"Meeting in Hawaii?" LaTour repeated. "With an open return?"

"What're you implying?"

"It's a little odd, don't you think. Flying off to the South Seas a few days after your parents die? Not going to the funeral?"

"Funerals're for the survivors. I've made peace with my parents and their deaths. They wouldn't've wanted me to blow off an important meeting. Dad was as much a businessman as a father. I'm as much a businesswoman as a daughter."

Her eyes slipped to Tal and she gave a sour laugh. "Okay, you got me, Simms." Emphasizing the name was presumably to remind him again that his name would be prominently included in the court documents she filed. She nodded to the purse. "It's all in there. The evidence about me escaping the country after—what?—stealing my parents' money? What *exactly* do you think I've done?"

"We're not accusing you of anything. We just want to—"

"—ask you a few questions."

"So ask, goddamn it."

LaTour was reading a lengthy document he'd found in her purse.

He frowned and handed it to Tal, then asked her, "Can you tell me where you were the night your parents died?"

"Why?"

"Look, lady, you can cooperate or you can clam up and we'll—"

"Go downtown. Yadda, yadda, yadda. I've heard this before."

LaTour frowned at Tal and mouthed, "What's downtown?" Tal shrugged and returned to the document. It was a business plan for a company that was setting up an energy joint venture in Hawaii. Her law firm was representing it. The preliminary meeting seemed to be scheduled for two days from now in Hawaii. There was a memo saying that the meetings could go on for weeks and recommended that the participants get open-return tickets.

Oh.

"Since I have to get to the airport now," she snapped, "and I don't have time for any bullshit, okay, I'll tell you where I was on the night of the quote crime. On an airplane. I flew back on United Airlines from San Francisco, the flight that got in about 11 P.M. My boarding pass is probably in there—" A contemptuous nod at the purse LaTour held. "And if it isn't, I'm sure there's a record of the flight at the airline. With security being what it is nowadays, picture IDs and everything, that's probably a pretty solid alibi, don't you think?"

Did seem to be, Tal agreed silently. And it got even more solid when LaTour found the boarding pass and ticket receipt in her purse.

Tal's phone began ringing and he was happy for the chance to escape from Sandra's searing fury. He heard Shellee speak from the receiver. "Hey, Boss, 's'me."

"What's up?"

"Crime Scene called. They went through all the ash in the Whitleys' fireplace, looking for a letter or something about changing the will. They didn't find anything about that at all. Something had been burned but it was all just a bunch of information on companies—computer and biotech companies. The Crime Scene guy was thinking Mr. Whitley might've just used some old junk mail or something to start the fire."

Once again: Oh.

Then: Damn.

"Thanks."

He nodded LaTour aside and told him what Crime Scene had reported.

"Shit on the street," he whispered. "Jumped a little fast here . . . Okay, let's go kiss some ass. Brother."

The groveling time was quite limited—Sandra was adamant about catching her plane. She sped out of the driveway, leaving behind a blue cloud of tire smoke.

"Aw, she'll forget about it," LaTour said.

"You think?" Tal asked.

A pause. "Nope. We're way fucked." He added, "We still gotta find the mysterious babe in the sunglasses and hat." They climbed into the car and LaTour pulled into traffic.

Tal wondered if Mac McCaffrey might've seen someone like that around the Whitleys' place. Besides, it'd be a good excuse to see her again. Tal said, "I'll look into that one."

"You?" LaTour laughed.

"Yeah. Me. What's so funny about that?"

"I don't know. Just you never investigated a case before."

"So? You think I can't interview witnesses on my own? You think I should just go back home and hump my calculator?"

Silence. Tal hadn't meant to say it.

"You heard that?" LaTour finally asked, no longer laughing.

"I heard."

"Hey, I didn't mean it, you know."

"Didn't mean it?" Tal asked, giving an exaggerated squint. "As in you didn't mean for me to hear you? Or as in you don't actually believe I have sex with adding machines?"

"I'm sorry, okay? . . . I bust people's chops sometimes. It's the way I am. I do it to everybody. Fuck, people do it to me. They call me Bear 'causa my gut. They call you Einstein 'cause you're smart."

"Not to my face."

LaTour hesitated. "You're right. Not to your face. . . . You know, you're too polite, Tal. You can give me a lot more shit. I wouldn't mind. You're too uptight. Loosen up."

"So it's *my* fault that I'm pissed 'cause you dump on me?"

"It was . . ." He began defensively but then he stopped. "Okay, I'm sorry. I am. . . . Hey, I don't apologize a lot, you know. I'm not very good at it."

"That's an apology?"

"I'm doing the best I can . . . Whatta you want?"

Silence.

"All right," Tal said finally.

LaTour sped the car around a corner and wove frighteningly through the heavy traffic. Finally he said, "It's okay, though, you know."

"What's okay?"

"If you want to."

"Want to what?" Tal asked.

"You know, you and your calculator. . . . Lot safer than some of the weird shit you see nowadays."

"LaTour," Tal said, "you can—"

"You just seemed defensive about it, you know. Figure I probably hit close to home, you know what I'm saying?"

"You can go fuck yourself."

The huge cop was laughing hard. "Shit, don'tcha feel like we're finally breaking the ice here? I think we are. Now, I'll drop you off back at your car, Einstein, and you can go on this secret mission all by your lonesome."

His stated purpose was to ask her if she'd ever seen the mysterious woman in the baseball cap and sunglasses, driving a small car, at the Whitleys' house.

Lame, Tal thought.

Lame *and* transparent—since he could've asked her that on the phone. He was sure the true mission here was so obvious that it was laughable: To get a feel for what would happen if he asked Mac Mc-Caffrey out to dinner. Not to actually *invite* her out at this point, of course; she was, after all, a potential witness. No, he just wanted to test the waters.

Tal parked along Elm Street and climbed out of the car, enjoying the complicated smells of the April air, the skin-temperature breeze, the golden snowflakes of fallen forsythia petals covering the lawn.

Walking toward the park where he'd arranged to meet her, Tal reflected on his recent romantic life.

Fine, he concluded. It was fine.

He dated 2.66 women a month. The median age of his dates in

the past 12 months was approximately 31 (a number skewed some-what by the embarrassing—but highly memorable—outlier of a Co-lumbia University senior). And the mean IQ of the women was around 140 or up—and that latter statistic was a very sharp bell curve with a very narrow standard deviation; Talbot Simms went for intel-lect before anything else.

It was this latter criteria, though, he'd come to believe lately, that led to the tepid adjective "fine."

Yes, he'd had many interesting evenings with his 2⅔ dates every month. He'd discussed with them Cartesian hyperbolic doubt. He'd argue about the validity of analyzing objects in terms of their primary qualities ("No way! *I'm* suspicious of secondary qualities too. . . . I mean, how 'bout that? We have a lot in com-mon!") They'd draft mathematical formulae in crayon on the paper table coverings at the Crab House. They'd discuss Fermat's Last Theorem until 2:00 or 3:00 A.M. (These were not wholly academic encounters, of course; Tal Simms happened to have a full-size chalkboard in his bedroom).

He was intellectually stimulated by most of these women. He even learned things from them.

But he didn't really have a lot of fun.

Mac McCaffrey, he believed, would be fun.

She'd sounded surprised when he'd called. Cautious too at first. But after a minute or two she'd relaxed and had seemed almost pleased at the idea that he wanted to meet with her.

He now spotted her in the park next to the Knickerbocker Home, which appeared to be a nursing facility, where she suggested they get together.

"Hey," he said.

"Hi there. Hope you don't mind meeting outside. I hate to be cooped up."

He recalled the Sierra Club posters in her office. "No, it's beauti-ful here."

Her sharp green eyes, set in her freckled face, looked away and took in the sights of the park. Tal sat down and they made small talk for five minutes or so. Finally she asked, "You started to tell me that you're, what, a mathematician?"

"That's right."

She smiled. There was crookedness to her mouth, an asymmetry, which he found charming. "That's pretty cool. You could be on a TV series. Like *CSI* or *Law and Order*, you know. Call it *Math Cop*."

They laughed. He glanced down at her shoes, old black Reeboks, and saw they were nearly worn out. He noticed too a bare spot on the knee of her jeans. It'd been rewoven. He thought of cardiologist Anthony Sheldon's designer wardrobe and huge office, and reflected that Mac worked in an entirely different part of the health care universe.

"So I was wondering," she asked. "Why this interest in the Whitleys' deaths?"

"Like I said. They were out of the ordinary."

"I guess I mean, why are *you* interested? Did you lose somebody? To suicide, I mean."

"Oh, no. My father's alive. My mother passed away a while ago. A stroke."

"I'm sorry. She must've been young."

"Was, yes."

She waved a bee away. "Is your dad in the area?"

"Nope. Professor in Chicago."

"Math?"

"Naturally. Runs in the family." He told her about Wall Street, the financial crimes, statistics.

"All that adding and subtracting. Doesn't it get, I don't know, boring?"

"Oh, no, just the opposite. Numbers go on forever. Infinite questions, challenges. And remember, math is a lot more than just calculations. What excites me is that numbers let us understand the world. And when you understand something you have control over it."

"Control?" she asked, serious suddenly. "Numbers won't keep you from getting hurt. From dying."

"Sure they can," he replied. "Numbers make car brakes work and keep airplanes in the air and let you call the fire department. Medicine, science."

"I guess so. Never thought about it." Another crooked smile. "You're pretty enthusiastic about the subject."

Tal asked, "Pascal?"

"Heard of him."

"A philosopher. He was a prodigy at math but he gave it up completely. He said math was so enjoyable it had to be related to sex. It was sinful."

"Hold on, mister," she said, laughing. "You got some math porn you want to show me?"

Tal decided that the preliminary groundwork for the date was going pretty well. But, apropos of which, enough about himself. He asked, "How'd you get into your field?"

"I always liked taking care of people . . . or animals," she explained. "Somebody's pet'd get hurt, I'd be the one to try to help it. I hate seeing anybody in pain. I was going to go to med school but my mom got sick and, without a father around, I had to put that on hold—where it's been for. . . . well, for a few years."

No explanation about the missing father. But he sensed that, like him, she didn't want to discuss dad. A common denominator among these particular members of the Four Percent Club.

She continued, looking at the nursing home door. "Why I'm doing *this* particularly? My mother, I guess. Her exit was pretty tough. Nobody really helped her. Except me, and I didn't know very much. The hospital she was in didn't give her any support. So after she passed I decided I'd go into the field myself. Make sure patients have a comfortable time at the end."

"It doesn't get you down?"

"Some times are tougher than others. But I'm lucky. I'm not all that religious but I do think there's something there after we die."

Tal nodded but he said nothing. He'd always wanted to believe in that *something* too but religion wasn't allowed in the Simms household—nothing, that is, except the cold deity of numbers his father worshiped—and it seemed to Tal that if you don't get hooked early by some kind of spiritualism, you'll rarely get the bug later. Still, people do change. He recalled that the Bensons had been atheists but apparently toward the end had come to believe differently.

Together forever . . .

Mac was continuing, speaking of her job at the Cardiac Support Center. "I like working with the patients. And I'm good, if I do say so myself. I stay away from the sentiment, the maudlin crap. I knock back some scotch or wine with them. Watch movies, pig out on low-fat chips and popcorn, tell some good death and dying jokes."

"No," Tal said, frowning. "Jokes?"

"You bet. Here's one: When I die, I want to go peacefully in my sleep, like my grandfather. . . . Not screaming like the passengers in the car with him."

Tal blinked then laughed hard. She was pleased he'd enjoyed it, he could tell. He said, "Hey, there's a statistician joke. Want to hear it?"

"Sure."

"Statistics show that a person gets robbed every four minutes. And, man, is he getting tired of it."

She smiled. "That really sucks."

"Best we can do," Tal said. Then after a moment he added, "But Dr. Dehoeven said that your support center isn't all death and dying. There's a lot of things you do to help before and after surgery."

"Oh, sure," she said. "Didn't mean to neglect that. Exercise, diet, care giving, getting the family involved, psychotherapy."

Silence for a moment, a silence that, he felt, was suddenly asking: what exactly was he doing here?

He said, "I have a question about the suicides. Some witnesses said they saw a woman in sunglasses and a beige baseball cap, driving a small car, at the Bensons' house just before they killed themselves. I was wondering if you ever saw anyone like that around their house."

A pause. "Me?" she asked, frowning. "I wasn't seeing the Bensons, remember?"

"No, I mean at the Whitleys."

"Oh." She thought for a moment. "Their daughter came by a couple of times."

"No, it wasn't her."

"They had a cleaning lady. But she drove a van. And I never saw her in a hat."

Her voice had grown weaker and Tal knew that her mood had changed quickly. Probably the subject of the Whitleys had done it—raised the issue of whether there was anything else she might've done to keep them from dying.

Silence surrounded them, as dense as the humid April air, redolent with the scent of lilac. He began to think that it was a bad idea to mix a personal matter with a professional one—especially when it involved patients who had just died. Conversation resumed but it was now different, superficial, and, as if by mutual decision, they both glanced at their watches, said goodbye, then rose and headed down the same sidewalk in different directions.

Shellee appeared in the doorway of Tal's office, where the statistician and LaTour were parked. "Found something," she said in her Beantown accent.

"Yeah, whatsat?" LaTour asked, looking over a pile of documents that she was handing her boss.

She leaned close to Tal and whispered, "He just gonna move in here?"

Tal smiled and said to her, "Thanks, Detective."

An eye-roll was her response.

"Where'd you get all that?" LaTour asked, pointing at the papers but glancing at her chest.

"The Internet," Shellee snapped as she left. "Where else?"

"She got all that information from there?" the big cop asked, taking the stack and flipping through it.

Tal saw a chance for a bit of cop-cop jibe, now that, yeah, the ice was broken, and he nearly said to LaTour, you'd be surprised, there's a lot more on line than wicked-sluts.com that you browse through in the wee hours. But then he recalled the silence when he asked about the cop's family life.

That's something else . . .

And he decided a reference to lonely nights at home was out of line. He kept the joke to himself.

LaTour handed the sheets to Tal. "I'm not gonna read all this crap. It's got fucking numbers in it. Gimme the bottom line."

Tal skimmed the information, much of which might have contained numbers but was still impossible for him to understand. It was mostly chemical jargon and medical formulae. But toward the end he found a summary. He frowned and read it again.

"Jesus."

"What?"

"We maybe have our perps."

"No shit."

The documents Shellee had found were from a consumer protection Web site devoted to medicine. They reported that the FDA was having doubts about Luminux because the drug trials showed that it had hallucinogenic properties. Several people in the trials had had psychotic episodes believed to have been caused by the drug. Others reported violent mood swings. Those with serious problems were a small minority of those in the trials, less than a tenth of one percent. But the reactions were so severe that the FDA was very doubtful about approving it.

But Shellee also found that the agency had approved Luminux a year ago, despite the dangers.

"Okay, got it," LaTour said. "How's this for a maybe, Einstein? Montrose slipped some money to somebody to get the drug approved and then kept an eye on the patients taking it, looking for anybody who had bad reactions."

The cops speculated that he'd have those patients killed—making it look like suicide—so that no problems with Luminux ever surfaced. LaTour wondered if this was a realistic motive—until Tal found a printout that revealed that Luminux was Montrose's only money-maker, to the tune of $78 million a year.

Their other postulate was that it had been Karen Billings—as patient relations director—who might have been the woman in the hat and sunglasses at the Bensons and who'd left the tire tracks and worn the gloves at the Whitleys. She'd spent time with them, given them overdoses, talked them into buying the suicide manual and helped them—what had Mac said? That was it: Helped them "exit."

"Some fucking patient relations," LaTour said. "That's harsh." Using his favorite adjective. "Let's go see 'em."

Ignoring—with difficulty—the clutter on his desk, Tal opened the top drawer of his desk and pulled out his pistol. He started to mount it to his belt but the holster clip slipped and the weapon dropped to the floor. He winced as it hit. Grimacing, Tal bent down and retrieved then hooked it on successfully.

As he glanced up he saw LaTour watching him with a faint smile on his face. "Do me a favor. It probably won't come to it but if it does, lemme do the shooting, okay?"

∞

Nurse McCaffrey would be arriving soon.

No, "Mac" was her preferred name, Robert Covey reminded himself.

He stood in front of his liquor cabinet and finally selected a nice vintage port, a 1977. He thought it would go well with the Saga blue cheese and shrimp he'd had laid out for her, and the water crackers and nonfat dip for himself. He'd driven to the Stop 'N' Shop that morning to pick up the groceries.

Covey arranged the food, bottle and glasses on a silver tray. Oh, napkins. Forgot the napkins. He found some under the counter and set them out on the tray, which he carried into the living room. Next to it were some old scrapbooks he'd unearthed from the basement. He wanted to show her pictures—snapshots of his brother, now long gone, and his nieces, and his wife, of course. He also had many pictures of his son.

Oh, Randall . . .

Yep, he liked Mac a lot. It was scary how in minutes she saw right into him, perfectly.

It was irritating. It was good.

But one thing she couldn't see through was the lie he'd told her.

"You see him much?"

"All the time."

"When did you talk to him last?"

"The other day."

"And you've told him all about your condition?"

"You bet."

Covey called his son regularly, left messages on his phone at work and at home. But Randy never returned the calls. Occasionally he'd pick up, but it was always when Covey was calling from a different phone, so that the son didn't recognize the number (Covey even wondered in horror if the man bought a caller ID phone mostly to avoid his father).

In the past week he'd left two messages at his son's house. He'd never seen the place but pictured it being a beautiful high-rise somewhere in L.A., though Covey hadn't been to California in years and didn't even know if they had real high-rises there, the City of Angels being to earthquakes what trailer parks in the Midwest are to twisters.

In any case, whether his home was high-rise, low- or a hovel, his son had not returned a single call.

Why? he often wondered in despair. *Why?*

He looked back on his days as a young father. He'd spent much time at the office and traveling, yes, but he'd also devoted many, many hours to the boy, taking him to the Yankees games and movies, attending Randy's recitals and Little League.

Something had happened, though, and in his twenties he'd drifted away. Covey had thought maybe he'd gone gay, since he'd never married, but when Randy came home for Ver's funeral he brought a beautiful young woman with him. Randy had been polite but distant and a few days afterward he'd headed back to the coast. It had been some months before they'd spoken again.

Why? . . .

Covey now sat down on the couch, poured himself a glass of the port, slowly to avoid the sediment, and sipped it. He picked up another scrapbook and began flipping through it.

He felt sentimental. And then sad and anxious. He rose slowly from the couch, walked into the kitchen and took two of his Luminux pills.

In a short while the drugs kicked in and he felt better, giddy. Almost carefree.

The book sagged in his hands. He reflected on the big question: Should he tell Randy about his illness and the impending surgery? Nurse Mac would want him to, he knew. But Covey wouldn't do that. He wanted the young man to come back on his own or not at all. He wasn't going to use sympathy as a weapon to force a reconciliation.

A glance at the clock on the stove. Mac would be here in fifteen minutes.

He decided to use the time productively and return phone calls. He confirmed his next appointment with Dr. Jenny and left a message with Charley Hanlon, a widower up the road, about going to the movies next weekend. He also made an appointment for tomorrow about some alternative treatments the hospital had suggested he look into. "Long as it doesn't involve colonics, I'll think about it," Covey grumbled to the soft-spoken director of the program, who'd laughed and assured him that it did not.

He hung up. Despite the silky calm from the drug Covey had a moment's panic. Nothing to do with his heart, his surgery, his mortality, his estranged son, tomorrow's non-colonic treatment.

No, what troubled him: What if Mac didn't like blue cheese?

Covey rose and headed into the kitchen, opened the refrigerator and began to forage for some other snacks.

"You can't go in there."

But in there they went.

LaTour and Tal pushed past the receptionist into the office of Daniel Montrose.

At the circular glass table sat the president of the company and the other suspect, Karen Billings.

Montrose leaned forward, eyes wide in shock. He stood up slowly. The woman too pushed back from the table. The head of the company was as rumpled as before; Billings was in a fierce crimson dress.

"You, don't move!" LaTour snapped.

The red-dress woman blinked, unable to keep the anger out of her face. Tal could hear the tacit rejoinder: Nobody talks to me that way.

"Why didn't you tell us about the problems with Luminux?"

The president exchanged a look with Billings.

He cleared his throat. "Problems?"

Tal dropped the downloaded material about the FDA issues with Luminux on Montrose's desk. The president scooped it up and read.

LaTour had told Tal to watch the man's eyes. The eyes tell if someone's lying, the homicide cop had lectured. Tal squinted and studied them. He didn't have a clue what was going on behind his expensive glasses.

LaTour said to Billings, "Can you tell me where you were on April seventh and the ninth?"

"What the fuck are you talking about?"

"Simple question, lady. Where were you?"

"I'm not answering any goddamn questions without our lawyer." She crossed her arms, sat back and contentedly began a staring contest with LaTour.

"Why didn't you tell us about this?" Tal nodded at the documents.

Montrose said to Billings, "The dimethylamino."

"They found out about that?" she asked.

"Yeah, we found out about it," LaTour snapped. "Surprise."

Montrose turned to Tal. "What exactly did you find in the victims' blood?"

Unprepared for the question, he frowned. "Well, Luminux."

"You have the coroner's report?"

Tal pulled it out of his briefcase and put it on the table. "There."

Montrose frowned in an exaggerated way. "Actually, it doesn't say 'Luminux.'"

"The fuck you talking about? It's—"

Montrose said, "I quote: '9-fluoro, 7-chloro-1,3-dihydro-1-methyl-5-phenyl-2H-1, 4-benzodiazepin, 5-hydroxytryptamine and N-(1-phenethyl-4-piperidyl) propionanilide citrate.'"

"Whatever," LaTour snapped, rolling his eyes. "That *is* Luminux. The medical examiner said so."

"That's right," Karen snapped right back. "That's the approved version of the drug."

LaTour started to say something but fell silent.

"Approved?" Tal asked uncertainly.

Montrose said, "Look at the formula for the early version."

"Early?"

"The one the FDA rejected. It's in that printout of yours."

Tal was beginning to see where this was headed and he didn't like the destination. He found the sheet in the printout and compared it to the formula in the medical examiner's report. They were the same except that the earlier version of the Luminux contained another substance, dimethylamino ethyl phosphate ester.

"What's—"

"A mild antipsychotic agent known as DEP. That's what caused the problems in the first version. In combination it had a slight psychedelic effect. As soon as we took it out the FDA approved the drug. That was a year ago. You didn't find any DEP in the bodies. The victims were taking the approved version of the drug. No DEP-enhanced Luminux was every released to the public."

Billings muttered, "And we've never had a single incidence of suicide among the six million people worldwide on the drug—a lot of whom are probably alive today because they were taking Luminux and *didn't* kill themselves."

Montrose pulled a large binder off his desk and dropped it on his desk. "The complete study and FDA approval. No detrimental side effects. It's even safe with alcohol in moderation."

"Though we don't recommend it," Billings snapped, just as icily as she had at their first meeting.

"Why didn't you tell us before?" LaTour grumbled.

"You didn't ask. All drugs go through a trial period while we make them safe." Montrose wrote a number on a memo pad. "If you still don't believe us—this's the FDA's number. Call them."

Billings's farewell was "You found your way in here. You can find your way out."

Tal slouched in his office chair. LaTour was across from him with his feet up on Tal's desk again.

"Got a question," Tal asked. "You ever wear spurs?"

"Spurs? Oh, you mean like for horses? Why would I wear spurs? Or is that some kind of math nerd joke about putting my feet on your fucking desk?"

"You figure it out," Tal muttered as the cop swung his feet to the floor. "So where do we go from here? No greedy daughters, no evil drug maker. And we've pretty much humiliated ourselves in front of two *harsh* women. We're batting oh for two." The statistician sighed. Maybe they *did* kill themselves. Hell, sometimes life is just too much for some people."

"You don't think that, though."

"I don't *feel* it but I do *think* it and I do better thinking. When I start feeling I get into trouble."

"And the world goes round and round," LaTour said. "Shit. It time for a beer yet?"

But a beer was the last thing on Tal's mind. He stared at the glacier of paper on his desk, the printouts, the charts, the lists, the photographs, hoping that he'd spot one fact, one *datum*, that might help them.

Tal's phone rang. He grabbed it. " 'Lo?"

"Is this Detective Simms?" a meek voice asked.

"That's right."

"I'm Bill Fendler, with Oak Creek Books in Barlow Heights. Somebody from your office called and asked to let you know if we sold any copies of *Making the Final Journey: The Complete Guide to Suicide and Euthanasia*."

Tal sat up. "That's right. Have you?"

"I just noticed the inventory showed one book sold in the last couple of days."

LaTour frowned. Tal held up a wait-a-minute finger.

"Can you tell me who bought it"

"That's what I've been debating. . . . I'm not sure it's ethical. I was thinking if you had a court order it might be better."

"We have reason to believe that somebody might be using that book to cover up a series of murders. That's why we're asking about it. Maybe it's not ethical. But I'm asking you, please, give me the name of the person who bought it."

A pause. The man said, "Okay. Got a pencil."

Tal found one. "Go ahead."

The mathematician started to write the name. Stunned, he paused. "Are you sure?" he asked.

"Positive, Detective. The receipt's right here in front of me."

The phone sagged in Tal's hand. He finished jotting the name, showed it to LaTour. "What do we do now?" he asked.

LaTour lifted a surprised eyebrow. "Search warrant," he said. "That's what we do."

The warrant was pretty easy, especially since LaTour was on good terms with nearly every judge and magistrate in Westbrook County personally, and a short time later they were halfway through their search of the modest bungalow located in even more modest Harrison Village. Tal and LaTour were in the bedroom, three uniformed county troopers were downstairs.

Drawers, closets, beneath the bed . . .

Tal wasn't exactly sure what they were looking for. He followed LaTour's lead. The big cop had considerable experience sniffing out hiding places, it seemed, but it was Tal who found the jacket, which was shedding off-white fibers that appeared to match the one they'd found at the Whitleys' death scene.

This was *some* connection, though a tenuous one.

"Sir, I found something outside!" a cop called up the stairs.

They went out to the garage, where the officer was standing over a suitcase, hidden under stacks of boxes. Inside were two large bottles of Luminux, with only a few pills remaining in each. There were no personal prescription labels attached but they seemed to be the containers that were sold directly to hospitals. This one had been sold to the Cardiac Support Center. Also in the suitcase were articles cut from magazines and newspapers—one was from several years ago. It was about a nurse who'd killed elderly patients in a nursing home in Ohio with lethal drugs. The woman was quoted as saying, "I did a good thing, helping those people die with dignity. I never got a penny from their deaths. I only wanted them to be at peace. My worst crime is I'm an Angel of Mercy." There were a half-dozen others, too, the theme being the kindness of euthanasia. Some actually gave practical advice on "transitioning" people from life.

Tal stepped back, arms crossed, staring numbly at the find.

Another officer walked outside. "Found these hidden behind the desk downstairs."

In his latex-gloved hands Tal took the documents. They were the Bensons' files from the Cardiac Support Center. He opened and read through the first pages.

LaTour said something but the statistician didn't hear. He'd hoped up until now that the facts were wrong, that this was all a huge misunderstanding. But true mathematicians will always accept where the truth leads, even if it shatters their most heart-felt theorem.

There was no doubt that Mac McCaffrey was the killer.

She'd been the person who'd just bought the suicide book. And it was here, in her house, that they'd found the jacket, the Luminux bottles and the euthanasia articles. As for the Bensons' files, her name was prominently given as the couple's nurse/counselor. She'd lied about working with them.

The homicide cop spoke again.

"What'd you say?" Tal muttered.

"Where is she, you think?"

"At the hospital, I'd guess. The Cardiac Support Center."

"So you ready?" LaTour asked.

"For what?"

"To make your first collar."

The blue cheese, in fact, turned out to be a bust.

But Nurse Mac—the only way Robert Covey could think of her now—seemed to enjoy the other food he'd laid out.

"Nobody's ever made appetizers for me," she said, touched.

"They don't make gentlemen like me anymore."

And bless her, here was a woman who didn't whine about her weight. She smeared a big slab of paté on a cracker and ate it right down, then went for the shrimp.

Covey sat back on the couch in the den, a bit perplexed. He recalled her feistiness from their first meeting and was anticipating—and looking forward to—a fight about diet and exercise. But she made only one exercise comment—after she'd opened the back door.

"Beautiful yard."

"Thanks. Ver was the landscaper."

"That's a nice pool. You like to swim?"

He told her he loved to, though since he'd been diagnosed with the heart problem he didn't swim alone, worried he'd faint or have a heart attack and drown.

Nurse Mac had nodded. But there was something else on her mind. She finally turned away from the pool. "You're probably wondering what's on the agenda for this session?"

"Yes'm, I am."

"Well, I'll be right up front. I'm here to talk you into doing something you might not want to do."

"Ah, negotiating, are we? This involve the fourth glass of port?"

She smiled. "It's a little more important than that. But now that you've brought it up . . ." She rose and walked to the bar. "You don't mind, do you?" She picked up a bottle of old Taylor-Fladgate, lifted an eyebrow.

"I'll mind if you pour it down the drain. I don't mind if we drink some."

"Why don't you refill the food," she said. "I'll play bartender."

When Covey returned from the kitchen Nurse Mac had poured him a large glass of port. She handed it to him then poured one for herself. She lifted hers. He did too and the crystal rang.

They both sipped.

"So what's this all about, you acting so mysterious?"

"What's it about?" she mused. "It's about eliminating pain, finding peace. And sometimes you just can't do that alone. Sometimes you need somebody to help you."

"Can't argue with the sentiment. What've you got in mind? Specific, I mean."

Mac leaned forward, tapped her glass to his. "Drink up." They downed the ruby-colored liquor.

"Go, go, go!"

"You wanna drive?" LaTour shouted over the roar of the engine. They skidded sharply around the parkway, over the curb and onto the grass, nearly scraping the side of the unmarked car against a jutting rock.

"At least I know *how* to drive," Tal called. Then: "Step on it!"

"Shut the fuck up. Let me concentrate."

As the wheel grated against another curb Tal decided that shutting up was a wise idea and fell silent.

Another squad car was behind them.

"There, that's the turn-off." Tal pointed.

LaTour controlled the skid and somehow managed to keep them out of the oncoming traffic lane.

Another three hundred yards. Tal directed the homicide cop down the winding road then up a long driveway, at the end of which was a small, dark-blue sedan. The same car the witnesses had seen outside the Bensons' house, the same car that had left the tread marks at the Whitley's the day they died.

Killing the siren, LaTour skidded to a stop in front of the car. The squad car parked close behind, blocking the sedan in.

All four officers leapt out. As they ran past the vehicle Tal glanced in the backseat and saw the tan baseball cap that the driver of the car, Mac McCaffrey, had worn outside the Bensons' house, the day she'd engineered their deaths.

In a movement quite smooth for such a big man LaTour unlatched the door and shoved inside, not even breaking stride. He pulled his gun from his holster.

They and the uniformed officers charged into the living room and then the den.

They stopped, looking at the two astonished people on the couch.

One was Robert Covey, who was unharmed.

The other, the woman who'd been about to kill him, was standing over him, eyes wide. Mac was just offering the old man one of the tools of her murderous trade: a glass undoubtedly laced with enough Luminux to render him half conscious and suggestible to suicide. Tal noticed that the back door was open, revealing a large swimming pool. So, not a gun or carbon monoxide. Death by drowning this time.

"Tal!" she gasped.

But he said nothing. He let LaTour step forward to cuff her and arrest her. The homicide cop was, of course, much better versed in such matters of protocol.

The homicide detective looked through her purse and found the suicide book inside.

Robert Covey was in the ambulance outside, being checked out by the medics. He'd seemed okay but they were taking their time, just to make sure.

After they found the evidence at Mac's house, Tal and LaTour had sped to the hospital. She was out but Dr. Dehoeven at the CRC had pulled her client list and they'd gone through her calendar, learning that she was meeting with Covey at that moment. He hadn't answered the phone, and they'd raced to the elderly man's house.

LaTour would've been content to ship Mac off to Central Booking but Tal was a bit out of control; he couldn't help confronting her. "You *did* know Don and Sy Benson. Don was your client. You lied to me."

Mac started to speak then looked down, her tearful eyes on the floor.

"We found Benson's files in your house. And the computer logs at CSC showed you erased his records. You *were* at their house the day they died. It was you the witness saw in the hat and sunglasses. And the Whitleys? You killed them too."

"I didn't kill anybody!"

"Okay, fine—you *helped* them kill themselves. You drugged them and talked them into it. And then cleaned up after." He turned to the uniformed deputy. "Take her to Booking."

And she was led away, calling, "I didn't do anything wrong!"

"Bullshit," LaTour muttered.

Though, staring after her as the car eased down the long drive, Tal reflected that in a way—some abstract, moral sense—she truly *did* believe she hadn't done anything wrong.

But to the people of the state of New York, the evidence was irrefutable. Nurse Claire "Mac" McCaffrey had murdered four people and undoubtedly intended to murder scores of others. She'd gotten the Bensons doped up on Friday and helped them kill themselves. Then on

Sunday she'd called the Whitleys from a pay phone, made sure they were home then went over there and arranged for their suicides too. She'd cleaned up the place, taken the Luminux and hadn't left until *after* they died: (Tal had learned that the opera show she listened to wasn't on until 7:00 P.M. Not 4:00, as she'd told him. That's why he hadn't been able to find it when he'd surfed the frequencies in LaTour's car.)

She'd gone into this business to ease the suffering of patients—because her own mother had had such a difficult time dying. But what she'd meant by "easing suffering" was putting them down like dogs.

Robert Covey returned to his den. He was badly shaken but physically fine. He had some Luminux in his system but not a dangerously high dosage. "She seemed so nice, so normal," he whispered.

Oh, you bet, Tal thought bitterly. A goddamn perfect member of the Four Percent Club.

He and LaTour did some paperwork—Tal so upset that he didn't even think about his own questionnaire—and they walked back to LaTour's car. Tal sat heavily in the front seat, staring straight ahead. The homicide cop didn't start the engine. He said, "Sometimes closing a case is harder than not closing it. That's something they don't teach you at the academy. But you did what you had to. People'll be alive now because of what you did."

"I guess," he said sullenly. He was picturing Mac's office. Her crooked smile when she'd look over the park. Her laugh.

"Let's file the papers. Then we'll go get a beer. Hey, you do drink beer, don'tcha?"

"Yeah, I drink beer," Tal said.

"We'll make a cop outta you yet, Einstein."

Tal clipped his seatbelt on, deciding that being a real cop was the last thing in the world he wanted.

A beep on the intercom. "Mr. Covey's here, sir."

"I'll be right there." Dr. William Farley rose from his desk, a glass-sheet-covered Victorian piece his business partner had bought for him in New England on one of the man's buying sprees. Farley would have been content to have a metal desk or even a card table.

But in the *business* of medicine, not the *practice*, appearances count. The offices of the Lotus Research Foundation, near the mall containing Neiman Marcus and Saks Fifth Avenue, were filled with many antiques. Farley had been amused when they'd moved here three years ago to see the fancy furniture, paintings, objets d'art. Now, they were virtually invisible to him. What he greatly preferred was the huge medical facility itself behind the offices. As a doctor and researcher, that was the only place he felt truly at home.

Forty-eight, slim to the point of being scrawny, hair with a mind of its own, Farley had nonetheless worked hard to rid himself of his backroom medical researcher's image. He now pulled on his thousand-dollar suit jacket and applied a comb. He paused at the door, took a deep breath, exhaled and stepped into a lengthy corridor to the foundation's main lobby. It was deserted except for the receptionist and one elderly man, sitting in a deep plush couch.

"Mr. Covey?" the doctor asked, extending his hand.

The man set down the coffee cup he'd been given by the receptionist and they shook hands.

"Dr. Farley?"

A nod.

"Come on into my office."

They chatted about the weather as Farley led him down the narrow corridor to his office. Sometimes the patients here talked about sports, about their families, about the paintings on the walls.

Sometimes they were so nervous they said nothing at all.

Entering the office, Farley gestured toward a chair and then sat behind the massive desk. Covey glanced at it, unimpressed. Farley looked him over. He didn't appear particularly wealthy—an off-the-rack suit, a tie with stripes that went one way while those on his shirt went another. Still, the director of the Lotus Foundation had learned enough about rich people to know that the wealthiest were those who drove hybrid Toyota gas-savers and wore raincoats until they were threadbare.

Farley poured more coffee and offered Covey a cup.

"Like I said on the phone yesterday, I know a little about your condition. Your cardiologist is Jennifer Lansdowne, right?"

"That's right."

"And you're seeing someone from the Cardiac Support Center at the hospital."

Covey frowned. "I *was*."

"You're not any longer?"

"A problem with the nurse they sent me. I haven't decided if I'm going back. But that's a whole 'nother story."

"Well, we think you might be a good candidate for our services here, Mr. Covey. We offer a special program to patients in certain cases."

"What kind of cases?"

"Serious cases."

"The Lotus Research Foundation for *Alternative* Treatment," Covey recited. "Correct me if I'm wrong but I don't think ginseng and acupuncture work for serious cases."

"That's not what we're about." Farley looked him over carefully. "You a businessman, sir?"

"Was. For half a century."

"What line?"

"Manufacturing. Then venture capital."

"Then I imagine you generally like to get straight to the point."

"You got that right."

"Well, then let me ask you this, Mr. Covey. How would you like to live forever?"

"How's that?"

In the same way that he'd learned to polish his shoes and speak in words of fewer than four syllables, Farley had learned how to play potential patients like trout. He knew how to pace the pitch. "I'd like to tell you about the foundation. But first would you mind signing this?" He opened the drawer of his desk and passed a document to Covey.

He read it. "A nondisclosure agreement."

"It's pretty standard."

"I know it is," the old man said. "I've written 'em. Why do you want me to sign it?"

"Because what I'm going to tell you can't be made public."

He was intrigued now, the doctor could tell, though trying not to show it.

"If you don't want to, I understand. But then I'm afraid we won't be able to pursue our conversation further."

Covey read the sheet again. "Got a pen?"

Farley handed him a Mont Blanc; Covey took the heavy barrel with a laugh suggesting he didn't like ostentation very much. He signed and pushed the document back.

Farley put it into his desk. "Now, Dr. Lansdowne's a good woman. And she'll do whatever's humanly possible to fix your heart and give you a few more years. But there're limits to what medical science can do. After all, Mr. Covey, we all die. You, me, the children being born at this minute. Saints and sinners . . . we're all going to die."

"You got an interesting approach to medical services, Doctor. You cheer up all your patients this way?"

Dr. Farley smiled. "We hear a lot about aging nowadays."

"Can't turn on the TV without it."

"And about people trying to stay young forever."

"Second time you used that word. Keep going."

"Mr. Covey, you ever hear about the Hayflick rule?"

"Nope. Never have."

"Named after the man who discovered that human cells can reproduce themselves a limited number of times. At first, they make perfect reproductions of themselves. But after a while they can't keep up that level of quality control, you could say; they become more and more inefficient."

"Why?"

Covey, he reflected, was a sharp one. Most people sat there and nodded with stupid smiles on their faces. He continued. "There's an important strand of DNA that gets shorter and shorter each time the cells reproduce. When it gets too short, the cells go haywire and they don't duplicate properly. Sometimes they stop altogether."

"I'm following you in general. But go light on the biology bullshit. Wasn't my strong suit."

"Fair enough, Mr. Covey. Now, there're some ways to cheat the Hayflick limit. In the future it may be possible to extend life span significantly, dozens, maybe hundreds of years."

"That ain't forever."

"No, it's not."

"So cut to the chase."

"We'll never be able to construct a human body that will last more than a few hundred years at the outside. The laws of physics and nature just don't allow it. And even if we could we'd still have disease and illness and accidents that shorten life spans."

"This's getting cheerier and cheerier."

"Now, Dr. Lansdowne'll do what she can medically and the Cardiac Support Center will give you plenty of help."

"Depending on the nurse," Covey muttered. "Go on."

"And you might have another five, ten, fifteen years. . . . Or you can consider our program." Farley handed Covey a business card and tapped the logo of the Lotus Foundation, a golden flower. "You know what the lotus signifies in mythology?"

"Not a clue."

"Immortality."

"Does it now?"

"Primitive people'd see lotuses grow up out of the water in riverbeds that'd been dry for years. They assumed the plants were immortal."

"You said you can't keep people from dying."

"We can't. You will die. What we offer is what you might call a type of reincarnation."

Covey sneered. "I stopped going to church thirty years ago."

"Well, Mr. Covey. I've never gone to church. I'm not talking about spiritual reincarnation. No, I mean scientific, provable reincarnation."

The old man grunted. "This's about the time you start losing people, right?"

Farley laughed hard. "That's right. Pretty much at that sentence."

"Well, you ain't lost me yet. Keep going."

"It's very complex but I'll give it to you in a nutshell—just a little biology."

The old man sipped more coffee and waved his hand for the doctor to continue.

"The foundation holds the patent on a process that's known as neuro stem cell regenerative replication. . . . I know, it's a mouthful. Around here we just call it consciousness cloning."

"Explain that."

"What is consciousness?" Farley asked. "You look around the room, you see things, smell them, have reactions. Have thoughts. I sit in the same room, focus on different things, or focus on the same things, and have different reactions. Why? Because our brains are unique."

A slow nod. This fish was getting close to the fly.

"The foundation's developed a way to genetically map your brain and then program embryonic cells to grow in a way that duplicates it perfectly. After you die your identical consciousness is re-created in a fetus. You're—" A slight smile. "—born again. In a secular, biological sense, of course. The sensation you have is as if your brain were transplanted into another body."

Farley poured more coffee, handed it to Covey, who was shaking his head.

"How the hell do you do this?" Covey whispered.

"It's a three-step process." The doctor was always delighted to talk about his work. "First, we plot the exact structure of your brain as it exists now—the parts where the consciousness resides. We use supercomputers and micro-MRI machines."

"MRI. . . . that's like a fancy X-ray, right?"

"Magnetic resonance. We do a perfect schematic of your consciousness. Then step two: you know about genes, right? They're the blueprints for our bodies, every cell in your body contains them. Well, genes decide not only what your hair color is and your height and susceptibility to certain diseases but also how your brain develops. After a certain age the brain development gene shuts off; your brain's structure is determined and doesn't change—that's why brain tissue doesn't regenerate if it's destroyed. The second step is to extract and reactivate the development gene. Then we implant it into a fetus."

"You clone me?"

"No, not your body. We use donor sperm and egg and a surrogate mother. There's an in vitro clinic attached to the foundation. You're 'placed,' we call it, with a good family from the same social-economic class as you live in now."

Covey wanted to be skeptical, it seemed, but he was still receptive.

"The final part is to use chemical and electromagnetic intervention to make sure the brain develops identically to the map we made of your present one. Stimulate some cells' growth, inhibit others'. When you're born again, your perceptions will be exactly what they are from your point of view now. Your sensibilities, interests, desires."

Covey blinked.

"You won't look like you. Your body type will be different.

Though you will be male. We insist on that. It's not our job to work out gender-identity issues."

"Not a problem," he said shortly, frowning at the absurdity of the idea. Then: "Can you eliminate health problems? I had skin cancer. And the heart thing, of course."

"We don't do that. We don't make supermen or superwomen. We simply boost your consciousness into another generation, exactly as you are now."

Covey considered this for a moment. "Will I remember meeting you, will I have images of this life?"

"Ah, memories . . . We didn't quite know about those at first. But it seems that, yes, you will remember, to some extent—because memories are hard-wired into some portions of the brain. We aren't sure how many yet, since our first clients are only three or four years old now—in their second lives, of course—and we haven't had a chance to fully interview them yet."

"You've actually *done* this?" he whispered.

Farley nodded. "Oh, yes, Mr. Covey. We're up and running."

"What about will I go wacko or anything? That sheep they cloned died? She was a mess, I heard."

"No, that can't happen because we control development, like I was explaining. Every step of the way."

"Jesus," he whispered. "This isn't a joke?"

"Oh, no, not at all."

"You said, 'Forever.' So, how does it work—we do the same thing in seventy years or whatever?"

"It's literally a lifetime guarantee, even if that lifetime lasts ten thousand years. The Lotus Foundation will stay in touch with all our clients over the years. You can keep going for as many generations as you want."

"How do I know you'll still be in business?"

A slight chuckle. "Because we sell a product there's an infinite demand for. Companies that provide that don't ever go out of business."

Covey eyed Farley and the old man said coyly, "Which brings up your fee."

"As you can imagine . . ."

"Forever don't come cheap. Gimme a number."

"One half of your estate with a minimum of ten million dollars."

"One half? That's about twenty-eight million. But it's not liquid. Real estate, stocks, bonds. I can't just write you a check for it."

"We don't want you to. We're keeping this procedure very low-key. In the future we hope to offer our services to more people but now our costs are so high we can work only with the ones who can cover the expenses. . . . And, let's be realistic, we prefer people like you in the program."

"Like me?"

"Let's say higher in the gene pool than others."

Covey grunted. "Well, how *do* you get paid?"

"You leave the money to one of our charities in your will."

"Charities?"

"The foundation owns dozens of them. The money gets to us eventually."

"So you don't get paid until I die."

"That's right. Some clients wait until they actually die of their disease. Most, though, do the paperwork and then transition themselves."

"Transition?"

"They end their own life. That way they avoid a painful end. And, of course, the sooner they leave, the sooner they come back."

"How many people've done this?"

"Eight."

Covey looked out the window for a moment, at the trees in Central Park, waving slowly in a sharp breeze. "This's crazy. The whole thing's nuts."

Farley laughed. "*You'd* be nuts if you didn't think that at first. . . . Come on, I'll give you a tour of the facility."

Setting down his coffee, Covey followed the doctor out of the office. They walked down the hallway through an impressive-looking security door into the laboratory portion of the foundation. Farley pointed out first the massive supercomputers used for brain mapping and then the genetics lab and cryogenic facility itself, which they couldn't enter but could see from windows in the corridor. A half dozen white-coated employees dipped pipettes into tubes, grew cultures in petri dishes and hunched over microscopes.

Covey was intrigued but not yet sold, Farley noted.

"Let's go back to the office."

When they'd sat again the old man finally said, "Well, I'll think about it."

Sheldon nodded with a smile and said, "You bet. A decision like this . . . Some people just can't bring themselves to sign on. You take your time." He handed Covey a huge binder. "Those're case studies, genetic data for comparison with the transitioning clients and their next-life selves, interviews with them. There's nothing identifying them but you can read about the children and the process itself." Farley paused and let Covey flip through the material. He seemed to be reading it carefully. The doctor added, "What's so nice about this is that you never have to say good-bye to your loved ones. Say you've got a son or daughter . . . we could contact them when they're older and propose our services to them. You could reconnect with them a hundred years from now."

At the words *son or daughter*, Covey had looked up, blinking. His eyes drifted off and finally he said, "I don't know. . . ."

"Mr. Covey," Farley said, "let me just add one thing. I understand your skepticism. But you tell me you're a businessman? Well, I'm going to treat you like one. Sure, you've got doubts. Who wouldn't? But even if you're not one hundred percent sure, even if you think I'm trying to sell you a load of hooey, what've you got to lose? You're going to die anyway. Why don't you just roll the dice and take the chance?"

He let this sink in for a minute and saw that the words—as so often—were having an effect. Time to back off. He said, "Now, I've got some phone calls to make, if you'll excuse me. There's a lounge through that door. Take your time and read through those things."

Covey picked up the files and stepped into the room the doctor indicated. The door closed.

Farley had pegged the old man as shrewd and deliberate. And accordingly the doctor gave him a full forty-five minutes to examine the materials. Finally he rose and walked to the doorway. Before he could say anything Covey looked up from the leather couch he was sitting in and said, "I'll do it. I want to do it."

"I'm very happy for you," Farley said sincerely.

"What do I need to do now?"

"All you do is an MRI scan and then give us a blood sample for the genetic material."

"You don't need part of my brain?"

"That's what's so amazing about genes. All of us is contained in a cell of our own blood."

Covey nodded.

"Then you change your will and we take it from there." He looked in a file and pulled out a list of the charities the foundation had set up recently.

"Any of these appeal? You should pick three or four. And they ought to be something in line with interests or causes you had when you were alive."

"There." Covey circled three of them. "I'll leave most to the Metropolitan Arts Assistance Association." He looked up. "Veronica, my wife, was an artist. That okay?"

"It's fine." Farley copied down the names and some other information and then handed a card to Covey. "Just take that to your lawyer."

The old man nodded. "His office is only a few miles from here. I could see him today."

"Just bring us a copy of the will." He didn't add what Covey, of course, a savvy businessman, knew. That if the will was not altered, or if he changed it later, the foundation wouldn't do the cloning. They had the final say.

"What about the . . . transition?"

Farley said, "That's your choice. Entirely up to you. Tomorrow or next year. Whatever you're comfortable with."

At the door Covey paused and turned back, shook Farley's hand. He gave a faint laugh. "Who would've thought? Forever."

∞

In Greek mythology Eos was the goddess of dawn and she was captivated with the idea of having human lovers. She fell deeply in love with a mortal, Tithonos, the son of the king of Troy, and convinced Zeus to let him live forever.

The god of gods agreed. But he neglected one small detail: granting him youth as well as immortality. While Eos remained unchanged Tithonos grew older and more decrepit with each passing year until he was so old he was unable to move or speak. Horrified, Eos turned him into an insect and moved on to more suitable paramours.

Dr. William Farley thought of this myth now, sitting at his desk in the Lotus Research Foundation. The search for immortality's always been tough on us poor humans, he reflected. But how doggedly we ignore the warning in Tithonos's myth—and the logic of science—and continue to look for ways to cheat death.

Farley glanced at a picture on his desk. It showed a couple, arm in arm—younger versions of those in a second picture on his credenza. His parents, who'd died in an auto accident when Farley was in medical school.

An only child, desperately close to them, he took months to recover from the shock. When he was able to resume his studies, he decided he'd specialize in emergency medicine—devoting his to saving lives threatened by trauma.

But the young man was brilliant—too smart for the repetitious mechanics of ER work. Lying awake nights he would reflect about his parents' deaths and he took some reassurance that they were, in a biochemical way, still alive within him. He developed an interest in genetics, and that was the subject he began to pursue in earnest.

Months, then years, of manic twelve-hour days doing research in the field resulted in many legitimate discoveries. But this also led to some ideas that were less conventional, even bizarre—consciousness cloning, for instance.

Not surprisingly, he was either ignored or ridiculed by his peers. His papers were rejected by professional journals, his grant requests turned down. The rejection didn't discourage him, though he grew more and more desperate to find the millions of dollars needed to research his theory. One day—about seven years ago—nearly penniless and living in a walk-up beside one of Westbrook's commuter train lines, he'd gotten a call from an old acquaintance. The man had heard about Farley's plight and had an idea.

"You want to raise money for your research?" he'd asked the impoverished medico. "It's easy. Find really sick, really wealthy patients and sell them immortality."

"What?"

"Listen," the man had continued. "Find patients who're about to die anyway. They'll be desperate. You package it right, they'll buy it."

"I can't sell them anything yet," Farley had replied. "I *believe* I can make this work. But it could take years."

"Well, sometimes sacrifices have to be made. You can pick up ten million overnight, twenty. That'd buy some pretty damn nice research facilities."

Farley had been quiet, considering those words. Then he'd said, "I *could* keep tissue samples, I suppose, and then when we actually can do the cloning, I could bring them back then."

"Hey, there you go," said the doctor. Something in the tone suggested to Farley that he didn't think the process would ever work. But the man's disbelief was irrelevant if he could help Farley get the money he needed for research.

"Well, all right," Farley said to his colleague—whose name was Anthony Sheldon, of the cardiology department at Westbrook Hospital, a man who was as talented an entrepreneur as he was a cardiovascular surgeon.

Six years ago they'd set up the Lotus Research Foundation, an in vitro clinic and a network of bogus charities. Dr. Sheldon, whose office was near the Cardiac Support Center, would finagle a look at the files of patients there and would find the richest and sickest. Then he'd arrange for them to be contacted by the Lotus Foundation and Farley would sell them the program.

Farley had truly doubted that anybody would buy the pitch but Sheldon had coached him well. The man had thought of everything. He found unique appeals for each potential client and gave Farley this information to snare them. In the case of the Bensons, for instance, Sheldon had learned how much they loved each other. His pitch to them was that this was the chance to be together forever, as they so poignantly noted in their suicide note. With Robert Covey, Sheldon had learned about his estranged son, so Farley added the tactical mention that a client could have a second chance to connect with children.

Sheldon had also come up with one vital part of the selling process. He made sure the patients got high doses of Luminux (even the coffee that Covey had just been drinking, for instance, was laced with the drug). Neither doctor believed that anyone would sign up for such a far-fetched idea without the benefit of some mind-numbing Mickey Finn.

The final selling point was, of course, the desperate desire of people facing death to believe what Farley promised them.

And that turned out to be one hell of a hook. The Lotus Research Foundation had earned almost 93 million in the past six years.

Everything had gone fine—until recently, when their greed got the better of them. Well, got the better of Sheldon. They'd decided that the cardiologist would never refer his own patients to the foundation—and would wait six months or a year between clients. But Tony Sheldon apparently had a mistress with very expensive taste and had lost some serious money in the stock market recently. Just after the Bensons signed up, the Whitleys presented themselves. Although Sam Whitley was a patient, they were far too wealthy to pass up and so Farley reluctantly yielded to Sheldon's pressure to go ahead with the plan.

But they learned that, though eager to proceed, Sam Whitley had wanted to reassure himself that this wasn't pure quackery and he'd tracked down some technical literature about the computers used in the technique and genetics in general. After the patients had died, Farley and Sheldon had to find this information in his house, burn it and scour the place for any other evidence that might lead back to the foundation.

The intrusion, though, must've alerted the police to the possibility that the families' deaths were suspicious. Officers had actually interviewed Sheldon, sending a jolt of panic through Farley. But then a scapegoat stumbled into the picture: Mac McCaffrey, a young nurse/counselor at the Cardiac Support Center. She was seeing their latest recent prospect—Robert Covey—as she'd been working with the Bensons and the Whitleys. This made her suspect to start with. Even better was her reluctance to admit she'd seen the Bensons; after their suicide the nurse had apparently lied about them and had stolen their files from the CSC. A perfect setup. Sheldon had used his ample resources to bribe a pharmacist at the CSC to doctor the logs and give him a couple of wholesale bottles containing a few Luminux tablets, to make it look like she'd been drugging patients for some time. Farley, obsessed with death and dying, had a vast library of articles on euthanasia and suicide. He copied several dozen of these. The drugs and the articles they planted in the nurse's garage—insurance in case they needed somebody to take the fall.

Which they had. And now the McCaffrey woman had just been hauled off to jail.

A whole 'nother story, as Covey had said.

The nurse's arrest had troubled Farley. He'd speculated out loud about telling the police that she was innocent. But Sheldon reminded him coolly what would happen to them and the foundation if Farley did that and he relented.

Sheldon had said, "Look, we'll do one more—this Covey—and then take a break. A year. Two years."

"No. Let's wait."

"I checked him out," Sheldon said, "He's worth over fifty million."

"I think it's too risky."

"I've thought about that." With the police still looking into the Benson and Whitley suicides, Sheldon explained, it'd be better to have the old man die in a mugging or hit and run, rather than killing himself.

"But," Farley had whispered, "you mean murder?"

"A suicide'll be way too suspicious."

"We can't."

But Sheldon had snapped, "Too late for morality, Doctor. You made your deal with the devil. You can't renegotiate now." And hung up.

Farley stewed for a while but finally realized the man was right; there was no going back. And, my, what he could do with another $25 million. . . .

His secretary buzzed him on the intercom.

"Mr. Covey's back, sir."

"Show him in."

Covey walked into the office. They shook hands again and Covey sat. As cheerful and blinky as most patients on seventy-five milligrams of Luminux. He happily took another cup of special brew then reached into his jacket pocket and displayed a copy of the codicil to the will. "Here you go."

Though Farley wasn't a lawyer he knew what to look for; the document was in proper form.

They shook hands formally.

Covey finished his coffee and Farley escorted him to the lab, where he would undergo the MRI and give a blood sample, making the nervous small talk that the clients always made at this point in the process.

The geneticist shook his hand and told him he'd made the right decision. Covey thanked Farley sincerely, with a hopeful smile on his face that was, Farley knew, only partly from the drug. He returned to his office and the doctor picked up the phone, called Anthony Sheldon. "Covey's changed the will. He'll be leaving here in about fifteen minutes."

"I'll take care of him now," Sheldon said and hung up.

Farley sighed and dropped the received into the cradle. He stripped off his suit jacket then pulled on a white lab coat. He left his office and fled up the hall to the research lab, where he knew he would find solace in the honest world of science, safe from all his guilt and sins, as if they were barred entry by the double-sealed doors of the airlock.

Robert Covey was walking down the street, feeling pretty giddy, odd thoughts going through his head.

Thinking of his life—the way he'd lived it. And the people who'd touched him and whom he'd touched. A foreman in the Bedford plant, who'd worked for the company for forty years . . . The men in his golfing foursome . . . Veronica . . . His brother . . .

His son, of course.

Still no call from Randy. And for the first time it occurred to him that maybe there *was* a reason the boy—well, young man—had been ignoring him. He'd always assumed he'd been such a good father. But maybe not.

Nothing makes you question your life more closely than when somebody's trying to sell you immortality.

Walking toward the main parking garage, Covey noted that the area was largely deserted. He saw only a few grungy kids on skateboards, a pretty redhead across the street, two men getting out of a white van parked near an alley.

He paid attention only to the men, because they were large, dressed in what looked like cheap suits and, with a glance up and down, started in his direction.

Covey soon forgot them, though, and concentrated again on his son. Thinking about his decision not to tell the boy about his illness. Maybe withholding things like this had been a pattern in Covey's life. Maybe the boy had felt excluded.

He laughed to himself. Maybe he should leave a message about what he and Farley had just been talking about. Lord have mercy, what he wouldn't give to see Randy's reaction when he listened to that! He could—

Covey slowed, frowning.

What was this?

The two men from the van were now jogging—directly toward him. He hesitated and shied back. Suddenly the men split up. One stopped and turned his back to Covey, scanning the sidewalk, while the other sped up, springing directly toward the old man. Then simultaneously they both pulled guns from under their coats.

No!

He turned to run, thinking that sprinting would probably kill him faster than the bullets. Not that it mattered. The man approaching him was fast and before Covey had a chance to take more than a few steps he was being pulled roughly into the alleyway behind him.

∞

"No, what are you doing? Who are—"

"Quiet!"

The man pressed Covey against the wall.

The other joined them but continued to gaze out over the street as he spoke into a walkie-talkie. "We've got him. No sign of hostiles. Move in, all units, move in!"

From out on the street came the rushing sound of car engines and the bleats of siren.

"Sorry, Mr. Covey. We had a little change of plans." The man speaking was the one who'd pulled him into the alley. They both produced badges and ID cards of the Westbrook County Sheriff's Department. "We work with Greg LaTour."

Oh, LaTour . . . He was the burly officer who, along with that skinny young officer named Talbot Simms, had come to his house early this morning with a truly bizarre story. This outfit called the Lotus Research Foundation might be running some kind of scam, targeting sick people, but the police weren't quite sure how it worked. Had he been contacted by anyone there? When Covey had told them, yes, and that he was in fact meeting with its director, Farley, that afternoon they wondered if he'd be willing to wear a wire to find out what it was all about.

Well, what it was all about was immortality . . . and it *had* been one hell of a scam.

The plan was that after he stopped at Farley's office and dropped off the fake codicil to his will (he executed a second one at the same time, voiding the one he'd given Farley), he was going to meet La-Tour and Simms at a Starbucks not far away.

But now the cops had something else in mind.

"Who're you?" Covey now asked. "Where're Laurel and Hardy?" Meaning Simms and LaTour.

The young officer who'd shoved him into the alley had blinked, not understanding the reference. He said, "Well, sir, what happened was we had a tap on the phone in Farley's office. He called Sheldon to tell him about you and it seems they weren't going to wait to try to talk you into killing yourself. Sheldon was going to kill you right away—make it look like a mugging or hit and run, we think."

Covey muttered, "You might've thought about that possibility up front."

There was a crackle in the mike/speaker of one of the officers. Covey couldn't hear too well but the gist of it was that they'd arrested Dr. Anthony Sheldon just outside his office. They now stepped out of the alley and Covey observed a half dozen police officers escorting William Farley and three men in lab coats out of the Lotus Foundation offices in handcuffs.

Covey observed the procession coolly, feeling contempt for the depravity of the foundation's immortality scam, though also with a grudging admiration. A businessman to his soul, Robert Covey couldn't help be impressed by someone who'd identified an inexhaustible market demand. Even if that product he sold was completely bogus.

The itch had yet to be scratched. Tal's office was still as sloppy as La-Tour's. The mess was driving him crazy, though Shellee seemed to think it was a step up on the evolutionary chain—for him to have digs that looked like everyone else's.

Captain Dempsey was sitting in the office, playing with one rolled-up sleeve, then the other. Greg LaTour too, his booted feet on the floor for a change, though the reason for this propriety seemed to be that Tal's desk was piled too high with paper to find a place to rest them.

"How'd you tip to this scam of theirs?" the captain asked. "The Lotus Foundation?"

Tal said, "Some things just didn't add up."

"Haw." From LaTour.

Both the captain and Tal glanced at him.

LaTour stopped smiling. "He's the math guy. He says something didn't *add* up. I thought it was a joke." He grumbled, "Go on."

Tal explained that after he'd returned to the office following Mac's arrest, he couldn't get her out of his head.

"Women do that," LaTour said.

"No, I mean there was something odd about the whole case," he continued. "Issues I couldn't reconcile. So I checked with Crime Scene—there *was* no Luminux in the port Mac was giving Covey. Then I went to see her in the lockup. She admitted she'd lied about not being the Bensons' nurse. She said she destroyed their records at the Cardiac Support Center and that she was the one that the witnesses had seen the day they died. But she lied because she was afraid she'd lose her job—two of her patients killing themselves? When, to her, they seemed to be doing fine? It shook her up bad. That's why she bought the suicide book. She bought it *after* I told her about it—she got the title from me. She wanted to know what to look for, to make sure nobody else died."

"And you believed her?" the captain asked.

"Yes, I did. I asked Covey if she'd ever brought up suicide. Did he have any sense that she was trying to get him to kill himself. But he said, no. All she'd talked about at that meeting—when we arrested her—was how painful and hard it is to go through a tough illness alone. She'd figured that he hadn't called his son, Randall, and told him, like he'd said. She gave him some port, got him relaxed and was trying to talk him into calling the boy."

"You said something about an opera show?" Dempsey continued, examining both sleeves and making sure they were rolled up to within a quarter inch of each other. Tal promised himself never to compulsively play with his tie knot again. His boss continued, "You said she lied about the time it was on."

"Oh. Right. Oops."

"Oops?"

"The Whitleys died on Sunday. The show's on at four then. But it's on at *seven* during the week, just after the business report. I checked the NPR program guide."

The captain asked, "And the articles about euthanasia? The ones they found in her house?"

"Planted. Her fingerprints weren't on them. Only glove-print smudges. The stolen Luminux bottle too. No prints. And, according to the inventory, those drugs disappeared from the clinic when Mac was out of town. Naw, she didn't have anything to do with the scam. It was Farley and Sheldon."

LaTour continued, "Quite a plan. Slipping the patients drugs, getting them to change their wills, then kill themselves and clean up afterwards.

"They did it all themselves? Farley and Sheldon?"

LaTour shook his head. "They must've hired muscle or used somebody in the foundation for the dirty work. We got four of 'em in custody. But they clammed up. Nobody's saying anything." LaTour sighed. "And they got the best lawyers in town. Big surprise, with all the fucking money they've got."

Tal said, "So, anyway, I knew Mac was being set up. But we still couldn't figure what was going on. You know, in solving an algebra problem you look for common denominators and—"

"Again with the fucking math," LaTour grumbled.

"Well, what was the denominator? We had two couples committing suicide and leaving huge sums of money to charities—more than half their estates. I looked up the statistics from the NAEPP."

"The—"

"The National Association of Estate Planning Professionals. When people have children, only two percent leave that much of their estate to charities. And even when they're childless, only twelve percent leave significant estates—that's over ten million dollars—to charities. So that made me wonder what was up with these nonprofits. I called the guy at the SEC I've been working with and he put me in touch with the people in charge of registering charities in New York, New Jersey, Massachusetts, and Delaware. I followed the trail of the nonprofits and found they were all owned ultimately by the Lotus Research Foundation. It's controlled by Farley and Sheldon. I checked them out. Sheldon was a rich cardiologist who'd been sued for malpractice a couple of times and been investigated for some securities fraud and insider trading. Farley? . . . Okay, now *he* was interesting. A crackpot. Trying to get funding for some weird cloning theory. I'd found his name on a card for the Lotus Foundation at the Whitleys'. It had something to do with alternative medical treatment but it didn't say what specifically."

LaTour explained about checking with Mac and the other Cardiac Support Center patients to see if they'd heard from the foundation. That led them to Covey.

"Immortality," Dempsey said slowly. "And people fell for it."

Together forever. . . .

"Well, they were pretty doped up on Luminux, remember," Tal said.

But LaTour offered what was perhaps the more insightful answer. "People always fall for shit they wanta fall for."

"That McCaffrey woman been released yet?" Dempsey asked uneasily. Arresting the wrong person was probably as embarrassing as declaring a bum 2124 (and as expensive; Sandra Whitley's lawyer—a guy as harsh as she was—had already contacted the Sheriff's Department, threatening suit).

"Oh, yeah. Dropped all charges," Tal said. Then he looked over his desk. "I'm going to finish up the paperwork and ship it off to the prosecutor. Then I've got some spreadsheets to get back to."

He glanced up to see a cryptic look pass between LaTour and the captain. He wondered what it meant.

Naiveté.

The tacit exchange in Tal's office between the two older cops was a comment on Tal's naiveté. The paperwork didn't get "finished up" at all. Over the next few days it just grew and grew and grew.

As did his hours. His working day expanded from an average 8.3 hours to 12 plus.

LaTour happily pointed out, "You call a twenty-one-twenty-four, you're the case officer. You stay with it all the way till the end. Ain't life sweet?"

And the end was nowhere in sight. Analyzing the evidence—the hundreds of cartons removed from the Lotus Foundation and from Sheldon's office—Tal learned that the Bensons hadn't been the first victims. Farley and Sheldon had engineered other suicides, going back several years, and had stolen tens of millions of dollars. The prior suicides were like the Bensons and the Whitleys—upper class and quite ill, though not necessarily terminally. Tal was shocked to find that he was familiar with one of the earlier victims: Mary Stemple, a physicist who'd taught at the Princeton Institute for Advanced Study, the famed think-tank where Einstein had worked. Tal had read some of her papers. A trained mathematician, she'd done most of her work in physics and astronomy and made important discoveries about the size and nature of the universe. It was a true shame that she'd been tricked into taking her life; she might have had years of important discoveries ahead of her.

He was troubled by the deaths, yes, but he was even more shocked to find that the foundation had actually supervised the in vitro fertilization of six eggs, which had been implanted in surrogate mothers, three of whom had already given birth to children. They were ultimately placed with parents who could not otherwise conceive.

This had been done, Tal, LaTour, and the district attorney concluded, so that Farley and Sheldon could prove to potential clients that they were actually doing the cloning (though another reason, it appeared, was to make an additional fee from childless couples).

The main concern was for the health of the children and the county hired several legitimate genetics doctors and pediatricians to see if the three children who'd been born and the three fetuses within the surrogate mothers were healthy. They were examined and found to be fine and, despite the immortality scam, the surrogate births and the adoption placements were completely legal, the attorney general concluded.

One of the geneticists Tal and LaTour had consulted said, "So Bill Farley was behind this?" The man had shaken his head. "We've been hearing about his crazy ideas for years. A wacko."

"There any chance," Tal wondered, "that someday somebody'll actually be able to do what he was talking about?"

"Cloning consciousness?" The doctor laughed. "You said you're a statistician, right?"

"That's right."

"You know what the odds are of being able to perfectly duplicate the structure of any given human brain?"

"Small as a germ's ass?" LaTour suggested.

The doctor considered this and said, "That sums it up pretty well."

The day was too nice to be inside so Mac McCaffrey and Robert Covey were in the park. Tal spotted them on a bench overlooking a duck pond. He waved and veered toward them.

She appeared to be totally immersed in the sunlight and the soft breeze; Tal remembered how much this member of the Four Percent Club loved the out-of-doors.

Covey, Mac had confided to Tal, was doing pretty well. His blood pressure was down and he was in good spirits as he approached his surgery. She was breaching confidentiality rules by telling Tal this but she justified it on the grounds that Tal was a police officer investigating a case involving her patient. Another reason was simply that Tal liked the old guy and was concerned about him.

Mac also told him that Covey had finally called his son and left a message about his condition and the impending surgery. There'd been no reply, though Covey'd gotten a hang-up on his voice mail, the caller ID on the phone indicating "Out of Area." Mac took the optimistic position that it had indeed been his son on the other end of the line and the man hadn't left a message because he preferred to talk to his father in person. Time would tell.

In his office an hour ago, on the phone, Tal had been distracted as he listened to Mac's breathy, enthusiastic report about her patient. He'd listened attentively but was mostly waiting for an appropriate lull in the conversation to leap in with a dinner invitation. None had presented itself, though, before she explained she had to get to a meeting. He'd hurriedly made plans to meet here.

Tal now joined them and she looked up with that charming crooked smile that he really liked (and was more than just a little sexy).

"Hey," he said.

"Officer," Robert Covey said. They warmly shook hands. Tal hesitated for a moment in greeting Mac but then thought, hell with it, bent down and kissed her on the cheek. This seemed unprofessional on several levels—his as well as hers—but she didn't seem to care; he knew *he* certainly didn't have a problem with the lapse.

Tal proceeded to explain to Covey that since he was the only victim who'd survived the Lotus Foundation scam the police needed a signed and notarized copy of his statement.

"In case I croak when I'm under the knife you'll still have the evidence to put the pricks away."

That was it exactly. Tal shrugged. "Well . . ."

"Don'tcha worry," the old man said. "I'm happy to."

Tal handed him the statement. "Look it over, make any changes you want. I'll print out a final version and we'll get it notarized."

"Will do." Covey skimmed it and then looked up. "How 'bout something to drink? There's a bar—"

"Coffee, tea or soda," Mac said ominously. "It's not even noon yet."

"She claims she negotiates," Covey muttered to Tal. "But she don't."

The old man pointed toward the park's concession stand at the top of a hill some distance away. "Coffee's not bad there—for an outfit that's not named for a whaler."

"I'll get it."

"I'll have a large with cream."

"He'll have a medium, skim milk," Mac said. "Tea for me, please. Sugar." She fired a crooked smile Tal's way.

About a hundred yards from the bench where the old man sat chatting away with his friend, a young woman walked along the park path. The redhead was short, busty, attractive, wearing a beautiful tennis bracelet and a diamond/emerald ring, off which the sunlight glinted fiercely.

She kept her eyes down as she walked, so nobody could see her abundant tears.

Margaret Ludlum had been crying on and off for several days. Ever since her boss and lover, Dr. Anthony Sheldon, had been arrested.

Margaret had greeted the news of his arrest—and Farley's too—with horror, knowing that she'd probably be the next to be picked up. After all, she'd been the one that Sheldon and Farley had sent as a representative of the Lotus Research Foundation to the couples who were planning to kill themselves. It was she who'd slipped them plenty of Luminux during their last few weeks on earth, then suggested they buy the blueprint for their deaths—the suicide books—and coerced them into killing themselves and afterwards cleaned up any evidence linking them to the Foundation or its two principals.

But the police had taken her statement—denying everything, of course—and let her go. It was clear they suspected Sheldon and Farley had an accomplice but seemed to think that it was one of Farley's research assistants. Maybe they thought that only a man was capable of killing defenseless people.

Wrong. Margaret had been completely comfortable with assisted suicide. And more: She'd been only a minute away from murdering Robert Covey the other day as he walked down the street after leaving the Lotus Research Foundation. But just as she started toward him a van stopped nearby and two men jumped out, pulling him to safety. Other officers had raided the foundation. She'd veered down a side street and called Sheldon to warn him. But it was too late. They got him outside his office at the hospital as he'd tried to flee.

Oh, yes, she'd been perfectly willing to kill Covey then.

And was perfectly willing to kill him now.

She watched that detective who'd initially come to interview Tony Sheldon walk away from the bench and up the path toward the refreshment stand. It didn't matter that he was leaving; he wasn't her target.

Only Covey. With the old man gone it would be much harder to get a conviction, Sheldon explained. He might get off altogether or serve only a few years—that's what they doled out in most cases of assisted suicides. The cardiologist promised he'd finally get divorced and he and Margaret would move to Europe. . . . They'd taken some great trips to the south of France and the weeks there had been wonderful. Oh, how she missed him.

Missed the money too, of course. That was the other reason she had to get Tony out of jail, of course. The doctor had been meaning to set up an account for her but hadn't gotten around to it. She'd let it slide for too long and the paperwork never materialized.

In her purse, banging against her hip, she felt the heavy pistol, the one she'd been planning to use on Covey several days ago. She was familiar with guns—she'd helped several of the other foundation clients "transition" by shooting themselves. And though she'd never actually pulled the trigger and murdered someone, she knew she could do it.

The tears were gone now. She was thinking of how best to handle the shooting. Studying the old man and that woman—who'd have to die too, of course; she'd be a witness against Margaret herself for the murder today. Anyway, the double murder would make the scenario more realistic. It would look like a mugging. Margaret would demand the wallet and the woman's purse and when they handed the items over, she'd shoot them both in the head.

Pausing now, next to a tree, Margaret looked over the park. A few passersby, but no one was near Covey and the woman. The detective—Simms, she recalled—was still hiking up the hill to the concession stand. He was two hundred yards from the bench; she could kill them both and be in her car speeding away before he could sprint back to the bench.

She waited until he disappeared into a stand of trees then reached into her purse, cocking the pistol. Margaret stepped out from behind the tree and moved quickly down the path that led to the bench. A glance around her. Nobody was present.

Closer now, closer. Along the asphalt path, damp from an earlier rain and the humid spring air.

She was twenty feet away . . . ten . . .

She stepped quickly up behind them. They looked up. The woman gave a faint smile in greeting—a smile that faded as she noted Margaret's cold eyes.

"Who are you?" the woman asked, alarm in her voice.

Margaret Ludlum said nothing. She pulled the gun from her purse.

∞

"Wallet!" Pointing the pistol directly at the old man's face.

"What?"

"Give me your wallet!" Then turning to the woman, "And the purse! Now!"

"You want—?"

They were confused, being mugged by someone outfitted by Neiman Marcus.

"Now!" Margaret screamed.

The woman thrust the purse forward and stood, holding her hands out. "Look, just calm down."

The old man was frantically pulling his wallet from his pocket and holding it out unsteadily.

Margaret grabbed the items and shoved them into her shoulder bag. Then she looked at the man's eyes and—rather than feel any sympathy, she felt that stillness she always did when slipping someone drugs or showing them how to grip the gun or seal the garage with duct tape to make the most efficient use of the carbon monoxide.

The woman was saying, "Please, don't do anything stupid. Just take everything and leave!"

Then Robert Covey squinted. He was looking at Margaret with certain understanding. He knew what this was about. "Leave her alone," he said. "Me, it's okay. It's all right. Just let her go."

But she thrust the gun forward at Covey as the woman with him screamed and dropped to the ground. Margaret began to pull the trigger, whispering the phrase she always did when helping transition the foundation's clients, offering a prayer for a safe journey. "God be with—"

A flash of muddy light filled her vision as she felt, for a tiny fragment of a second, a fist or rock slam into her chest.

"But . . . what . . ."

Then nothing but numb silence.

A thousand yards away, it seemed.

If not miles.

Talbot Simms squinted toward the bench, where he could see the forms of Robert Covey and Mac on their feet, backing away from the body of the woman he'd just shot. Mac was pulling out her cell phone, dropping it, picking it up again, looking around in panic.

Tal lowered the gun and stared.

A moment before, Tal had paid the vendor and was turning from the concession stand, holding the tray of drinks. Frowning, he saw a woman standing beside the bench, pointing something toward Mac and Covey, Mac rearing away then handing her purse over, the old man giving her something, his wallet, it seemed.

And then Tal had noticed that what she held was a gun.

He knew that she was in some way connected to Sheldon or Farley and the Lotus Foundation. The red hair . . . Yes! Sheldon's secretary, unsmiling Celtic Margaret. He'd known too that she'd come here to shoot the only living eyewitness to the scam—and probably Mac too.

Dropping the tray of tea and coffee, he'd drawn his revolver. He'd intended to sprint back toward them, calling for her to stop, threatening her. But when he saw Mac fall to the ground, futilely covering her face, and Margaret shoving the pistol forward, he'd known she was going to shoot.

Tal had cocked his own revolver to single-action and stepped into a combat firing stance, left hand curled under and around his right, weight evenly distributed on both feet, aiming high and slightly to the left, compensating for gravity and a faint breeze.

He'd fired, felt the kick of the recoil and heard the sharp report, followed by screams behind him of bystanders diving for cover.

Remaining motionless, he'd cocked the gun again and prepared to fire a second time in case he'd missed.

But he saw immediately that another shot wouldn't be necessary.

Tal Simms carefully lowered the hammer of his weapon, replaced it in his holster and began running down the path.

"Excuse me, you were standing *where*?"

Tal ignored Greg LaTour's question and asked them both one more time, "You're okay? You're sure?"

The bearded cop persisted. "You were on *that* hill. Way the fuck up *there*?"

Mac told Tal that she was fine. He instinctively put his arm around her. Covey too said that he was unhurt, though he added that, as a heart patient, he could do without scares like that one.

Margaret Ludlum's gun had fired but it was merely a reflex after Tal's bullet had struck her squarely in the chest. The slug from her pistol had buried itself harmlessly in the ground.

Tal glanced at her body, now covered with a green tarp from the Medical Examiner's Office. He waited to feel upset, or shocked or guilty, but he was only numb. Those feelings would come later, he supposed. At the moment he was just relieved to find that Mac and Robert Covey were all right—and that the final itch in the case had been alleviated: The tough Irish girl, Margaret, was the missing link.

*They must've hired muscle or used somebody in the foundation for the
dirty work.*

As the Crime Scene techs picked up evidence around the body
and looked through the woman's purse, LaTour persisted. "That hill
up there? No fucking way."

Tal glanced up. "Yeah. Up there by the concession stand. Why?"

The bearded cop glanced at Mac. "He's kidding. He's jerking
my chain, right?"

"No, that's where he was."

"That's a fucking long shot. Wait . . . how big's your barrel?"

"What?"

"On your service piece."

"Three inch."

LaTour said. "You made that shot with a three-inch barrel?"

"We've pretty much established that, Greg. Can we move on?"
Tal turned back to Mac and smiled, feeling weak, he was so relieved
to see her safe.

But LaTour said, "You told me you don't shoot."

"I didn't say that at all. You *assumed* I don't shoot. I just didn't
want to go the range the other day. I've shot all my life. I was captain
of the rifle team at school."

LaTour squinted at the distant concession stand. He shook his
head. "No way."

Tal glanced at him and asked, "Okay, you want to know how I
did it? There's a trick."

"What?" the big cop asked eagerly.

"Easy. Just calculate the correlation between gravity as a con-
stant and the estimated mean velocity of the wind over the time it
takes the bullet to travel from points A to B—that's the muzzle to the
target. Got that? Then you just multiply distance times that corre-
lated factor divided by the mass of the bullet times its velocity
squared."

"You—" The big cop squinted again. "Wait, you—"

"It's a joke, Greg."

"You son of a bitch. You had me."

"Haven't you noticed it's not that hard to do?"

The cop mouthed words that Mac couldn't see but Tal had no
trouble deciphering.

LaTour squinted one last time toward the knoll and exhaled a laugh. "Let's get statements." He nodded to Robert Covey and escorted him toward his car, calling back to Tal, "You get hers. That okay with you, Einstein?"

"Sure."

Tal led Mac to a park bench out of sight of Margaret's body and listened to what she had to say about the incident, jotting down the facts in his precise handwriting. An officer drove Covey home and Tal found himself alone with Mac. There was silence for a moment and he asked, "Say, one thing? Could you help me fill out this questionnaire?"

"I'd be happy to."

He pulled one out of his briefcase, looked at it, then back to her. "How 'bout dinner tonight?"

"Is that one of the questions?"

"It's one of *my* questions. Not a police question."

"Well, the thing is I've got a date tonight. Sorry."

He nodded. "Oh, sure." Couldn't think of anything to follow up with. He pulled out his pen and smoothed the questionnaire, thinking: Of *course* she had a date. Women like her, high-ranking members of the Four Percent Club, always had dates. He wondered if it'd been the Pascal-sex comment that had knocked him out of the running. Note for the future: Don't bring that one up too soon.

Mac continued, "Yeah, tonight I'm going to help Mr. Covey find a health club with a pool. He likes to swim but he shouldn't do it alone. So we're going to find a place that's got a lifeguard."

"Really? Good for him." He looked up from Question 1.

"But I'm free Saturday," Mac said.

"Saturday? Well, I am too."

Silence. "Then how's Saturday?" she asked.

"I think it's great . . . Now how 'bout those questions?"

A week later the Lotus Research Foundation case was nearly tidied up—as was Tal's office, much to his relief—and he was beginning to think about the other tasks awaiting him: the SEC investigation, the statistical analysis for next year's personnel assignments and, of course, hounding fellow officers to get their questionnaires in on time.

The prosecutor still wanted some final statements for the Farley and Sheldon trials, though, and he'd asked Tal to interview the parents who'd adopted the three children born following the in vitro fertilization at the foundation.

Two of the three couples lived nearby and he spent one afternoon taking their statements. The last couple was in Warwick, a small town outside of Albany, over an hour away. Tal made the drive on a Sunday afternoon, zipping down the picturesque roadway along the Hudson River, the landscape punctuated with blooming azaleas, forsythia, and a billion spring flowers, the car filling with the scent of mulch and hot loam and sweet asphalt.

He found both Warwick and the couple's bungalow with no difficulty. The husband and wife, in their late twenties, were identically pudgy and rosy skinned. Uneasy too, until Tal explained that his mission there had nothing to do with any challenges to the adoption. It was merely a formality for a criminal case.

Like the other parents they provided good information that would be helpful in prosecuting Farley and Sheldon. For a half hour Tal jotted careful notes and then thanked them for their time. As he was leaving he walked past a small, cheery room decorated in a circus motif.

A little girl, about four, stood in the doorway. It was the youngster the couple had adopted from the foundation. She was adorable—blond, gray-eyed, with a heart-shaped face.

"This is Amy," the mother said.

"Hello, Amy," Tal offered.

She nodded shyly.

Amy was clutching a piece of paper and some crayons. "Did you draw that?" he asked.

"Uh-huh. I like to draw."

"I can tell. You've got lots of pictures." He nodded at the girl's walls.

"Here," she said, holding the sheet out. "You can have this. I just drew it."

"For me?" Tal asked. He glanced at her mother, who nodded her approval. He studied the picture for a moment. "Thank you, Amy. I love it. I'll put it up on my wall at work."

The girl's face broke into a beaming smile.

Tal said good-bye to her parents and ten minutes later he was cruising south on the parkway. When he came to the turnoff that would take him to his house and his Sunday retreat into the world of mathematics, though, Tal continued on. He drove instead to his office at the County Building.

A half hour later he was on the road again. En route to an address in Chesterton, a few miles away.

He pulled up in front of a split-level house surrounded by a small but immaculately trimmed yard. Two plastic tricycles and other assorted toys sat in the driveway.

But this wasn't the right place, he concluded with irritation. Damn. He must've written the address down wrong.

The house he was looking for had to be nearby and Tal decided to ask the owner here where it was. Walking to the door, Tal pushed the bell then stood back.

A pretty blonde in her thirties greeted him with a cheerful, "Hi. Help you?"

"I'm looking for Greg LaTour's house."

"Well, you found it. Hi, I'm his wife, Joan."

"He lives *here*?" Tal asked, glancing past her into a suburban home right out of a Hollywood sitcom. Thinking too: *And he's married?*

She laughed. "Hold on. I'll get him."

A moment later Greg LaTour came to the door, wearing shorts, sandals, and a green Izod shirt. He blinked in surprise and looked back over his shoulder into the house. Then he stepped outside and pulled the door shut after him. "What're you doing here?"

"Needed to tell you something about the case. . . ." But Tal's voice faded. He was staring at two cute blond girls, twins, about eight years old, who'd come around the side of the house and were looking at Tal curiously.

One said, "Daddy, the ball's in the bushes. We can't get it."

"Honey, I've got to talk to my friend here," he said in a singsong, fatherly voice. "I'll be there in a minute."

"Okay." They disappeared.

"You've got two kids?"

"*Four* kids."

"How long you been married?"

"Eighteen years."

"But I thought you were single. You never mentioned family. You didn't wear a ring. Your office, the biker posters, the bars after work . . ."

"That's who I need to be to do my job," LaTour said in a low voice. "That life—" He nodded vaguely in the direction of the Sheriff's Department. "—and this life I keep separate. Completely."

That's something else . . .

Tal now understood the meaning of the phrase. It wasn't about tragedies in his life, marital breakups, alienated children. And there was nothing LaTour was hiding from Tal. This was a life kept separate from everybody in the department.

"So you're mad I'm here," Tal said.

A shrug. "Just wish you'd called first."

"Sorry."

LaTour shrugged. "You go to church today?"

"I don't go to church. Why?"

"Why're you wearing a tie on Sunday?"

"I don't know. I just do. Is it crooked?"

The big cop said, "No it's not crooked. So. What're you doing here?"

"Hold on a minute."

Tal got his briefcase out of the car and returned to the porch. "I stopped by the office and checked up on the earlier suicides Sheldon and Farley arranged."

"You mean from a few years ago?"

"Right. Well, one of them was a professor named Mary Stemple. I'd heard of her—she was a physicist at Princeton. I read some of her work a while ago. She was brilliant. She spent the last three years of her life working on this analysis of the luminosity of stars and measuring blackbody radiation—"

"I've got burgers about to go on the grill," LaTour grumbled.

"Okay. Got it. Well, this was published just before she killed herself." He handed LaTour what he'd downloaded from the *Journal of Advanced Astrophysics* Web site:

THE INFINITE JOURNEY OF LIGHT:
A NEW APPROACH TO MEASURING
DISTANT STELLAR RADIATION
BY PROF. MARY STEMPLE, PH.D.

He flipped to the end of the article, which consisted of several pages of complicated formulae. They involved hundreds of numbers and Greek and English letters and mathematical symbols. The one that occurred most frequently was the sign for infinity: ∞

LaTour looked up. "There a punch line to all this?"

"Oh, you bet there is." He explained about his drive to Warwick to interview the adoptive couple.

And then he held up the picture that their daughter, Amy, had given him. It was a drawing of the earth and the moon and a spaceship—and all around them, filling the sky, were infinity symbols, growing smaller and smaller as they receded into space.

Forever . . .

Tal added, "And this wasn't the only one. Her walls were *covered* with pictures she'd done that had infinity signs in them. When I saw this I remembered Stemple's work. I went back to the office and I looked up her paper."

"What're you saying?" LaTour frowned.

"Mary Stemple killed herself five years ago. The girl who drew this was conceived at the foundation's clinic a month after she died."

"Jesus . . ." The big cop stared at the picture. "You don't think . . . Hell, it can't be real, that cloning stuff. That doctor we talked to, he said it was impossible."

Tal said nothing, continued to stare at the picture.

LaTour shook his head. "Naw, naw. You know what they did, Sheldon or that girl of his? Or Farley? They showed the kid pictures of that symbol. You know, so they could prove to other clients that the cloning worked. That's all."

"Sure," Tal said. "That's what happened. . . . Probably."

Still, they stood in silence for a long moment, this trained mathematician and this hardened cop, staring, captivated, at a clumsy, crayon picture drawn by a cute four-year-old.

"It can't be," LaTour muttered. "Germ's ass, remember?"

"Yeah, it's impossible," Tal said, staring at the symbol. He repeated: "Probably."

"Daddy!" Came a voice from the backyard.

LaTour called, "Be there in a minute, honey!" Then he looked up at Tal and said, "Hell, as long as you're here, come on in. Have dinner. I make great burgers."

Tal considered the invitation but his eyes were drawn back to the picture, the stars, the moon, the infinity signs. "Thanks but think I'll pass. I'm going back to the office for a while. All that evidence we took out of the foundation? I wanta look over the data a little more."

"Suit yourself, Einstein," the homicide cop said. He started back into the house but paused and turned back. "Data plural," he said, pointing a huge finger at Tal's chest.

"Data plural," Tal agreed.

LaTour vanished inside, the screen door swinging shut behind him with a bang.

ED MCBAIN

Ed McBain was born in 1956, when Evan Hunter was thirty years old. I am both of these people. What happened was that Pocket Books, Inc., had published the paperback edition of *The Blackboard Jungle* (by Evan Hunter) and wanted to know if I had any ideas for a mystery series. I came up with the notion of the 87th Precinct, and they gave me a contract for three paperback books, "to see how it goes." I was advised to put a pseudonym on the new series because "If it becomes known that Evan Hunter is writing mystery novels, it could be damaging to your career as a serious novelist," quote, unquote. When I finished the first book, *Cop Hater*, I still didn't have a new name. I went out into the kitchen, where my wife was feeding my twin sons, and I said, "How's Ed McBain?" She thought for a moment, and then said, "Good."

Fiddlers, which will be published this year, is the fifty-sixth title in the 87th Precinct series; frankly, I can't see that the Evan Hunter career has suffered at all. Between them, Hunter and McBain have written more than a hundred novels. McBain has never written a screenplay, but Hunter has written several, including *The Birds* for Alfred Hitchcock. The most recent Hunter novel was *The Moment She Was Gone*. The most recent McBain was *Alice in Jeopardy*, the first in a new mystery series.

But only once have they ever *actually* written anything together: Hunter wrote the first half of *Candyland* and McBain wrote the second half.

They still speak to each other.

MERELY HATE

Ed McBain

A blue Star of David had been spray-painted on the windshield of the dead driver's taxi.

"This is pretty unusual," Monoghan said.

"The blue star?" Monroe asked.

"Well, that, too," Monoghan agreed.

The two homicide detectives flanked Carella like a pair of bookends. They were each wearing black suits, white shirts, and black ties, and they looked somewhat like morticians, which was not a far cry from their actual calling. In this city, detectives from Homicide Division were overseers of death, expected to serve in an advisory and supervisory capacity. The actual murder investigation was handled by the precinct that caught the squeal—in this case, the Eight-Seven.

"But I was referring to a cabbie getting killed," Monoghan explained. "Since they started using them plastic partitions . . . what, four, five years ago? . . . yellow-cab homicides have gone down to practically zip."

Except for tonight, Carella thought.

Tall and slender, standing in an easy slouch, Steve Carella looked like an athlete, which he wasn't. The blue star bothered him. It bothered his partner, too. Meyer was hoping the blue star wasn't the start of something. In this city—in this world—things started too fast and took too long to end.

"Trip sheet looks routine," Monroe said, looking at the clipboard he'd recovered from the cab, glancing over the times and locations handwritten on the sheet. "Came on at midnight, last fare was dropped off at one-forty. When did you guys catch the squeal?"

Car four, in the Eight-Seven's Adam Sector, had discovered the cab parked at the curb on Ainsley Avenue at two-thirty in the morning. The driver was slumped over the wheel, a bullet hole at the base of his skull. Blood was running down the back of his neck, into his collar. Blue paint was running down his windshield. The uniforms had phoned the detective squadroom some five minutes later.

"We got to the scene at a quarter to three," Carella said.

"Here's the ME, looks like," Monoghan said.

Carl Blaney was getting out of a black sedan marked with the seal of the Medical Examiner's Office. Blaney was the only person Carella knew who had violet eyes. Then again, he didn't know Liz Taylor.

"What's this I see?" he asked, indicating the clipboard in Monroe's hand. "You been compromising the crime scene?"

"Told you," Monoghan said knowingly.

"It was in plain sight," Monroe explained.

"This the vic?" Blaney asked, striding over to the cab and looking in through the open window on the driver's side. It was a mild night at the beginning of May. Spectators who'd gathered on the sidewalk beyond the yellow CRIME SCENE tapes were in their shirt sleeves. The detectives in sport jackets and ties, Blaney and the homicide dicks in suits and ties, all looked particularly formal, as if they'd come to the wrong street party.

"MCU been here yet?" Blaney asked.

"We're waiting," Carella said.

Blaney was referring to the Mobile Crime Unit, which was called the CSI in some cities. Before they sanctified the scene, not even the ME was supposed to touch anything. Monroe felt this was another personal jab, just because he'd lifted the goddamn clipboard from the front seat. But he'd never liked Blaney, so fuck him.

"Why don't we tarry over a cup of coffee?" Blaney suggested, and without waiting for company, started walking toward an all-night diner across the street. This was a black neighborhood, and this stretch of turf was largely retail, with all of the shops closed at three-fifteen in the morning. The diner was the only place ablaze with illumination, although lights had come on in many of the tenements above the shuttered shops.

The sidewalk crowd parted to let Blaney through, as if he were a visiting dignitary come to restore order in Baghdad. Carella and Meyer ambled along after him. Monoghan and Monroe lingered near the taxi, where three or four blues stood around scratching their asses. Casually, Monroe tossed the clipboard through the open window and onto the front seat on the passenger side.

There were maybe half a dozen patrons in the diner when Blaney and the two detectives walked in. A man and a woman sitting in one of the booths were both black. The girl was wearing a purple silk dress and strappy high-heeled sandals. The man was wearing a beige linen suit with wide lapels. Carella and Meyer each figured them for a hooker and her pimp, which was profiling because for all they knew, the pair could have been a gainfully employed, happily married couple coming home from a late party. Everyone sitting on stools at the counter was black, too. So was the man behind it. They all knew this was the Law here, and the Law frequently spelled trouble in the hood, so they all fell silent when the three men took stools at the counter and ordered coffee.

"So how's the world treating you these days?" Blaney asked the detectives.

"Fine," Carella said briefly. He had come on at midnight, and it had already been a long night.

The counterman brought their coffees.

Bald and burly and blue-eyed, Meyer picked up his coffee cup, smiled across the counter, and asked, "How you doing?"

"Okay," the counterman said warily.

"When did you come to work tonight?"

"Midnight."

"Me, too," Meyer said. "Were you here an hour or so ago?"

"I was here, yessir."

"Did you see anything going down across the street?"

"Nossir."

"Hear a shot?"

"Nossir."

"See anyone approaching the cab there?"

"Nossir."

"Or getting out of the cab?"

"I was busy in here," the man said.

"What's your name?" Meyer asked.

"Whut's my name got to do with who got aced outside?"

"Nothing," Meyer said. "I have to ask."

"Deaven Brown," the counterman said.

"We've got a detective named Arthur Brown up the Eight-Seven," Meyer said, still smiling pleasantly.

"That right?" Brown said indifferently.

"Here's Mobile," Carella said, and all three men hastily downed their coffees and went outside again.

The chief tech was a Detective/First named Carlie . . .

"For Charles," he explained.

. . . Epworth. He didn't ask if anyone had touched anything, and Monroe didn't volunteer the information either. The MCU team went over the vehicle and the pavement surrounding it, dusting for prints, vacuuming for fibers and hair. On the cab's dashboard, there was a little black holder with three miniature American flags stuck in it like an open fan. In a plastic holder on the partition facing the back seat, there was the driver's pink hack license. The name to the right of the photograph was Khalid Aslam. It was almost four A.M. when Epworth said it would be okay to examine the corpse.

Blaney was thorough and swift.

Pending a more thorough examination at the morgue, he proclaimed cause of death to be a gunshot wound to the head—

Big surprise, Monroe thought, but did not say.

—and told the assembled detectives that they would have his written report by the end of the day. Epworth promised likewise, and one of the MCU team drove the taxi off to the police garage where it would be sealed as evidence. An ambulance carried off the stiff. The blues took down the CRIME SCENE tapes, and told everybody to go home, nothing to see here anymore, folks.

Meyer and Carella still had four hours to go before their shift ended.

"Khalid Aslam, Khalid Aslam," the man behind the computer said. "Must be a Muslim, don't you think?"

The offices of the License Bureau at the Taxi and Limousine Commission occupied two large rooms on the eighth floor of the old brick building on Emory Street all the way downtown. At five in the morning, there were only two people on duty, one of them a woman at another computer across the room. Lacking population, the place seemed cavernous.

"Most of the drivers nowadays are Muslims," the man said. His name was Lou Foderman, and he seemed to be close to retirement age, somewhere in his mid-sixties, Meyer guessed.

"Khalid Aslam, Khalid Aslam," he said again, still searching. "The names these people have. You know how many licensed yellow-cab drivers we have in this city?" he asked, not turning from the computer screen. "Forty-two thousand," he said, nodding. "Khalid Aslam, where are you hiding, Khalid Aslam? Ninety percent of them are immigrants, seventy percent from India, Pakistan, and Bangladesh. You want to bet Mr. Aslam here is from one of those countries? How much you wanna bet?"

Carella looked up at the wall clock.

It was five minutes past five.

"Back when *I* was driving a cab," Foderman said, "this was during the time of the Roman Empire, most of your cabbies were Jewish or Irish or Italian. We still got a couple of Jewish drivers around, but they're mostly from Israel or Russia. Irish and Italian, forget about it. You get in a cab nowadays, the driver's talking Farsi to some other guy on his cell phone, you think they're planning a terrorist attack. I wouldn't be surprised Mr. Aslam was talking on the phone to one of his pals, and the passenger shot him because he couldn't take it anymore, you said he was shot, correct?"

"He was shot, yes," Meyer said.

He looked up at the clock, too.

"Because he was babbling on the phone, I'll bet," Foderman said. "These camel jockeys think a taxi is a private phone booth, never mind the passenger. You ask them to please stop talking on the phone, they get insulted. We get more complaints here about drivers talking on the phone than anything else. Well, maybe playing the radio. They play their radios with all this string music from the Middle East, sitars, whatever they call them. Passengers are trying to have a decent conversation, the driver's either playing the radio or talking on the phone. You tell him please lower the radio, he gives you a look could kill you on the spot. Some of them even wear turbans and carry little daggers in their boots, Sikhs, they call themselves. 'All Singhs are Sikhs,'" Forderman quoted, "'but not all Sikhs are Singhs,' that's an expression they have. Singhs is a family name. Or the other way around, I forget which. Maybe it's 'All Sikhs are Singhs,' who knows? Khalid Aslam, here he is. What do you want to know about him?'"

Like more than thousands of other Muslim cab drivers in this city, Khalid Aslam was born in Bangladesh. Twelve years ago, he came to America with his wife and one child. According to his updated computer file, he now had three children and lived with his family at 3712 Locust Avenue in Majesta, a neighborhood that once—like the city's cab drivers—was almost exclusively Jewish, but which now was predominately Muslim.

Eastern Daylight Savings Time had gone into effect three weeks ago. This morning, the sun came up at six minutes to six. There was already heavy early-morning rush-hour traffic on the Majesta Bridge. Meyer was driving. Carella was riding shotgun.

"You detect a little bit of anti-Arab sentiment there?" Meyer asked.

"From Foderman, you mean?"

"Yeah. It bothers me to hear another Jew talk that way."

"Well, it bothers me, too," Carella said.

"Yeah, but you're not Jewish."

Someone behind them honked a horn.

"What's with him?" Meyer asked.

Carella turned to look.

"Truck in a hurry," he said.

"I have to tell you," Meyer said, "that blue star on the windshield bothers me. Aslam being Muslim. A bullet in the back of his head, and a Star of David on the windshield, that bothers me."

The truck driver honked again.

Meyer rolled down the window and threw him a finger. The truck driver honked again, a prolonged angry blast this time.

"Shall we give him a ticket?" Meyer asked jokingly.

"I think we should," Carella said.

"Why not? Violation of Section Two Twenty-One, Chapter Two, Subchapter Four, Noise Control."

"Maximum fine, eight hundred and seventy-five smackers," Carella said, nodding, enjoying this.

"Teach him to honk at cops," Meyer said.

The driver behind them kept honking his horn.

"So much hate in this city," Meyer said softly. "So much hate."

Shalah Aslam opened the door for them only after they had both held up their shields and ID cards to the three inches of space allowed by the night chain. She was wearing a blue woolen robe over a long white cotton nightgown. There was a puzzled look on her pale face. This was six-thirty in the morning, she had to know that two detectives on her doorstep at this hour meant something terrible had happened.

There was no diplomatic way to tell a woman that her husband had been murdered.

Standing in a hallway redolent of cooking smells, Carella told Shalah that someone had shot and killed her husband, and they would appreciate it if she could answer a few questions that might help them find whoever had done it. She asked them to come in. The apartment was very still. In contrast to the night before, the day had dawned far too cold for May. There was a bleak chill to the Aslam dwelling.

They followed her through the kitchen and into a small living room where the detectives sat on an upholstered sofa that probably had been made in the mountains of North Carolina. The blue robe Shalah Aslam was wearing most likely had been purchased at the Gap. But here on the mantel was a clock shaped in the form of a mosque, and there were beaded curtains leading to another part of the apartment, and there were the aromas of strange foods from other parts of the building, and the sounds of strange languages wafting up from the street through the open windows. They could have been somewhere in downtown Dhakar.

"The children are still asleep," Shalah explained. "Benazir is only six months old. The two other girls don't catch their school bus until eight-fifteen. I usually wake them at seven."

She had not yet cried. Her pale narrow face seemed entirely placid, her dark brown eyes vacant. The shock had registered, but the emotions hadn't yet caught up.

"Khalid was worried that something like this might happen," she said. "Ever since 9/11. That's why he had those American flags in his taxi. To let passengers know he's American. He got his citizenship five years ago. He's American, same as you. We're all Americans."

They had not yet told her about the Star of David painted on her husband's windshield.

"Seven Bangladesh people died in the towers, you know," she said. "It is not as if we were not victims, too. Because we are Muslim, that does not make us terrorists. The terrorists on those planes were Saudi, you know. Not people from Bangladesh."

"Mrs. Aslam, when you say he was worried, did he ever say specifically . . . ?"

"Yes, because of what happened to some other drivers at Regal."

"Regal?"

"That's the company he works for. A Regal taxi was set on fire in Riverhead the very day the Americans went into Afghanistan. And another one parked in Calm's Point was vandalized the week after we invaded Iraq. So he was afraid something might happen to him as well."

"But he'd never received a specific death threat, had he? Or . . ."

"No."

". . . a threat of violence?"

"No, but the fear was always there. He has had rocks thrown at his taxi. He told me he was thinking of draping a small American flag over his hack license, to hide his picture and name. When passengers ask if he's Arab, he tells them he's from Bangladesh."

She was still talking about him in the present tense. It still hadn't sunk in.

"Most people don't even know where Bangladesh is. Do you know where Bangladesh is?" she asked Meyer.

"No, ma'am, I don't," Meyer said.

"Do you?" she asked Carella.

"No," Carella admitted.

"But they know to shoot my husband because he is from Bangladesh," she said, and burst into tears.

The two detectives sat opposite her clumsily, saying nothing.

"I'm sorry," she said.

She took a tiny, crochet-trimmed handkerchief from the pocket of the robe, dabbed at her eyes with it.

"Khalid was always so careful," she said. "He never picked up anyone wearing a ski cap," drying her cheeks now. "If he got sleepy, he parked in front of a twenty-four-hour gas station or a police precinct. He never picked up anyone who didn't look right. He didn't care what color a person was. If that person looked threatening, he wouldn't pick him up. He hid his money in his shoes, or in an ashtray, or in the pouch on the driver-side door. He kept only a few dollars in his wallet. He was a very careful man."

Meyer bit the bullet.

"Did your husband know any Jewish people?" he asked.

"No," she said. "Why?"

"Mama?" a child's voice asked.

A little girl in a white nightgown, six, seven years old, was standing in the doorway to one of the other rooms. Her dark eyes were big and round in a puzzled face Meyer had seen a thousand times on television these past several years. Straight black hair. A slight frown on the face now. Wondering who these strange men were in their living room at close to seven in the morning.

"Where's Daddy?" she asked.

"Daddy's working," Shalah said, and lifted her daughter onto her lap. "Say hello to these nice men."

"Hello," the little girl said.

"This is Sabeen," Shalah said. "Sabeen is in the first grade, aren't you, Sabeen?"

"Uh-huh," Sabeen said.

"Hello, Sabeen," Meyer said.

"Hello," she said again.

"Sweetie, go read one of your books for a while, okay?" Shalah said. "I have to finish here."

"I have to go to school," Sabeen said.

"I know, darling. I'll just be a few minutes."

Sabeen gave the detectives a long look, and then went out of the room, closing the door behind her.

"Did a Jew kill my husband?" Shalah asked.

"We don't know that," Carella said.

"Then why did you ask if he knew any Jews?"

"Because the possibility exists that this might have been a hate crime," Meyer said.

"My husband was not a Palestinian," Shalah said. "Why would a Jew wish to kill him?"

"We don't know for a fact . . ."

"But you must at least *suspect* it was a Jew, isn't that so? Otherwise, why would you ask such a question? Bangladesh is on the Bay of Bengal, next door to India. It is nowhere near Israel. So why would a Jew . . . ?"

"Ma'am, a Star of David was painted on his windshield," Meyer said.

The room went silent.

"Then it *was* a Jew," she said, and clasped her hands in her lap. She was silent for perhaps twenty seconds.

Then she said, "The rotten bastards."

"I shouldn't have told her," Meyer said.

"Be all over the papers, anyway," Carella said. "Probably make the front page of the afternoon tabloid."

It was ten minutes past seven, and they were on their way across the bridge again, to where Regal Taxi had its garage on Abingdon and Hale. The traffic was even heavier than it had been on the way out. The day was warming up a little, but not much. This had been the worst damn winter Carella could ever remember. He'd been cold since October. And every time it seemed to be warming up a little, it either started snowing or raining or sleeting or some damn thing to dampen the spirits and crush all hope. Worst damn shitty winter ever.

"What?" Meyer said.

"Nothing."

"You were frowning."

Carella merely nodded.

"When do you think she'll tell the kids?" Meyer asked.

"I think she made a mistake saying he was working. She's got to tell them sooner or later."

"Hard call to make."

"Well, she's not gonna send them to school today, is she?"

"I don't know."

"Be all over the papers," Carella said again.

"I don't know what I'd do in a similar situation."

"When my father got killed, I told my kids that same day," Carella said.

"They're older," Meyer said.

"Even so."

He was silent for a moment.

"They really loved him," he said.

Meyer figured he was talking about himself.

There are times in this city when it is impossible to catch a taxi. Stand on any street corner between three-fifteen and four o'clock and you can wave your hand at any passing blur of yellow, and—forget about it. That's the forty-five minutes when every cabbie is racing back to the garage to turn in his trip sheet and make arrangements for tomorrow's tour of duty. It was the same with cops. The so-called night shift started at four P.M. and ended at midnight. For the criminally inclined, the shift change was a good time for them to do their evil thing because that's when all was confusion.

Confusion was the order of the day at the Regal garage when Meyer and Carella got there at seven-thirty that morning. Cabs were rolling in, cabs were rolling out. Assistant managers were making arrangements for tomorrow's short-terms, and dispatchers were sending newly gassed taxis on their way through the big open rolling doors. This was the busiest time of the day. Even busier than the pre-theater hours. Nobody had time for two flatfoots investigating a homicide.

Carella and Meyer waited.

Their own shift would end in—what was it now?—ten minutes, and they were bone-weary and drained of all energy, but they waited patiently because a man had been killed and Carella had been First Man Up when he answered the phone. It was twelve minutes after eight before the manager, a man named Dennis Ryan, could talk to them. Tall, and red-headed, and fortyish, harried-looking even though all of his cabs were on their way now, he kept nodding impatiently as they told him what had happened to Khalid Aslam.

"So where's my cab?" he asked.

"Police garage on Courtney," Meyer told him.

"When do I get it back? That cab is money on the hoof."

"Yes, but a man was killed in it," Carella said.

"When I saw Kal didn't show up this morning . . ."

Kal, Carella thought. Yankee Doodle Dandy.

". . . I figured he stopped to say one of his bullshit prayers."

Both detectives looked at him.

"They're supposed to pray five times a day, you know, can you beat it? Five times! Sunrise, early afternoon, late afternoon, sunset, and then before they go to bed. Five friggin times! And two *optional* ones if they're *really* holy. Most of them recognize they have a job to do here, they don't go flopping all over the sidewalk five times a day. Some of them pull over to a mosque on their way back in, for the late afternoon prayer. Some of them just do the one before they come to work, and the sunset one if they're home in time, and then the one before they go to bed. I can tell you anything you need to know about these people, we got enough of them working here, believe me."

"What kind of a worker was Aslam?" Carella asked.

"I guess he made a living."

"Meaning?"

"Meaning, it costs eighty-two bucks a shift to lease the cab. Say the driver averages a hundred above that in fares and tips. Gasoline costs him, say, fifteen, sixteen bucks? So he ends up taking home seventy-five, eighty bucks for an eight-hour shift. That ain't bad, is it?"

"Comes to around twenty grand a year," Meyer said.

"Twenty, twenty-five. That ain't bad," Ryan said again.

"Did he get along with the other drivers?" Carella asked.

"Oh, sure. These friggin Arabs are thick as thieves."

"How about your non-Arab drivers? Did he get along with them?"

"What non-Arab drivers? Why? You think one of my drivers done him?"

"Did he ever have any trouble with one of the other drivers?"

"I don't think so."

"Ever hear him arguing with one of them?"

"Who the hell knows? They babble in Bangla, Urdu, Sindi, Farsi, who the hell knows what else? They all sound the same to me. And they *always* sound like they're arguing. Even when they got smiles on their faces."

"Have you got any Jewish drivers?" Meyer asked.

"Ancient history," Ryan said. "I ain't *ever* seen a Jewish driver at Regal."

"How about anyone who might be sympathetic to the Jewish cause?"

"Which cause is that?" Ryan asked.

"Anyone who might have expressed pro-Israel sympathies?"

"Around here? You've got to be kidding."

"Did you ever hear Aslam say anything *against* Israel? Or the Jewish people?"

"No. Why? Did a Jew kill him?"

"What time did he go to work last night?"

"The boneyard shift goes out around eleven-thirty, quarter to twelve, comes in around seven, seven-thirty—well, you saw. I guess he must've gone out as usual. Why? What time was he killed?"

"Around two, two-thirty."

"Where?"

"Up on Ainsley and Twelfth."

"Way up there, huh?" Ryan said. "You think a nigger did it?"

"We don't know if who did it was white, purple, or black, was the word you meant, right?" Carella said, and looked Ryan dead in the eye.

And fuck you, too, Ryan thought, but said only, "Good luck catching him," making it sound like a curse.

Meyer and Carella went back to the squadroom to type up their interim report on the case.

It was almost a quarter to nine when they finally went home.

The day shift had already been there for half an hour.

Detectives Arthur Brown and Bert Kling made a good salt-and-pepper pair.

Big and heavyset and the color of his surname, Brown looked somewhat angry even when he wasn't. A scowl from him was usually enough to cause a perp to turn to Kling for sympathy and redemption. A few inches shorter than his partner—*everybody* was a few inches shorter than Brown—blond and hazel-eyed, Kling looked like a broad-shouldered farm boy who'd just come in off the fields after working since sunup. God Cop-Bad Cop had been invented for Kling and Brown.

It was Brown who took the call from Ballistics at 10:27 that Friday morning.

"You handling this cabbie kill?" the voice said.

Brown immediately recognized the caller as a brother.

"I've been briefed on it," he said.

"This is Carlyle, Ballistics. We worked that evidence bullet the ME's office sent over, you want to take this down for whoever's running the case?"

"Shoot," Brown said, and moved a pad into place.

"Nice clean bullet, no deformities, must've lodged in the brain matter, ME's report didn't say exactly where they'd recovered it. Not that it matters. First thing we did here, bro . . ."

He had recognized Brown's voice as well.

". . . was compare a rolled impression of the evidence bullet against our specimen cards. Once we got a first-sight match, we did a microscopic examination of the actual bullet against the best sample bullet in our file. Way we determine the make of an unknown firearm is by examining the grooves on the bullet and the right or left direction of twist—but you don't want to hear all that shit, do you?"

Brown had heard it only ten thousand times before.

"Make a long story short," Carlyle said, "what we got here is a bullet fired from a .38-caliber Colt revolver, which is why you didn't find an ejected shell in the taxi, the gun being a revolver and all. Incidentally, there are probably a hundred thousand unregistered, illegal .38-caliber Colts in this city, so the odds against you finding it are probably eighty to one. End of story."

"Thanks," Brown said. "I'll pass it on."

"You see today's paper?" Carlyle asked.

"No, not yet."

"Case made the front page. Makes it sound like the Israeli army invaded Majesta with tanks, one lousy Arab. Is this true about a Jewish star on the windshield?"

"That's what our guys found."

"Gonna be trouble, bro," Carlyle said.

He didn't know the half of it.

While Carella and Meyer slept like hibernating grizzlies, Kling and Brown read their typed report, noted that the dead driver's widow had told them the Aslams' place of worship was called Majid Hazrat-i-Shabazz, and went out at eleven that morning to visit the mosque.

If either of them had expected glistening white minarets, arches, and domes, they were sorely disappointed. There were more than a hundred mosques in this city, but only a handful of them had been originally designed as such. The remainder had been converted to places of worship from private homes, warehouses, storefront buildings, and lofts. There were, in fact, only three requirements for any building that now called itself a mosque: that males and females be separated during prayer; that there be no images of animate objects inside the building; and that the *quibla*—the orientation of prayer in the direction of the Kabba in Mecca—be established.

A light rain began falling as they got out of the unmarked police sedan and began walking toward a yellow brick building that had once been a small supermarket on the corner of Lowell and Franks. Metal shutters were now in place where earlier there'd been plate glass display windows. Grafitti decorated the yellow brick and the green shutters. An ornately hand-lettered sign hung above the entrance doors, white on a black field, announcing the name of the mosque: Majid Hazrat-i-Shabazz. Men in flowing white garments and embroidered prayer caps, other men in dark business suits and pillbox hats milled about on the sidewalk with young men in team jackets, their baseball caps turned backward. Friday was the start of the Muslim sabbath, and now the faithful were being called to prayer.

On one side of the building, the detectives could see women entering through a separate door.

"My mother knows this Muslim lady up in Diamondback," Brown said, "she goes to this mosque up there—lots of blacks are Muslims, you know . . ."

"I know," Kling said.

"And where she goes to pray, they got no space for this separation stuff. So the men and women all pray together in the same open hall. But the women sit *behind* the men. So this fat ole sister gets there late one Friday, and the hall is already filled with men, and they tell her there's no room for her. Man, she takes a fit! Starts yelling, 'This is America, I'm as good a Muslim as any man here, so how come they's only room for *brothers* to pray?' Well, the imam—that's the man in charge, he's like the preacher—he quotes scripture and verse that says only men are *required* to come to Friday prayer, whereas women are not. So they have to let the men in first. It's as simple as that. So she quotes right back at him that in Islam, women are *spose* to be highly respected and revered, so how come he's dissing her this way? And she walked away from that mosque and never went back. From that time on, she prayed at home. That's a true story," Brown said.

"I believe it," Kling said.

The imam's address that Friday was about the dead cab driver. He spoke first in Arabic—which, of course, neither Kling nor Brown understood—and then he translated his words into English, perhaps for their benefit, perhaps in deference to the younger worshippers in the large drafty hall. The male worshippers knelt at the front of the hall. Behind a translucent, moveable screen, Brown and Kling could perceive a small number of veiled female worshippers.

The imam said he prayed that the strife in the Middle East was not now coming to this city that had known so much tragedy already. He said he prayed that an innocent and hard-working servant of Allah had not paid with his life for the acts of a faraway people bent only on destruction—

The detectives guessed he meant the Israelis.

—prayed that the signature star on the windshield of the murdered man's taxi was not a promise of further violence to come.

"It is foolish to grieve for our losses," he said, "since all is ordained by Allah. Only by working for the larger nation of Islam can we understand the true meaning of life."

Men's foreheads touched the cement floor.

Behind the screen, the women bowed their heads as well.

The imam's name was Muhammad Adham Akbar.

"What we're trying to find out," Brown said, "is whether or not Mr. Aslam had any enemies that you know of."

"Why do you even ask such a question?" Akbar said.

"He was a worshipper at your mosque," Kling said. "We thought you might know."

"Why would he have enemies here?"

"Men have enemies everywhere," Brown said.

"Not in a house of prayer. If you want to know who Khalid's enemy was, you need only look at his windshield."

"Well, we have to investigate every possibility," Kling said.

"The star on his windshield says it all," Akbar said, and shrugged. "A Jew killed him. That would seem obvious to anyone."

"Well, a Jew may have committed those murders," Kling agreed. "But . . ."

"May," the imam said, and nodded cynically.

"But until we catch him, we won't know for sure, will we?" Kling said.

Akbar looked at him.

Then he said, "The slain man had no enemies that I know of."

Just about when Carella and Meyer were each and separately waking up from eight hours of sleep, more or less, the city's swarm of taxis rolled onto the streets for the four-to-midnight shift. And as the detectives sat down to late afternoon meals which for each of them were really hearty breakfasts, many of the city's more privileged women were coming out into the streets to start looking for taxis to whisk them homeward. Here was a carefully coiffed woman who'd just enjoyed afternoon tea, chatting with another equally stylish woman as they strolled together out of a midtown hotel. And here was a woman who came out of a department store carrying a shopping bag in each hand, shifting one of the bags to the other hand, freeing it so she could hail a taxi. And here was a woman coming out of a Korean nail shop, wearing paper sandals to protect her freshly painted toenails. And another coming out of a deli, clutching a bag with baguettes showing, raising one hand to signal a cab. At a little before five, the streets were suddenly alive with the leisured women of this city, the most beautiful women in all the world, all of them ready to kill if another woman grabbed a taxi that had just been hailed.

This was a busy time for the city's cabbies. Not ten minutes later, the office buildings would begin spilling out men and women who'd been working since nine this morning, coming out onto the pavements now and sucking in great breaths of welcome spring air. The rain had stopped, and the sidewalk and pavements glistened, and there was the strange aroma of freshness on the air. This had been one hell of a winter.

The hands went up again, typists' hands, and file clerks' hands, and the hands of lawyers and editors and agents and producers and exporters and thieves, yes, even thieves took taxis—though obvious criminal types were avoided by these cabbies steering their vehicles recklessly toward the curb in a relentless pursuit of passengers. These men had paid eighty-two dollars to lease their taxis. These men had paid fifteen, twenty bucks to gas their buggies and get them on the road. They were already a hundred bucks in the hole before they put foot to pedal. Time was money. And there were hungry mouths to feed. For the most part, these men were Muslims, these men were gentle strangers in a strange land.

But someone had killed one of them last night.

And he was not yet finished.

Salim Nazir and his widowed mother left Afghanistan in 1994, when it became apparent that the Taliban were about to take over the entire country. His father had been one of the mujahideen killed fighting the Russian occupation; Salim's mother did not wish the wrath of "God's Students" to fall upon their heads if and when a new regime came to power.

Salim was now twenty-seven years old, his mother fifty-five. Both had been American citizens for three years now, but neither approved of what America had done to their native land, the evil Taliban notwithstanding. For that matter they did not appreciate what America had done to Iraq in its search for imaginary weapons of mass destruction. (Salim called them "weapons of mass deception.") In fact, Salim totally disapproved of the mess America had made in what once was his part of the world, but he rarely expressed these views out loud, except when he was among other Muslims who lived—as he and his mother did now—in a ghettolike section of Calm's Point.

Salim knew what it was like to be an outsider in George W. Bush's America, no matter how many speeches the president made about Islam being a peaceful religion. With all his heart, Salim knew this to be true, but he doubted very much that Mr. Bush believed what he was saying.

Just before sundown that Friday, Salim pulled his yellow taxi into the curb in front of a little shop on a busy street in Majesta. Here in Ikram Hassan's store, devout Muslims could purchase whatever food and drink was considered *halal*—lawful or permitted for consumption as described in the Holy Koran.

The Koran decreed, "Eat of that over which the name of Allah hath been mentioned, if ye are believers in His revelations." Among the acceptable foods were milk (from cows, sheep, camels, or goats), honey, fish, plants that were not intoxicant, fresh or naturally frozen vegetables, fresh or dried fruits, legumes (like peanuts, cashews, hazelnuts, and walnuts), and grains such as wheat, rice, barley, and oats.

Many animals, large and small, were considered *halal* as well, but they had to be slaughtered according to Islamic ritual. Ikram Hassan was about to slay a chicken just as his friend Salim came into the shop. He looked up when a small bell over his door sounded.

"Hey there, Salim," he said in English.

There were two major languages in Afghanistan, both of them imported from Iran, but Pushto was the official language the two men had learned as boys growing up in Kandahar, and this was the language they spoke now.

Salim fidgeted and fussed as his friend hunched over the chicken; he did not want to be late for the sunset prayer. Using a very sharp knife, and making certain that he cut the main blood vessels without completely severing the throat, Ikram intoned "*Bismillah Allah-u-Albar*" and completed the ritual slaughter.

Each of the men then washed his hands to the wrists, and cleansed the mouth and the nostrils with water, and washed the face and the right arm and left arm to the elbow, and washed to the ankle first the right foot and then the left, and at last wiped the top of the head with wet hands, the three middle fingers of each hand joined together.

Salim consulted his watch yet another time.

Both men donned little pillbox hats.

Ikram locked the front door to his store, and together they walked to the mosque four blocks away.

The sun had already set.

It was ten minutes to seven.

———

Among other worshippers, Salim and Ikram stood facing Mecca, their hands raised to their ears, and they uttered the words, "*Allahu Akbar*," which meant "Allah is the greatest of all." Then they placed the right hand just below the breast and recited in unison the prayer called *istiftah*.

"Surely I have turned myself, being upright holy to Him Who originated the heavens and the earth and I am not of the polytheists. Surely my prayer and my sacrifice and my life and my death are for Allah, the Lord of the worlds, no associate has He; and this I am commanded and I am one of those who submit. Glory to Thee, O Allah, and Thine is the praise, and blessed is Thy name, and exalted is Thy majesty, and there is none to be served besides Thee."

A'udhu bi-llahi minash-shaitani-r-rajim.

"I seek the refuge of Allah from the accursed devil."

Six hours later, Salim Nazir would be dead.

In this city, all the plays, concerts, and musicals let out around eleven, eleven-thirty, the cabarets around one, one-thirty. The night clubs wouldn't break till all hours of the night. It was Salim's habit during the brief early-morning lull to visit a Muslim friend who was a short-order cook at a deli on Culver Avenue, a mile and a half distant from all the midtown glitter. He went into the deli at one-thirty, enjoyed a cup of coffee and a chat with his friend, and left twenty minutes later. Crossing the street to where he'd parked his taxi, he got in behind the wheel, and was just about to start the engine when he realized someone was sitting in the dark in the back seat.

Startled, he was about to ask what the hell, when the man fired a bullet through the plastic divider and into his skull.

The two Midtown South detectives who responded to the call immediately knew this killing was related to the one that had taken place uptown the night before; a blue Star of David had been spray-painted on the windshield. Nonetheless, they called their lieutenant from the scene, and he informed them that this was a clear case of First Man Up, and advised them to wait right there while he contacted the Eight-Seven, which had caught the original squeal. The detectives were still at the scene when Carella and Meyer got there at twenty minutes to three.

Midtown South told Carella that both MCU and the ME had already been there and gone, the corpse and the vehicle carried off respectively to the morgue and the PD garage to be respectively dissected and impounded. They told the Eight-Seven dicks that they'd talked to the short-order cook in the deli across the street, who informed them that he was a friend of the dead man, and that he'd been in there for a cup of coffee shortly before he got killed. The vic's name was Salim Nazir, and the cab company he worked for was called City Transport. They assumed the case was now the Eight-Seven's and that Carella and Meyer would do all the paper shit and send them dupes. Carella assured them that they would.

"We told you about the blue star, right?" one of the Midtown dicks said.

"You told us," Meyer said.

"Here's the evidence bullet we recovered," he said, and handed Meyer a sealed manila envelope. "Chain of Custody tag on it, you sign next. Looks like you maybe caught an epidemic."

"Or maybe a copycat," Carella said.

"Either way, good luck," the other Midtown dick said.

Carella and Meyer crossed the street to the deli.

Like his good friend, Salim, the short-order cook was from Afghanistan, having arrived here in the city seven years ago. He offered at once to show the detectives his green card, which made each of them think he was probably an illegal with a counterfeit card, but they had bigger fish to fry and Ajmal Khan was possibly a man who could help them do just that.

Ajmal meant "good-looking" in his native tongue, a singularly contradictory description for the man who now told them he had heard a shot outside some five minutes after Salim finished his coffee. Dark eyes bulging with excitement, black mustache bristling, bulbous nose twitching like a rabbit's, Ajmal reported that he had rushed out of the shop the instant he heard the shot, and had seen a man across the street getting out of Salim's taxi on the driver's side, and leaning over the windshield with a can of some sort in his hand.

Ajmal didn't know what he was doing at the time but he now understood the man was spray-painting a Jewish star on the windshield.

"Can you describe this man?" Carella asked.

"Is that what he was doing? Painting a Star of David on the windshield?"

"Apparently," Meyer said.

"That's bad," Ajmal said.

The detectives agreed with him. That was bad. They did not believe this was a copycat. This was someone specifically targeting Muslim cab drivers. But they went through the routine anyway, asking the questions they always asked whenever someone was murdered: Did he have any enemies that you know of, did he mention any specific death threats, did he say he was being followed or harassed, was he in debt to anyone, was he using drugs?

Ajmal told them that his good friend Salim was loved and respected by everyone. This was what friends and relatives always said about the vic. He was a kind and gentle person. He had a wonderful sense of humor. He was thoughtful and generous. He was devout. Ajmal could not imagine why anyone would have done this to a marvelous person like his good friend Salim Nazir.

"He was always laughing and friendly, a very warm and outgoing man. Especially with the ladies," Ajmal said.

"What do you mean?" Carella asked.

"He was quite a ladies' man, Salim. It is written that men may have as many as four wives, but they must be treated equally in every way. That is to say, emotionally, sexually, and materially. If Salim had been a wealthy man, I am certain he would have enjoyed the company of many wives."

"How many wives did he actually *have*?" Meyer asked.

"Well, none," Ajmal said. "He was single. He lived with his mother."

"Do you know where?"

"Oh yes. We were very good friends. I have been to his house many times."

"Can you give us his address?"

"His phone number, too," Ajmal said. "His mother's name is Gulalai. It means 'flower' in my country."

"You say he was quite a ladies' man, is that right?" Carella asked.

"Well, yes. The ladies liked him."

"More than one lady?" Carella said.

"Well, yes, more than one."

"Did he ever mention any jealousy among these various ladies?"

"I don't even know who they were. He was a discreet man."

"No reason any of these ladies might have wanted to shoot him?" Carella said.

"Not that I know of."

"But he *did* say he was seeing several women, is that it?"

"In conversation, yes."

"He said he was in *conversation* with several women?"

"No, he said to *me* in conversation that he was enjoying the company of several women, yes. As I said, he was quite a ladies' man."

"But he didn't mention the names of these women."

"No, he did not. Besides, it was a man I saw getting out of his taxi. A very tall man."

"Could it have been a very tall woman?"

"No, this was very definitely a man."

"Can you describe him?"

"Tall. Wide shoulders. Wearing a black raincoat and a black hat." Ajmal paused. "The kind rabbis wear," he said.

Which brought them right back to that Star of David on the windshield.

Two windshields.

This was not good at all.

This was a mixed lower-class neighborhood—white, black, Hispanic. These people had troubles of their own, they didn't much care about a couple of dead Arabs. Matter of fact, many of them had sons or husbands who'd fought in the Iraqi war. Lots of the people Carella and Meyer spoke to early that morning had an "Army of One," was what it was called nowadays, who'd gone to war right here from the hood. Some of these young men had never come back home except in a box.

You never saw nobody dying on television. All them reporters embedded with the troops, all you saw was armor racing across the desert. You never saw somebody taking a sniper bullet between the eyes, blood spattering. You never saw an artillery attack with arms and legs flying in the air. You could see more people getting killed right here in the hood than you saw getting killed in the entire Iraqi war. It was an absolute miracle, all them embedded newspeople out there reporting, and not a single person getting killed for the cameras. Maybe none of them had a camera handy when somebody from the hood got killed. So who gave a damn around here about a few dead Arabs more or less?

One of the black women they interviewed explained that people were asleep, anyway, at two in the morning, wun't that so? So why go axin a dumb question like did you hear a shot that time of night? A Hispanic man they interviewed told them there were *always* shots in the barrio; nobody ever paid attention no more. A white woman told them she'd got up to go pee around that time, and thought she heard something but figured it was a backfire.

At 4:30 A.M., Meyer and Carella spoke to a black man who'd been blinded in Iraq. He was in pajamas and a bathrobe, and he was wearing dark glasses. A white cane stood angled against his chair. He could remember President Bush making a little speech to a handful of veterans like himself at the hospital where he was recovering, his eyes still bandaged. He could remember Bush saying something folksy like, "I'll bet those Iraqi soldiers weren't happy to meet *you* fellas!" He could remember thinking, I wun't so happy to meet *them*, either. I'm goan be blind the ress of my life, Mr. Pres'dunt, how you feel about *that*?

"I heerd a shot," he told the detectives.

Travon Nelson was his name. He worked as a dishwasher in a restaurant all the way downtown. They stopped serving at eleven, he was usually out by a little before one, took the number 17 bus uptown, got home here around two. He had just got off the bus, and was walking toward his building, his white cane tapping the sidewalk ahead of him . . .

He had once thought he'd like to become a Major League ballplayer.

. . . when he heard the sharp crack of a small-arms weapon, and then heard a car door slamming, and then a hissing sound, he didn't know what it was . . .

The spray paint, Meyer thought.

. . . and then a man yelling.

"Yelling at *you*?" Carella asked.

"No, sir. Must've been some girl."

"What makes you think that?"

"Cause whut he yelled was 'You *whore*!' An' then I think he must've hit her, cause she screamed an' kepp right on screamin an' screamin."

"Then what?" Meyer asked.

"He run off. She run off, too. I heerd her heels clickin away. High heels. When you blind . . ."

His voice caught.

They could not see his eyes behind the dark glasses.

". . . you compensate with yo' other senses. They was the sound of the man's shoes runnin off and then the click of the girl's high heels."

He was silent for a moment, remembering again what high heels on a sidewalk sounded like.

"Then evy'thin went still again," he said.

Years of living in war-torn Afghanistan had left their mark on Gulalai Nazir's wrinkled face and stooped posture; she looked more like a woman in her late sixties than the fifty-five-year-old mother of Salim. The detectives had called ahead first, and several grieving relatives were already in her apartment when they got there at six that Saturday morning. Gulalai—although now an American citizen—spoke very little English. Her nephew—a man who at the age of sixteen had fought with the mujahideen against the Russians—translated for the detectives.

Gulalai told them what they had already heard from the short-order cook.

Her son was loved and respected by everyone. He was a kind and gentle person. A loving son. He had a wonderful sense of humor. He was thoughtful and generous. He was devout. Gulalai could not imagine why anyone would have done this to him.

"Unless it was that Jew," she said.

The nephew translated.

"Which Jew?" Carella asked at once.

"The one who killed that other Muslim cab driver uptown," the nephew translated.

Gulalai wrung her hands and burst into uncontrollable sobbing. The other women began wailing with her.

The nephew took the detectives aside.

His name was Osman, he told them, which was Turkish in origin, but here in America everyone called him either Ozzie or Oz.

"Oz Kiraz," he said, and extended his hand. His grip was firm and strong. He was a big man, possibly thirty-two, thirty-three years old, with curly black hair and an open face with sincere brown eyes. Carella could visualize him killing Russian soldiers with his bare hands. He would not have enjoyed being one of them.

"Do you think you're going to get this guy?" he asked.

"We're trying," Carella said.

"Or is it going to be the same song and dance?"

"Which song and dance is that, sir?" Meyer said.

"Come on, this city is run by Jews. If a Jew killed my cousin, it'll be totally ignored."

"We're trying to make sure that doesn't happen," Carella said.

"I'll bet," Oz said.

"You'd win," Meyer said.

The call from Detective Carlyle in Ballistics came at a quarter to seven that Saturday morning.

"You the man I spoke to yesterday?" he asked.

"No, this is Carella."

"You workin this Arab shit?"

"Yep."

"It's the same gun," Carlyle said. "This doesn't mean it was the same *guy*, it coulda been his cousin or his uncle or his brother pulled the trigger. But it was the same .38-caliber Colt that fired the bullet."

"That it?"

"Ain't that enough?"

"More than enough," Carella said. "Thanks, pal."

"Buy me a beer sometime," Carlyle said, and hung up.

At 8:15 that morning, just as Carella and Meyer were briefing Brown and Kling on what had happened the night before, an attractive young black woman in her mid twenties walked into the squadroom. She introduced herself as Wandalyn Holmes, and told the detectives that she'd been heading home from baby-sitting her sister's daughter last night—walking to the corner to catch the number 17 bus down-town, in fact—when she saw this taxi sitting at the curb, and a man dressed all in black spraying paint on the windshield.

"When he saw I was looking at him, he pointed a finger at me . . ."

"Pointed . . . ?"

"Like this, yes," Wandalyn said, and showed them how the man had pointed his finger. "And he yelled 'You! Whore!' and I screamed and he came running after me."

"You whore?"

"No, two words. First 'You!' and *then* 'Whore!' "

"Did you know this man?"

"Never saw him in my life."

"But he pointed his finger at you and called you a whore."

"Yes. And when I ran, he came after me and caught me by the back of the coat, you know what I'm saying? The collar of my coat? And pulled me over, right off my feet."

"What time was this, Miss Holmes?" Carella asked.

"About two in the morning, a little after."

"What happened then?"

"He kicked me. While I was laying on the ground. He seemed mad as hell. I thought at first he was gonna rape me. I kept scream-ing, though, and he ran off."

"What'd you do then?" Brown asked.

"I got up and ran off, too. Over to my sister's place. I was scared he might come back."

"Did you get a good look at him?"

"Oh yes."

"Tell us what he looked like," Meyer said.

"Like I said, he was all in black. Black hat, black raincoat, black everything."

"Was he himself black?" Kling asked.

"Oh no, he was a white man."

"Did you see his face?"

"I did."

"Describe him."

"Dark eyes. Angry. Very angry eyes."

"Beard? Mustache?"

"No."

"Notice any scars or tattoos?"

"No."

"Did he say anything to you?"

"Well, yes, I told you. He called me a whore."

"*After* that."

"No. Nothing. Just pulled me over backward, and started kicking me when I was down. I thought he was gonna rape me, I was scared to death." Wandalyn paused a moment. The detectives caught the hesitation.

"Yes?" Carella said. "Something else?"

"I'm sorry I didn't come here right away last night, but I was too scared," Wandalyn said. "He was very angry. *So* angry. I was scared he might come after me if I told the police anything."

"You're here now," Carella said. "And we thank you."

"He *won't* come after me, right?" Wandalyn asked.

"I'm sure he won't," Carella said. "It's not you he's angry with."

Wandalyn nodded. But still looked skeptical.

"You'll be okay, don't worry," Brown said, and led her to the gate in the slatted wooden railing that divided the squadroom from the corridor outside.

At his desk, Carella began typing up their Detective Division report. He was still typing when Brown came over and said, "You know what time it is?"

Carella nodded and kept typing.

It was 9:33 A.M. when he finally printed up the report and carried it over to Brown's desk.

"Go home," Brown advised, scowling.

They had worked important homicides before, and these had also necessitated throwing the schedule out the window. What was new this time around—

Well, no, there was also a murder that had almost started a race riot, this must've been two, three years back, they hadn't got much sleep that time, either. This was similar, but different. This was two Muslim cabbies who'd been shot to death by someone, obviously a Jew, eager to take credit for both murders.

Meyer didn't know whether he dreamt it, or whether it was a brilliant idea he'd had before he fell asleep at nine that morning.

Dream or brilliant idea, the first thing he did when the alarm clock rang at three that afternoon was find a fat felt-tipped pen and a sheet of paper and draw a big blue Star of David on it.

He kept staring at the star and wondering if the department's handwriting experts could tell them anything about the man or men who had spray-painted similar stars on the windshields of those two cabs.

He was almost eager to get to work.

Six hours of sleep wasn't bad for what both detectives considered a transitional period, similar to the decompression a deep-sea diver experienced while coming up to the surface in stages. Actually, they were moving back from the midnight shift to the night shift, a passage that normally took place over a period of days, but which given the exigency of the situation occurred in the very same day. Remarkably, both men felt refreshed and—in Meyer's case at least—raring to go.

"I had a great idea last night," he told Carella. "Or maybe it was just a dream. Take a look at this," he said, and showed Carella the Star of David he'd drawn.

"Okay," Carella said.

"I'm right-handed," Meyer said. "So what I did . . ."

"So am I," Carella said.

"What I did," Meyer said, "was start the first triangle here at the northernmost point of the star . . . there are six points, you know, and they mean something or other, I'm not really sure what. I am not your ideal Jew."

"I never would have guessed."

"But religious Jews know what the six points stand for."

"So what's your big idea?"

"Well, I was starting to tell you. I began the first triangle at the very top, and drew one side down to this point here," he said, indicating the point on the bottom right . . .

". . . and then I drew a line across to the left . . ."

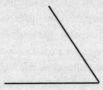

". . . and another line up to the northern point again, completing the first triangle."

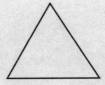

"Okay," Carella said, and picked up a pen and drew a triangle in exactly the same way.

"Then I started the second triangle at the western point—the one here on the left—and drew a line over to the east here . . ."

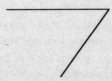

". . . and then down on an angle to the south . . ."

". . . and back up again to . . . northwest, I guess it is . . . where I started."

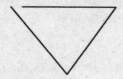

Carella did the same thing.

"That's right," he said. "That's how you do it."

"Yes, but we're both right-handed."

"So?"

"I think a left-handed person might do it differently."

"Ah," Carella said, nodding.

"So I think we should call Documents and get them to look at both those cabs. See if the same guy painted those two stars, and find out if he was right-handed or left-handed."

"I think that's brilliant," Carella said.

"You don't."

"I do."

"I can tell you don't."

"I'll make the call myself," Carella said.

He called downtown, asked for the Documents Section, and spoke to a detective named Jackson who agreed that there would be a distinct difference between left- and right-handed handwriting, even if the writing instrument—so to speak—was a spray can. Carella told him they were investigating a double homicide . . .

"Those Muslim cabbies, huh?"

. . . and asked if Documents could send someone down to the police garage to examine the spray-painting on the windshields of the two impounded taxis. Jackson said it would have to wait till tomorrow morning, they were a little short-handed today.

"While I have you," Carella said, "can you switch me over to the lab?"

The lab technician he spoke to reported that the paint scrapings from the windshields of both cabs matched laboratory samples of a product called Redi-Spray, which was manufactured in Milwaukee, Wisconsin, distributed nationwide, and sold in virtually every hard-

ware store and supermarket in this city. Carella thanked him and
hung up.

He was telling Meyer what he'd just learned, when Rabbi Avi
Cohen walked into the squadroom.

"I think I may be able to help you with the recent cab driver murders," the rabbi said.

Carella offered him a chair alongside his desk.

"If I may," the rabbi said, "I would like to go back to the beginning."

Would you be a rabbi otherwise? Meyer thought.

"The beginning was last month," the rabbi said, "just before
Passover. Today is the sixteenth day of the Omer, which is one week
and nine days from the second day of Passover, so this would have
been before Passover. Around the tenth of April, a Thursday I seem
to recall it was."

As the rabbi remembers it . . .

This young man came to him seeking guidance and assistance.
Was the rabbi familiar with a seventeen-year-old girl named Rebecca
Schwartz, who was a member of the rabbi's own congregation? Well,
yes, of course, Rabbi Cohen knew the girl well. He had, in fact, offi-
ciated at her *bat mitzvah* five years ago. Was there some problem?

The problem was that the young man was in love with young
Rebecca, but he was not of the Jewish faith—which, by the way, had
been evident to the rabbi at once, the boy's olive complexion, his
dark brooding eyes. It seemed that Rebecca's parents had forbidden
her from seeing the boy ever again, and this was why he was here in
the synagogue today, to ask the rabbi if he could speak to Mr.
Schwartz and convince him to change his mind.

Well.

The rabbi explained that this was an Orthodox congregation and
that anyway there was a solemn prohibition in Jewish religious law
against a Jew marrying anyone but another Jew. He went on to explain that this ban against intermarriage was especially pertinent to
our times, when statistics indicated that an alarming incidence of intermarriage threatened the very future of American Jewry.

"In short," Rabbi Cohen said, "I told him I was terribly sorry, but
I could never approach Samuel Schwartz with a view toward encour-

aging a relationship between his daughter and a boy of another faith. Do you know what he said to me?"

"What?" Carella asked.

"'Thanks for nothing!' He made it sound like a threat."

Carella nodded. So did Meyer.

"And then the e-mails started," the rabbi said. "Three of them all together. Each with the same message. 'Death to all Jews.' And just at sundown last night . . ."

"When was this?" Meyer asked. "The e-mails?"

"Last week. All of them last week."

"What happened last night?" Carella asked.

"Someone threw a bottle of whiskey with a lighted wick through the open front door of the synagogue."

The two detectives nodded again.

"And you think this boy . . . the one who's in love with Rebecca . . . ?"

"Yes," the rabbi said.

"You think he might be the one responsible for the e-mails and the Molotov . . ."

"Yes. But not only that. I think he's the one who killed those cab drivers."

"I don't understand," Carella said. "Why would a Muslim want to kill *other* Mus . . . ?"

"But he's *not* Muslim. Did I say he was Muslim?"

"You said this was related to the . . ."

"Catholic. He's a Catholic."

The detectives looked at each other.

"Let me understand this," Carella said. "You think this kid . . . how old is he, anyway?"

"Eighteen, I would guess. Nineteen."

"You think he got angry because you wouldn't go to Rebecca's father on his behalf . . ."

"That's right."

"So he sent you three e-mails, and tried to fire-bomb your temple . . ."

"Exactly."

". . . and also killed two Muslim cab drivers?"

"Yes."

"Why? The Muslims, I mean."

"To get even."

"With?"

"With me. And with Samuel Schwartz. And Rebecca. With the entire Jewish population of this city."

"How would killing two . . . ?"

"The *magen David*," the rabbi said.

"The Star of David," Meyer explained.

"Painted on the windshields," the rabbi said. "To let people think a Jew was responsible. To enflame the Muslim community against Jews. To cause trouble between us. To cause more killing. That is why."

The detectives let this sink in.

"Did this kid happen to give you a name?" Meyer asked.

Anthony Inverni told the detectives he didn't wish to be called Tony.

"Makes me sound like a wop," he said. "My grandparents were born here, my parents were born here, my sister and I were both born here, we're Americans. You call me Tony, I'm automatically *Italian*. Well, the way I look at it, Italians are people who are born in Italy and live in Italy, not Americans who were born here and live here. And we're not *Italian*-Americans, either, by the way, because *Italian*-Americans are people who came here from Italy and *became* American citizens. So don't call me Tony, okay?"

He was nineteen years old, with curly black hair, and an olive complexion, and dark brown eyes. Sitting at sunset on the front steps of his building on Merchant Street, all the way downtown near Ramsey University, his arms hugging his knees, he could have been any Biblical Jew squatting outside a baked-mud dwelling in an ancient world. But Rabbi Cohen had spotted him for a *goy* first crack out of the box.

"Gee, who called you Tony?" Carella wanted to know.

"You were about to. I could feel it coming."

Calling a suspect by his first name was an old cop trick, but actually Carella hadn't been about to use it on the Inverni kid here. In fact, he agreed with him about all these proliferating hyphenated Americans in a nation that broadcast the words "United We Stand" as if they were a newly minted advertising slogan. But his father's name had been Anthony. And his father had called himself Tony.

"What would you like us to call you?" he asked.

"Anthony. Anthony could be British. In fact, soon as I graduate, I'm gonna change my last name to Winters. Anthony Winters. I could be the prime minister of England, Anthony Winters. That's what Inverni means anyway, in Italian. Winters."

"Where do you go to school, Anthony?" Carella asked.

"Right here," he said, nodding toward the towers in the near distance. "Ramsey U."

"You studying to be a prime minister?" Meyer asked.

"A writer. Anthony Winters. How does that sound for a writer?"

"Very good," Meyer said, trying the name, "Anthony Winters, excellent. We'll look for your books."

"Meanwhile," Carella said, "tell us about your little run-in with Rabbi Cohen."

"What run-in?"

"He seems to think he pissed you off."

"Well, he did. I mean, why *wouldn't* he go to Becky's father and put in a good word for me? I'm a straight-A student, I'm on the dean's list, am I some kind of pariah? You know what that means, 'pariah'?"

Meyer figured this was a rhetorical question.

"I'm not even *Catholic*, no less pariah," Anthony said, gathering steam. "I gave up the church the minute I tipped to what they were selling. I mean, am I supposed to believe a *virgin* gave birth? To the son of *God*, no less? That goes back to the ancient Greeks, doesn't it? All their Gods messing in the affairs of humans? I mean, give me a break, man."

"Just how pissed off were you?" Carella asked.

"Enough," Anthony said. "But you should've seen *Becky*! When I told her what the rabbi said, she wanted to go right over there and kill him."

"Then you're still seeing her, is that it?"

"Of course I'm still seeing her! We're gonna get married, what do you think? You think her bigoted father's gonna stop us? You think Rabbi Cohen's gonna stop us? We're in *love*!"

Good for you, Meyer thought. And *mazeltov*. But did you kill those two cabbies, as the good *rov* seems to think?

"Are you on the internet?" he asked.

"Sure."

"Do you send e-mails?"

"That's the main way Becky and I communicate. I can't phone her because her father hangs up the minute he hears my voice. Her mother's a little better, she at least lets me talk to her."

"Ever send an e-mail to Rabbi Cohen?"

"No. Why? An e-mail? Why would . . . ?"

"Three of them, in fact."

"No. What kind of e-mails?"

" 'Death to all Jews,' " Meyer quoted.

"Don't be ridiculous," Anthony said. "I love a Jewish *girl*! I'm gonna *marry* a Jewish girl!"

"Were you anywhere near Rabbi Cohen's synagogue last night?" Carella asked.

"No. Why?"

"You didn't throw a fire-bomb into that synagogue last night, did you?"

"No, I did not!"

"Sundown last night? You didn't . . . ?"

"Not at sundown and not at *any* time! I was with *Becky* at sundown. We were walking in the park outside school at sundown. We were trying to figure out our next *move*."

"You may love a Jewish girl," Meyer said, "but how do you feel about *Jews*?"

"I don't know what that means."

"It means how do you feel about all these *Jews* who are trying to keep you from marrying this Jewish *girl* you love?"

"I did not throw a fucking fire-bomb . . ."

"Did you kill two Muslim cabbies . . . ?"

"What!"

". . . and paint Jewish stars on their windshields?"

"Holy shit, is *that* what this is about?"

"Did you?"

"Who said I did?" Anthony wanted to know. "Did the rabbi say I did such a thing?"

"Did you?"

"No. Why would . . . ?"

"Because you were pissed off," Meyer said. "And you wanted to get even. So you killed two Muslims and made it look like a Jew did it. So Muslims would start throwing fire-bombs into . . ."

"I don't give a damn about Muslims or Jews *or* their fucking problems," Anthony said. "All I care about is Becky. All I care about is marrying Becky. The rest is all bullshit. I did not send any e-mails to that jackass rabbi. I did not throw a fire-bomb into his dumb temple, which by the way won't let women sit with men. I did not kill any Muslim cab drivers who go to stupid temples of their own, where *their* women aren't allowed to sit with men, either. That's a nice little plot you've cooked up there, and I'll use it one day, when I'm Anthony Winters the best-selling writer. But right now, I'm still just Tony Inverni, right? And that's the only thing that's keeping me from marrying the girl I love, and that is a shame, gentlemen, that is a fucking crying shame. So if you'll excuse me, I really don't give a damn about *your* little problem, because Becky and I have a major problem of our own."

He raised his right hand, touched it to his temple in a mock salute, and went back into his building.

At nine the next morning, Detective Wilbur Jackson of the Documents Section called to say they'd checked out the graffiti—

He called the Jewish stars graffiti.

—on the windshields of those two evidence cabs and they were now able to report that the handwriting was identical in both instances and that the writer was right-handed.

"Like ninety percent of the people in this city," he added.

That night, the third Muslim cabbie was killed.

"Let's hear it," Lieutenant Byrnes said.

He was not feeling too terribly sanguine this Monday morning. He did not like this at all. First off, he did not like murder epidemics. And next, he did not like murder epidemics that could lead to full-scale riots. White-haired and scowling, eyes an icy-cold blue, he glowered across his desk as though the eight detectives gathered in his corner office had themselves committed the murders.

Hal Willis and Eileen Burke had been riding the midnight horse when the call came in about the third dead cabbie. At five-eight, Willis had barely cleared the minimum height requirement in effect before women were generously allowed to become police officers, at which time five-foot-two-eyes-of-blue became threatening when one was carrying a nine-millimeter Glock on her hip. That's exactly what Eileen was carrying this morning. Not on her hip, but in a tote bag slung over her shoulder. At five-nine, she topped Willis by an inch. Red-headed and green-eyed, she provided Irish-setter contrast to his dark, curly-haired, brown-eyed, cocker-spaniel look. Byrnes was glaring at both of them. Willis deferred to the lady.

"His name is Ali Al-Barak," Eileen said. "He's a Saudi. Married with three . . ."

"That's the most common Arabic name," Andy Parker said. He was slumped in one of the chairs near the windows. Unshaven and unkempt, he looked as if he'd just come off a plant as a homeless wino. Actually, he'd come straight to the squadroom from home, where he'd dressed hastily, annoyed because he wasn't supposed to come in until four, and now another fuckin Muslim had been aced.

"Al-Barak?" Brown asked.

"No, Ali," Parker said. "More than five million men in the Arab world are named Ali."

"How do you know that?" Kling asked.

"I know such things," Parker said.

"And what's it got to do with the goddamn price of fish?" Byrnes asked.

"In case you run into a lot of Alis," Parker explained, "you'll know it ain't a phenomenon, it's just a fact."

"Let me hear it," Byrnes said sourly, and nodded to Eileen.

"Three children," she said, picking up where she'd left off. "Lived in a Saudi neighborhood in Riverhead. No apparent connection to either of the two other vics. All three even worshipped at different mosques. Shot at the back of the head, same as the other two. Blue star on the windshield . . ."

"The other two were the same handwriting," Meyer said.

"Right-handed writer," Carella said.

"Anything from Ballistics yet?" Byrnes asked Eileen.

"Slug went to them, too soon to expect anything."

"Two to one, it'll be the same," Richard Genero said.

He was the newest detective on the squad and rarely ventured comments at these clambakes. Taller than Willis—hell, *everybody* was taller than Willis—he nonetheless looked like a relative, what with the same dark hair and eyes. Once, in fact, a perp had asked them if they were brothers. Willis, offended, had answered, "I'll give you brothers."

"Which'll mean the same guy killed all three," Byrnes said.

Genero felt rewarded. He smiled in acknowledgment.

"Or the same gun, anyway," Carella said.

"Widow been informed?"

"We went there directly from the scene," Willis said.

"What've we got on the paint?"

"Brand name sold everywhere," Meyer said.

"What's with this Inverni kid?"

"He's worth another visit."

"Why?"

"He has a thing about religion."

"What kind of thing?"

"He thinks it's all bullshit."

"Doesn't everyone?" Parker said.

"I don't," Genero said.

"That doesn't mean he's going around killing Muslims," Byrnes said. "But talk to him again. Find out where he was last night at . . . Hal? What time did the cabbie catch it?"

"Twenty past two."

"Be nice if Inverni's our man," Brown said.

"Yes, that would be very nice."

"In your dreams," Parker said.

"You got a better idea?"

Parker thought this over.

"You're such an expert on Arabian first names . . ."

"Arabic."

". . . I thought maybe you might have a better idea," Byrnes said.

"How about we put undercovers in the cabs?"

"Brilliant," Byrnes said. "You know any Muslim cops?"

"Come to think of it," Parker said, and shrugged again.

"Where'd this last one take place?"

"Booker and Lowell. In Riverhead," Eileen said. "Six blocks from the stadium."

"He's ranging all over the place."

"Got to be random," Brown said.

"Let's scour the hood," Kling suggested. "Must be somebody heard a shot at two in the morning."

"Two-twenty," Parker corrected.

"I'm going to triple-team this," Byrnes said. "Anybody not on vacation or out sick, I want him on this case. I'm surprised the commissioner himself hasn't called yet. Something like this . . ."

The phone on his desk rang.

"Let's get this son of a bitch," Byrnes said, and waved the detectives out of his office.

His phone was still ringing.

He rolled his eyes heavenward and picked up the receiver.

THIRD HATE KILLING
Muslim Murders Mount

All over the city, busy citizens picked up the afternoon tabloid, and read its headline, and then turned to the story on page three. Unless the police were withholding vital information, they still did not have a single clue. This made people nervous. They did not want these stupid killings to escalate into the sort of situation that was a daily occurrence in Israel. They did not want retaliation to follow retaliation. They did not want hate begetting more hate.

But they were about to get it.

The first of what the police hoped would be the last of the bombings took place that very afternoon, the fifth day of May.

Parker—who knew such things—could have told the other detectives on the squad that the fifth of May was a date of vast importance in Mexican and Chicano communities, of which there were not a few in this sprawling city. *Cinco de Mayo*, as it was called in Spanish, celebrated the victory of the Mexican Army over the French in 1862. Hardly anyone today—except Parker maybe—knew that *La Battala de Puebla* had been fought and won by Mestizo and Zapotec Indians. Nowadays, many of the Spanish-speaking people in this city thought the date commemorated Mexican independence, which Parker could have told you was September 16, 1810, and not May 5, 1862.

Some people suspected Parker was an idiot savant, but this was only half true. He merely read a lot.

On that splendid, sunny, fifth day of May, as the city's Chicano population prepared for an evening of folklorico dancing and mariachi music and margaritas, and as the weary detectives of the Eight-Seven spread out into the three sections of the city that had so far been stricken with what even the staid morning newspaper labeled "The Muslim Murders," a man carrying a narrow Gucci dispatch case walked into a movie theater that was playing a foreign film about a Japanese prostitute who aspires to become an internationally famous violinist, took a seat in the center of the theater's twelfth row, watched the commercials for furniture stores and local restaurants and antique shops, and then watched the coming attractions, and finally, at 1:37 P.M.—just as the feature film was about to start—got up to go to the men's room.

He left the Gucci dispatch case under the seat.

There was enough explosive material in that sleek leather case to blow up at least seven rows of seats in the orchestra. There was also a ticking clock set to trigger a spark at 3:48 P.M., just about when the Japanese prostitute would be accepted at Juilliard.

Spring break had ended not too long ago, and most of the students at Ramsey U still sported tans they'd picked up in Mexico or Florida. There was an air of bustling activity on the downtown campus as Meyer and Carella made their way through crowded corridors to the Registrar's Office, where they hoped to acquire a program for Anthony Inverni. This turned out to be not as simple as they'd hoped. Each and separately they had to show first their shields and next their ID cards, and still had to invoke the sacred words "Homicide investigation," before the yellow-haired lady with a bun would reveal the whereabouts of Anthony Inverni on this so-far eventless Cinco de Mayo.

The time was 1:45 P.M.

They found Inverni already seated in the front row of a class his program listed as "Shakespearean Morality." He was chatting with a girl wearing a blue scarf around her head and covering her forehead. The detectives assumed she was Muslim, though this was probably pro-filing. They asked Inverni if he would mind stepping outside for a moment, and he said to the girl, "Excuse me, Halima," which more or less confirmed their surmise, but which did little to reinforce the profile of a hate criminal.

"So what's up?" he asked.

"Where were you at two this morning?" Meyer asked, going straight for the jugular.

"That, huh?"

"That," Carella said.

"It's all over the papers," Inverni said. "But you're still barking up the wrong tree."

"So where were you?"

"With someone."

"Who?"

"Someone."

"The someone wouldn't be Rebecca Schwartz, would it? Be-cause as an alibi . . ."

"Are you kidding? You think old Sam would let her out of his sight at two in the morning?"

"Then who's this 'someone' we're talking about?"

"I'd rather not get her involved."

"Oh? Really? We've got three dead cabbies here. You'd better start worrying about *them* and not about getting *someone* involved. Who is she? Who's your alibi?"

Anthony turned to look over his shoulder, into the classroom. For a moment, the detectives thought he was going to name the girl with the blue scarf. Hanima, was it? Halifa? He turned back to them again. Lowering his voice, he said, "Judy Manzetti."

"Was with you at two this morning?"

"Yes."

His voice still a whisper. His eyes darting.

"Where?"

"My place."

"Doing what?"

"Well . . . you know."

"Spell it out."

"We were in bed together."

"Give us her address and phone number," Carella said.

"Hey, come on. I told you I didn't want to get her involved."

"She's already involved," Carella said. His notebook was in his hand.

Inverni gave him her address and phone number.

"Is that it?" he asked. "Cause class is about to start."

"I thought you planned to marry Becky," Meyer said.

"Of *course* I'm marrying Becky!" Inverni said. "But mean-while . . ."—and here he smiled conspiratorially—". . . I'm fucking Judy."

No, Meyer thought. It's Becky who's getting fucked.

The time was two P.M.

As if to confirm Parker's fact-finding acumen, the two witnesses who'd heard the shot last night were both named Ali. They'd been coming home from a party at the time, and each of them had been a little drunk. They explained at once that this was not a habit of theirs. They fully understood that the imbibing of alcoholic beverages was strictly forbidden in the Koran.

"*Haram*," the first Ali said, shaking his head. "Most definitely *haram*."

"Oh yes, unacceptable," the second Ali agreed, shaking his head as well. "Forbidden. Prohibited. In the Koran, it is written, 'They ask thee concerning wine and gambling. In them is great sin, and some profit, for men; but the sin is greater than the profit.'"

"But our friend was celebrating his birthday," the first Ali said, and smiled apologetically.

"It was a party," the second Ali explained.

"Where?" Eileen asked.

The two Alis looked at each other.

At last, they admitted that the party had taken place at a club named Buffers, which Eileen and Willis both knew was a topless joint, but the Alis claimed that no one in their party had gone back to the club's so-called private room but had instead merely enjoyed the young ladies dancing around their poles.

Eileen wondered *whose* poles?

The young ladies' poles?

Or the poles of Ali and Company?

She guessed she maybe had a dirty mind.

At any rate, the two Alis were staggering out of Buffers at two o'clock in the morning when they spotted a yellow cab parked at the curb up the block. They were planning on taking the subway home, but one never argued with divine providence so they decided on the spot to take a taxi instead. As they tottered and swayed toward the idling cab—the first Ali raising his hand to hail it, the second Ali breaking into a trot toward it and almost tripping—they heard a single shot from inside the cab. They both stopped dead still in the middle of the pavement.

"A man jumped out," the first Ali said now, his eyes wide with the excitement of recall.

"What'd he look like?" Eileen asked.

"A tall man," the second Ali said. "Dressed all in black."

"Black suit, black coat, black hat."

"Was he bearded or clean-shaven?"

"No beard. No."

"You're sure it was a man?"

"Oh yes, positive," the second Ali said.

"What'd he do after he got out of the cab?"

"Went to the windshield."

"Sprayed the windshield."

"You saw him spraying the windshield?"

"Yes."

"Oh yes."

"Then what?"

"He ran away."

"Up the street."

"Toward the subway."

"There's an entrance there."

"For the subway."

Which could have taken him anywhere in the city, Eileen thought.

"Thanks," Willis said.

It was 2:15 P.M.

Parker and Genero were the two detectives who spoke once again to Ozzie Kiraz, the cousin of the second dead cabbie.

Kiraz was just leaving for work when they got there at a quarter past three that afternoon. He introduced them to his wife, a diminutive woman who seemed half his size, and who immediately went into the kitchen of their tiny apartment to prepare tea for the men. Fine-featured, dark-haired and dark-eyed, Badria Kiraz was a woman in her late twenties, Parker guessed. Exotic features aside, she looked very American to him, sporting lipstick and eye shadow, displaying a nice ass in beige tailored slacks, and good tits in a white cotton blouse.

Kiraz explained that he and his wife both worked night shifts at different places in different parts of the city. He worked at a pharmacy in Majesta, where he was manager of the store. Badria worked as a cashier in a supermarket in Calm's Point. They both started work at four, and got off at midnight. Kiraz told them that in Afghanistan he'd once hoped to become a schoolteacher. That was before he started fighting the Russians. Now, here in America, he was the manager of a drugstore.

"Land of the free, right?" he said, and grinned.

Genero didn't know if he was being a wise guy or not.

"So tell us a little more about your cousin," he said.

"What would you like to know?"

"One of the men interviewed by our colleagues . . ."

Genero liked using the word "colleagues." Made him sound like a university professor. He consulted his notebook, which made him feel even more professorial.

"Man named Ajmal, is that how you pronounce it?"

"Yes," Kiraz said.

"Ajmal Khan, a short-order cook at a deli named Max's in Midtown South. Do you know him?"

"No, I don't."

"Friend of your cousin's," Parker said.

He was eyeing Kiraz's wife, who was carrying a tray in from the kitchen. She set it down on the low table in front of the sofa, smiled, and said, "We drink it sweet, but I didn't add sugar. It's there if you want it. Cream and lemon, too. Oz," she said, "do you know what time it is?"

"I'm watching it, Badria, don't worry. Maybe you should leave."

"Would that be all right?" she asked the detectives.

"Yes, sure," Genero said, and both detectives rose politely. Kiraz kissed his wife on the cheek. She smiled again and left the room.

They heard the front door to the apartment closing. The men sat again. Through the open windows, they could hear the loud-speakered cry of the muezzin calling the faithful to prayer.

"The third prayer of the day," Kiraz explained. "The *Salat al-'Asr*," and added almost regretfully, "I never pray anymore. It's too difficult here in America. If you want to be American, you follow American ways, am I right? You do what Americans do."

"Oh sure," Parker agreed, even though he'd never had any problem following American ways or doing what Americans do.

"Anyway," Genero said, squeezing a little lemon into one of the tea glasses, and then picking it up, "this guy at the deli told our colleagues your cousin was dating quite a few girls . . ."

"That's news to me," Kiraz said.

"Well, that's what we wanted to talk to you about," Parker said. "We thought you might be able to help us with their names."

"The names of these girls," Genero said.

"Because this guy in the deli didn't know who they might be," Parker said.

"I don't know, either," Kiraz said, and looked at his watch.

Parker looked at his watch, too.

It was twenty minutes past three.

"Ever *talk* to you about any of these girls?" Genero asked.

"Never. We were not that close, you know. He was single, I'm married. We have our own friends, Badria and I. This is America. There are different customs, different ways. When you live here, you do what Americans do, right?"

He grinned again.

Again, Genero didn't know if he was getting smart with them.

"You wouldn't know if any of these girls were Jewish, would you?" Parker asked.

"Because of the blue star, you mean?"

"Well . . . yes."

"I would sincerely doubt that my cousin was dating any Jewish girls."

"Because sometimes . . ."

"Oh sure," Kiraz said. "Sometimes things aren't as simple as they appear. You're thinking this wasn't a simple hate crime. You're thinking this wasn't a mere matter of a Jew killing a Muslim simply because he *was* a Muslim. You're looking for complications. Was

Salim involved with a Jewish girl? Did the Jewish girl's father or brother become enraged by the very *thought* of such a relationship? Was Salim killed as a warning to any other Muslim with interfaith aspirations? Is that why the Jewish star was painted on the windshield? Stay away! Keep off!"

"Well, we weren't thinking *exactly* that," Parker said, "but, yes, that's a possibility."

"But you're forgetting the *other* two Muslims, aren't you?" Kiraz said, and smiled in what Genero felt was a superior manner, fuckin guy thought he was Chief of Detectives here.

"No, we're not forgetting them," Parker said. "We're just trying to consider all the possibilities."

"A mistake," Kiraz said. "I sometimes talk to this doctor who comes into the pharmacy. He tells me, 'Oz, if it has stripes like a zebra, don't look for a horse.' Because people come in asking me what I've got for this or that ailment, you know? Who knows why?" he said, and shrugged, but he seemed pleased by his position of importance in the workplace. "I'm only the manager of the store, I'm not a pharmacist, but they ask me," he said, and shrugged again. "What's good for a headache, or a cough, or the sniffles, or this or that? They ask me all the time. And I remember what my friend the doctor told me," he said, and smiled, seemingly pleased by this, too, the fact that his friend was a doctor. "If it has the symptoms of a common cold, don't go looking for SARS. Period." He opened his hands to them, palms up, explaining the utter simplicity of it all. "Stop looking for zebras," he said, and smiled again. "Just find the fucking Jew who shot my cousin in the head, hmm?"

The time was 3:27 P.M.

In the movies these days, it was not unusual for a working girl to become a princess overnight, like the chambermaid who not only gets the hero onscreen but in real life as well, talk about Cinderella stories! In other movies of this stripe, you saw common working class girls who aspired to become college students. Or soccer players. It was a popular theme nowadays. America was the land of opportunity. So was Japan, apparently, although Ruriko—the prostitute in the film all these people were waiting on line to see— was a "working girl" in the truest sense, and she didn't even want to become a

princess, just a concert violinist. She was about to become just that in
about three minutes.

The two girls standing on line outside the theater box office also
happened to be true working girls, which was why they were here to
catch the four o'clock screening of the Japanese film. They had each
separately seen *Pretty Woman*, another Working Girl Becomes Princess
film, and did not for a moment believe that Julia Roberts had ever
blown anybody for fifty bucks, but maybe it would be different with
this Japanese actress, whatever her name was. Maybe this time,
they'd believe that these One in a Million fairy tales could really
happen to girls who actually did this sort of thing for a living.

The two girls, Heidi and Roseanne, looked and dressed just like
any secretary who'd got out of work early today . . .

It was now 3:46 P.M.

. . . and even sounded somewhat like girls with junior college ed-
ucations. As the line inched closer to the box office, they began talking about what Heidi was going to do to celebrate her birthday
tonight. Heidi was nineteen years old today. She'd been hooking for
two years now. The closest she'd got to becoming a princess was
when one of her old-fart regulars asked her to come to London with
him on a weekend trip. He rescinded the offer when he learned she
was expecting her period, worse luck.

"You doing anything special tonight?" Roseanne asked.

"Jimmy's taking me out to dinner," Heidi said.

Jimmy was a cop she dated. He knew what profession she was in.

"That's nice."

"Yeah."

In about fifteen seconds, it would be 3:48 P.M.

"I still can't get over it," Roseanne said.

"What's that, hon?"

"The *coincidence*!" Roseanne said, amazed. "Does your birthday
always fall on Cinco de Mayo?"

A couple sitting in the seats just behind the one under which the
Gucci dispatch case had been left were seriously necking when the
bomb exploded.

The boy had his hand under the girl's skirt, and she had her hand
inside his unzipped fly, their fitful manual activity covered by the

raincoat he had thrown over both their laps. Neither of them really gave a damn about whether or not Ruriko passed muster with the judges at Juilliard, or went back instead to a life of hopeless despair in the slums of Yokohama. All that mattered to them was achieving mutual orgasm here in the flickering darkness of the theater while the soulful strains of Aram Khacaturian's *Spartacus* flowed from Ruriko's violin under the expert coaxing of her talented fingers.

When the bomb exploded, they both thought for the tiniest tick of an instant that they'd died and gone to heaven.

Fortunately for the Eight-Seven, the movie-theater bombing occurred in the Two-One downtown. Since there was no immediate connection between this new outburst of violence and the Muslim Murders, nobody from the Two-One called uptown in an attempt to unload the case there. Instead, because this was an obvious act of terrorism, they called the Joint Terrorist Task Force at One Federal Square further downtown, and dumped the entire matter into their laps. This did not, however, stop the talking heads on television from linking the movie bombing to the murders of the three cabbies.

The liberal TV commentators noisily insisted that the total mess we'd made in Iraq was directly responsible for this new wave of violence here in the United States. The conservative commentators wagged their heads in tolerant understanding of their colleagues' supreme ignorance, and then sagely suggested that if the police in this city would only learn how to handle the problems manifest in a gloriously diverse population, there wouldn't be any civic violence at all.

It took no more than an hour and a half before all of the cable channels were demanding immediate arrests in what was now perceived as a single case. On the six-thirty network news broadcasts, the movie-theater bombing was the headline story, and without fail the bombing was linked to the cab-driver killings, the blue Star of David on the windshields televised over and over again as the unifying leitmotif.

Ali Al-Barak, the third Muslim victim, had worked for a company that called itself simply Cabco. Its garage was located in the shadow of the Calm's Point Bridge, not too distant from the market under the massive stone supporting pillars on the Isola side of the bridge. The market was closed and shuttered when Meyer and Carella drove past it at a quarter to seven that evening. They had trouble finding Cabco's garage and drove around the block several times, getting entangled in bridge traffic. At one point, Carella suggested that they hit the hammer, but Meyer felt use of the siren might be excessive.

They finally located the garage tucked between two massive apartment buildings. It could have been the underground garage for either of them, but a discreet sign identified it as Cabco. They drove down the ramp, found the dispatcher's office, identified themselves, and explained why they were there.

"Yeah," the dispatcher said, and nodded. His name was Hazhir Demirkol. He explained that like Al-Barak, he too was a Muslim, though not a Saudi. "I'm a Kurd," he told them. "I came to this country ten years ago."

"What can you tell us about Al-Barak?" Meyer asked.

"I knew someone would kill him sooner or later," Demirkol said. "The way he was shooting up his mouth all the time."

Shooting *off*, Carella thought, but didn't correct him.

"In what way?" he asked.

"He kept complaining that Israel was responsible for all the trouble in the Arab world. If there was no Israel, there would have been no Iraqi war. There would be no terrorism. There would be no 9/11. Well, he's a Saudi, you know. His countrymen were the ones who *bombed* the World Trade Center! But he was being foolish. It doesn't matter how you feel about Jews. I feel the same way. But in this city, I have learned to keep my thoughts to myself."

"Why's that?" Meyer asked.

Demirkol turned to him, looked him over. One eyebrow arched. Sudden recognition crossed his face. This man was a Jew. This detective was a Jew.

"It doesn't matter why," he said. "Look what happened to Ali. *That* is why."

"You think a Jew killed him, is that it?"

"No, an angel from Paradise painted that blue star on his windshield."

"Who might've heard him when he was airing all these complaints?" Carella asked.

"Who knows? Ali talked freely, *too* freely, you ask me. This is a democracy, no? Like the one America brought to Iraq, no?" Demirkol asked sarcastically. "He talked everywhere. He talked here in the garage with his friends, he talked to his passengers, I'm sure he talked at the mosque, too, when he went to prayer. Freedom of speech, correct? Even if it gets you killed."

"You think he expressed his views to the wrong person, is that it?" Meyer asked. "The wrong *Jew*."

"The *same* Jew who killed the other drivers," Demirkol said, and nodded emphatically, looking Meyer dead in the eye, challenging him.

"This mosque you mentioned," Carella said. "Would you know . . . ?"

"Majid At-Abu," Demirkol said at once. "Close by here," he said, and gestured vaguely uptown.

Now *this* was a mosque.

This was what one conjured when the very word was uttered. This was straight out of *Arabian Nights*, minarets and domes, blue tile and gold leaf. This was the real McCoy.

Opulent and imposing, Majid At-Abu was not as "close by" as Demirkol had suggested, it was in fact a good mile and a half uptown. When the detectives got there at a little past eight that night, the faithful were already gathered inside for the sunset prayer. The sky beyond the mosque's single glittering dome was streaked with the last red-purple streaks of a dying sun. The minaret from which the muezzin called worshippers to prayer stood tall and stately to the right of the arched entrance doors. Meyer and Carella stood on the sidewalk outside, listening to the prayers intoned within, waiting for an opportune time to enter.

Across the street, some Arabic-looking boys in T-shirts and jeans were cracking themselves up. Meyer wondered what they were saying. Carella wondered why they weren't inside praying.

"Ivan Sikimiavuçlyor!" one of the kids shouted, and the others all burst out laughing.

"How about Alexandr Siksallandr?" one of the other kids suggested, and again they all laughed.

"Or Madame Döllemer," another boy said.

More laughter. Carella was surprised they didn't all fall to the sidewalk clutching their bellies. It took both of the detectives a moment to realize that these were *names* the boys were bandying about. They had no idea that in Turkish "Ivan Sikimiavuçlyor" meant "Ivan Holding My Cock," or that "Alexandr Siksallandr" meant "Alexander Who Swings a Cock," or that poor "Madame Döllemer" was just a lady "Sucking Sperm." Like the dirty names Meyer and Carella had attached to fictitious book titles when they themselves were kids . . .

The Open Robe by Seymour Hare.
The Russian Revenge by Ivana Kutchakokoff.
The Chinese Curse by Wan Hong Lo.
Hawaiian Paradise by A'wana Leia Oo'aa.

. . . these Arab teenagers growing up here in America were now making puns on their parents' native tongue.

"Fenasi Kerim!" one of the boys shouted finally and triumphantly, and whereas neither of the detectives knew that this invented name meant "I Fuck You Bad," the boys' ensuing exuberant laughter caused them to laugh as well.

The sunset prayer had ended.

They took off their shoes and placed them outside in the foyer—alongside the loafers and sandals and jogging shoes and boots and laced brogans parked there like autos in a used-car lot—and went inside to find the imam.

"I never heard Ali Al-Barak utter a single threatening word about the Jewish people, or the Jewish state, or any Jew in particular," Mohammad Talal Awad said.

They were standing in the vast open hall of the mosque proper, a white space the size of a ballroom, with arched windows and tiled floors and an overhead clerestory through which the detectives could see the beginnings of a starry night. The imam was wearing white baggy trousers and a flowing white tunic and a little while pillbox hat. He had a long black beard, a narrow nose and eyes almost black, and he directed his every word to Meyer.

"Nor is there anything in the Koran that directs Muslims to kill anyone," he said. "Not Jews, not anyone. There is nothing there. Search the Koran. You will find not a word about murdering in the name of Allah."

"We understand Al-Barak made remarks some people might have found inflammatory," Carella said.

"Political observations. They had nothing to do with Islam. He was young, he was brash, perhaps he was foolish to express his opinions so openly. But this is America, and one may speak freely, isn't that so? Isn't that what democracy is all about?"

Here we go again, Meyer thought.

"But if you think Ali's murder had anything to do with the bombing downtown . . ."

Oh? Carella thought.

". . . you are mistaken. Ali was a pious young man who lived with another man his own age, recently arrived from Saudi Arabia. In their native land, they were both students. Here, one drove a taxi and the other bags groceries in a supermarket. If you think Ali's friend, in revenge for his murder, bombed that theater downtown . . ."

Oh? Carella thought again.

". . . you are very sadly mistaken."

"We're not investigating that bombing," Meyer said. "We're investigating Ali's murder. And the murder of two other Muslim cab drivers. If you can think of anyone who might possibly . . ."

"I know no Jews," the imam said.

You know one now, Meyer thought.

"This friend he lived with," Carella said. "What's his name, and where can we find him?"

The music coming from behind the door to the third-floor apartment was very definitely rap. The singers were very definitely black, and the lyrics were in English. But the words weren't telling young kids to do dope or knock women around or even up. As they listened at the wood, the lyrics the detectives heard spoke of intentions alone not being sufficient to bring reward . . .

When help is needed, prayer to Allah is the answer . . .

Allah alone can assist in . . .

Meyer knocked on the door.

"Yes?" a voice yelled.

"Police," Carella said.

The music continued to blare.

"Hello?" Carella said. "Mind if we ask you some questions?"

No answer.

"Hello?" he said again.

He looked at Meyer.

Meyer shrugged. Over the blare of the music, he yelled, "Hello in there!"

Still no answer.

"This is the police!" he yelled. "Would you mind coming to the door, please?"

The door opened a crack, held by a night chain.

They saw part of a narrow face. Part of a mustache. Part of a mouth. A single brown eye.

"Mr. Rajab?"

"Yes?"

Wariness in the voice and in the single eye they could see.

"Mind if we come in? Few questions we'd like to ask you."

"What about?"

"You a friend of Ali Al-Barak?"

"Yes?"

"Do you know he was murdered last . . . ?"

The door slammed shut.

They heard the sudden click of a bolt turning.

Carella backed off across the hall. His gun was already in his right hand, his knee coming up for a jackknife kick. The sole of his shoe collided with the door, just below the lock. The lock held.

"The yard!" he yelled, and Meyer flew off down the stairs.

Carella kicked at the lock again. This time, it sprang. He followed the splintered door into the room. The black rap group was still singing praise to Allah. The window across the room was open, a curtain fluttering in the mild evening breeze. He ran across the room, followed his gun hand out the window and onto a fire escape. He could hear footsteps clattering down the iron rungs to the second floor.

"Stop!" he yelled. "Police!"

Nobody stopped.

He came out onto the fire escape, took a quick look below, and started down.

From below, he heard Meyer racketing into the backyard. They had Rajab sandwiched.

"Hold it right there!" Meyer yelled.

Carella came down to the first-floor fire escape, out of breath, and handcuffed Rajab's hands behind his back.

They listened in total amazement as Ishak Rajab told them all about how he had plotted instant revenge for the murder of his friend and roommate, Ali Al-Barak. They listened as he told them how he had constructed the suitcase bomb . . .

He called the Gucci dispatch case a suitcase.

. . . and then had carefully chosen a movie theater showing so-called art films because he knew Jews pretended to culture, and there would most likely be many Jews in the audience. Jews had to be taught that Arabs could not wantonly be killed without reprisal.

"Ali was killed by a Jew," Rajab said. "And so it was fitting and just that Jews be killed in return."

Meyer called the JTTF at Fed Square and told them they'd accidentally lucked into catching the guy who did their movie-theater bombing.

Ungrateful humps didn't even say thanks.

It was almost ten o'clock when he and Carella left the squad-room for home. As they passed the swing room downstairs, they looked in through the open door to where a uniformed cop was half-dozing on one of the couches, watching television. One of cable's most vociferous talking heads was demanding to know when a terrorist was *not* a terrorist.

"Here's the story," he said, and glared out of the screen. "A green-card Saudi-Arabian named Ishak Rajab was arrested and charged with the wanton slaying of sixteen movie patrons and the wounding of twelve others. Our own police and the Joint Terrorist Task Force are to be highly commended for their swift actions in this case. It is now to be hoped that a trial and conviction will be equally swift.

"However . . .

"Rajab's attorneys are already indicating they'll be entering a plea of insanity. Their reasoning seems to be that a man who *deliberately* leaves a bomb in a public place is not a terrorist—have you got that? *Not* a terrorist! Then what is he, huh, guys? Well, according to

his attorneys, he was merely a man blinded by rage and seeking retaliation. The rationale for Rajab's behavior would seem to be his
close friendship with Ali Al-Barak, the third victim in the wave of
taxi-driver slayings that have swept the city since last Friday: Rajab
was Al-Barak's roommate.

"Well, neither I nor any right-minded citizen would condone the
senseless murder of Muslim cab drivers. That goes without saying.
But to invoke a surely inappropriate Biblical—*Biblical*, mind you—
'eye for an eye' defense by labeling premeditated mass murder 'insanity' is in itself insanity. A terrorist is a terrorist, and this was an act
of terrorism, pure and simple. Anything less than the death penalty
would be gross injustice in the case of Ishak Rajab. That's my opinion, now let's hear yours. You can e-mail me at . . ."

The detectives walked out of the building and into the night.

In four hours, another Muslim cabbie would be killed.

The police knew at once that this wasn't their man.

To begin with, none of the other victims had been robbed.

This one was.

All of the other victims had been shot only once, at the base of
the skull.

This one was shot three times through the open driver-side window of his cab, two of the bullets entering his face at the left temple
and just below the cheek, the third passing through his neck and
lodging in the opposite door panel.

Shell casings were found on the street outside the cab, indicating
that the murder weapon had been an automatic, and not the revolver
that had been used in the previous three murders. Ballistics confirmed this. The bullets and casings were consistent with samples
fired from a Colt .45 automatic.

Moreover, two witnesses had seen a man leaning into the cab
window moments before they heard shots, and he was definitely not
a tall white man dressed entirely in black.

There were only two similarities in all four murders. The drivers
were all Muslims, and a blue star had been spray-painted onto each
of their windshields.

But the Star of David had six points, and this new one had only five, and it was turned on end like the inverted pentagram used by devil-worshippers.

They hoped to hell yet *another* religion wasn't intruding its beliefs into this case.

But they knew for sure this wasn't their man.

This was a copycat.

CABBIE SHOT AND KILLED
FOURTH MUSLIM MURDER

So read the headline in the Metro Section of the city's staid morning newspaper. The story under it was largely put together from details supplied in a Police Department press release. The flak that had gone out from the Public Relations Office on the previous three murders had significantly withheld any information about the killer himself or his MO. None of the reporters—print, radio, or television—had been informed that the killer had been dressed in black from head to toe, or that he'd fired just a single shot into his separate victims' heads. They were hoping the killer himself—if ever they caught him—would reveal this information, thereby incriminating himself.

But this time around, because the police knew this was a copycat, the PR release was a bit more generous, stating that the cabbie had been shot three times, that he'd been robbed of his night's receipts, and that his assailant, as described by two eyewitnesses, was a black man in his early twenties, about five feet seven inches tall, weighing some hundred and sixty pounds and wearing blue jeans, white sneakers, a brown leather jacket, and a black ski cap pulled low on his forehead.

The man who'd murdered the previous three cabbies must have laughed himself silly.

Especially when another bombing took place that Tuesday afternoon.

The city's Joint Terrorist Task Force was an odd mix of elite city detectives, FBI Special Agents, Homeland Security people, and a handful of CIA spooks. Special Agent in Charge Brian Hooper and a team of four other Task Force officers arrived at The Merrie Coffee

Bean at three that afternoon, not half an hour after a suicide bomber had killed himself and a dozen patrons sitting at tables on the sidewalk outside. Seven wounded people had already been carried by ambulance to the closest hospital, Abingdon Memorial, on the river at Condon Street.

The coffee shop was a shambles.

Wrought iron tables and chairs had been twisted into surreal and smoldering bits of modern sculpture. Glass shards lay all over the sidewalk and inside the shop gutted and flooded by the Fire Department.

A dazed and dazzled waitress, wide-eyed and smoke-smudged but remarkably unharmed otherwise, told Hooper that she was at the cappuccino machine picking up an order when she heard someone yelling outside. She thought at first it was one of the customers, sometimes they got into arguments over choice tables. She turned from the counter to look outside, and saw this slight man running toward the door of the shop, yelling at the top of his lungs . . .

"What was he yelling, miss, do you remember?" Hooper asked.

Hooper was polite and soft-spoken, wearing a blue suit, a white shirt, a blue tie, and polished black shoes. Two detectives from the Five-Oh had also responded. Casually, dressed in sport jackets, slacks, and shirts open at the throat, they looked like bums in contrast. They stood by trying to look interested and significant while Hooper conducted the questioning.

"Something about Jews," the waitress said. "He had a foreign accent, you know, so it was hard to understand him to begin with. And this was like a rant, so that made it even more difficult. Besides, it all happened so fast. He was running from the open sidewalk down this, like, *space* we have between the tables? Like an *aisle* that leads to the front of the shop? And he was yelling Jews-this, Jews-that, and waving his arms in the air like some kind of nut? Then all at once there was this terrific explosion, it almost knocked *me* off my feet, and I was all the way inside the shop, near the cap machine. And I saw . . . there was like sunshine outside, you know? Like shining through the windows? And all of a sudden I saw all body parts flying in the air in the sunshine. Like in silhouette. All these people getting blown apart. It was, like, awesome."

Hooper and his men went picking through the rubble.

The two detectives from the Five-Oh were thinking this was very bad shit here.

If I've already realized what I hoped to accomplish, why press my luck, as they say? The thing has escalated beyond my wildest expectations. So leave it well enough alone, he told himself.

But that idiot last night has surely complicated matters. The police aren't fools, they'll recognize at once that last night's murder couldn't possibly be linked to the other three. So perhaps another one *was* in order, after all. To nail it to the wall. Four would round it off, wouldn't it?

To the Navajo Indians—well, Native Americans, as they say—the number four was sacred. Four different times of day, four sacred mountains, four sacred plants, four different directions. East was symbolic of Positive Thinking. South was for Planning. West for Life itself. North for Hope and Strength. They believed all this, the Navajo people. Religions were so peculiar. The things people believed. The things he himself had once believed, long ago, so very long ago.

Of course the number four wasn't *truly* sacred, that was just something the Navajos believed. The way Christians believed that the number 666 was the mark of the beast, who was the Antichrist and who—well, of course, what else?—had to be Jewish, right? There were even people who believed that the Internet acronym "www" for "World Wide Web" really transliterated into the Hebrew letter "*vav*" repeated three times, *vav, vav, vav*, the numerical equivalent of 666, the mark of the beast. *Let him that hath understanding count the number of the beast: for it is the number of a man; and his number is six hundred threescore and six*, Revelations 13. Oh yes, I've read the Bible, thank you, *and* the Koran, *and* the teachings of Buddha, and they're all total bullshit, as they say. But there are people who believe in a matrix, too, and not all of them are in padded rooms wearing straitjackets.

So, yes, I think there should be another one tonight, a tip of the hat, as they say, to the Navajo's sacred number four, and that will be the end of it. The last one. The same signature mark of the beast, the six-pointed star of the Antichrist. Then let them go searching the synagogues for me. Let them try to find the murdering Jew. After tonight, I will be finished!

Tonight, he thought.

Yes.

Abbas Miandad was a Muslim cab driver, and no fool.

Four Muslim cabbies had already been killed since Friday night, and he didn't want to be number five. He did not own a pistol—carrying a pistol would be exceedingly stupid in a city already so enflamed against people of the Islamic faith—nor did he own a dagger or a sword, but his wife's kitchen was well stocked with utensils and before he set out on his midnight shift he took a huge bread knife from the rack . . .

"Where are you going with that?" his wife asked.

She was watching television.

They were reporting that there'd been a suicide bombing that afternoon. They were saying the bomber had not been identified as yet.

"Never mind," he told her, and wrapped a dishtowel around the knife and packed it in a small tote bag that had BARNES & NOBLE lettered on it.

He had unwrapped the knife the moment he drove out of the garage. At three that Wednesday morning, it was still in the pouch on the driver's side of the cab. He had locked the cab when he stopped for a coffee break. Now, he walked up the street to where he'd parked the cab near the corner, and saw a man dressed all in black, bending to look into the back seat. He walked to him swiftly.

"Help you, sir?" he asked.

The man straightened up.

"I thought you might be napping in there," he said, and smiled.

"No, sir," he said. "Did you need a taxi?"

"Is this your cab?"

"It is."

"Can you take me to Majesta?" he said.

"Where are you going, sir?"

"The Boulevard and a Hundred Twelfth."

"Raleigh Boulevard?"

"Yes."

Abbas knew the neighborhood. It was residential and safe, even at this hour. He would not drive anyone to neighborhoods that he knew to be dangerous. He would not pick up black men, even if they were accompanied by women. Nowadays, he would not pick up anyone who looked Jewish. If you asked him how he knew whether a person was Jewish or not, he would tell you he just knew. This man dressed all in black did not look Jewish.

"Let me open it," he said, and took his keys from the right-hand pocket of his trousers. He turned the key in the door lock and was opening the door when, from the corner of his eye, he caught a glint of metal. Without turning, he reached for the bread knife tucked into the door's pouch.

He was too late.

The man in black fired two shots directly into his face, killing him at once.

Then he ran off into the night.

"Changed his MO," Byrnes said. "The others were shot from the back seat, single bullet to the base of the skull . . ."

"Not the one Tuesday night," Parker said.

"Tuesday was a copycat," Genero said.

"Maybe this one was, too," Willis suggested.

"Not if Ballistics comes back with a match," Meyer said.

The detectives fell silent.

They were each and separately hoping this newest murder would not trigger another suicide bombing someplace. The Task Force downtown still hadn't been able to get a positive ID from the smoldering remains of the Merrie Coffee Bean bomber.

"Anybody see anything?" Byrnes asked.

"Patrons in the diner heard shots, but didn't see the shooter."

"Didn't see him painting that blue star again?"

"I think they were afraid to go outside," Carella said. "Nobody wants to get shot, Pete."

"Gee, no kidding?" Byrnes said sourly.

"Also, the cab was parked all the way up the street, near the corner, some six cars back from the diner, on the same side of the street. The killer had to be standing on the passenger side . . ."

"Where he could see the driver's hack license . . ." Eileen said.

"Arab name on it," Kling said.

"Bingo, he had his victim."

"Point is," Carella said, "standing where he was, the people in the diner couldn't have seen him."

"Or just didn't *want* to see him."

"Well, sure."

"Cause they *could've* seen him while he was painting the star," Parker said.

"That's right," Byrnes said. "He had to've come around to the windshield."

"They could've at least seen his back."

"Tell us whether he was short, tall, what he was wearing . . ."

"But they didn't."

"Talk to them again."

"We talked them deaf, dumb, and blind," Meyer said.

"Talk to them *again*," Byrnes said. "And talk to anybody who was in those coffee shops, diners, delis, whatever, at the scenes of the other murders. These cabbies stop for coffee breaks, two, three in the morning, they go back to their cabs and get shot. That's no co-incidence. Our man knows their habits. And he's a night-crawler. What's with the Inverni kid? Did his alibi stand up?"

"Yeah, he was in bed with her," Carella said.

"In bed with who?" Parker asked, interested.

"Judy Manzetti. It checked out."

"Okay, so talk to everybody *else* again," Byrnes said. "See who might've been lurking about, hanging around, casing these various sites *before* the murders were committed."

"We *did* talk to everybody again," Genero said.

"Talk to them *again* again!"

"They all say the same thing," Meyer said. "It was a Jew who killed those drivers, all we have to do is look for a goddamn Jew."

"You're too fucking sensitive," Parker said.

"I'm telling you what we're getting. Anybody we talk to thinks it's an open-and-shut case. All we have to do is round up every Jew in the city . . ."

"Take forever," Parker said.

"What does that mean?"

"It means there are millions of Jews in this city."

"And what does *that* mean?"

"It means you're too fucking sensitive."

"Knock it off," Byrnes said.

"Anyway, Meyer's right," Genero said. "That's what we got, too. You know that, Andy."

"What do I know?" Parker said, glaring at Meyer.

"They keep telling us all we have to do is find the Jew who shot those guys in the head."

"Who told you that?" Carella said at once.

Genero looked startled.

"Who told you they got shot in the head?"

"Well . . . they *all* did."

"No," Parker said. "It was just the cousin, whatever the fuck his name was."

"What cousin?"

"The second vic. His cousin."

"Salim Nazir? *His* cousin?"

"Yeah, Ozzie something."

"Osman," Carella said. "Osman Kiraz."

"That's the one."

"And he said these cabbies were shot in the *head*?"

"Said his cousin was."

"Told us to stop looking for zebras."

"What the hell is that supposed to mean?" Byrnes asked.

"Told us to just find the Jew who shot his cousin in the head."

"The *fucking* Jew," Parker said.

Meyer looked at him.

"Were his exact words," Parker said, and shrugged.

"How did he know?" Carella asked.

"Go get him," Byrnes said.

Ozzie Kariz was asleep when they knocked on his door at nine-fifteen that Wednesday morning. Bleary-eyed and unshaven, he came to the door in pajamas over which he had thrown a shaggy blue robe, and explained that he worked at the pharmacy until midnight each night and did not get home until one, one-thirty, so he normally slept late each morning.

"May we come in?" Carella asked.

"Yes, sure," Kariz said, "but we'll have to be quiet, please. My wife is still asleep."

They went into a small kitchen and sat at a wooden table painted green.

"So what's up?" Kariz asked.

"Few more questions we'd like to ask you."

"Again?" Kariz said. "I told those other two . . . what were their names?"

"Genero and Parker."

"I told them I didn't know any of my cousin's girlfriends. Or even their names."

"This doesn't have anything to do with his girlfriends," Carella said.

"Oh? Something new then? Is there some new development?"

"Yes. Another cab driver was killed last night."

"Oh?"

"You didn't know that."

"No."

"It's already on television."

"I've been asleep."

"Of course."

"Was he a Muslim?"

"Yes."

"And was there another . . . ?"

"Yes, another Jewish star on the windshield."

"This is bad," Kiraz said. "These killings, the bombings . . ."

"Mr. Kiraz," Meyer said, "can you tell us where you were at three o'clock this morning?"

"Is that when it happened?"

"Yes, that's exactly when it happened."

"Where?"

"You tell us," Carella said.

Kiraz looked at them.

"What is this?" he asked.

"How'd you know your cousin was shot in the head?" Meyer asked.

"Was he?"

"That's what you told Genero and Parker. You told them a Jew shot your cousin in the head. How did you . . . ?"

"And did a Jew also shoot this man last night?" Kiraz asked. "In the head?"

"Twice in the face," Carella said.

"I asked you a question," Meyer said. "How'd you know . . . ?"

"I saw his body."

"You saw your cousin's . . ."

"I went with my aunt to pick up Salim's corpse at the morgue. After the people there were finished with him."

"When was this?" Meyer asked.

"The day after he was killed."

"That would've been . . ."

"Whenever. I accompanied my aunt to the morgue, and an ambulance took us to the mosque where they bathed the body according to Islamic law . . . they have rules, you know. Religious Muslims. They have many rules."

"I take it you're not religious."

"I'm American now," Kiraz said. "I don't believe in the old ways anymore."

"Then what were you doing in a mosque, washing your cousin's . . . ?"

"My aunt asked me to come. You saw her. You saw how distraught she was. I went as a family duty."

"I thought you didn't believe in the old ways anymore," Carella said.

"I don't believe in any of the *religious* bullshit," Kiraz said. "I went with her to help her. She's an old woman. She's alone now that her only son was killed. I went to help her."

"So you washed the body . . ."

"No, the *imam* washed the body."

"But you were there when he washed the body."

"I was there. He washed it three times. That's because it's written that when the daughter of Muhammad died, he instructed his followers to wash her three times, or more than that if necessary. Five times, seven, whatever. But always an *odd* number of times. Never an *even* number. That's what I mean about all the religious *bullshit*. Like having to wrap the body in *three* white sheets. That's because when Muhammad died, he himself was wrapped in three white sheets. From Yemen. That's what's written. So God forbid you should wrap a Muslim corpse in *four* sheets! Oh no! It has to be three. But you have to use *four* ropes to tie the sheets, not *three*, it has to be four. And the ropes each have to be seven feet long. Not three, or four, but *seven*! Do you see what I mean? All mumbo-jumbo bullshit."

"So you're saying you saw your cousin's body . . ."

"Yes."

". . . while he was being washed."

"Yes."

"And that's how you knew he was shot in the head."

"Yes. I saw the bullet wound at the base of his skull. Anyway, where *else* would he have been shot? If his murderer was sitting behind him in the taxi . . ."

"How do you know that?"

"What?"

"How do you know his murderer was inside the taxi?"

"Well, if Salim was shot at the back of the head, his murderer *had* to be sitting . . ."

"Oz?"

She was standing in the doorway to the kitchen, a diminutive woman with large brown eyes, her long ebony hair trailing down the back of the yellow silk robe she wore over a long white nightgown.

"Badria, good morning," Kiraz said. "My wife, gentlemen. I'm sorry, I've forgotten your names."

"Detective Carella."

"Detective Meyer."

"How do you do?" Badria said. "Have you offered them coffee?" she asked her husband.

"I'm sorry, no."

"Gentlemen? Some coffee?"

"None for me, thanks," Carella said.

Meyer shook his head.

"Oz? Would you like some coffee?"

"Please," he said. There was a faint amused smile on his face now. "As an illustration," he said, "witness my wife."

The detectives didn't know what he was talking about.

"The wearing of silk is expressly forbidden in Islamic law," he said. " 'Do not wear silk, for one who wears it in the world will not wear it in the Hereafter.' That's what's written. You're not allowed to wear yellow clothing, either, because 'these are the clothes usually worn by nonbelievers,' quote unquote. But here's my beautiful wife wearing a yellow silk robe, oh shame unto her," Kiraz said, and suddenly began laughing.

Badria did not laugh with him.

Her back to the detectives, she stood before a four-burner

stove, preparing her husband's coffee in a small brass pot with a tin lining.

"'A man was wearing clothes dyed in saffron,'" Kiraz said, apparently quoting again, his laughter trailing, his face becoming serious again. "'And finding that Muhammad disapproved of them, he promised to wash them. But the Prophet said, *Burn* them!'" That's written, too. So tell me, Badria. Should we burn your pretty yellow silk robe? What do you think, Badria?"

Badria said nothing.

The aroma of strong Turkish coffee filled the small kitchen.

"You haven't answered our very first question," Meyer said.

"And what was that? I'm afraid I've forgotten it."

"Where were you at three o'clock this morning?"

"I was here," Kiraz said. "Asleep. In bed with my beautiful wife. Isn't that so, Badria?"

Standing at the stove in her yellow silk robe, Badria said nothing.

"Badria? Tell the gentlemen where I was at three o'clock this morning."

She did not turn from the stove.

Her back still to them, her voice very low, Badria Kiraz said, "I don't know where you were, Oz."

The aroma of the coffee was overpowering now.

"But you weren't here in bed with me," she said.

Nellie Brand left the District Attorney's Office at eleven that Wednesday morning and was uptown at the Eight-Seven by a little before noon. She had cancelled an important lunch date, and even before the detectives filled her in, she warned them that this better be real meat here.

Osman Kiraz had already been read his rights and had insisted on an attorney before he answered any questions. Nellie wasn't familiar with the man he chose. Gulbuddin Amin was wearing a dark-brown business suit, with a tie and vest. Nellie was wearing a suit, too. Hers was a Versace, and it was a deep shade of green that complimented her blue eyes and sand-colored hair. Amin had a tidy little mustache and he wore eyeglasses. His English was impeccable, with a faint Middle-Eastern accent. Nellie guessed he might originally have come from Afghanistan, as had his client. She guessed he was some-where in his mid fifties. She herself was thirty-two.

The police clerk's fingers were poised over the stenotab ma-chine. Nellie was about to begin the questioning when Amin said, "I hope this was not a frivolous arrest, Mrs. Brand."

"No, counselor . . ."

". . . because that would be a serious mistake in a city already fraught with Jewish-Arab tensions."

"I would not use the word frivolous to describe this arrest," Nel-lie said.

"In any case, I've already advised my client to remain silent."

"Then we have nothing more to do here," Nellie said, briskly dusting the palm of one hand against the other. "Easy come, easy go. Take him away, boys, he's all yours."

"Why are you afraid of her?" Kiraz asked his lawyer.

Amin responded in what Nellie assumed was Arabic.

"Let's stick to English, shall we?" she said. "What'd you just say, counselor?"

"My comment was privileged."

"Not while your man's under oath, it isn't."

Amin sighed heavily.

"I told him I'm afraid of no woman."

"Bravo!" Nellie said, applauding, and then looked Kiraz dead in the eye. "How about you?" she asked. "Are *you* afraid of me?"

"Of course not!"

"So would you like to answer some questions?"

"I have nothing to hide."

"Yes or no? It's your call. I haven't got all day here."

"I would like to answer her questions," Kiraz told his lawyer.

Amin said something else in Arabic.

"Let us in on it," Nellie said.

"I told him it's his own funeral," Amin said.

Q: Mr. Kiraz, would you like to tell us where you were at three this morning?
A: I was at home in bed with my wife.
Q: You wife seems to think otherwise.
A: My wife is mistaken.
Q: Well, she'll be subpoenaed before the grand jury, you know, and

she'll have to tell them under oath whether you were in bed with her or somewhere else.

A: I was home. She was in bed with me.

Q: You yourself are under oath right this minute, you realize that, don't you?

A: I realize it.

Q: You swore on the Koran, did you not? You placed your left hand on the Koran and raised your right hand . . .

A: I know what I did.

Q: Or does that mean anything to you?

Q: Mr. Kiraz?

Q: Mr. Kiraz, does that mean anything to you? Placing your hand on the Islamic holy book . . .

A: I heard you.

Q: May I have your answer, please?

A: My word is my bond. It doesn't matter whether I swore on the Koran or not.

Q: Well, good, I'm happy to hear that. So tell me, Mr. Kiraz, where were you on these *other* dates at around two in the morning? Friday, May second . . . Saturday, May third . . . and Monday, May fifth. All at around two in the morning, where were you, Mr. Kiraz?

A: Home asleep. I work late. I get home around one, one-fifteen. I go directly to bed.

Q: Do you know what those dates signify?

A: I have no idea.

Q: You don't read the papers, is that it?

A: I read the papers. But those dates . . .

Q: Or watch television? You don't watch television?

A: I work from four to midnight. I rarely watch television.

Q: Then you don't know about these Muslim cab drivers who were shot and killed, is that it?

A: I know about them. Is that what those dates are? Is that when they were killed?

Q: How about Saturday, May third? Does that date hold any particular significance for you?

A: Not any more than the other dates.

Q: Do you know who was killed on that date?

A: No.

Q: Your cousin. Salil Nazir.

A: Yes.

Q: Yes what?

A: Yes. Now I recall that was the date.

Q: Because the detectives spoke to you that morning, isn't that so?

In your aunt's apartment? Gulalai Nazir, right? Your aunt? You spoke to the detectives at six that morning, didn't you?

A: I don't remember the exact time, but yes, I spoke to them.

Q: And told them a Jew had killed your cousin, isn't that so?

A: Yes. Because of the blue star.

Q: Oh, is that why?

A: Yes.

Q: And you spoke to Detective Genero and Parker, did you not, after a third Muslim cab driver was killed? This would have been on Monday, May fifth, at around three in the afternoon, when you spoke to them. And at that time you said, correct me if I'm wrong, you said, "Just find the fucking Jew who shot my cousin in the head," is that correct?

A: Yes, I said that. And I've already explained how I knew he was shot in the head. I was there when the imam washed him. I saw the bullet wound ?. .

Q: Did you know any of these other cab drivers?

A: No.

Q: Khalid Aslam . . .

A: No.

Q: Ali Al-Barak?

A: No.

Q: Or the one who was killed last night, Abbas Miandad, did you know any of these drivers?

A: I told you no.

Q: So the only one you knew was your cousin, Salim Nazir.

A: Of course I knew my cousin.

Q: And you also knew he was shot in the head.

A: Yes. I told you . . .

Q: Like all the other drivers.

A: I don't know how the other drivers were killed. I didn't see the other drivers.

Q: But you saw your cousin while he was being washed, is that correct?

A: That is correct.

Q: Would you remember the name of the imam who washed him?

A: No, I'm sorry.

Q: Would it have been Ahmed Nur Kabir?

A: It could have. I had never seen him before.

Q: If I told you his name was Ahmed Nur Kabir, and that the name of the mosque where your cousin's body was prepared for burial is Masjid Al-Barbrak, would you accept that?

A: If you say that's where . . .

Q: Yes, I say so.

A: Then, of course, I would accept it.

Q: Would it surprise you to learn that the detectives here—
   Detectives Carella and Meyer—spoke to the imam at Masjid
   Al-Barbrak?
A: I would have no way of knowing whether or not they . . .
Q: Will you accept my word that they spoke to him?
A: I would accept it.
Q: They spoke to him and he told them he was alone when he
   washed your cousin's body, alone when he wrapped the body in
   its shrouds. There was no one in the room with him. He was
   alone, Mr. Kiraz.
A: I don't accept that. I was with him.
Q: He says you were waiting outside with your aunt. He says he was
   alone with the corpse.
A: He's mistaken.
Q: If he was, in fact, alone with your cousin's body . . . ?
A: I told you he's mistaken.
Q: You think he's lying?
A: I don't know what . . .
Q: You think a holy man would lie?
A: *Holy* man! *Please*!
Q: If he was alone with the body, how do you explain seeing a bullet
   wound at the back of your cousin's head?
Q: Mr. Kiraz?
Q: Mr. Kiraz, how did you know your cousin was shot in the head?
   None of the newspaper or television reports . . .
Q: Mr. Kiraz? Would you answer my question, please?
Q: Mr. Kiraz?
A: Any man would have done the same thing.
Q: What would any man . . . ?
A: She is not one of his *whores*! She is my *wife*!

I knew, of course, that Salim was seeing a lot of women. That's
okay, he was young, he was good-looking, the Koran says a man can
take as many as four wives, so long as he can support them emotionally and financially. Salim wasn't even married, so there's nothing
wrong with dating a lot of girls, four, five, a dozen, who cares? This is
America, Salim was American, we're all Americans, right? You watch
television, the bachelor has to choose from *fifteen* girls, isn't that so?
This is America. So there was nothing wrong with Salim dating all
these girls.
   But not my wife.
   Not Badria.
   I don't know when it started with her. I don't know when it

started between them. I know one night I called the supermarket where she works. This was around ten o'clock one night, I was at the pharmacy. I manage a pharmacy, you know. People ask me all sorts of questions about what they should do for various ailments. I'm not a pharmacist, but they ask me questions. I know a lot of doctors. Also, I read a lot. I have time during the day, I don't start work till four in the afternoon. So I read a lot. I wanted to be a teacher, you know.

They told me she had gone home early.

I said, Gone home? Why?

I was alarmed.

Was Badria sick?

The person I spoke to said my wife had a headache. So she went home.

I didn't know what to think.

I immediately called the house. There was no answer. Now I became really worried. Was she seriously ill? Why wasn't she answering the phone? Had she fainted? So I went home, too. I'm the manager, I can go home if I like. This is America. A manager can go home if he likes. I told my assistant I thought my wife might be sick.

I was just approaching my building when I saw them. This was now close to eleven o'clock that night. It was dark, I didn't recognize them at first. I thought it was just a young couple. Another young couple. Only that. Coming up the street together. Arm in arm. Heads close. She turned to kiss him. Lifted her head to his. Offered him her lips. It was Badria. My wife. Kissing Salim. My cousin.

Well, they knew each other, of course. They had met at parties, they had met at family gatherings, this was my *cousin*! "Beware of getting into houses and meeting women," the Prophet said. "But what about the husband's brother?" someone asked, and the Prophet replied, "The husband's brother is like death." He often talked in riddles, the Prophet, it's all such bullshit. The Prophet believed that the influence of an evil eye is *fact*. Fact, mind you. The evil eye. The Prophet believed that he himself had once been put under a spell by a Jew and his daughters. The Prophet believed that the fever associated with plague was due to the intense heat of Hell. The Prophet once said, "Filling the belly of a person with pus is better than stuffing his brain with poetry." Can you believe that? I *read* poetry! I read a lot. The Prophet believed that if you had a bad dream, you should spit three times on your left side. That's what Jews do when they want to take the curse off something, you know, they spit on their fingers, ptui, ptui, ptui. I've seen elderly Jews doing that on the street. It's the same thing, am I right? It's all bullshit, all of it. Jesus turning water into wine, Jesus raising the dead! I mean, come on! Raising the *dead*? Moses parting the Red Sea? I'd love to see that one!

It all goes back to the time of the dinosaurs, when men huddled in caves in fear of thunder and lightning. It all goes back to God-fearing men arguing violently about which son of Abraham was the true descendant of the one true God, and whether or not Jesus was, in fact, the Messiah. As if a one *true* God, if there *is* a God at all, doesn't know who the hell he himself is! All of them killing each other! Well, it's no different today, is it? It's all about killing each other in the name of God, isn't it?

In the White House, we've got a born-again Christian who doesn't even realize he's fighting a holy war. An angry dry-drunk, as they say, full of hate, thirsting for white wine, and killing Arabs wherever he can find them. And in the sand out there, on their baggy-pantsed knees, we've got a zillion Muslim fanatics, full of hate, bowing to Mecca and vowing to drive the infidel from the Holy Land. Killing each other. All of them killing each other in the name of a one true God.

In my homeland, in my village, the tribal elders would have appointed a council to rape my wife as punishment for her transgression. And then the villagers would have stoned her to death.

But this is America.

I'm an American.

I knew I had to kill Salim, yes, that is what an American male would do, protect his wife, protect the sanctity of his home, kill the intruder. But I also knew I had to get away with it, as they say, I had to kill the violator and still be free to enjoy the pleasures of my wife, my position, I'm the manager of a pharmacy!

I bought the spray paint, two cans, at a hardware store near the pharmacy. I thought that was a good idea, the Star of David. Such symbolism! The six points of the star symbolizing God's rule over the universe in all six directions, north, south, east, west, up and down. Such bullshit! I didn't kill Salim until the second night, to make it seem as if he wasn't the true target, this was merely hate, these were hate crimes. I should have left it at three. Three would have been convincing enough, weren't you convinced after three?

Especially with the bombings that followed? Weren't you convinced? But I had to go for four. Insurance. The Navajos think four is a sacred number, you know. Again, it has to do with religion, with the four directions. They're all related, these religions. Jews, Christians, Muslims, they're all related. And they're all the same bullshit.

Salim shouldn't have gone after my wife.

He had enough whores already.

My wife is not a whore.

I did the right thing.

I did the American thing.

They came out through the back door of the station house—a Catholic who hadn't been to church since he was twelve, and a Jew who put up a tree each and every Christmas—and walked to where they'd parked their cars early this morning. It was a lovely bright afternoon. They both turned their faces up to the sun and lingered a moment. They seemed almost reluctant to go home. It was often that way after they cracked a tough one. They wanted to savor it a bit.

"I've got a question," Meyer said.

"Mm?"

"Do you think I'm too sensitive?"

"No. You're not sensitive at all."

"You mean that?"

"I mean it."

"You'll make me cry."

"I just changed my mind."

Meyer burst out laughing.

"I'll tell you one thing," he said. "I'm sure glad this didn't turn out to be what it looked like at first. I'm glad it wasn't hate."

"Maybe it was," Carella said.

They got into their separate cars and drove toward the open gate in the cyclone fence, one car behind the other. Carella honked "Shave-and-a-hair-cut," and Meyer honked back "Two-bits!" As Carella made his turn, he waved so long. Meyer tooted the horn again.

Both men were smiling.

JOYCE CAROL OATES

From the publication of her first book of short stories, *By the North Gate*, in 1963, **Joyce Carol Oates** has been the most prolific of major American writers, turning out novels, short stories, reviews, essays, and plays in an unceasing flow as remarkable for its quality as its volume. Writers who are extremely prolific often risk not being taken as seriously as they should—if one can write it that fast, how good can it be? Oates, however, has largely escaped that trap, and even her increasing identification with crime fiction, at a time when the field has attracted a number of other mainstream literary figures, has not lessened her reputation as a formidable author in the least. Many of Oates's works contain at least some elements of crime and mystery, from the National Book Award winner *them*, through the Chappaquiddick fictionalization *Black Water* and the Jeffrey Dahmer-inspired serial-killer novel *Zombie*, to her controversial 738-page fictionalized biography of Marilyn Monroe, *Blonde*. The element of detection becomes explicit with the investigations of amateur sleuth Xavier Kilgarvan in the novel *The Mysteries of Winterthurn*, which, the author explains in an afterword to the 1985 paperback edition, "is the third in a quintet of experimental novels that deal, in genre form, with nineteenth- and early twentieth-century America." Why would a literary writer like Oates choose to work in such "deliberately confining structures"? Because "the formal discipline of 'genre' . . . forces us inevitably to a radical re-visioning of the world and the craft of fiction." Oates, who numbers among her honors in a related genre the Bram Stoker Award of the Horror Writers of America, did not establish an explicit crime-fiction identity until *Lives of the Twins* appeared under the pseudonym Rosamund Smith. Initially intended to be a secret, the identity of Smith was revealed almost immediately, and later novels were bylined Joyce Carol Oates (large print) writing as Rosamund Smith (smaller print). Her recent novels include *The Falls*, *I'll Take You There*, and *Rape: A Love Story*.

THE CORN MAIDEN:
A LOVE STORY

Joyce Carol Oates

APRIL

YOU ASSHOLES!

Whywhy you're asking here's why her hair.

I mean *her hair*! I mean like I saw it in the sun it's pale silky gold like corn tassels and in the sun sparks might catch. And her eyes that smiled at me sort of nervous and hopeful like she could not know (but who could know?) what is Jude's wish. For I am Jude the Obscure, I am the Master of Eyes. I am not to be judged by crude eyes like yours, assholes.

There was her mother. I saw them together. I saw the mother stoop to kiss *her*. That arrow entered my heart. I thought *I will make you see me*. I would not forgive.

Okay then. More specific. Some kind of report you assholes will type up. Maybe there's a space for the medical examiner's verdict *cause of death*.

---

* Note: The Sacrifice of the Corn Maiden is a composite drawn from traditional sacrificial rituals of the Iroquois, Pawnee, and Blackfoot Indian tribes.

Assholes don't have a clue do you. If you did you'd know it is futile to type up reports as if such will grant you truth or even "facts."

Whywhy in the night at my computer clickclickclicking through galaxies and there was revealed on my birthday (March 11) the Master of Eyes granting me my wish that is why. *All that you wish will be made manifest in Time. If you are Master.*

Jude the Obscure he named me. In cyberspace we were twinned.

Here's why in sixth grade a field trip to the museum of natural history and Jude wandered off from the silly giggling children to stare at the Onigara exhibit of the Sacrifice of the Corn Maiden. *This exhibit is graphic in nature and not recommended for children younger than sixteen unless with parental guidance* you stepped through an archway into a fluorescent-lit interior of dusty display cases to stare at the Corn Maiden with braided black bristles for hair and flat face and blind eyes and mouth widened in an expression of permanent wonder beyond even terror and it was that vision that entered Jude's heart powerful as any arrow shot into the Corn Maiden's heart that is why.

Because it was an experiment to see if God would allow it that is why.

Because there was no one to stop me that is why.

DISCIPLES

We never thought Jude was serious!

We never thought it would turn out like it did.

We never thought . . .

. . . just *didn't*!

Never meant . . .

. . . *never*!

Nobody had anything against . . .

. . . . .

(Jude said it's Taboo to utter that name.)

Jude was the Master of Eyes. She was our leader all through school. Jude was just so cool.

Fifth grade, Jude instructed us how to get HIGH sniffing S. Where Jude got S., we didn't know.

Seventh grade, Jude gave us E. Like the older kids take. From her secret contact at the high school Jude got E.

When you're HIGH you love everybody but the secret is basically you don't give a damn.

That is what's so nice! HIGH floating above Skatskill like you could drop a bomb on Skatskill Day or your own house and there's your own family rushing out their clothes and hair on fire and screaming for help and you would smile because it would not touch you. That is HIGH.

Secrets no one else knew.

XXX videos at Jude's house.

Jude's grandmother Mrs. Trahern the widow of somebody famous.

Feral cats we fed. Cool!

Ritalin and Xanax Jude's doctors prescribed, Jude only just pretended to take that shit. In her bathroom, a supply of years.

Haagen Dazs French Vanilla ice cream we fed the Corn Maiden.

The Corn Maiden was sleepy almost at once, yawning. Ice cream tastes so good! Just one pill ground up, a half teaspoon. It was magic. We could not believe it.

Jude said you can't believe the magic you possess until somebody instructs how to unleash it.

The Corn Maiden had never been to Jude's house before. But Jude was friendly to her beginning back in March. Told us the Master of Eyes had granted her a wish on her birthday. And we were counted in that wish.

The plan was to *establish trust*.

The plan was to prepare for the Corn Maiden in the knowledge that one day there would be the magic hour when (Jude predicted) like a lightning flash lighting up the dark all would become clear.

This was so. We were in readiness, and the magic hour was so.

There is a rear entrance to the Trahern house. We came that way.

The Corn Maiden walked! On her own two feet the Corn Maiden walked, she was not forced, or carried.

Of her own volition Jude said.

It was not so in the Onigara Indian ceremony. There, the Corn Maiden did not come of her own volition but was kidnapped.

An enemy tribe would kidnap her. She would never return to her people.

The Corn Maiden would be buried, she would be laid among the corn seed in the sun and the earth covered over her. Jude told us of this like an old fairy tale to make you smile, but not to ask *Why*.

Jude did not like us to ask *Why*.

The Corn Maiden was never threatened. The Corn Maiden was treated with reverence, respect, and kindness.

(Except we had to scare her, a little. There was no other way Jude said.)

On Tuesdays and Thursdays she would come by the 7-Eleven store on the way home from school. Why this was, Jude knew. Mostly high school kids hang out there. Older kids, smoking. Crummy mini-mall on the state highway. Rug remnant store, hair and nails salon, Chinese takeout & the 7-Eleven. Behind are Dumpsters and a stink like something rotten.

Feral cats hide in the scrub brush behind the Dumpsters. Where it's like a jungle, nobody ever goes.

(Except Jude. To feed the feral cats she says are her Totem.)

At the 7-Eleven Jude had us walk separate so we would not be seen walking together.

Four girls together, somebody might notice.

A girl by herself, or two girls, nobody would notice.

Not that anybody was watching. We came by the back way.

Some old long-ago time when servants lived down the hill. When they climbed the hill to the big houses on Highgate Avenue. *Historic old Skatskill estate*. That was where Jude lived with just her grandmother. On TV it would be shown. In the newspapers. In *The New York Times* it would be shown on the front page. The house would be called *an eighteenth-century Dutch-American manor house*. We never knew about that. We never saw the house from the front. We only just went into Jude's room and a few other rooms. And there was the cellar.

From Highgate Avenue you can't see the Trahern house very well, there is a ten-foot stone wall surrounding it. This wall is old and crumbling but still you can't see over it. But through the gate that's wrought iron you can see if you look fast, while you're driving by.

Lots of people drive by now I guess.

NO PARKING   NO PARKING   NO PARKING on Highgate. Skatskill does not welcome strangers except to shop.

The Trahern estate it would be called. The property is eleven
acres. But there is a shortcut from the rear. When we brought the
Corn Maiden to the house, we came from the rear. Mostly the property is woods. Mostly it is wild, like a jungle. But there are old stone
steps you can climb if you are careful. An old service road that's
grown over with brambles and blocked off at the bottom of the hill
by a concrete slab but you can walk around the slab.

This back way, nobody would guess. Three minutes' walk from
the mini-mall.

Nobody would guess! The big old houses on Highgate, way up
the hill, how the rear of their property slopes down to the state
highway.

Jude warned *The Corn Maiden must be treated with reverence, respect,
kindness, and firmness. The Corn Maiden must never guess the fate that will
be hers.*

SUBURBAN SINGLE MOM, LATCHKEY DAUGHTER

"Marissa"

The first signal something was wrong, no lights in the apartment.

The second, too quiet.

"Marissa, honey . . . ?"

Already there was an edge to her voice. Already her chest felt as
if an iron band was tightening around it.

Stepped inside the darkened apartment. She would swear, no
later than 8 P.M.

In a dreamlike suspension of emotion shutting the door behind
her, switching on a light. Aware of herself as one might see oneself
on a video monitor behaving with conspicuous normality though the
circumstances have shifted, and are not normal.

A mother learns not to panic, not to betray weakness. Should a
child be observing.

"Marissa? Aren't you . . . are you *home*?"

If she'd been home, Marissa would have the lights on. Marissa would be doing her homework in the living room with the TV on, loud. Or the CD player on, loud. When she was home alone Marissa was made uneasy by quiet.

Made her nervous she said. Made her think scary thoughts like about dying she said. Hear her own heartbeat she said.

But the apartment was quiet. In the kitchen, quiet.

Leah switched on more lights. She was still observing herself, she was still behaving calmly. Seeing, from the living room, down the hall to Marissa's room that the door to that room was open, darkness inside.

It was possible—it was! if only for a blurred desperate moment— to think that Marissa had fallen asleep on her bed, that was why . . . But Leah checked, there was no slender figure lying on the bed.

No one in the bathroom. Door ajar, darkness inside.

The apartment did not seem familiar somehow. As if furniture had been moved. (It had not, she would determine later.) It was chilly, drafty as if a window had been left open. (No window had been left open.)

"Marissa? Marissa?"

There was a tone of surprise and almost-exasperation in the mother's voice. As if, if Marissa heard, she would know herself just mildly scolded.

In the kitchen that was empty, Leah set the groceries down. On a counter. Wasn't watching, the bag slumped slowly over. Scarcely saw, a container of yogurt fell out.

Marissa's favorite, strawberry.

So quiet! The mother, beginning to shiver, understood why the daughter hated quiet.

She was walking through the rooms, and would walk through the few rooms of the small first-floor apartment calling *Marissa? Honey?* in a thin rising voice like a wire pulled tight. She would lose track of time. She was the mother, she was responsible. For eleven years she had not lost her child, every mother's terror of losing her child, an abrupt physical loss, a theft, a stealing-away, a *forcible abduction*.

"No. She's here. Somewhere . . ."

Retracing her steps through the apartment. There were so few rooms for Marissa to be in! Again opening the bathroom door, wider. Opening a closet door. Closet doors. Stumbling against . . . Struck her shoulder on . . . Collided with Marissa's desk chair, stinging her thigh. "Marissa? Are you *hiding*?"

As if Marissa would be hiding. At such a time.

Marissa was eleven years old. Marissa had not hidden from her mother to make Mommy seek her out giggling and squealing with excitement in a very long time.

She would protest she was not a negligent mother.

She was a working mother. A single mother. Her daughter's father had disappeared from their lives, he paid neither alimony nor child support. How was it her fault, she had to work to support her daughter and herself, and her daughter required special education instruction and so she'd taken her out of public school and enrolled her at Skatskill Day . . .

They would accuse her. In the tabloids they would crucify her.

Dial 911 and your life is public fodder. Dial 911 and your life is not yours. Dial 911 and your life is forever changed.

Suburban Single Mom. Latchkey Daughter.

Eleven-Year-Old Missing, South Skatskill.

She would protest it was not that way at all! It was not.

Five days out of seven *it was not*.

Only Tuesdays and Thursdays she worked late at the clinic. Only since Christmas had Marissa been coming home to an empty apartment.

No. It was not ideal. And maybe she should have hired a sitter except . . .

She would protest she had no choice but to work late, her shift had been changed. On Tuesdays/Thursdays she began at 10:30 A.M. and ended at 6:30 P.M. Those nights, she was home by 7:15 P.M., by 7:30 P.M. at the latest she was home. She would swear, she was! Most nights.

How was it her fault, slow-moving traffic on the Tappan Zee Bridge from Nyack then north on route 9 through Tarrytown, Sleepy Hollow, to the Skatskill town limits, and route 9 under repair. Traffic in pelting rain! Out of nowhere a cloudburst, rain! She had wanted to sob in frustration, in fury at what her life had become, blinding headlights in her eyes like laser rays piercing her brain.

But usually she was home by 8 P.M. At the latest.

Before dialing 911 she was trying to think: to calculate.

Marissa would ordinarily be home by about 4 P.M. Her last class ended at 3:15 P.M. Marissa would walk home, five and a half suburban blocks, approximately a half mile, through (mostly) a residential neighborhood. (True, 15th Street was a busy street. But Marissa didn't need to cross it.) And she would walk with school friends. (Would she?) Marissa didn't take a school bus, there was no bus for private school children, and in any case Marissa lived near the school because Leah Bantry had moved to the Briarcliff Apts. in order to be near Skatskill Day.

She would explain! In the interstices of emotion over her *missing child* she would explain.

Possibly there had been something special after school that day, a sports event, choir practice, Marissa had forgotten to mention to Leah . . . Possibly Marissa had been invited home by a friend.

In the apartment, standing beside the phone, as if waiting for the phone to ring, trying to think what it was she'd just been thinking. Like trying to grasp water with her fingers, trying to think . . .

A friend! That was it.

What were the names of girls in Marissa's class . . . ?

Of course, Leah would telephone! She was shaky, and she was upset, but she would make these crucial calls before involving the police, she wasn't a hysterical mother. She might call Leah's teacher whose name she knew, and from her she would learn the names of other girls, she would call these numbers, she would soon locate Marissa, it would be all right. And the mother of Marissa's friend would say apologetically, *But I'd thought Marissa had asked you, could she stay for supper. I'm so very sorry!* And Leah would say quickly laughing in relief, *You know how children are, sometimes. Even the nice ones.*

Except: Marissa didn't have many friends at the school.

That had been a problem in the new, private school. In public school she'd had friends, but it wasn't so easy at Skatskill Day where most students were privileged, well-to-do. Very privileged, and very well-to-do. And poor Marissa was so sweet, trusting and hopeful and easy to hurt if other girls chose to hurt her.

Already in fifth grade it had begun, a perplexing girl-meanness.

In sixth grade, it had become worse.

"Why don't they like me, Mommy?"

"Why do they make fun of me, Mommy?"

For in Skatskill if you lived down the hill from Highgate Avenue and/or east of Summit Street you were known to be *working class*. Marissa had asked what it meant? Didn't everybody work? And what was a *class* was it like . . . a class in school? A class*room?*)

But Leah had to concede: even if Marissa had been invited home by an unknown school friend, she wouldn't have stayed away so long.

Not past 5 P.M. Not past dark.

Not without calling Leah.

"She isn't the type of child to . . ."

Leah checked the kitchen again. The sink was empty. No package of chicken cutlets defrosting.

Tuesdays/Thursdays were Marissa's evenings to start supper. Marissa loved to cook, Mommy and Marissa loved to cook together. Tonight they were having chicken jambalaya which was their favorite fun meal to prepare together. "Tomatoes, onions, peppers, cajun powder. Rice . . ."

Leah spoke aloud. The silence was unnerving.

If I'd come home directly. Tonight.

The 7-Eleven out on the highway. That's where she had stopped on the way home.

Behind the counter, the middle-aged Indian gentleman with the wise sorrowful eyes would vouch for her. Leah was a frequent customer, he didn't know her name but he seemed to like her.

Dairy products, a box of tissues. Canned tomatoes. Two six-packs of beer, cold. For all he knew, Leah had a husband. *He* was the beer drinker, the husband.

Leah saw that her hands were trembling. She needed a drink, to steady her hands.

"Ma*ris*sa!"

She was thirty-four years old. Her daughter was eleven. So far as anyone in Leah's family knew, including her parents, she had been "amicably divorced" for seven years. Her former husband, a medical school drop-out, had disappeared somewhere in Northern California; they had lived together in Berkeley, having met at the university in the early 1990s.

Impossible to locate the former husband/father whose name was not Bantry.

She would be asked about him, she knew. She would be asked about numerous things.

She would explain: eleven is too old for day care. Eleven is fully capable of coming home alone . . . Eleven can be responsible for . . .

At the refrigerator she fumbled for a can of beer. She opened it and drank thirstily. The liquid was freezing cold, her head began to ache immediately: an icy spot like a coin between her eyes. *How can you! At a time like this!* She didn't want to panic and call 911 before she'd thought this through. Something was staring her in the face, some explanation, maybe?

Distraught Single Mom. Modest Apartment.

Missing Eleven-Year-Old. "Learning Disabilities."

Clumsily Leah retraced her steps through the apartment another time. She was looking for . . . Throwing more widely open those doors she'd already opened. Kneeling beside Marissa's bed to peer beneath in a burst of desperate energy.

And finding—what? A lone sock.

As if Marissa would be hiding beneath a bed!

Marissa who loved her mother, would never never wish to worry or upset or hurt her mother. Marissa who was young for her age, never rebellious, sulky. Marissa whose idea of badness was forgetting to make her bed in the morning. Leaving the bathroom mirror above the sink splattered with water.

Marissa who'd asked Mommy, "Do I have a daddy somewhere like other girls, and he knows about me?"

Marissa who'd asked, blinking back tears, "Why do they make fun of me, Mommy? Am I *slow*?"

In public school classes had been too large, her teacher hadn't had time or patience for Marissa. So Leah had enrolled her at Skatskill Day where classes were limited to fifteen students and Marissa would have special attention from her teacher and yet: still she was having trouble with arithmetic, she was teased, called "slow" . . . Laughed at even by girls she'd thought were her friends.

"Maybe she's run away."

Out of nowhere this thought struck Leah.

Marissa had run away from Skatskill. From the life Mommy had worked so hard to provide for her.

"That can't be! Never."

Leah swallowed another mouthful of beer. Self-medicating, it was. Still her heart was beating in rapid thumps, then missing a beat. Hoped to God she would not faint . . .

"Where? Where would Marissa go? *Never.*"

Ridiculous to think that Marissa would run away!

She was far too shy, passive. Far too uncertain of herself. Other children, particularly older children, intimidated her. Because Marissa was unusually attractive, a beautiful child with silky blond hair to her shoulders, brushed by her proud mother until it shone, sometimes braided by her mother into elaborate plaits, Marissa often drew unwanted attention; but Marissa had very little sense of herself and of how others regarded her.

She had never ridden a bus alone. Never gone to a movie alone. Rarely entered any store alone, without Leah close by.

Yet it was the first thing police would suspect, probably: Marissa had run away.

"Maybe she's next door. Visiting the neighbors."

Leah knew this was not likely. She and Marissa were on friendly terms with their neighbors but they never visited one another. It wasn't that kind of apartment complex, there were few other children.

Still, Leah would have to see. It was expected of a mother looking for her daughter, to check with neighbors.

She spent some time then, ten or fifteen minutes, knocking on doors in the Briarcliff Apts. Smiling anxiously into strangers' startled faces. Trying not to sound desperate, hysterical.

"Excuse me . . ."

A nightmare memory came to her, of a distraught young mother knocking on their door, years ago in Berkeley when she'd first moved in with her lover who would become Marissa's father. They'd been interrupted at a meal, and Leah's lover had answered the door, an edge of annoyance in his voice; and Leah had come up behind him, very young at the time, very blond and privileged, and she'd stared at a young Filipino woman blinking back tears as she'd asked them *Have you seen my daughter . . .* Leah could not remember anything more.

Now it was Leah Bantry who was knocking on doors. Interrupting strangers at mealtime. Apologizing for disturbing them, asking in a tremulous voice *Have you seen my daughter . . .*

In the barracks-like apartment complex into which Leah had moved for economy's sake two years before, each apartment opened directly out onto the rear of the building, into the parking area. This was a brightly lit paved area, purely functional, ugly. In the apartment complex there were no hallways. There were no interior stairs, no foyers. There were no meeting places for even casual exchanges. This was not an attractive condominium village overlooking the Hudson River but Briarcliff Apts, South Skatskill.

Leah's immediate neighbors were sympathetic and concerned, but could offer no help. They had not seen Marissa, and of course she hadn't come to visit them. They promised Leah they would "keep an eye out" and suggested she call 911.

Leah continued to knock on doors. A mechanism had been triggered in her brain, she could not stop until she had knocked on every door in the apartment complex. As she moved farther from her own first-floor apartment, she was met with less sympathy. One tenant shouted through the door to ask what she wanted. Another, a middle-aged man with a drinker's flushed indignant face, interrupted her faltering query to say he hadn't seen any children, he didn't know any children, and he didn't have time for any children.

Leah returned to her apartment staggering, dazed. Saw with a thrill of alarm she'd left the door ajar. Every light in the apartment appeared to be on. Almost, she thought Marissa must be home now, in the kitchen.

She hurried inside. "Marissa . . . ?"

Her voice was eager, piteous.

The kitchen was empty of course. The apartment was empty.

A new, wild idea: Leah returned outside, to the parking lot, to check her car which was parked a short distance away. She peered inside, though knowing it was locked and empty. Peered into the back seat.

Am I going mad? What is happening to me . . .

Still, she'd had to look. She had a powerful urge, too, to get into the car and drive along 15th Street to Skatskill Day School, and check out the building. Of course, it would be locked. The parking lot to the rear . . .

She would drive on Van Buren. She would drive on Summit. She would drive along Skatskill's small downtown of boutiques, novelty restaurants, high-priced antique and clothing stores. Out to the highway past gas stations, fast-food restaurants, mini-malls.

Expecting to see—what? Her daughter walking in the rain?

Leah returned to the apartment, thinking she'd heard the phone ring but the phone was not ringing. Another time, unable to stop herself she checked the rooms. This time looking more carefully through Marissa's small closet, pushing aside Marissa's neatly hung clothes. (Marissa had always been obsessively neat. Leah had not wished to wonder why.) Stared at Marissa's shoes. Such small shoes! Trying to remember what Marissa had worn that morning . . . So many hours ago.

Had she plaited Marissa's hair that morning? She didn't think she'd had time. Instead she had brushed it, lovingly. Maybe she was a little too vain of her beautiful daughter and now she was being punished . . . No, that was absurd. You are not punished for loving your child. She had brushed Marissa's hair until it shone and she had fastened it with barrettes, mother-of-pearl butterflies.

"Aren't you pretty! Mommy's little angel."

"Oh, Mommy. I am not."

Leah's heart caught. She could not understand how the child's father had abandoned them both. She was sick with guilt, it had to be her fault as a woman and a mother.

She'd resisted an impulse to hug Marissa, though. At eleven, the girl was getting too old for spontaneous unexplained hugs from Mommy.

Displays of emotion upset children, Leah had been warned. Of course, Leah hadn't needed to be warned.

Leah returned to the kitchen for another beer. Before dialing 911. Just a few swallows, she wouldn't finish the entire can.

She kept nothing stronger than beer in the apartment. That was a rule of her mature life.

No hard liquor. No men overnight. No exposure to her daughter, the emotions Mommy sometimes felt.

She knew: she would be blamed. For she was blameable.

Latchkey child. Working mom.

She'd have had to pay a sitter nearly as much as she made at the clinic as a medical assistant, after taxes. It was unfair, and it was impossible. She could not.

Marissa was not so quick-witted as other children her age but she was not *slow*! She was in sixth grade, she had not fallen behind. Her tutor said she was "improving." And her attitude was so hopeful. *Your daughter tries so hard, Mrs. Bantry! Such a sweet, patient child.*

Unlike her mother, Leah thought. Who wasn't sweet, and who had given up patience long ago.

"I want to report a child missing . . ."

She rehearsed the words, struck by their finality. She hoped her voice would not sound slurred.

Where was Marissa? It was impossible to think she wasn't somehow in the apartment. If Leah looked again . . .

Marissa knew: to lock the front door behind her, and to bolt the safety latch when she was home alone. (Mommy and Marissa had practiced this maneuver many times.) Marissa knew: not to answer the door if anyone knocked, if Mommy was not home. Not to answer the telephone immediately but to let the answering machine click on, to hear if it was Mommy calling.

Marissa knew: never let strangers approach her. No conversations with strangers. Never climb into vehicles with strangers or even with people she knew unless they were women, people Mommy knew or the mothers of classmates for instance.

Above all Marissa knew: come home directly from school.

Never enter any building, any house, except possibly the house of a classmate, a school friend . . . Even so, Mommy must be told about this beforehand.

(Would Marissa remember? Could an eleven-year-old be trusted to remember so much?)

Leah had totally forgotten; she'd intended to call Marissa's teacher. From Miss Fletcher, Leah would learn the names of Marissa's friends. This, the police would expect her to know. Yet she stood by the phone indecisively, wondering if she dared call the woman; for if she did, Miss Fletcher would know that something was wrong.

The ache between Leah's eyes had spread, her head was wracked with pain.

Four-year-old Marissa would climb up onto the sofa beside Leah, and stroke her forehead to smooth out the "worry lines." Wet kisses on Mommy's forehead. "Kiss to make go away!"

Mommy's vanity had been somewhat wounded, that her child saw worry lines in her face. But she'd laughed, and invited more kisses. "All right, sweetie. Kiss-to-make-go-away."

It had become their ritual. A frown, a grimace, a mournful look—either Mommy or Marissa might demand, "Kiss-to-make-go-away."

Leah was paging through the telephone directory. *Fletcher.* There were more than a dozen *Fletchers.* None of the initials seemed quite right. Marissa's teacher's first name was—Eve? Eva?

Leah dialed one of the numbers. A recording clicked on, a man's voice.

Another number, a man answered. Politely telling Leah no: there was no one named "Eve" or "Eva" at that number.

This is hopeless, Leah thought.

She should be calling ERs, medical centers, where a child might have been brought, struck by a vehicle for instance crossing a busy street . . .

She fumbled for the can of beer. She would drink hurriedly now. Before the police arrived.

Self-medicating a therapist had called it. Back in high school she'd begun. It was her secret from her family, they'd never known. Though her sister Avril had guessed. At first Leah had drunk with her friends, then she hadn't needed her friends. It wasn't for the elevated sensation, the buzz, it was to calm her nerves. To make her less anxious. Less disgusted with herself.

I need to be beautiful. More beautiful.

He'd said she was beautiful, many times. The man who was to be Marissa's father. Leah was beautiful, he adored her.

They were going to live in a seaside town somewhere in northern California, Oregon. It had been their fantasy. In the meantime he'd been a medical student, resentful of the pressure. She had taken the easier route, nursing school. But she'd dropped out when she became pregnant.

Later he would say sure she was beautiful, but he did not love her. *Love wears out. People move on.*

Still, there was Marissa. Out of their coupling, Marissa.

Gladly would Leah give up the man, any man, so long as she had her daughter back.

If she had not stopped on the way home from the clinic! If she had come directly home.

She knew this: she would have to tell police where she had been, before returning home. Why she'd been unusually late. She would have to confess that, that she had been late. Her life would be turned inside-out like the pockets of an old pair of pants. All that was private, precious, rudely exposed.

The single evening in weeks, months . . . She'd behaved out of character.

But she'd stopped at the 7-Eleven, too. It was a busy place in the early evening. This wasn't out of character, Leah frequently stopped at the convenience store which was two blocks from Briarcliff Apts. The Indian gentleman at the cash register would speak kindly of her to police officers. He would learn that her name was Leah Barnty and that her daughter was missing. He would learn that she lived close by, on 15th Street. He would learn that she was a single mother, she was not married. The numerous six-packs of Coors she bought had not been for a husband but for her.

He'd seen her with Marissa, certainly. And so he would remember Marissa. Shy blond child whose hair was sometimes in plaits. He would pity Leah as he'd never had reason to pity her in the past, only just to admire her in his guarded way, the blond shining hair, the American-healthy good looks.

Leah finished the beer, and disposed of the can in the waste basket beneath the sink. She thought of going outside and dumping all the cans into a trash can, for police would possibly search the house, but there was no time, she had delayed long enough waiting for Marissa to return and everything to be again as it had been. Thinking *Why didn't I get a cell phone for Marissa, why did I think the expense wasn't worth it?* She picked up the receiver, and dialed 911.

Her voice was breathless as if she'd been running.

"I want—I want—to report a child missing."

LONE WOLVES

I am meant for a special destiny. I am!

He lived vividly inside his head. She lived vividly inside her head.

He was a former idealist. She was an unblinking realist.

He was thirty-one years old. She was thirteen.

He was tall/lanky/ropey-muscled five feet ten inches (on his New York State driver's license he'd indicated 5'11"), weighing one hundred fifty-five pounds. She was four feet eleven, eighty-three pounds.

He thought well of himself, secretly. She thought very well of herself, not so secretly.

He was a substitute math teacher/ "computer consultant" at Skatskill Day School. She was an eighth grader at Skatskill Day School.

His official status at the school was *part-time employee*.

Her official status at the school was *full-tuition pupil, no exceptions*.

Part-time employee meant no medical/dental insurance coverage, less pay per hour than full-time employees, and no possibility of tenure. *Full-tuition, no exceptions* meant no scholarship aid or tuition deferral.

He was a relatively new resident of Skatskill-on-Hudson, eight miles north of New York City. She was a longtime resident who'd come to live with her widowed grandmother when she was two years old, in 1992.

To her, to his face, he was *Mr. Zallman*; otherwise, *Mr. Z*.

To him, she had no clear identity. One of those Skatskill Day girls of varying ages (elementary grades through high school) to whom he gave computer instructions and provided personal assistance as requested.

Even sixth grader Marissa Bantry with the long straight corn-tassel hair he would not recall, immediately.

The kids he called them. In a voice that dragged with reluctant affection; or in a voice heavy with sarcasm. *Those kids!*

Depending on the day, the week. Depending on his mood.

Those others she called them in a voice quavering with scorn.

They were an alien race. Even her small band of disciples she had to concede were losers.

In his confidential file in the office of the principal of Skatskill Day it was noted *Impressive credentials/recommendations, interacts well with brighter students. Inclined to impatience. Not a team player. Unusual sense of humor. (Abrasive?)*

In her confidential file (1998–present) in the principal's office it was noted in reports by numerous parties *Impressive background (maternal grandmother/legal guardian Mrs. A. Trahern, alumna/donor/trustee/ emeritus), impressive I.Q. (measured 149, 161, 113, 159 ages 6, 9, 10, 12), flashes of brilliance, erratic academic performance, lonely child, gregarious child, interacts poorly with classmates, natural leader, antisocial tendencies, lively presence in class, disruptive presence in class, hyperactive, apathetic, talent for "fantasy," poor communication skills, immature tendencies, ver-*

bal fluency, imagination stimulated by new projects, easily bored, sullen, mature for age, poor motor coordination skills, diagnosed Attention Deficit Syndrome age 5/prescribed Ritalin with good results/mixed results, diagnosed borderline dyslexic age 7, prescribed special tutoring with good results/mixed results, honor roll fifth grade, low grades/failed English seventh grade, suspended for one week Oct. 2002 "threatening" girl classmate, reinstated after three days/legal action brought against school by guardian/mandated psychological counseling with good/mixed results. (On the outside of the folder, in the principal's handwriting *A challenge*!)

He was swarthy skinned, with an olive complexion. She had pale translucent skin.

He was at the school Monday/Tuesday/Thursday unless he was subbing for another teacher which he did, on the average, perhaps once every five weeks. She was at the school five days a week, Skatskill Day was her turf!

Hate/love she felt for Skatskill Day. *Love/hate.*

(Often, as her teachers noted, she "disappeared" from classes and later "reappeared." Sulky/arrogant with no explanation.)

He was a lone wolf and yet: the great-grandson of immigrant German Jews who had come to the United States in the early 1900s. The grandson and son of partners at Cleary, McCorkle, Mace & Zallman, Wall Street brokers. She was the lone grandchild of New York State Supreme Court Justice Elias Trahern who had died before she was born and was of no more interest to her than the jut-jawed and bewigged General George Washington whose idealized image hung in the school rotunda.

His skin was dotted with moles. Not disfiguring exactly but he'd see people staring at these moles as if waiting for them to move.

Her skin was susceptible to angry-looking rashes. Nerve-rashes they'd been diagnosed, also caused by picking with her nails.

He was beginning to lose his thick-rippled dark hair he had not realized he'd been vain about. Receding at the temples so he wore it straggling over his collar. Her hair exploded in faded-rust fuzz like dandelion seed around her pointy pinched face.

He was Mikal. She was Jude.

He'd been born Michael but there were so many damn Michaels!

She'd been born Judith but—*Judith! Enough to make you want to puke.*

Lone wolves who scorned the crowd. Natural aristocrats who had no use for money, or for family connections.

He was estranged from the Zallmans. Mostly.

She was estranged from the Traherns. Mostly.

He had a quick engaging ironic laugh. She had a high-pitched nasal-sniggering laugh that surprised her suddenly, like a sneeze.

His favored muttered epithet was *What next?* Her favored muttered epithet was *Bor-ing!*

He knew: prepubescent/adolescent girls often have crushes on their male teachers. Yet somehow it never seemed very real to him, or very crucial. Mikal Zallman living in his own head.

She detested boys her own age. And most men, any age.

Making her disciples giggle and blush, at lunchtime flashing a paring knife in a swooping circular motion to indicate *cas-tra-tion: know what that is?* as certain eighth grade boys passed noisily by carrying cafeteria trays.

Boys rarely saw her. She'd learned to go invisible like a playing card turned sideways.

He lived—smugly, it seemed to some observers—inside an armor of irony. (Except when alone. Staring at images of famine, war, devastation he felt himself blinking hot tears from his eyes. He'd shocked himself and others crying uncontrollably at his father's funeral in an Upper East Side synagogue the previous year.)

She had not cried in approximately four years. Since she'd fallen from a bicycle and cut a gash in her right knee requiring nine stitches.

He lived alone, in three sparely furnished rooms, in Riverview Heights, a condominium village on the Hudson River in North Tarrytown. She lived alone, except for the peripheral presence of her aging grandmother, in a few comfortably furnished rooms in the main wing of the Trahern estate at 83 Highgate Avenue; the rest of the thirty-room mansion had long been closed off for economy's sake.

He had no idea where she lived, as he had but the vaguest idea of who she was. She knew where he lived, it was three miles from 83 Highgate Avenue. She'd bicycled past Riverview Heights more than once.

He drove a not-new metallic blue Honda CR-V, New York li-

cense TZ 6063. She knew he drove a not-new metallic blue Honda
CR-V, New York license TZ 6063.

Actually he didn't always think so well of himself. Actually she
didn't always think so well of herself.

He wished to think well of himself. He wished to think well of
all of humanity. He did not want to think *Homo sapiens is hopeless, let's
pull the plug.* He wanted to think *I can make a difference in others' lives.*

He'd been an idealist who had *burnt out, crashed* in his late twenties. These were worthy clichés. These were clichés he had earned.
He had taught in Manhattan, Bronx, and Yonkers public schools
through his mid-and late twenties and after an interim of recovery he
had returned to Columbia University to upgrade his credentials with a
master's degree in computer science and he had returned to teaching
for his old idealism yet clung to him like lint on one of his worn-at-the-
elbow sweaters, one thing he knew he would never emulate his father
in the pursuit of money, here in Skatskill-on-Hudson where he knew
no one he could work part-time mostly helping kids with computers
and he would be respected here or in any case his privacy would be respected, he wasn't an ambitious private school teacher, wasn't angling
for a permanent job, in a few years he'd move on but for the present
time he was contentedly employed, he had freedom to *feed my rat* as he
called it.

Much of the time she did not think so well of herself. Secretly.

*Suicide fantasies are common to adolescents. Not a sign of mental illness
so long as they remain fantasies.*

He'd had such fantasies, too. Well into his twenties, in fact. He'd
outgrown them now. That was what *feeding my rat* had done for Mikal
Zallman.

Her suicide fantasies were cartoons, you could say. A plunge
from the Tappan Zee Bridge/George Washington Bridge, footage on
the 6 P.M. news. A blazing fireball on a rooftop. (Skatskill Day? It was
the only roof she had access to.) If you swallowed like five, six Ecstasy pills your heart would explode (maybe). If you swallowed a
dozen barbiturates you would fall asleep and then into a coma and
never wake up (maybe). With drugs there was always the possibility
of vomiting, waking up in an ER your stomach being pumped or

waking up brain damaged. There were knives, razor blades. Bleed-
ing into a bathtub, the warm water gushing.

Eve of her thirteenth birthday and she'd been feeling shitty and
her new friend/mentor the Master of Eyes (in Alaska, unless it was
Antarctica) advised her why hate yourself Jude it's bor-ing. Better to
hate *those others* who surround.

She never cried, though. Really really never cried.

Like Jude O's tear ducts are dried out. Cool!

Ducts reminded her of *pubes* she had first encountered as a word
in a chat room, she'd looked up in the dictionary seeing *pubes* was a
nasty word for those nasty crinkly/kinky hairs that had started to
sprout in a certain place, between her legs. And in her armpits where
she refused to apply *deodorant* until Grandmother nagnagged.

Grandmother Trahern was half blind but her sense of smell was
acute. Grandmother Trahern was skilled at nagnagnagging, you
might say it was the old woman's predominant skill in the eighth de-
cade of her life.

Mr. Z! Maybe he'd smelled her underarms. She hoped he had
not smelled her crotch.

Mr. Z. in computer lab making his way along the aisle answering
kids' questions most of them pretty elementary/dumb ass she'd have
liked to catch his eye and exchange a knowing smirk but Mr. Z.
never seemed to be looking toward her and then she was stricken
with shyness, blood rushing into her face as he paused above her to
examine the confusion on her screen and she heard herself mutter
with childish bravado *Guess I fucked up, Mr. Zallman, huh?* wiping her
nose on the edge of her hand beginning to giggle and there was
sexy/cool Mr. Z. six inches from her not breaking into a smile even of
playful reproach giving not the slightest hint he'd heard the forbidden F-word from an eighth grade girl's innocent mouth.

In fact Mr. Z. had heard. Sure.

Never laugh, never encourage them. If they swear or use obscene or sug-
gestive language.

And never touch them.

Or allow them to touch you.

The (subterranean) connection between them.

He had leaned over her, typed on her keyboard. Repaired the
damage. Told her she was doing very well. Not to be discouraged!
He didn't seem to know her name but maybe that was just pretense,
his sense of humor. Moving on to the next raised hand.

Still, she'd known there was the (subterranean) connection.

As she'd known, first glimpsing the Corn Maiden in the seventh
grade corridor. Silky blond corn-tassel hair. Shy, frightened.

A new girl. Perfect.

One morning she came early to observe the Corn Maiden's
mother dropping her off at the curb. Good-looking woman with the
same pale blond hair, smiling at the girl and hastily leaning over to
kiskiss.

Some connections go through you like a laser ray.

Some connections, you just know.

Mr. Z. she'd sent an e-message *you are a master mister z*. Which
was not like Jude O. to do because any message in cyberspace can
never be erased. But Mr. Z. had not replied.

So easy to reply to a fucking e-message! But Mr. Z. had not.

Mr. Z. did not exchange a knowing smile/wink with her as you'd
expect.

Ignored her!

Like he didn't know which one of them she was.

Like he could confuse her with *those others* her inferiors.

And so something turned in her heart like a rusty key and she
thought calmly, *You will pay for this mister asshole Z and all your progeny*.

Thought of calling the FBI reporting a suspected terrorist, Mr.
Z. was dark like an Arab, and shifty-eyed. Though probably he was
a Jew.

Afterward vaguely he would recall *you are a master mister z* but of
course he'd deleted it. So easy to delete an e-message.

Afterward vaguely he would recall the squirmy girl at the computer with the frizz hair and glassy staring eyes, a startling smell as of
unwashed flesh wafting from her (unusual at Skatskill Day as it was
unusual in the affluent suburban village of Skatskill) he had not
known at the time, this was January/February, was Jude Trahern. He
had no homeroom students, he met with more than one hundred
students sometimes within days, couldn't keep track of them and

had no interest in keeping track. Though a few days later he would come upon the girl in the company of a fattish friend, the two of them rummaging in a waste basket in the computer lab but he'd taken no special note of them as they'd hurried away embarrassed and giggling together as if he'd opened a door and seen them naked.

But he would remember: the same frizz-haired girl boldly seated at his computer after school one day frowning at the screen and click-clicking keys with as much authority as if the computer were her own and this time he'd spoken sharply to her, "Excuse me?" and she'd looked up at him cringing and blind-seeming as if she thought he might hit her. And so he joked, "Here's the famous hacker, eh?"—he knew it was the kindest as it was the wisest strategy to make a joke of the audacious/inexplicable behavior of adolescents, it wasn't a good idea to confront or embarrass. Especially not a girl. And this stunted-seeming girl hunched over like she was trying make herself smaller. Papery-thin skin, short upper lip exposing her front teeth, a guarded rodent look, furtive, anxious, somehow appealing. Her eyes were of the no-color of grit, moist and widened. Eyebrows and lashes scanty, near-invisible. She was so fiercely plain and her unbeautiful eyes stared at him so *rawly* . . . He felt sorry for her, poor kid. Bold, nervy, but in another year or so she'd be left behind entirely by her classmates, no boy would glance at her twice. He could not have guessed that the tremulous girl was the lone descendent of a family of reputation and privilege though possibly he might have guessed that her parents were long divorced from one another and perhaps from her as well. She was stammering some feeble explanation *Just needed to look something up, Mr. Zallman*. He laughed and dismissed her with a wave of his hand. Had an impulse, out of character for him, to reach out and tousle that frizzed floating hair as you'd rub a dog's head partly in affection and partly to chastise.

Didn't touch her, though. Mikal Zallman wasn't crazy.

"101 DALMATIANS"

Is she breathing, d'you think?
  She is! Sure she is.
  Oh God what if . . .
  . . . she *is*. See?

The Corn Maiden slept by candlelight. The heavy open-mouthed sleep of the sedated.

We observed her in wonder. The Corn Maiden, in our power!

Jude removed the barrettes from her hair so we could brush it. Long straight pale blond hair. We were not jealous of the Corn Maiden's hair because *It is our hair now*.

The Corn Maiden's hair was spread out around her head like she was falling.

She was breathing, yes you could see. If you held a candle close to her face and throat you could see.

We had made a bed for the Corn Maiden, that Jude called a *bier*. Out of beautiful silk shawls and a brocaded bedspread, cashmere blanket from Scotland, goose-feather pillows. From the closed-off guest wing of the house Jude brought these, her face shining.

We fumbled to remove the Corn Maiden's clothes.

You pull off your own clothes without hardly thinking but another person, even a small girl who is lying flat on her back, arms and legs limp but heavy, that's different.

When the Corn Maiden was bare it was hard not to giggle. Hard not to snort with laughter . . .

More like a little girl than she was like us.

We were shy of her suddenly. Her breasts were flat against her rib cage, her nipples were tiny as seeds. There were no hairs growing between her legs that we could see.

She was very cold, shivering in her sleep. Her lips were putty-colored. Her teeth were chattering. Her eyes were closed but you could see a thin crescent of white. So (almost!) you worried the Corn Maiden was watching us paralyzed in sleep.

It was Xanax Jude had prepared for the Corn Maiden. Also she had codeine and Oxycodone already ground to powder, in reserve.

We were meant to "bathe" the Corn Maiden, Jude said. But maybe not tonight.

We rubbed the Corn Maiden's icy fingers, her icy toes, and her icy cheeks. We were not shy of touching her suddenly, we wanted to touch her and touch and *touch*.

Inside here, Jude said, touching the Corn Maiden's narrow chest, there is a heart beating. An actual *heart*.

Jude spoke in a whisper. In the quiet you could hear the heart beat.

We covered the Corn Maiden then with silks, brocades, cashmere wool. We placed a goose-feather pillow beneath the Corn Maiden's head. Jude sprinkled perfume on the Corn Maiden with her fingertips. It was a blessing Jude said. The Corn Maiden would sleep and sleep for a long time and when she woke, she would know only our faces. The faces of her friends.

It was a storage room in the cellar beneath the guest wing we brought the Corn Maiden. This was a remote corner of the big old house. This was a closed-off corner of the house and the cellar was yet more remote, nobody would ever ever come here Jude said.

And you could scream your head off, nobody would ever hear.

Jude laughed, cupping her hands to her mouth like she was going to scream. But all that came out was a strangled choked noise.

There was no heat in the closed-off rooms of the Trahern house. In the cellar it was a damp cold like winter. Except this was meant to be a time of nuclear holocaust and no electricity we would have brought a space heater to plug in. Instead we had candles.

These were fragrant hand-dipped candles old Mrs. Trahern had been saving in a drawer since 1994, according to the gift shop receipt.

Jude said, Grandma won't miss 'em.

Jude was funny about her grandmother. Sometimes she liked her okay, other times she called her the old bat, said fuck her she didn't give a damn about Jude she was only worried Jude would embarrass her somehow.

Mrs. Trahern had called up the stairs, when we were in Jude's room watching a video. The stairs were too much for her, rarely she came upstairs to check on Jude. There was an actual elevator in the house (we had seen it) but Jude said she'd fucked it up, fooling with it so much when she was a little kid. Just some friends from school, Denise and Anita, Jude called back. You've met them.

Those times Mrs. Trahern saw us downstairs with Jude she would ask politely how we were and her snail-mouth would stretch in a grudging little smile but already she wasn't listening to anything we said, and she would never remember our names.

101 Dalmatians Jude played, one of her old videos she'd long outgrown. (Jude had a thousand videos she'd outgrown!) It was a young-kids' movie we had all seen but the Corn Maiden had never seen. Sitting cross-legged on the floor in front of the TV eating ice cream from a bowl in her lap and we finished ours and waited for her and Jude asked would she like a little more and the Corn Maidden hesitated just a moment then said *Yes thank you*.

We all had more Haagen Dazs French Vanilla ice cream. But it was not the same ice cream the Corn Maiden had not exactly!

Her eyes shining, so happy. Because we were her friends.

A sixth grader, friends with eighth graders. A guest in Jude Trahern's house.

Jude had been nice to her at school for a long time. Smiling, saying hello. Jude had a way of fixing you with her eyes like a cobra or something you could not look away. You were scared but sort of thrilled, too.

In the 7-Eleven she'd come inside to get a Coke and a package of nachos. She was on her way home from school and had no idea that two of us had followed her and one had run ahead, to wait. She was smiling to see Jude who was so friendly. Jude asked where was her mom and she said her mom was a nurse's aide across the river in Nyack and would not be home till after dark.

She laughed saying her mom didn't like her eating junk food but her mom didn't know.

Jude said what our moms don't know don't hurt them.

The Sacrifice of the Corn Maiden was a ritual of the Onigara Indians, Jude told us. In school we had studied Native Americans as they are called but we had not studied the Onigara Indians, Jude said had been extinct for two hundred years. The Iroquois had wiped out the Onigaras, it was survival of the fittest.

The Corn Maiden would be our secret. Beforehand we seemed to know it would be the most precious of our secrets.

Jude and the Corn Maiden walked ahead alone. Denise and Anita behind. Back of the stores, past the Dumpsters, we ran to catch up.

Jude asked would the Corn Maiden like to visit her house and the Corn Maiden said yes but she could not stay long. Jude said it was just a short walk. Jude pretended not to know where the Corn Maiden lived (but she knew: crummy apartments at 15th Street and Van Buren) and this was a ten-minute walk, approximately.

We climbed the back way. Nobody saw. Old Mrs. Trahern would be watching TV in her room, and would not see.

If she saw she would not seriously *see*. For at a distance her eyes were too weak.

The guest wing was a newer part of the house. It overlooked a swimming pool. But the pool was covered with a tarpaulin, Jude said nobody had swum in it for years. She could remember wading in the shallow end but it was long ago like the memory belonged to someone else.

The guest wing was never used either, Jude said. Most of the house was never used. She and her grandmother lived in just a few rooms and that was fine with them. Sometimes Mrs. Trahern would not leave the house for weeks. She was angry about something that had happened at church. Or maybe the minister had said something she found offensive. She had had to dismiss the black man who'd driven her "limo-zene." She had dismissed the black woman who'd been her cook and house cleaner for twenty years. Groceries were delivered to the house. Meals were mostly heat up in the microwave. Mrs. Trahern saw a few of her old friends in town, at the Village Woman's Club, the Hudson Valley Friends of History, and the Skatskill Garden Club. Her friends were not invited to the house to see her.

Do you love your mom? Jude asked the Corn Maiden.

The Corn Maiden nodded yes. Sort of embarrassed.

Your mom is real pretty. She's a nurse, I guess?

The Corn Maiden nodded yes. You could see she was proud of her mom but shy to speak of her.

Where is your dad? Jude asked.

The Corn Maiden frowned. She did not know.

Is your dad living?

Did not know.

When did you see your dad last?

Was not sure. She'd been so little . . .

Did he live around here, or where?

California, the Corn Maiden said. Berkeley.

My mom is in California, Jude said. Los Angeles.

The Corn Maiden smiled, uncertainly.

Maybe your dad is with my dad now, Jude said.

The Corn Maiden looked at Jude in wonderment.

In Hell, Jude said.

Jude laughed. That way she had, her teeth glistening.

Denise and Anita laughed. The Corn Maiden smiled not know-ing whether to laugh. Slower and slower the spoon was being lifted to her mouth, her eyelids were drooping.

We would carry the Corn Maiden from Jude's room. Along a corridor and through a door into what Jude called the guest wing, where the air was colder, and stale. And down a stairway in the guest wing and into a cellar to the storage room.

The Corn Maiden did not weigh much. Three of us, we weighed so much more.

On the outside of the storage room door, a padlock.

Anita and Denise had to leave by 6 P.M., to return to their houses for supper. So boring!

Jude would remain with the Corn Maiden for much of the night. To *watch over*. A *vigil*. She was excited by the candle flames, the incense-smell. The pupils of her eyes were dilated, she was highhigh on Ecstasy. She would not bind the Corn Maiden's wrists and ankles, she said, until it was necessary.

Jude had a Polaroid camera, she would take pictures of the Corn Maiden sleeping on her bier.

As the Corn Maiden was being missed the next morning we would all be at school as usual. For nobody had seen us, and nobody would think of *us*.

Some pre-vert they'll think of, Jude said. We can help them with that.

Remember, the Corn Maiden has come as our guest, Jude said. It is not *kidnapping*.

The Corn Maiden came to Jude on the Thursday before Palm Sun-day, in April of the year.

BREAKING NEWS

Dial 911 your life is no longer your own.
   Dial 911 you become a beggar.
   Dial 911 you are stripped naked.

She met them at the curb. Distraught mother awaiting police officers in the rain outside Briarcliff Apts., 15th St., South Skatskill, 8:20 P.M. Approaching officers as they emerged from the patrol car pleading, anxious, trying to remain calm but her voice rising, Help me please help my daughter is missing! I came home from work, my daughter isn't here, Marissa is eleven years old, I have no idea where she is, nothing like this has ever happened, please help me find her, I'm afraid that someone has taken my daughter!—Caucasian female, early thirties, blond, bare-headed, strong smell of beer on her breath.

They would question her. They would repeat their questions, and she would repeat her answers. She was calm. She tried to be calm. She began to cry. She began to be angry. She knew her words were being recorded, each word she uttered was a matter of public record. She would face TV cameras, interviewers with microphones out-thrust like sceptors. She would see herself performing clumsily and stumbling over her lines in the genre *missing child/pleading mother*. She would see how skillfully the TV screen leapt from her anxious drawn face and bloodshot eyes to the smiling innocent wide-eyed Marissa, sweet-faced Marissa with gleaming blond hair, eleven years old, sixth grader, the camera lingered upon each of three photos of Marissa provided by her mother; then, as the distraught mother continued to speak, you saw the bland sandstone facade of the "private"—"exclusive"—Skatskill Day School and next you were looking at the sinister nighttime traffic of 15th Street, South Skatskill along which, as a neutral-sounding woman's voice explained, eleven-year-old Marissa Branty normally walked home to let herself into an empty apartment and begin to prepare supper for her mother (who worked at a Nyack medical clinic, would not be home until 8 P.M.) and herself; then you were looking at the exterior, rear of Briarcliff Apts. squat and ugly as an army barracks in the rain, where a few hardy residents stood curious staring at police officers and camera crews; then you saw again the mother of the missing girl Leah Bantry, thirty-four, obviously a negligent mother, a sick-with-guilt mother publicly pleading If anyone has seen my daughter, if anyone has any idea what might have happened to Marissa . . .

Next news item, tractor-trailer overturned on the New Jersey Turnpike, pile-up involving eleven vehicles, two drivers killed, eight taken by ambulance to Newark hospital.

So ashamed! But I only want Marissa back.

It was BREAKING NEWS! which means exciting news and by 10 P.M. of that Thursday in April each of four local TV stations was carrying the *missing Marissa* story, and would carry it at regular intervals for as long as there were developments and as long as local interest remained high. But really it was not "new" news, everyone had seen it before. All that could be "new" were the specific players and certain details to be revealed in time, with the teasing punctuality of a suspense film.

It was a good thing, the distraught mother gathered, that cases of missing/abducted children were relatively rare in the affluent Hudson Valley suburbs north of New York City, as crimes of violence in these communities were rare. This meant dramatically focused police attention, cooperation with neighboring police departments in Tarrytown, Sleepy Hollow, Irvington. This meant dramatically focused media coverage, replication of Marissa Banty's likeness, public concern and participation in the search. *Outpouring of sympathy*, it would be called. *Community involvement.* You would not find such a response in a high-crime area, Leah was told.

"Something to be grateful for. Thank you!"

She wasn't speaking ironically. Tears shone in her bloodshot eyes, she wanted only to be believed.

It was in the distraught mother's favor, too, that, if her daughter had been abducted and hadn't simply run away of her own volition, hers would be the first such case in Skatskill's history.

That was remarkable. That was truly a novelty.

"But she didn't run away. Marissa did not run away. I've tried to explain . . ."

Another novelty in the affluent Hudson Valley suburbs was the mysterious/suspicious circumstance of the "considerable" time lapse between the child's probable disappearance after school and the recorded time the mother reported her missing at 8:14 P.M. The most vigilant of the local TV stations was alert to the dramatic possibilities here. *Skatskill police will neither confirm nor deny that the department is said to be considering charging Branty, who has no previous police record, with child endangerment.*

And how it would be leaked to this same TV station, the distraught mother had evidenced signs of "inebriation" when police arrived at her home, no one at the station was in a position to say.

So ashamed! I want to die.
   If I could exchange my life for Marissa's

Hours, days. Though each hour was singular, raw as a stone forced down the throat. And what were days but unchartable and unfathomable durations of time too painful to be borne except as singular hours or even minutes. She was aware of a great wheel turning, and of herself caught in this wheel, helpless, in a state of suspended panic and yet eager to cooperate with the very turning of the wheel, if it might bring Marissa back to her. For she was coming to feel, possibly yes there was a God, a God of mercy and not just justice, and she might barter her life for Marissa's.

Through most of it she remained calm. On the surface, calm. She believed she was calm, she had not become hysterical. She had called her parents in Spokane, Washington, for it could not be avoided. She had called her older sister in Washington, D.C. She had not seemed to hear in their shocked and incredulous voices any evidence of reproach, accusation, disgust; but she understood that that was to come, in time.

I am to blame. I know.
   It doesn't matter about me.

She believed she was being damned calm! Answering their impudent questions and reanswering them and again repeating as in a deranged tape loop the answers that were all she had in the face of their suspicion, their doubt. She answered the officers' questions with the desperation of a drowning woman clutching a rope already fraying to haul herself into a lifeboat already leaking water. She had no idea, she had told them immediately she had no idea where Marissa's father was, for the past seven years there had been no contact between them, she had last seen him in Berkeley, California, thousands of miles away and he had had no interest in Marissa, he had sought no interest in his own daughter, and so truly she did not believe she could not believe that there was any likelihood of that man having abducted Marissa, truly she did not want to involve him, did not wish to seem in the most elliptical way to be accusing him . . . Yet they continued to question her. It was an interrogation, they sensed that she had something to hide, had she? And what was that, and why? Until finally she heard herself say in a broken defeated voice all right, yes I will give you his name and his last-known address and telephone number that was surely inoperative after so long, all right I will tell you: we were never married, his name is not my child's name, he'd pretended even to doubt that Marissa was his child, we had only lived together, he had no interest in marriage, are you satisfied now?

Her shame, she'd never told her parents. Never told her sister.

Now they would know Leah's pathetic secret. It would be another shock, a small one set beside the other. It would cause them to think less of her, and to know that she was a liar. And now she must telephone to tell them before they discovered it in the media. *I lied to you, I was never married to Andrew. There was no marriage, and there was no divorce.*

Next, they needed to know exactly where she'd been after she had left the Nyack clinic at 6:30 P.M. of the day her daughter had disappeared. Now they knew she was a liar, and a desperate woman, now they had scented blood. They would track the wounded creature to its lair.

At first Leah had been vague about time. In the shock of her daughter missing, it had been natural for the mother to be vague, confused, uncertain about time.

She'd told them that she had been stuck in traffic returning home from Nyack. The Tappan Zee Bridge, route 9 and road repair and rain but yes, she had stopped at the 7-Eleven store near her apartment to buy a few things as she often did . . .

And was that all, had that been her only stop?

Yes. Her only stop. The 7-Eleven. The clerk at the cash register would recognize her.

This was a question, a probing, that had to do with Leah Bantry's male friends. If she had any, who would have known Marissa. Who would have met Marissa. Who might simply have glimpsed Marissa.

Any male friend of the missing girl's mother who might have been attracted to the girl. Might have "abducted" her.

For Marissa might have willingly climbed into a vehicle, if it was driven by someone she knew. Yes?

Calmly Leah insisted no, no one.

She had no male friends at the present time. No serious involvements.

No one she was "seeing"?

Leah flared up, angry. In the sense of—what? What did "seeing" mean?

She was being adamant, and she was speaking forcibly. Yet her interrogators seemed to know. Especially the female detective seemed to know. An evasiveness in Leah's bloodshot eyes that were the eyes of a sick, guilty mother. A quavering in Leah's voice even as she spoke impatiently, defiantly. I told you! God damn I have told you.

There was a pause. The air in the room was highly charged.

There was a pause. Her interrogators waited.

It was explained to Leah then that she must answer the officers' questions fully and truthfully. This was a police investigation, she would be vulnerable to charges of obstruction of justice if she lied.

If she lied.

A known liar.

An exposed, humiliated liar.

And so, another time, Leah heard her voice break. She heard herself say all right, yes. She had not gone directly to the 7-Eleven store from Nyack, she had stopped first to see a friend and, yes he was a close male friend, separated from his wife and uncertain of his future and he was an intensely private man whose identity she could not reveal for he and Leah were not exactly lovers though, yes they had made love . . .

Just once, they had made love. One time.

On Sunday evening, the previous Sunday evening they had made love.

For the first time they had made love. And it wasn't certain that . . . Leah had no way of knowing whether . . .

She was almost pleading now. Blood seemed to be hemorrhaging into her swollen face.

The police officers waited. She was wiping at her eyes with a wadded tissue. There was no way out of this was there! Somehow she had known, with the sickening sensation of a doomed cow entering a slaughter chute, she had known that a part of her life would be over, when she'd dialed 911.

Your punishment, for losing your daughter.

Of course, Leah had to provide the police officers with the man's name. She had no choice.

She was sobbing, crushed. Davitt would be furious with her.

Davitt Stoop, M.D. Director of the medical clinic. He was Dr. Stoop, her superior. Her employer. He was a kindly man, yet a short-tempered man. He was not in love with Leah Banty, she knew; nor was Leah in love with him, exactly; and yet, they were relaxed together, they got along so very well together, both were parents of single children of about the same age, both had been hurt and deceived in love, and were wary of new involvements.

Davitt was forty-two, he had been married for eighteen years. He was a responsible husband and father as he had a reputation at the clinic for being an exacting physician and it had been his concern that he and Leah might be seen together prematurely. He did not want his wife to know about Leah, not yet. Still less did he want Leah's coworkers at the clinic to know. He dreaded gossip, innuendo. He dreaded any exposure of his private life.

It was the end, Leah knew.

Before it had begun between them, it would end.

They would humiliate him, these police officers. They would ask him about Leah Bantry and Leah's missing daughter, did he know the child, how well did he know the child, had he ever seen the child without the mother present, had he ever been alone with the child, had he ever given the child a ride in his car for instance this past Thursday?

Possibly they would want to examine the car. Would he allow a search, or would he insist upon a warrant?

Davitt had moved out of his family home in February and lived in an apartment in Nyack, the very apartment Leah Bantry had visited on Thursday evening after her shift. Impulsively she had dropped by. Davitt might have expected her, it hadn't been certain.

They were in the early stages of a romance, excited in each other's presence but uncertain.

This apartment. Had Marissa ever been there?

No! Certainly not.

In a faltering voice telling the officers that Davitt scarcely knew Marissa. Possibly he'd met her, once. But they had spent no time together, certainly not.

Leah had stayed in Davitt's apartment approximately a half hour. Possibly, forty minutes.

No. They had not had sex.

Not exactly.

They had each had a drink. They had been affectionate, they had talked.

Earnestly, seriously they had talked! About the clinic, and about their children. About Davitt's marriage, and Leah's own.

(It would be revealed, Leah had led Davitt Stoop to believe she had been married, and divorced. It had seemed such a trivial and inconsequential lie at the time.)

Leah was saying, stammering, Davitt would never do such a thing! Not to Marissa, not to any child. He was the father of a ten-year-old boy, himself. He was not the type . . .

The female detective asked bluntly what did Leah mean, "type"? Was this a "type" she believed she could recognize?

Davitt forgive me! I had no choice.

I could not lie to police. I had to tell them about you. I am so very sorry, Davitt, you can understand can't you I must help them find Marissa I had no choice.

Still, Marissa remained missing.

"People who do things like this, take children, they're not rational. What they do, they do for their own purposes. We can only track them. We can try to stop them. We can't understand them."

And, "When something like this happens, it's natural for people to want to cast blame. You'd be better off not watching TV or reading the papers right now, Miss Bantry."

One of the Skatskill detectives spoke so frankly to her, she could not believe he too might be judging her harshly.

There were myriad calls, e-mail messages. Blond-haired Marissa Bantry had been sighted in a car exiting the New York Thruway at Albany. She had been sighted in the company of "hippie-type males" on West Houston Street, New York City. A Skatskill resident would recall, days after the fact, having seen "that pretty little pig-tailed blond girl" getting into a battered-looking van driven by a Hispanic male in the parking lot of the 7-Eleven store a few blocks from her home.

Still, Marissa remained missing.

... hours in rapid succession jarring and discontinuous as a broken film projected upon a flimsy screen she would not sleep for more than two or three hours even with sedatives and she slept without dreaming like one who has been struck on the head with a mallet and she woke hollow-headed and parch-mouthed and her heart beating in her chest like something with a broken wing.

Always as she woke in that split-second before awareness rushed upon her like a mouthful of filthy water *My daughter is gone, Marissa is lost* there was a sense of grace, a confusion in time like a prayer *It has not happened yet has it? Whatever it will be.*

HAVE YOU SEEN ME?

Like a sudden bloom of daffodils there appeared overnight, everywhere in Skatskill, the smiling likeness of MARISSA BANTRY, 11.

In store windows. On public bulletin boards, telephone poles. Prominent in the foyers of the Skatskill Post Office, the Skatskill Food Mart, the Skatskill Public Library. Prominent though already dampening in April rain, on the fences of construction sites.

MISSING SINCE APRIL 10. SKATSKILL DAY SCHOOL/15TH ST. AREA.

Hurriedly established by the Skatskill police department was a

MARISSA Web site posting more photos of the missing blond girl, a detailed description of her, background information. ANYONE KNOWING ANYTHING ABOUT MARISSA BANTRY PLEASE CONTACT SKATSKILL POLICE AT THIS NUMBER.

Initially, no reward was posted. By Friday evening, an anonymous donor (prominent Skatskill philanthropist, retired) had come forward to offer fifteen thousand dollars.

It was reported by the media that Skatskill police were working *round the clock*. They were *under intense pressure*, they were investigating *all possible leads*. It was reported that *known pedophiles, sex offenders, child molesters* in the area were being questioned. (Information about such individuals was confidential of course. Still, the most vigilant of area tabloids learned from an anonymous source that a sixty-year-old Skatskill resident, a retired music teacher with a sexual misdemeanor record dating back to 1987, had been visited by detectives. Since this individual refused to speak with a reporter, or consent to be photographed, the tabloid published a photograph of his front door at 12 Amwell Circle on its cover, beneath the strident headline LOCAL SEX OFFENDER QUERIED BY COPS: WHERE IS MARISSA?)

Each resident of Briarcliff Apts. was questioned, some more than once. Though no search warrants had been issued, several residents cooperated with police allowing both their apartments and their motor vehicles to be searched.

Storekeepers in the area of the Skatskill Day School and along Marissa Bantry's route home were questioned. At the 7-Eleven store in the mini-mall on the highway, so often frequented by young people, several clerks examined photographs of the missing girl, solemnly shook their heads and told police officers no, they did not believe that Marissa Bantry had been in the store recently, or ever. "There are so many children . . ." Questioned about Leah Bantry, whose photograph they were also shown, the eldest clerk said, carefully, that yes, he recognized this woman, she was a friendly woman; friendlier than most of his customers; but he could not say with certainty if she had been in his store on Thursday, with or without her daughter. "There are so many customers. And so many of them, they look like one another especially if they are blond."

Detectives queried teenagers, most of them from Skatskill High, and some no longer in school, who hung out at the mini-mall. Most of them stiffened at the approach of police officers and hurriedly shook their heads no, they had not seen the little blond girl who was missing, or anyway could not remember seeing her. A striking girl with electric blue hair and a glittering pin in her left eyebrow frowned at the photo and said finally yeah she'd maybe seen Marissa "like with her mother? But when, like maybe it wasn't yesterday because I don't think I was here yesterday, might've been last week? I don't know."

Skatskill Day School was in a stage of siege. TV crews on the front walk, reporters and press photographers at all the entrances. Crisis counsellors met with children in small groups through the day following Marissa's disappearance and there was an air in all the classrooms of shock, as if in the wake of a single violent tremor of the earth. A number of parents had kept their children home from school, but this was not advised by school authorities: "There is no risk at Skatskill Day. Whatever happened to Marissa did not happen on school grounds, and would never have happened on school grounds." It was announced that school security had been immediately strengthened, and new security measures would be begun on Monday. In Marissa Bantry's sixth grade class children were subdued, uneasy. After the counsellor spoke, and asked if anyone had a question, the class sat silent until a boy raised his hand to ask if there would be a search party "like on TV, people going through woods and fields until they find the body?"

Not after a counsellor spoke with eighth graders, but later in the day, an eighth-grade girl named Anita Helder came forward hesitantly to speak with her teacher. Anita was a heavyset girl with a low C average who rarely spoke in class, and often asked to be excused for mysterious health reasons. She was a suspected drug-taker, but had never been caught. In class, she exuded a sulky, defiant manner if called upon by her teacher. Yet now she was saying, in an anxious, faltering voice, that maybe she had seen Marissa Bantry the previous day, on 15h Street and Trinity, climbing into a minivan after school.

". . . I didn't know it was her then for sure, I don't know Marissa Bantry at all but I guess now it must've been her. Oh God I feel so bad I didn't try to stop her! I was like close enough to call out to her, 'Don't get in!' What I could see, the driver was leaning over and sort of pulling Marissa inside. It was a man, he had real dark hair kind of long on the sides but I couldn't see his face. The minivan was like silver-blue, the license plate was something like TZ 6 . . . Beyond that, I can't remember."

Anita's eyes welled with tears. She was visibly trembling, the memory so upset her.

By this time Skatskill detectives had questioned everyone on the school staff except for Mikal Zallman, thirty-one years old, computer consultant and part-time employee, who wasn't at the Skatskill Day School on Fridays.

FEEDING MY RAT

It was an ugly expression. It was macho-ugly, the worst kind of ugly. It made him smile.

Feeding my rat. Alone.

IN CUSTODY

Alone he'd driven out of Skatskill on Thursday afternoon immediately following his final class of the week. Alone driving north in his trim Honda minivan along the Hudson River where the river landscape so mesmerizes the eye, you wonder why you'd ever given a damn for all that's petty, inconsequential. Wondering why you'd ever given a damn for the power of others to hurt you. Or to accuse you with tearful eyes of hurting them.

He'd tossed a valise, his backpack, a few books, hiking boots and a supply of trail food into the back of the van. Always he traveled light. As soon as he left Skatskill he ceased to think of his life there. It was of little consequence really, a professional life arranged to provide him with this freedom. *Feeding my rat.*

There was a woman in Skatskill, a married woman. He knew the signs. She was lonely in her marriage and yearning to be saved from her loneliness. Often she invited him as if impulsively, without premeditation. *Come to dinner, Mikal? Tonight?* He had been vague about accepting, this time. He had not wanted to see the disappointment in her eyes. He felt a tug of affection for her, he recognized her hurt, her resentment, her confusion, she was a colleague of his at the Skatskill School whom he saw often in the company of others, there was a rapport between them, Zallman acknowledged, but he did not want to be involved with her or with any woman, not now. He was thirty-one, and no longer naive. More and more he lived for *feeding my rat*.

It was arrogant, was it, this attitude? Selfish. He'd been told so, more than once. Living so much in his own head, and for himself.

He hadn't married, he doubted he would ever marry. The prospect of children made his heart sink: bringing new lives into the uncertainty and misery of this world, in the early twenty-first century!

He much preferred his secret life. It was an innocent life. Running each morning, along the river. Hiking, mountain climbing. He did not hunt or fish, he had no need to destroy life to enhance his own. Mostly it was exulting in his body. He was only a moderately capable hiker. He hadn't the endurance or the will to run a marathon. He wasn't so fanatic, he wanted merely to be alone where he could exert his body pleasurably. Or maybe to the edge of pain.

One summer in his mid-twenties he'd gone backpacking alone in Portugal, Spain, northern Morocco. In Tangier he'd experimented with the hallucinatory *kif* which was the most extreme form of aloneness and the experience had shaken and exhilarated him and brought him back home to reinvent himself. Michael, now Mikal.

Feeding my rat meant this freedom. Meant he'd failed to drop by her house as she had halfway expected he would. And he had not telephoned, either. It was a way of allowing the woman to know he didn't want to be involved, he would not be involved. In turn, she and her her husband would not provide Mikal Zallman with an alibi for those crucial hours.

When, at 5:18 P.M. of Friday, April 11, returning to his car along a steep hiking trail, he happening to see what appeared to be a New York State troopers' vehicle in the parking lot ahead, he had no reason to think *They've come for me.* Even when he saw that two uniformed officers were looking into the rear windows of his minivan, the lone vehicle in the lot parked near the foot of the trail, because it had been the first vehicle of the day parked in the lot, the sight did not alarm or alert him. So confident in himself he felt, and so guiltless.

"Hey. What d'you want?"

Naively, almost conversationally he called to the troopers, who were now staring at him, and moving toward him.

Afterward he would recall how swiftly and unerringly the men moved. One called out, "Are you Mikal Zallman" and the other called, sharply, before Zallman could reply, "Keep your hands where we can see them, sir."

Hands? What about his hands? What were they saying about his hands?

He'd been sweating inside his T-shirt and khaki shorts and his hair was sticking against the nape of his neck. He'd slipped and fallen on the trail once, his left knee was scraped, throbbing. He was not so exuberant as he'd been in the fresh clear air of morning. He held his hands before him, palms uplifted in a gesture of annoyed supplication.

What did these men want with *him*? It had to be a mistake.

. . . staring into the back of the minivan. He'd consented to a quick search. Trunk, interior. Glove compartment. What the hell, he had nothing to hide. Were they looking for drugs? A concealed weapon? He saw the way in which they were staring at two paperback books he'd tossed onto the rear window ledge weeks ago, Roth's The Dying Animal *and Ovid's* The Art of Love. *On the cover of the first was a sensuously reclining Modligliani nude in rich flesh tones, with prominent pink-nippled breasts. On the cover of the other was a classical nude, marmoreal white female with a full, shapely body and blank, blind eyes.*

TABOO

It was Taboo to utter aloud the Corn Maiden's name.

It was Taboo to touch the Corn Maiden except as Jude guided.

For Jude was the Priest of the Sacrifice. No one else.

What does Taboo mean, it means death. If you disobey.

––––––––

Jude took Polaroid pictures of the Corn Maiden sleeping on her bier. Arms crossed on her flat narrow chest, cornsilk hair spread like pale flames around her head. Some pictures, Jude was beside the Corn Maiden. We took pictures of her smiling, and her eyes shiny and dilated.

For posterity, Jude said. For the record.

It was Taboo to utter the Corn Maiden's actual name aloud and yet: everywhere in Skatskill that name was being spoken! And everywhere in Skatskill her face was posted!

Missing Girl. Abduction Feared. State of Emergency.

It is so easy, Jude said. To make the truth your own.

But Jude was surprised too, we thought. That it was so real, what had only been for so long Jude O's *idea*.

Ju*dith*!

Mrs. Trahern called in her whiny old-woman voice, we had to troop into her smelly bedroom where she was propped up in some big old antique brass bed like a nutty queen watching TV where footage of the *missing Skatskill Day girl* was being shown. Chiding, You girls! Look what has happened to one of your little classmates! Did you know this poor child?

Jude mumbled no Grandma.

Well. You would not be in a class with a retarded child, I suppose.

Jude mumbled no Grandma.

Well. See that you never speak with strangers, Judith! Report anyone who behaves strangely with you, or is seen lurking around the neighborhood. Promise me!

Jude mumbled okay. Grandma, I promise.

Denise and Anita mumbled Me, too, Mrs. Trahern. For it seemed to be expected.

Next, Mrs. Trahern made Jude come to her bed, to take Jude's hands in her clawy old-woman hands. I have not always been a good grandma, I know. As the judge's widow there are so many demands on my time. But I am your grandma, Judith. I am your only blood kin who cares for you, dear. You know that, I hope?

Jude mumbled Yes Grandma, I know.

THE WORLD AS WE HAVE KNOWN IT

Has vanished.

We are among the few known survivors.

. . . terrorist attack. Nuclear war. Fires.

New York City is a gaping hole. The George Washington Bridge is crashed into the river. Washington, D.C., is gone.

So the Corn Maiden was told. So the Corn Maiden believed in her Rapture.

Many times we said these words. Jude had made us memorize. The world as we have known it has vanished. There is no TV now. No newspapers. No electricity. We are among the few known survivors. We must be brave, everyone else is gone. All the adults are gone. All our mothers.

The Corn Maiden opened her mouth to shriek but she had not the strength. Her eyes welled with tears, lapsing out of focus.

All our mothers. So exciting!

Only candles to be lighted, solemnly. To keep away the night.

The Corn Maiden was informed that we had to ration our food supplies. For there were no stores now, all of Skatskill was gone. The Food Mart was gone. Main Street was gone. The Mall.

Jude knew, to maintain the Rapture the Corn Maiden must be fed very little. For Jude did not wish to bind her wrists and ankles, that were so fragile-seeming. Jude did not wish to gag her, to terrify her. For then the Corn Maiden would fear us and not trust and adore us as her protectors.

The Corn Maiden must be treated with reverence, respect, kindness, and firmness. She must never guess the fate that will be hers.

The Corn Maiden's diet was mostly liquids. Water, transparent fruit juices like apple, grapefruit. And milk.

It was Taboo Jude said for the Corn Maiden to ingest any foods except white foods. And any foods containing bones or skins.

These foods were soft, crumbly or melted foods. Cottage cheese, plain yogurt, ice cream. The Corn Maiden was not a retarded child as some of the TV stations were saying but she was not shrewd-witted, Jude said. For these foods we fed her were refrigerated, and she did not seem to know.

Of course, finely ground in these foods were powdery-white tranquilizers, to maintain the Rapture.

The Corn Maiden of the Onigara Sacrifice was to pass into the next world in a Rapture. Not in fear.

We took turns spooning small portions of food into the Corn Maiden's mouth that sucked like an infant's to be fed. So hungry, the Corn Maiden whimpered for more. No, no! There is no more she was told.

(How hungry we were, after these feedings! Denise and Anita went home to stuffstuff their faces.)

Jude did not want the Corn Maiden to excrete solid waste she said. Her bowels must be clean and pure for the Sacrifice. Also we had to take her outside the storage room for this, half-carrying her to a bathroom in a corner of the cobwebby cellar that was a "recreation room" of some bygone time Jude said the 1970s that is ancient history now.

Only two times did we have to take the Corn Maiden to this bathroom, half-carried out, groggy and stumbling and her head lolling on her shoulders. All other times the Corn Maiden used the pot Jude had brought in from one of the abandoned greenhouses. A fancy Mexican ceramic pot, for the Corn Maiden to squat over, as we held her like a clumsy infant.

The Corn Maiden's pee! It was hot, bubbly. It had a sharp smell different from our own.

Like a big infant the Corn Maiden was becoming, weak and trusting all her bones. Even her crying when she cried saying she wanted to go home, she wanted her mommy, where was her mommy she wanted her mommy was an infant's crying, with no strength or anger behind it.

Jude said all our mommies are gone, we must be brave without them. She would be safe with us Jude said stroking her hair. See, we would protect her better than her mommy had protected her.

Jude took Polaroid pictures of the Corn Maiden sitting up on her bier her face streaked with tears. The Corn Maiden was chalky

white and the colors of the bier were so rich and silky. The Corn
Maiden was so thin, you could see her collarbone jutting inside the
white muslin nightgown Jude had clothed her in.

We did not doubt Jude. What Jude meant to do with the Corn
Maiden we would not resist.

In the Onigara ceremony Jude said the Corn Maiden was slowly
starved and her bowels cleaned out and purified and she was tied on
an altar still living and a priest shot an arrow that had been blessed
into her heart. And the heart was scooped out with a knife that had
been blessed and touched to the lips of the priest and others of the
tribe to bless them. And the heart and the Corn Maiden's body were
then carried out into a field and buried in the earth to honor the
Morning Star which is the sun and the Evening Star which is the
moon and beg of them their blessing for the corn harvest.

Will the Corn Maiden be killed we wished to know but we could
not ask Jude for Jude would be angered.

To ourselves we said Jude will kill the Corn Maiden, maybe! We
shivered to think so. Denise smiled, and bit at her thumbnail, for she
was jealous of the Corn Maiden. Not because the Corn Maiden had
such beautiful silky hair but because Jude fussed over the Corn
Maiden so, as Jude would not have fussed over Denise.

The Corn Maiden wept when we left her. When we blew out the
candles and left her in darkness. We had to patrol the house we said.
We had to look for fires and "gas leakage" we said. For the world as
we have known it has come to an end, there were no adults now. We
were the adults now.

We were our own mommies.

Jude shut the door, and padlocked it. The Corn Maiden's muffled sobs from inside. *Mommy! Mommy!* the Corn Maiden wept but
there was no one to hear and even on the steps to the first floor you
could no longer hear.

OUT THERE

HATEHATEHATE you assholes Out There. The Corn Maiden
was Jude O's perfect revenge.

At Skatskill Day we saw our hatred like scalding-hot lava rushing through the corridors and into the classrooms and cafeteria to burn our enemies alive. Even girls who were okay to us mostly would perish for they would rank us below the rest, wayway below the Hot Shit Cliques that ran the school and also the boys—all the boys. And the teachers, some of them had pissed us off and deserved death. Jude said Mr. Z. had "dissed" her and was the "target enemy" now.

Sometimes the vision was so fierce it was a rush better than E!

Out There it was believed that the *missing Skatskill girl* might have been kidnapped. A ransom note was awaited.

Or, it was believed the *missing girl* was the victim of a "sexual predator."

On TV came Leah Bantry, the mother, to appeal to whoever had taken her daughter saying, Please don't hurt Marissa, please release my daughter I love her so, begging please in a hoarse voice that sounded like she'd been crying a lot and her eyes haggard with begging so Jude stared at the woman with scorn.

Not so hot-shit now, are you Mrs. Brat-tee! Not so pretty-pretty.

It was surprising to Denise and Anita, that Jude hated Leah Bantry so. We felt sorry for the woman, kind of. Made us think how our mothers would be, if we were gone, though we hated our mothers we were thinking they'd probably miss us, and be crying, too. It was a new way of seeing our moms. But Jude did not have a mom even to hate. Never spoke of her except to say she was Out West in L.A. We wanted to think that Jude's mom was a movie star under some different name, that was why she'd left Jude with Mrs. Trahern to pursue a film career. But we would never say this to Jude, for sure.

Sometimes Jude scared us. Like she'd maybe hurt *us*.

Wild! On Friday 7 P.M. news came BULLETIN—BREAKING NEWS—SKATSKILL SUSPECT IN CUSTODY. It was Mr. Zallman!

We shrieked with laughter. Had to press our hands over our mouths so old Mrs. Trahern would not hear.

Jude is flicking through the channels and there suddenly is Mr.

Z. on TV! And some broadcaster saying in an excited voice that this man had been apprehended in Bear Mountain State Park and brought back to Skatskill to be questioned in the disappearance of Marissa Bantry and the shocker is: Mikal Zallman, thirty-one, is on the faculty of the Skatskill Day School.

Mr. Zallman's jaws were scruffy like he had not shaved in a while. His eyes were scared and guilty-seeming. He was wearing a T-shirt and khaki shorts like we would never see him at school and this was funny, too. Between two plainclothes detectives being led up the steps into police headquarters and at the top they must've jerked him under the arms, he almost turned his ankle.

We were laughing like hyenas. Jude crouched in front of the TV rocking back and forth, staring.

"Zallman claims to know nothing of Marissa Bantry. Police and rescue workers are searching the Bear Mountain area and will search through the night if necessary."

There was a cut to our school again, and 15th Street traffic at night. ". . . unidentified witness, believed to be a classmate of Marissa Bantry, has told authorities that she witnessed Marissa being pulled into a Honda CR-V at this corner, Thursday after school. This vehicle has been tentatively identified as . . ."

Unidentified witness. That's me! Anita cried.

And a second "student witness" had come forward to tell the school principal that she had seen "the suspect Zallman" fondling Marissa Bantry, stroking her hair and whispering to her in the computer lab when he thought no one was around, only last week.

That's *me*! Denise cried.

And police had found a mother-of-pearl butterfly barrette on the ground near Zallman's parking space, behind his condominium residence. This barrette had been "absolutely identified" by Marissa Bantry's mother as a barrette Marissa had been wearing on Thursday.

We turned to Jude who was grinning.

We had not known that Jude had planned *this*. On her bicycle she must've gone, to drop the barrette where it would be found.

We laughed so, we almost wet ourselves. Jude was just so *cool*.

But even Jude seemed surprised, kind of. That you could make the wildest truth your own and every asshole would rush to believe.

DESPERATE

Now she knew his name: *Mikal Zallman*.

The man who'd taken Marissa. One of Marissa's teachers at the Skatskill Day School.

It was a nightmare. All that Leah Bantry had done, what exertion of heart and soul, to enroll her daughter in a private school in which a pedophile was allowed to instruct elementary school children.

She had met Zallman, she believed. At one of the parents' evenings. Something seemed wrong, though: Zallman was young. You don't expect a young man to be a pedophile. An attractive man though with a hawkish profile, and not very warm. Not with Leah. Not that she could remember.

The detectives had shown her Zallman's photograph. They had not allowed her to speak with Zallman. Vaguely yes she did remember. But not what he'd said to her, if he had said anything. Very likely Leah has asked him about Marissa but what he'd said she could not recall.

And then, hadn't Zallman slipped away from the reception, early? By chance she'd seen him, the only male faculty member not to be wearing a necktie, hair straggling over his collar, disappearing from the noisy brightly lighted room.

He'd taken a polygraph, at his own request. The results were "inconclusive."

If I could speak with him. Please.

They were telling her no, Mrs. Bantry. Not a good idea.

This man who took Marissa if I could speak with him *please*.

In her waking state she pleaded. She would beg the detectives, she would throw herself on their mercy. Her entire conscious life was now begging, pleading, and bartering. And waiting.

Zallman is the one, isn't he? You have him, don't you? An eyewitness said she saw him. Saw him pull Marissa into a van with him. In broad daylight! And you found Marissa's barrette by his parking space *isn't that proof*!

To her, the desperate mother, it was certainly proof. The man had taken Marissa, he knew where Marissa was. The truth had to be wrung from him before it was too late.

On her knees she would beg to see Zallman promising not to become emotional and they told her no, for she would only become emotional in the man's presence. And Zallman, who had a lawyer now, would only become more adamant in his denial.

Denial! How could he . . . deny! He had taken Marissa, he knew where Marissa was.

She would beg *him*. She would show Zallman pictures of Marissa as a baby. She would plead with this man for her daughter's life if only if only if only for God's sake they would allow her.

Of course, it was impossible. The suspect was being questioned following a procedure, a strategy, to which Leah Bantry had no access. The detectives were professionals, Leah Bantry was an amateur. She was only the mother, an amateur.

The wheel, turning.

It was a very long Friday. The longest Friday of Leah's life.

Then abruptly it was Friday night, and then it was Saturday morning. And Marissa was still gone.

Zallman had been captured, yet Marissa was still gone.

He might have been tortured, in another time. To make him confess. The vicious pedophile, whose "legal rights" had to be honored.

Leah's heart beat in fury. Yet she was powerless, she could not intervene.

Saturday afternoon: approaching the time when Marissa would be missing for forty-eight hours.

Forty-eight hours! It did not seem possible.

She has drowned by now, Leah thought. She has suffocated for lack of oxygen.

She is starving. She has bled to death. Wild creatures on Bear Mountain have mutilated her small body.

She calculated: it would soon be fifty hours since Leah had last seen Marissa. Kissed her hurriedly good-bye in the car, in front of the school Thursday morning at eight. And (she forced herself to re-

member, she would not escape remembering) Leah hadn't troubled
to watch her daughter run up the walk, and into the school. Pale gold
hair shimmering behind her and just possibly (possibly!) at the door,
Marissa had turned to wave goodbye to Mommy but Leah was already driving away.

And so, she'd had her opportunity. She would confess to her sister Avril *I let Marissa slip away.*

The great wheel, turning. And the wheel was Time itself, without
pity.

She saw that now. In her state of heightened awareness bred of terror she saw. She had ceased to give a damn about "Leah Bantry" in the
public eye. The distraught/negligent mother. Working mom, single
mom, mom-with-a-drinking-problem. She'd been exposed as a liar.
She'd been exposed as a female avid to sleep with another woman's
husband and that husband her boss. She knew, the very police who
were searching for Marissa's abductor were investigating her, too.
Crude tabloids, TV journalism. Under a guise of sympathy, pity for her
"plight."

None of this mattered, now. What the jackals said of her, and
would say. She was bartering her life for Marissa's. Appealing to God
in whom she was trying in desperation to believe. *If You would. Let
Marissa be alive. Return Marissa to me. If You would hear my plea.* So
there was no room to give a damn about herself, she had no scruples
now, no shame. Yes she would consent to be interviewed on the cru-
elest and crudest of the New York City TV stations if that might help
Marissa, somehow. Blinking into the blinding TV lights, baring her
teeth in a ghastly nervous smile.

Never would she care again for the pieties of ordinary life. When
on the phone her own mother began crying, asking why, why on
earth had Leah left Marissa alone for so many hours, Leah had interrupted the older woman coldly, "That doesn't matter now, Mother.
Good-bye."

Neither of the elder Bantrys was in good health, they would not fly
east to share their daughter's vigil. But Leah's older sister Avril flew
up immediately from Washington to stay with her.

For years the sisters had not been close. There was a subtle rivalry between them, in which Leah had always felt belittled.

Avril, an investment attorney, was brisk and efficient answering the telephone, screening all e-mail. Avril checked the *Marissa* Web site constantly. Avril was on frank terms with the senior Skatskill detective working the case, who spoke circumspectly and with great awkwardness to Leah.

Avril called Leah to come listen to a voice-mail message that had come in while they'd been at police headquarters. Leah had told Avril about Davitt Stoop, to a degree.

It was Davitt, finally calling Leah. In a slow stilted voice that was not the warm intimate voice Leah knew he was saying *A terrible thing . . . This is a . . . terrible thing, Leah. We can only pray this madman is caught and that . . .* A long pause. You would have thought that Dr. Stoop had hung up but then he continued, more forcibly, *I'm sorry for this terrible thing but Leah please don't try to contact me again. Giving my name to the police! The past twenty-four hours have been devastating for me. Our relationship was a mistake and it can't be continued, I am sure you understand. As for your position at the clinic I am sure you understand the awkwardness among all the staff if . . .*

Leah's heart beat in fury, she punched *erase* to extinguish the man's voice. Grateful that Avril, who'd tactfully left the room, could be relied upon not to ask about Davitt Stoop, nor even to offer sisterly solicitude.

Take everything from me. If You will leave me Marissa, the way we were.

EMISSARIES

"Mommy!"

It was Marissa's voice, but muffled, at a distance.

Marissa was trapped on the far side of a barrier of thick glass, Leah heard her desperate cries only faintly. Marissa was pounding the glass with her fists, smearing her damp face against it. But the glass was too thick to be broken. "Mommy! Help me, Mommy . . ." And Leah could not move to help the child, Leah was paralyzed. Something gripped her legs, quicksand, tangled ropes. If she could break free . . .

Avril woke her, abruptly. There was someone to see her, friends of Marissa's they said they were.

"H-Hello, Mrs. Branty . . . Bant*ry*. My name is . . ."

Three girls. Three girls from Skatskill Day. One of them, with faded-rust-red hair and glistening stone-colored eyes, was holding out to Leah an astonishing large bouquet of dazzling white flowers: long-stemmed roses, carnations, paperwhites, mums. The sharp astringent fragrance of the paperwhites prevailed.

The bouquet must have been expensive, Leah thought. She took it from the girl and tried to smile. "Why, thank you."

It was Sunday, midday. She'd sunk into a stupor after twenty hours of wakefulness. Seeing it was a warm, incongruously brightly sunny April day beyond the partly-drawn blinds on the apartment windows.

She would have to focus on these girls. She'd been expecting, from what Avril had said, younger children, Marissa's age. But these were adolescents. Thirteen, fourteen. In eighth grade, they'd said. Friends of Marissa's?

The visit would not last long. Avril, disapproving, hovered near.

Possibly Leah had invited them, the girls were seated in her living room. They were clearly excited, edgy. They glanced about like nervous birds. Leah supposed she should offer them Cokes but something in her resisted. Hurriedly she'd washed her face, dragged a comb through her snarled hair that no longer looked blond, but dust-colored. How were these girls Marissa's friends? Leah had never seen them before in her life.

Nor did their names mean anything to her. "Jude Trahern," "Denise . . ." The third name she'd failed to catch.

The girls were moist-eyed with emotion. So many neighbors had dropped by to express their concern, Leah supposed she had to endure it. The girl who'd given Leah the bouquet, Jude, was saying in a faltering nasal voice how sorry they were for what had happened to Marissa and how much they liked Marissa who was just about the nicest girl at Skatskill Day. If something like this had to happen too bad it couldn't happen to—well, somebody else.

The other girls giggled, startled at their friend's vehemence.

"But Marissa is so nice, and so sweet. Ma'am, we are praying for her safe return, every minute."

Leah stared at the girl. She had no idea how to reply.

Confused, she lifted the bouquet to her face. Inhaled the almost too rich paperwhite smell. As if the purpose of this visit was to bring Leah . . . What?

The girls were staring at her almost rudely. Of course, they were young, they knew no better. Their leader, Jude, seemed to be a girl with some confidence, though she wasn't the eldest or the tallest or the most attractive of the three.

Not attractive at all. Her face was fiercely plain as if she'd scrubbed it with steel wool. Her skin was chalky, mottled. You could sense the energy thrumming through her like an electric current, she was wound up so tightly.

The other girls were more ordinary. One was softly plump with a fattish pug face, almost pretty except for something smirky, insolent in her manner. The other girl had a sallow blemished skin, limp grease-colored hair and oddly quivering, parted lips. All three girls wore grubby blue jeans, boys' shirts, and ugly square-toed boots.

". . . so we were wondering, Mrs. Bran-, Bantry, if you would like us to, like, pray with you? Like, now? It's Palm Sunday. Next Sunday is Easter."

"What? Pray? Thank you but . . ."

"Because Denise and Anita and me, we have a feeling, we have a really strong feeling, Mrs. Bantry, that Marissa is alive. And Marissa is depending on us. So, if—"

Avril came forward quickly, saying the visit was ended.

"My sister has been under a strain, girls. I'll see you to the door."

The flowers slipped through Leah's fingers. She caught at some of them, clumsily. The others fell to the floor at her feet.

Two of the girls hurried to the door, held open by Avril, with frightened expressions. Jude, pausing, continued to smile in her earnest, pinched way. She'd taken a small black object out of her pocket. "May I take a picture, Mrs. Bantry?"

Before Leah could protest, she raised the camera and clicked the shutter. Leah's hand had flown up to shield her face, instinctively.

Avril said sharply, "Please. The visit is over, girls."

Jude murmured, on her way out, "We will pray for you anyway, Mrs. Bantry. 'Bye!"

The other girls chimed in *Bye! bye!* Avril shut the door behind them.

———

Leah threw the flowers away in the trash. White flowers!

At least, they hadn't brought her calla lilies.

DUTCHWOMAN

. . . in motion. Tracing and retracing The Route. Sometimes on foot, sometimes in her car. Sometimes with Avril but more often alone. "I need to get out! I can't breathe in here! I need to see what Marissa saw."

These days were very long days. And yet, in all of the hours of these days, nothing happened.

Marissa was still gone, still gone.

Like a clock's ticking: still, still gone. Each time you checked, still gone.

She had her cell phone of course. If there was news.

She walked to the Skatskill Day School and positioned herself at the front door of the elementary grades wing, which was the door Marissa would have used, would have left by on Thursday afternoon. From this position she began The Route.

To the front sidewalk and east along Pinewood. Across Pinewood to Mahopac Avenue and continue east past 12th Street, 13th Street, 14th Street, 15th Street. At 15th and Trinity, the witness had claimed to see Mikal Zallman pull Marissa Bantry into his Honda CR-V van, and drive away.

Either it had happened that way, or it had not.

There was only the single witness, a Skatskill Day student whom police would not identify.

Leah believed that Zallman was the man and yet: there was something missing. Like a jigsaw puzzle piece. A very small piece, yet crucial.

Since the girls' visit. Since the bouquet of dazzling white flowers. That small twitchy smile Leah did not wish to interpret as taunting, of the girl named Jude.

We will pray for you anyway, Mrs. Bantry. Bye!

Important for Leah to walk briskly. To keep in motion.

There is a deep-sea creature, perhaps a shark, that must keep in motion constantly, otherwise it will die. Leah was becoming this creature, on land. She believed that news of Marissa's death would come to her only if she, the mother, were still; there was a kind of deadness in being still; but if she was in motion, tracing and retracting Marissa's route . . . "It's like Marissa is with me. Is *me*."

She knew that people along The Route were watching her. Everyone in Skatskill knew her face, her name. Everyone knew why she was out on the street, tracing and retracing The Route. A slender woman in shirt, slacks, dark glasses. A woman who had made a merely perfunctory attempt to disguise herself, dusty-blond hair partly hidden beneath a cap.

She knew the observers were pitying her. And blaming her.

Still, when individuals spoke to her, as a few did each time she traced The Route, they were invariably warm, sympathetic. Some of them, both men and women, appeared to be deeply sympathetic. Tears welled in their eyes. *That bastard* they spoke of Zallman. *Has he confessed yet?*

In Skatskill the name *Zallman* was known now, notorious. That the man was—had been—a member of the faculty at the Skatskill Day School had become a local scandal.

The rumor was, Zallman had a record of prior arrests and convictions as a sexual predator. He'd been fired from previous teaching positions but had somehow managed to be hired at the prestigious Skatskill School. The school's beleaguered principal had given newspaper and TV interviews vigorously denying this rumor, yet it prevailed.

Bantry, Zallman. The names now luridly linked. In the tabloids photos of the missing girl and "suspect" were printed side by side. Several times, Leah's photograph was included as well.

In her distraught state yet Leah was able to perceive the irony of such a grouping: a mock family.

Leah had given up hoping to speak with Zallman. She supposed it was a ridiculous request. If he'd taken Marissa he was a psychopath and you don't expect a psychopath to tell the truth. If he had not taken Marissa . . .

"If it's someone else. They will never find him."

The Skatskill police had not yet arrested Zallman. Temporarily, Zallman had been released. His lawyer had made a terse public statement that he was "fully cooperating" with the police investigation. But what he had told them, what could possibly be of worth that he had told them, Leah didn't know.

Along The Route, Leah saw with Marissa's eyes. The facades of houses. On 15th Street, storefronts. No one had corroborated the eyewitness's testimony about seeing Marissa pulled into a van in full daylight on busy 15th Street. Wouldn't anyone else have seen? And who had the eyewitness been? Since the three girls had dropped by to see her, Leah was left with a new sensation of unease.

Not Marissa's friends. Not those girls.

She crossed Trinity and continued. This was a slight extension of Marissa's route home from school. It was possible, Marissa dropped by the 7-Eleven to buy a snack on Tuesdays/Thursdays when Leah returned home late.

Taped to the front plate-glass door of the 7-Eleven was

HAVE YOU SEEN ME?
MARISSA BANTRY, 11
MISSING SINCE APRIL 10

Marissa's smiling eyes met hers as Leah pushed the door open.

Inside, trembling, Leah removed her dark glasses. She was feeling dazed. Wasn't certain if this was full wakefulness or a fugue state. She was trying to orient herself. Staring at a stack of thick Sunday *New York Times*. The front page headlines were of U.S.-Iraq issues and for a confused moment Leah thought *Maybe none of it has happened yet.*

Maybe Marissa was outside, waiting in the car.

The gentlemanly Indian clerk stood behind the counter in his usual reserved, yet attentive posture. He was staring at her strangely, Leah saw, as he would never have done in the past.

Of course, he recognized her now. Knew her name. All about her. She would never be an anonymous customer again. Leah saw, with difficulty, for her eyes were watering, a second HAVE YOU SEEN ME? taped conspicuously to the front of the cash register.

Wanting to embrace the man, wordless. Wanted to press herself into his arms and burst into tears.

Instead she wandered in one of the aisles. How like an overexposed photograph the store was. So much to see, yet you saw nothing.

Thank God, there were no other customers at the moment.

Saw her hand reach out for—what? A box of Kleenex.

Pink, the color Marissa preferred.

She went to the counter to pay. Smiled at the clerk who was smiling very nervously at her, clearly agitated by the sight of her. His always-so-friendly blond customer! Leah was going to thank him for having posted the notices, and she was going to ask him if he'd ever seen Marissa in his store alone, without her, when suddenly the man said, to her astonishment, "Mrs. Bantry, I know of your daughter and what has happened, that is so terrible. I watch all the time, to see what will come of it." Behind the counter was a small portable TV, volume turned down. "Mrs. Bantry, I want to say, when the police came here, I was nervous and not able to remember so well, but now I do remember, I am more certain, yes I did see your daughter that day, I believe. She did come into the store. She was alone, and then there was another girl. They went out together."

The Indian clerk spoke in a flood of words. His eyes were repentant, pleading.

"When? When was—"

"That day, Mrs. Bantry. That the police have asked about. Last week."

"Thursday? You saw Marissa on Thursday?"

But now he was hesitating. Leah spoke too excitedly.

"I think so, yes. I can not be certain. That is why I did not want to tell the police, I did not want to get into trouble with them. They are impatient with me, I don't know English so well. The questions they ask are not so easy to answer while they wait staring at you."

Leah didn't doubt that the Indian clerk was uneasy with the Caucasian Skatskill police, she was uneasy with them herself.

She said, "Marissa was with a girl, you say? What did this girl look like?"

The Indian clerk frowned. Leah saw that he was trying to be as accurate as possible. He had probably not looked at the girls very closely, very likely he could not distinguish among most of them. He said, "She was older than your daughter, I am sure. She was not too tall, but older. Not so blond-haired."

"You don't know her, do you? Her name?"

"No. I do not know their names any of them." He paused, frowning. His jaws tightened. "Some of them, the older ones, I think this girl is one of them, with their friends they come in here after school and take things. They steal, they break. They rip open bags, to eat. Like pigs they are. They think I can't see them but I know what they do. Five days a week they come in here, many of them. They are daring me to shout at them, and if I would touch them—"

His voice trailed off, tremulous.

"This girl. What did she look like?"

". . . a white skin. More than yours, Mrs. Bantry. A strange color of hair like . . . a color of something red, faded."

He spoke with some repugnance. Clearly, the mysterious girl was not attractive in his eyes.

Red-haired. Pale-red-haired. Who?

Jude Trahern. The girl who'd brought the flowers. The girl who spoke of praying for Marissa's safe return.

Were they friends, then? Marissa had had a friend?

Leah was feeling light-headed. The fluorescent lighting began to tilt and spin. There was something here she could not grasp. *Pray with you. Next Sunday is Easter.* She had more to ask of this kindly man but her mind had gone blank.

"Thank you. I . . . have to leave now."

"Don't tell them, Mrs. Bantry? The police? Please?"

Blindly Leah pushed through the door.

"Mrs. Bantry?" The clerk hurried after her, a bag in his hand. "You are forgetting."

The box of pink Kleenex.

Flying Dutchman. Dutchwoman. She was becoming. Always in motion, terrified of stopping. Returning home to her sister.

Any news?

None.

Behind the drab little mini-mall she was drifting, dazed. She would tell the Skatskill detectives what the Indian clerk had told her—she must tell them. If Marissa had been in the store on Thursday afternoon, then Marissa could not have been pulled into a minivan on 15th Street and Trinity, two blocks back toward school. Not by Mikal Zallman, or by anyone. Marissa must have continued past Trinity. After the 7-Eleven she would have circled back to 15th Street again, and walked another half block to home.

Unless she'd been pulled into the minivan on 15th Street and Van Buren. The eyewitness had gotten the streets wrong. She'd been closer to home.

Unless the Indian clerk was confused about days, times. Or, for what purpose Leah could not bear to consider, lying to her.

"Not him! Not him, too."

She refused to think that was a possibility. Her mind simply shut blank, in refusal.

She was walking now slowly, hardly conscious of her surroundings. A smell of rancid food assailed her nostrils. Only a few employees' cars were parked behind the mini-mall. The pavement was stained and littered, a single Dumpster overflowing trash. At the back of the Chinese takeout several scrawny cats were rummaging in food scraps and froze at Leah's approach before running away in panic.

"Kitties! I'm not going to hurt you."

The feral cats' terror mocked her own. Their panic was hers, misplaced, to no purpose.

Leah wondered: what were the things Marissa did, when Leah wasn't with her? For years they had been inseparable: mother, daughter. When Marissa had been a very small child, even before she could walk, she'd tried to follow her mother everywhere, from room to room. *Mom-my! Where Mom-my going!* Now, Marissa did many things by herself. Marissa was growing up. Dropping by the 7-Eleven, with other children after school. Buying a soft drink, a bag of something crunchy, salty. It was innocent enough. No child should be punished for it. Leah gave Marissa pocket change, as she called it, for just such impromptu purchases, though she disapproved of junk food.

Leah felt a tightening in her chest, envisioning her daughter in the 7-Eleven store the previous Thursday, buying something from the Indian clerk. Then, he had not known her name. A day or two later, everyone in Skatskill knew Marissa Bantry's name.

Of course it probably meant nothing. That Marissa had walked out of the store with a classmate from school. Nothing unusual about that. She could imagine with what polite stiff expressions the police would respond to such a "tip."

In any case, Marissa would still have returned to 15th Street on her way home. So busy, dangerous at that hour of day.

It was there on 15th Street that the "unidentified" classmate had seen Marissa being pulled into the Honda. Leah wondered if the witness was the red-haired Jude.

Exactly what the girl had told police officers, Leah didn't know. The detectives exuded an air, both assuring and frustrating, of knowing more than they were releasing at the present time.

Leah found herself at the edge of the paved area. Staring at a steep hill of uncultivated and seemingly worthless land. Strange how in the midst of an affluent suburb there yet remain these stretches of vacant land, uninhabitable. The hill rose to Highgate Avenue a half mile away, invisible from this perspective. You would not guess that "historical" old homes and mansions were located on the crest of this hill, property worth millions of dollars. The hill was profuse with crawling vines, briars, and stunted trees. The accumulation of years of wind-blown litter and debris made it look like an informal dump. There was a scurrying sound somewhere just inside the tangle of briars, a furry shape that appeared and disappeared so swiftly Leah scarcely saw it.

Behind the Dumpster, hidden from her view, the colony of wild cats lived, foraged for food, fiercely interbred, and died the premature deaths of feral creatures. They would not wish to be "pets"—they had no capacity to receive the affection of humans. They were, in clinical terms, undomesticable.

Leah was returning to her car when she heard a nasal voice in her wake:

"Mrs. Ban-try! H'lo."

Leah turned uneasily to see the frizz-haired girl who'd given her the flowers.

Jude. Jude Trahern.

Now it came to Leah: there was a Trahern Square in downtown Skatskill, named for a Chief Justice Trahern decades ago. One of the old Skatskill names. On Highgate, there was a Trahern estate, one of the larger houses, nearly hidden from the road.

This strange glistening-eyed girl. There was something of the sleek white rat about her. Yet she smiled uncertainly at Leah, clumsily straddling her bicycle.

"Are you following me?"

"Ma'am, no. I . . . just saw you."

Wide-eyed the girl appeared sincere, uneasy. Yet Leah's nerves were on edge, she spoke sharply: "What do you want?"

The girl stared at Leah as if something very bright glared from Leah's face that was both blinding and irresistible. She wiped nervously at her nose. "I . . . I want to say I'm sorry, for saying dumb things before. I guess I made things worse."

Made things worse! Leah smiled angrily, this was so absurd.

"I mean, Denise and Anita and me, we wanted to help. We did the wrong thing, I guess. Coming to see you."

"Were you the 'unidentified witness' who saw my daughter being pulled into a minivan?"

The girl blinked at Leah, blank-faced. For a long moment Leah would have sworn that she was about to speak, to say something urgent. Then she ducked her head, wiped again at her nose, shrugged self-consciously and muttered what sounded like, "I guess not."

"All right. Good-bye. I'm leaving now."

Leah frowned and turned away, her heart beating hard. How badly she wanted to be alone! But the rat-girl was too obtuse to comprehend. With the dogged persistence of an overgrown child she followed Leah at an uncomfortably close distance of about three feet, pedaling her bicycle awkwardly. The bicycle was an expensive Italian make of the kind a serious adult cyclist might own.

At last Leah paused, to turn back. "*Do* you have something to tell me, Jude?"

The girl looked astonished.

" 'Jude'! You remember my name?"

Leah would recall afterward this strange moment. The exultant look in Jude Trahern's face. Her chalky skin mottled with pleasure.

Leah said, "Your name is unusual, I remember unusual names. If you have something to tell me about Marissa, I wish you would."

"Me? What would I know?"

"You aren't the witness from school?"

"What witness?"

"A classmate of Marissa's says she saw a male driver pull Marissa into his minivan on 15th Street. But you aren't that girl?"

Jude shook her head vehemently. "You can't always believe 'eye-witnesses,' Mrs. Bantry."

"What do you mean?"

"It's well known. It's on TV all the time, police shows. An eyewitness swears she sees somebody, and she's wrong. Like, with Mr. Zallman, people are all saying it's him but, like, it might be somebody else."

The girl spoke rapidly, fixing Leah with her widened shining eyes.

"Jude, what do you mean, somebody else? Who?"

Excited by Leah's attention, Jude lost her balance on the bicycle, and nearly stumbled. Clumsily she began walking it again. Gripping the handlebars so tightly her bony knuckles gleamed white.

She was breathing quickly, lips parted. She spoke in a lowered conspiratorial voice.

"See, Mrs. Bantry, Mr. Zallman is like notorious. He comes on to girls if they're pretty-pretty like Marissa. Like some of the kids were saying on TV, he's got these laser-eyes." Jude shivered, thrilled.

Leah was shocked. "If everybody knows about Zallman, why didn't anybody tell? Before this happened? How could a man like that be allowed to teach?" She paused, anxious. Thinking *Did Marissa know? Why didn't she tell me?*

Jude giggled. "You got to wonder why any of them *teach*. I mean, why'd anybody want to hang out with *kids*! Not just some weird guy, but females, too." She smiled, seeming not to see how Leah stared at her. "Mr. Z. is kind of fun. He's this 'master'—he calls himself. Online, you can click onto him he's 'Master of Eyes.' Little kids, girls, he'd come onto after school, and tell them be sure not to tell anybody, see. Or they're be 'real sorry.'" Jude made a twisting motion with her hands as if wringing an invisible neck. "He likes girls with nice long hair he can brush."

"Brush?"

"Sure. Mr. Zallman has this wire brush, like. Calls it a little-doggy-brush. He runs it through your hair for fun. I mean, it used to be fun. I hope the cops took the brush when they arrested him, like for evidence. Hell, he never came on to me, I'm not pretty-pretty."

Jude spoke haughtily, with satisfaction. Fixing Leah with her curious stone-colored eyes.

Leah knew that she was expected to say, with maternal solicitude, *Oh, but you are pretty, Jude! One day, you will be.*

In different circumstances she was meant to frame the rat-girl's hot little face in her cool hands, comfort her. *One day you will be loved, Jude. Don't feel bad.*

"You were saying there might be—somebody else? Not Zallman but another person?"

Jude said, sniffing, "I wanted to tell you before, at your house, but you seemed, like, not to want to hear. And that other lady was kind of glaring at us. She didn't want us to stay."

"Jude, please. Who is this person you're talking about?"

"Mrs. Branly, Bant-ry, like I said Marissa is a good friend of mine. She is! Some kids make fun of her, she's a little slow they say but I don't think Marissa is slow, not really. She tells me all kinds of secrets, see?" Jude paused, drawing a deep breath. "She said, she missed her dad."

It was as if Jude had reached out to pinch her. Leah was speechless.

"Marissa was always saying she hates it here in Skatskill. She wanted to be with her dad, she said. Some place called 'Berkeley'—in California. She wanted to go there to live."

Jude spoke with the ingratiating air of one child informing on another to a parent. Her lips quivered, she was so excited.

Still Leah was unable to respond. Trying to think what to say except her brain seemed to be partly shutting down as if she'd had a small stroke.

Jude said innocently, "I guess you didn't know this, Mrs. Bantry?" She bit at her thumbnail, squinting.

"Marissa told you that? She told you—those things?"

"Are you mad at me, Mrs. Bantry? You wanted me to tell."

"Marissa told you—she wanted to live with her 'dad'? Not with her mother but with her 'dad'?"

Leah's peripheral vision had narrowed. There was a shadowy funnel-shape at the center of which the girl with the chalky skin and frizzed hair squinted and grinned, in a show of repentance.

"I just thought you would want to know, see, Mrs. Bantry? Like, maybe Marissa ran away? Nobody is saying that, everybody thinks it's Mr. Zallman, like the cops are thinking it's got to be him. Sure, maybe it is. But—maybe!—Marissa called her dad, and asked him to come get her? Something weird like that? And it was a secret from you? See, a lot of times Marissa would talk that way, like a little kid. Like, not thinking about her mother's feelings. And I told her, 'Your mom, she's real nice, she'd be hurt real bad, Marissa, if you—' "

Leah couldn't hold back the tears any longer. It was as if she'd lost her daughter for the second time.

MISTAKES

His first was to assume that, since he knew nothing of the disappearance of Marissa Bantry, he could not be "involved" in it.

His second was not to contact a lawyer immediately. As soon as he realized exactly why he'd been brought into police headquarters for questioning.

His third seemed to be to have lived the wrong life.

Pervert. Sex offender. Pedophile.
   Kidnapper/rapist/murderer.
   Mikal Zallman, thirty-one. Suspect.

"Mother, it's Mikal. I hope you haven't seen the news already, I have something very disturbing to tell you . . ."

Nothing! He knew nothing.

The name MARISSA BANTRY meant nothing to him.

Well, not initially. He couldn't be sure.

In his agitated state, not knowing what the hell they were getting at with their questions, he couldn't be sure.

"Why are you asking me? Has something happened to 'Marissa Bantry'?"

Next, they showed him photographs of the girl.

Yes: now he recognized her. The long blond hair, that was sometimes plaited. One of the quieter pupils. Nice girl. He recognized the picture but could not have said the girl's name because, look: "I'm not these kids' teacher, exactly. I'm a 'consultant.' I don't have a homeroom. I don't have regular classes with them. In the high school, one of the math instructors teaches computer science. I don't get to know the kids by name, like their other instructors do."

He was speaking quickly, an edge to his voice. It was uncomfortably cold in the room, yet he was perspiring.

As in a cartoon of police interrogation. *They sweated it out of the suspect.*

Strictly speaking, it wasn't true that Zallman didn't know students' names. He knew the names of many students. Certainly, he knew their faces. Especially the older students, some of whom were extremely bright, and engaging. But he had not known Marissa Bantry's name, the shy little blond child had made so little an impression on him.

Nor had he spoken with her personally. He was certain.

"Why are you asking me about this girl? If she's missing from home what is the connection with *me*?"

That edge to Zallman's voice. Not yet angry, only just impatient.

He was willing to concede, yes: if a child has been missing for more than twenty-four hours that was serious. If eleven-year-old Marissa Bantry was missing, it was a terrible thing.

"But it has nothing to do with *me*."

They allowed him to speak. They were tape recording his precious words. They did not appear to be passing judgment on him, he was not receiving the impression that they believed him involved with the disappearance, only just a few questions to put to him, to aid in their investigation. They explained to him that it was in his best interests to cooperate fully with them, to straighten out the misunderstanding, or whatever it was, a misidentification perhaps, before he left police headquarters.

"Misidentification"? What was that?

He was becoming angry, defiant. Knowing he was God-damned innocent of any wrongdoing, no matter how trivial: traffic violations, parking tickets. *He was innocent!* So he insisted upon taking a lie-detector test.

Another mistake.

Seventeen hours later an aggressive stranger now retained as Mikal Zallman's criminal lawyer was urging him, "Go home, Mikal. If you can, sleep. You will need your sleep. Don't speak with anyone except people you know and trust and assume yourself under surveillance and whatever you do, man—don't try to contact the missing girl's mother."

_____

*Please understand I am not the one. Not the madman who has taken your
beautiful child. There has been some terrible misunderstanding but I swear I
am innocent, Mrs. Bantry, we've never met but please allow me to commis-
erate with you, this nightmare we seem to be sharing.*

Driving home to North Tarrytown. Oncoming headlights blinding
his eyes. Tears streaming from his eyes. Now the adrenaline rush
was subsiding, leaking out like water in a clogged drain, he was beginning to feel a hammering in his head that was the worst headache
pain he'd ever felt in his life.

Jesus! What if it was a cerebral hemorrhage . . .

He would die. His life would be over. It would be judged that his
guilt had provoked the hemorrhage. His name would never be
cleared.

He'd been so cocky and arrogant coming into police headquarters,
confident he'd be released within the hour, and now. A wounded animal limping for shelter. He could not keep up with traffic on route 9,
he was so sick. Impatient drivers sounded their horns. A massive
SUV pulled up to within inches of Zallman's rear bumper.

He knew! Ordinarily he was an impatient driver himself. Disgusted with overly cautious drivers on route 9 and now he'd become
one of these, barely mobile at twenty miles an hour.

Whoever they were who hated him, who had entangled him in
this nightmare, they had struck a first, powerful blow.

Zallman's bad luck, one of his fellow tenants was in the rear lobby of
his building, waiting for the elevator, when Zallman staggered inside. He was unshaven, disheveled, smelling frankly of his body. He
saw the other man staring at him, at first startled, recognizing him;
then with undisguised repugnance.

But I didn't! I am not the one.

The police would not have released me if.

Zallman let his fellow tenant take the elevator up, alone.

Zallman lived on the fifth floor of the so-called condominium village. He had never thought of his three sparely furnished rooms as

"home" nor did he think of his mother's Upper East Side brownstone as "home" any longer: it was fair to say that Zallman had no home.

It was near midnight of an unnamed day. He'd lost days of his life. He could not have stated with confidence the month, the year. His head throbbed with pain. Fumbling with the key to his darkened apartment he heard the telephone inside ringing with the manic air of a telephone that has been ringing repeatedly.

Released for the time being. Keep your cell phone with you at all times for you may be contacted by police. Do not REPEAT DO NOT leave the area. A bench warrant will be issued for your arrest in the event that you attempt to leave the area.

"It isn't that I am innocent, Mother. I know that I am innocent! The shock of it is, people seem to believe that I might not be. A lot of people."

It was a fact. A lot of people.

He would have to live with that fact, and what it meant of Mikal Zallman's place in the world, for a long time.

Keep your hands in sight, sir.

That had been the beginning. His wounded brain fixed obsessively upon that moment, at Bear Mountain.

The state troopers. Staring at him. As if.

(Would they have pulled their revolvers and shot him down, if he'd made a sudden ambiguous gesture? It made him sick to think so. It should have made him grateful that it had not happened but in fact it made him sick.)

Yet the troopers had asked him politely enough if they could search his vehicle. He'd hesitated only a moment before consenting. Sure it annoyed him as a private citizen who'd broken no laws and as a (lapsed) member of the ACLU but why not, he knew there was nothing in the minivan to catch the troopers' eyes. He didn't even smoke marijuana any longer. He'd never carried a concealed weapon, never even owned a gun. So the troopers looked through the van, and found nothing. No idea what the hell they were looking for but he'd felt a gloating sort of relief that they hadn't found it. Seeing the way they were staring at the covers of the paperback books in the back seat he'd tossed there weeks ago and had more or less forgotten.

Female nudes, and so what?

"Good thing it isn't kiddie porn, officers, eh? That stuff is illegal."

Even as a kid Zallman hadn't been able to resist wisecracking at inopportune moments.

Now, he had a lawyer. "His" lawyer.

A criminal lawyer whose retainer was fifteen thousand dollars.

They are the enemy.

Neuberger meant the Skatskill detectives, and beyond them the prosecutorial staff of the district, whose surface civility Zallman had been misinterpreting as a tacit sympathy with him, his predicament. It was a fact they'd sweated him, and he'd gone along with it naively, frankly. Telling him he was not *under arrest* only just *assisting in their investigation*.

His body had known, though. Increasingly anxious, restless, needing to urinate every twenty minutes. He'd been flooded with adrenaline like a cornered animal.

His blood pressure had risen, he could feel pulses pounding in his ears. Damned stupid to request a polygraph at such a time but— he was an innocent man, wasn't he?

Should have called a lawyer as soon as they'd begun asking him about the missing child. Once it became clear that this was a serious situation, not a mere misunderstanding or misidentification by an unnamed "eyewitness." (One of Zallman's own students? Deliberately lying to hurt him? For Christ's sake *why?*) So at last he'd called an older cousin, a corporation attorney, to whom he had not spoken since his father's funeral, and explained the situation to him, this ridiculous situation, this nightmare situation, but he had to take it seriously since obviously he was a suspect and so: would Joshua recommend a good criminal attorney who could get to Skatskill immediately, and intercede for him with the police?

His cousin had been so stunned by Zallman's news he'd barely been able to speak. "Y-You? Mikal? You're arrested—?"

"No. I am not arrested, Andrew."

He believes I might be guilty. My own cousin believes I might be a sexual predator.

Still, within ninety minutes, after a flurry of increasingly desperate phone calls, Zallman had retained a Manhattan criminal lawyer named Neuberger who didn't blithely assure him, as Zallman halfway expected he would, that there was nothing to worry about.

TARRYTOWN RESIDENT QUESTIONED
IN ABDUCTION OF 11-YEAR-OLD

SEARCH FOR MARISSA CONTINUES
SKATSKILL DAY INSTRUCTOR IN POLICE CUSTODY

6TH GRADER STILL MISSING
SKATSKILL DAY INSTRUCTOR QUESTIONED BY POLICE
TENTATIVE IDENTIFICATION OF MINIVAN
BELIEVED USED IN ABDUCTION

MIKAL ZALLMAN, 31, COMPUTER CONSULTANT
QUESTIONED BY POLICE IN CHILD ABDUCTION

ZALLMAN: "I AM INNOCENT"
TARRYTOWN RESIDENT QUESTIONED BY POLICE
IN CHILD ABDUCTION CASE

Luridly spread across the front pages of the newspapers were photographs of the missing girl, the missing girl's mother, and "alleged suspect Mikal Zallman."

It was a local TV news magazine. Neuberger had warned him not to watch TV, just as he should not REPEAT SHOULD NOT answer the telephone if he didn't have caller I.D., and for sure he should not answer his door unless he knew exactly who was there. Still, Zallman was watching TV fortified by a half dozen double-strength Tylenols that left him just conscious enough to stare at the screen disbelieving what he saw and heard.

Skatskill Day students, their faces blurred to disguise their identities, voices eerily slurred, telling a sympathetic female broadcaster their opinions of Mikal Zallman.

Mr. Zallman, he's cool. I liked him okay.

Mr. Zallman is kind of sarcastic I guess. He's okay with the smart kids but the rest of us it's like he's trying real hard and wants us to know.

I was so surprised! Mr. Zallman never acted like that, you know—weird. Not in computer lab.

Mr. Zallman has, like, these laser eyes? I always knew he was scary.

Mr. Zallman looks at us sometimes! It makes you shiver.

Some kids are saying he had, like, a hairbrush? To brush the girls' hair? I never saw it.

This hairbrush Mr. Zallman had, it was so weird! He never used it on me, guess I'm not pretty-pretty enough for him.

He'd help you in the lab after school if you asked. He was real nice to me. All this stuff about Marissa, I don't know. It makes me want to cry.

And there was Dr. Adrienne Cory, principal of Skatskill Day, grimly explaining to a skeptical interviewer that Mikal Zallman whom she had hired two and a half years previously had excellent credentials, had come highly recommended, was a conscientious and reliable staff member of whom there had been no complaints.

No complaints! What of the students who'd just been on the program?

Dr. Cory said, twisting her mouth in a semblance of a placating smile, "Well. We never knew."

And would Zallman continue to teach at Skatskill Day?

"Mr. Zallman has been suspended with pay for the time being."

His first, furious thought was *I will sue.*

His second, more reasonable thought was *I must plead my case.*

He had friends at Skatskill Day, he believed. The young woman who thought herself less-than-happily married, and who'd several times invited Zallman to dinner; a male math teacher, whom he often met at the gym; the school psychologist, whose sense of humor dove-tailed with his own; and Dr. Cory herself, who was quite an intelligent woman, and a kindly woman, who had always seemed to like Zallman.

He would appeal to them. They must believe him!

Zallman insisted upon a meeting with Dr. Cory, face to face. He insisted upon being allowed to present his side of the case. He was informed that his presence at the school was "out of the question" at the present time; a mere glimpse of Zallman, and faculty members as well as students would be "distracted."

If he tried to enter the school building on Monday morning, Zallman was warned, security guards would turn him away.

"But why? What have I done? What have I done that is anything more than rumor?"

Not what Zallman had done but what the public perceived he might have done, that was the issue. Surely Zallman understood?

He compromised, he would meet Dr. Cory on neutral territory, 8 A.M. Monday in the Trahern Square office of the school's legal counsel. He was told to bring his own legal counsel but Zallman declined.

Another mistake, probably. But he couldn't wait for Neuberger, this was an emergency.

"I need to work! I need to return to school as if nothing is wrong, in fact *nothing is wrong*. I insist upon returning."

Dr. Cory murmured something vaguely supportive, sympathetic. She was a kind person, Zallman wanted to believe. She was decent, well-intentioned, she liked him. She'd always laughed at his jokes!

Though sometimes wincing, as if Zallman's humor was a little too abrasive for her. At least publicly.

Zallman was protesting the decision to suspend him from teaching without "due process." He demanded to be allowed to meet with the school board. How could he be suspended from teaching for no reason—wasn't that unethical, and illegal? Wouldn't Skatskill Day be liable, if he chose to sue?

"I swear I did not—*do it. I am not involved*. I scarcely know Marissa Bantry, I've had virtually no contact with the girl. Dr. Cory—Adrienne—these 'eyewitnesses' are lying. This 'barrette' that was allegedly found by police behind my building—someone must have placed it there. Someone who hates me, who wants to destroy me! This has been a nightmare for me but I'm confident it will turn out well. I mean, it can't be proven that I'm involved with—with—whatever has happened to the girl—because I am not involved! I need to come back to work, Adrienne, I need you to demonstrate that you have faith in me. I'm sure that my colleagues have faith in me. Please reconsider! I'm prepared to return to work this morning. I can explain to the students—something! Give me a chance, will you? Even if I'd been arrested—which I am not, Adrienne—under the law I am innocent until proven guilty and I can't be possibly be proven guilty because I—I did not—*I did not do anything wrong.*"

He was struck by a sudden stab of pain, as if someone had driven an ice pick into his skull. He whimpered and slumped forward gripping his hand in his hands.

A woman was asking him, in a frightened voice, "Mr. Zallman? Do you want us to call a doctor?—an ambulance?"

UNDER SURVEILLANCE

He needed to speak with her. He needed to console her.

On the fifth day of the vigil it became an overwhelming need.

For in his misery he'd begun to realize how much worse it was for the mother of Marissa Bantry, than for him who was merely the suspect.

It was Tuesday. Of course, he had not been allowed to return to teach. He had not slept for days except fitfully, in his clothes. He ate standing before the opened refrigerator, grabbing at whatever was inside. He lived on Tylenols. Obsessively he watched TV, switching from channel to channel in pursuit of the latest news of the missing girl and steeling himself for a glimpse of his own face, haggard and hollow-eyed and disfigured by guilt as by acne. *There he is! Zallman!* The only suspect in the case whom police had actually brought into custody, paraded before a phalanx of photographers and TV cameramen to arouse the excited loathing of hundreds of thousands of spectators who would not have the opportunity to see Zallman, and to revile him, in the flesh.

In fact, the Skatskill police had other suspects. They were following other "leads." Neuberger had told him he'd heard that they had sent men to California, to track down the elusive father of Marissa Bantry who had emerged as a "serious suspect" in the abduction.

Yet, in the Skatskill area, the search continued. In the Bear Mountain State Park, and in the Blue Mountain Reserve south of Peekskill. Along the edge of the Hudson River between Peekskill and Skatskill. In parkland and wooded areas east of Skatskill in the Rockefeller State Park. These were search and rescue teams comprised of both professionals and volunteers. Zallman had wanted to volunteer to help with the search for he was desperate to do something but Neuberger had fixed him with a look of incredulity. "Mikal, that is not a good idea. Trust me."

There had been reports of men seen "dumping" mysterious objects from bridges into rivers and streams and there had been further "sightings" of the living girl in the company of her captor or captors at various points along the New York State Thruway and the New England Expressway. Very blond fair-skinned girls between the ages of eight and thirteen resembling Marissa Bantry were being seen everywhere.

Police had received more than one thousand calls and Web site messages and in the media it was announced that *all leads will be followed* but Zallman wondered at this. *All* leads?

He himself called the Skatskill detectives, often. He'd memorized their numbers. Often, they failed to return his calls. He was made to understand that Zallman was no longer their prime suspect— maybe. Neuberger had told him that the girl's barrette, so conspicuously dropped by Zallman's parking space, had been wiped clean of fingerprints: "An obvious plant."

Zallman had had his telephone number changed to an unlisted number yet still the unwanted calls—vicious, obscene, threatening, or merely inquisitive—continued and so he'd had the phone disconnected and relied now upon his cell phone exclusively, carrying it with him as he paced through the shrinking rooms of his condominium apartment. From the fifth floor, at a slant, Zallman could see the Hudson River on overcast days like molten lead but on clear days possessed of an astonishing slate-blue beauty. For long minutes he lost himself in contemplation of the view: beauty that was pure, unattached to any individual, destined to outlive the misery that had become his life.

Nothing to do with me. Nothing to do with human evil.

Desperately he wanted to share this insight with the mother of Marissa Bantry. It was such a simple fact, it might be overlooked.

He went to 15th Street where the woman lived, he'd seen the exterior of the apartment building on TV numerous times. He had not been able to telephone her. He wanted only to speak with her for a few minutes.

It was near dusk of Tuesday. A light chill mist-rain was falling. For a while he stood indecisively on the front walk of the barracks-like building, in khaki trousers, canvas jacket, jogging shoes. His damp hair straggled past his collar. He had not shaved for several days. A sickly radiance shone in his face, he knew he was doing the right thing now crossing the lawn at an angle, to circle to the rear of the building where he might have better luck discovering which of the apartments belonged to Leah Bantry.

Please I must see you.

We must share this nightmare.

Police came swiftly to intercept him, grabbing his arms and cuffing his wrists behind his back.

SACRIFICE

Is she breathing?

. . . Christ!

She isn't . . . is she? *Is* she?

She is. She's okay.

. . . like maybe she's being . . . poisoned?

We were getting so scared! Anita was crying a lot, then Anita was laughing like she couldn't stop. Denise had this eating-thing, she was hungry all the time, stuffing her mouth at meals and in the cafeteria at school then poking a finger down her throat to make herself vomit into a toilet flush-flush-flushing the toilet so if she was at home nobody in her family would hear or if she was at school other girls wouldn't hear and tell on her.

More and more we could see how they were watching us at school, like *somehow they knew*.

Since giving the white flowers to the Corn Maiden's mother nothing felt right. Denise knew, and Anita. Jude maybe knew but would not acknowledge it.

Mothers don't give a shit about their kids. See, it's all pretend.

Jude believed this. She hated the Corn Maiden's mother worse than she hated anybody, just about.

Anita was worried the Corn Maiden was being poisoned, all the strong drugs Jude was making her swallow. The Corn Maiden was hardly eating anything now, you had to mush it up like cottage cheese with vanilla ice cream, open her jaws and spoon it into her mouth then close her jaws and try to make her to swallow, but half the time the Corn Maiden began choking and gagging and the white mush just leaked out of her mouth like vomit.

We were begging, Jude maybe we better . . .

. . . we don't want her to die, like do we?

Jude? *Jude?*

The fun was gone now. Seeing TV news, and all the newspapers even *The New York Times*, and the posters HAVE YOU SEEN ME? and the fifteen-thousand-dollar reward, and all that, that made us laugh like hyenas just a few days ago but wasn't anything to laugh at now, or anyway not much. Jude still scorned the assholes, she called them, and laughed at how they ran around looking for the Corn Maiden practically under their noses out Highgate Avenue.

Jude was doing these weird things. On Monday she came to school with one of the Corn Maiden's butterfly barrettes she was going to wear in her hair but we told her Oh no better not! and she laughed at us but didn't wear it.

Jude talked a lot about fire, "immolation." On the Internet she looked up some things like Buddhists had done a long time ago.

The Sacrifice of the Corn Maiden called for the heart of the captive cut out, and her blood collected in sacred vessels, but you could burn the Corn Maiden, too, and mix her ashes with the soil Jude said.

Fire is a cleaner way, Jude said. It would only hurt at the beginning.

Jude was taking Polaroids all the time now. By the end, Jude would have like fifty of these. We believed that Jude intended to post them on the Internet but that did not happen.

What was done with them, if the police took them away we would not know. They were not ever printed. Maybe they were destroyed.

These were pictures to stare at! In some of them the Corn Maiden was lying on her back in the bier in the beautiful silky fabrics and brocades and she was *so little*. Jude posed her naked and with her hair fanned out and her legs spread wide so you could see the little pink slip between her legs Jude called her cut.

The Corn Maiden's cut was not like ours, it was a little-girl cut and nicer, Jude said. It would never grow *pubic hairs* Jude said, the Corn Maiden would be spared that.

Jude laughed saying she would send the TV stations these pictures they could not use.

Other poses, the Corn Maiden was sitting up or kneeling or on her feet if Jude could revive her, and slap-slap her face so her eyes were open, you would think she was awake, and smiling this wan little smile leaning against Jude, their heads leaning together and Jude grinning like Jude O and the Corn Maiden were floating somewhere above the earth in some Heaven where nobody could reach them, only just look up at them wondering how they'd got there!

Jude had us take these pictures. One of them was her favorite, she said she wished the Corn Maiden's mother could see it and maybe someday she would.

That night, we thought the Corn Maiden would die.

She was shivering and twitching in her sleep like she'd been mostly doing then suddenly she was having like an epileptic fit, her mouth sprang open *Uh-uh-uh* and her tongue protruded wet with spittle and really ugly like a freak and Anita was backing off and whimpering She's going to die! oh God she's going to die! Jude do something she's going to die! and Jude slapped Anita's face to shut her up, Jude was so disgusted. Fat ass, get away. What the fuck do you know. Jude held the Corn Maiden down, the Corn Maiden's skinny arms and legs were shaking so, it was like she was trying to dance laying down and her eyes came open unseeing like a doll's dead glass eyes and Jude was kind of scared now and excited and climbed up onto the bier to lay on her, for maybe the Corn Maiden was cold, so skinny the cold had gotten into her bones, Jude's arms were stretched out like the Corn Maiden's arms and her hands were gripping the Corn Maiden's hands, her legs quivering stretched out the Corn Maiden's legs, and the side of her face against the Corn Maiden's face like they were twin girls hatched from the same egg. I am here, I am Jude I will protect you, in the Valley of the Shadow of Death I will protect you forever AMEN. Till finally the Corn Maiden ceased convulsing and was only just breathing in this long shuddering way, but she was breathing, she would be okay.

Still, Anita was freaked. Anita was trying not to laugh this wild hyena laugh you'd hear from her at school sometimes, like she was being tickled in a way she could not bear so Jude became disgusted and slapped Anita SMACK-SMACK on both cheeks calling her fat ass and stupid cunt and Anita ran out of the storage room like a kicked dog crying, we heard her on the stairs and Jude said, She's next.

On darkspeaklink.com where Jude O bonded with the Master of Eyes Jude showed us IF THERE IS A PERSON THERE IS A PROBLEM. IF THERE IS NO PERSON THERE IS NO PROBLEM. (STALIN)

Jude had never told the Master of Eyes that she was female or male and so the Master of Eyes believed her to be male. She had told him she had taken her captive, did he give her permission to Sacrifice? and the Master of Eyes shot back you are precocious/precious if 13 yrs old & where do you live Jude O? but the thought came to Jude suddenly the Master of Eyes was not her friend who dwelled in several places of the earth simultaneously but an FBI agent pretending to be her soul mate in order to capture her so Jude O disappeared from darkspeak-link.com forever.

YOU ASSHOLES! A SUICIDE NOTE

Jude O knew, it was ending. Four days preceding the Sacrifice and this was the sixth day. No turning back.

Denise was breaking down. Dull/dazed like she'd been hit over the head and in morning homeroom the teacher asked, Denise are you ill and at first Denise did not hear then shaking her head almost you could not hear her *no*.

Anita had not come to school. Anita was hiding away at home, and would betray Jude. And there was no way to get to Anita now, Jude was unable to silence the traitor.

Jude's disciples, she had trusted. Yet she had not truly trusted them knowing they were inferiors.

Denise was begging, Jude I think we better . . .

. . . let the Corn Maiden go?

Because because if she, if . . .

The Corn Maiden becomes Taboo. The Corn Maiden can never be released. Except if somebody takes the Corn Maiden's place the Corn Maiden can never be released.

You want to take the Corn Maiden's place?

Jude, she isn't the Corn Maiden she's M-Marissa Ban—

A flame of righteous fury came over Jude O, SMACK-SMACK with the palm and back of her hand she slapped the offensive face.

When spotted hyenas are born they are usually twins. One twin is stronger than the other and at once attacks the other hoping to tear out its throat and why, because the other would try to kill it otherwise. There is no choice.

At the table at the very rear of the cafeteria where Jude O and her disciples perceived as pathetic misfit losers by their Skatskill Day classmates usually ate their lunches together except today only Jude O and Denise Ludwig, and it was observed how Denise was whimpering and pleading with Jude wiping at her nose in a way repellent to the more fastidious girl who said through clenched jaws I forbid you to cry, I forbid you to make a spectacle of yourself, but Denise continued, and Denise whimpered and begged, and at last a flame of indignation swept over Jude who slapped Denise and Denise stumbled from the table overturning her chair, ran blubbering from the cafeteria in full view of staring others, and in that same instant it seemed that wily Jude O fled through a rear exit running crouched over to the middle school bicycle rack, and fueled by that same passion of indignation Jude bicycled 2.7 miles home to the old Trahern house on Highgate Avenue several times nearly struck by vehicles that swerved to avoid the blind-seeming cyclist and she laughed for she was feeling absolutely no fear now like a hawk riding the crest of an updraft scarcely needing to move its wings to remain aloft, and lethal. A hawk! Jude O was a hawk! If her bicycle had been struck and crushed, if she'd died on Highgate Avenue the Corn Maiden would molder in her bier of silks and brocades, unseen. No one would find the Corn Maiden for a long time.

It is better this way, we will die together.

She would not have requested a jury trial, you had to utter such bullshit to sway a jury. She would have requested a judge merely.

A judge is an aristocrat. Jude O was an aristocrat.

She would have been tried as an adult! Would have insisted.

In the gardener's shed there was a rusted old lawnmower. A can of gasoline half full. You poured the gasoline through the funnel if you could get it open. Jude had experimented, she could get it open.

Her grandmother's old silver lighter engraved with the initials *G.L.T.* Click-click-click and a transparent little bluish-orange flame appeared pretty as a flicking tongue.

She would immolate the Corn Maiden first.

No! Better to die together.

Telling herself calmly *It will only hurt at first. Just for a few seconds and by then it will be too late.*

She laughed to think of it. Like already it was done.

Stealthily entering the house by the rear door. So the old woman watching afternoon TV would not hear.

She was very excited! She was determined to make no error. Already forgetting that perhaps she had erred, allowing both her disciples to escape when she'd known that they were weakening. And confiding in the Master of Eyes believing she could trust him as her twin not recalling the spotted hyena twin, of course you could not trust.

Well, she had learned!

Forced herself to compose the Suicide Note. In her thoughts for a long time (it seemed so, now!) Jude had been composing this with care knowing its importance. It was addressed to *you assholes* for there was no one else.

Smiling to think how *you assholes* would be amazed.

On TV and on-line and in all the papers including *The New York Times* front page.

Whywhy you're asking here's why her hair.

I mean *her hair*! I mean like I saw it in the sun . . .

So excited! Heart beating fast like she'd swallowed a dozen E's. Unlocking the padlock with trembling hands. If Denise had told, already! *Should have killed them both last night. When I had the chance.* Inside the storage room, the Corn Maiden had shifted from the lying-on-her-side position in which Jude had left her that morning after making her eat. This was proof, the Corn Maiden was shrewdly pretending to be weaker than she was. Even in her sickness there was deceit.

Jude left the storage room door open, to let in light. She would not trouble to light the scented candles, so many candles there was not time. And flame now would be for a different purpose.

Squatting breathless over the Corn Maiden, with both thumbs lifting the bruised eyelids.

Milky eyes. Pupils shrunken.

Wake up! It's time it's time.

Feebly the Corn Maiden pushed at Jude. She was frightened, whimpering. Her breath smelled of something rotted. She had not been allowed to brush her teeth since coming to Jude's house, she had not been allowed to bathe herself. Only as Jude and her disciples had bathed her with wetted soapy washclothes.

Know what time it is it's time it's time it's timetimetime!

Don't hurt me please let me go . . .

Jude was the Taboo Priest. Seizing the Corn Maiden's long silky hair in her fist and forcing her down onto the bier scolding No no no no *no* like you would scold a baby.

A baby that is flesh of your flesh but you must discipline.

The immolation would have to be done swiftly, Jude knew. For that traitor-cunt Denise had babbled by now. Fat ass Anita had babbled. Her disciples had betrayed her, they were unworthy of her. They would be so sorry! She would not forgive them, though. Like she would not forgive the Corn Maiden's mother for staring at her like she was a bug or something, loathsome. What she regretted was she would not have time to cut out the Corn Maiden's heart as the Sacrifice demanded.

Lay still, I said it's *time*.

A new thought was coming to her now. She had not hold of it yet, the way you have not yet hold of a dream until it is fully formed like a magnificent bubble inside your head.

Jude had dragged the gasoline can into the storage room, and was spilling gasoline in surges. This could be the priest blessing the Corn Maiden and her bier. The stink of gasoline was strong, that was why the Corn Maiden was revived, her senses sharpening.

No! no! Don't hurt me let me go! I want my mother.

Jude laughed to see the Corn Maiden so rebellious. Actually pushing free of Jude, so weak she could not stand but on hands and knees naked crawling desperately toward the door. Never had Jude left the door open until now and yet the Corn Maiden saw, and comprehended this was escape. Jude smiled seeing how desperate the Corn Maiden, stark naked and her hair trailing the floor like an animal's mane. Oh so skin-and-bones! Her ribs, bony hips, even the ankle bones protruding. Skinny haunches no bigger than Jude's two hands fitted together. And her hinder. *Hinder* was a funny word, a word meant to make you smile. A long time ago a pretty curly-haired woman had been humming and singing daubing sweet-smelling white powder onto Jude's little *hinder* before drawing up her rubber underpants, pulling down Jude's smock embroidered with dancing kittens or maybe it had been a nightgown, and the underpants had been a diaper.

Jude watched, fascinated. She had never seen the Corn Maiden disobey her so openly! It was like a baby just learning to crawl. She had not known the Corn Maiden so desired to live. Thinking suddenly *Better for her to remain alive, to revere me. And I have made my mark on her she will never forget.*

The Priest was infused with the power. The power of life-and-death. She would confer life, it was her decision. Climbing onto the bier spilling gasoline in a sacred circle around her. The stink of gasoline made her sensitive nostrils constrict, her eyes were watering so she could barely see. But she had no need to see. All was within, that she wished to see. *It will only hurt at first. Then it will be too late.* Click-click-clicking the silver lighter with gasoline-slippery fingers until the bright little flame-tongue leapt out.

See what I can do assholes, you never could.

SEPTEMBER

The Little Family

It was their first outing together, at the Croton Falls Nature Preserve. The three of them, as a family.

Of course, Zallman was quick to concede, not an actual *family*.

For the man and woman were not married. Their status as friends/lovers was yet undefined. And the girl was the woman's child, alone.

Yet if you saw them, you would think *family*.

It was a bright warm day in mid-September. Zallman who now measured time in terms of before/after was thinking the date was exactly five months *after*. But this was a coincidence merely.

From Yonkers, where he now lived, Zallman drove north to Mahopac to pick up Leah Bantry and her daughter Marissa at their new home. Leah and Marissa had prepared a picnic lunch. The Croton Falls Nature Preserve, which Leah had only recently discovered, was just a few miles away.

A beautiful place, Leah had told Zallman. So quiet.

Zallman guessed this was a way of saying *Marissa feels safe here*.

Leah Bantry was working now as a medical technician at Woman/Space, a clinic in Mahopac, New York. Mikal Zallman was temporarily teaching middle school math at a large public school in Yonkers where he also assisted the soccer/basketball/baseball coach.

Marissa was enrolled in a small private school in Mahopac without grades or a formal curriculum in which students received special tutoring and counseling as needed.

Tuition at the Mahopac Day School was high. Mikal Zallman was helping with it.

No one can know what you and your daughter went through. I feel so drawn to you both, please let me be your friend!

Before Zallman had known Leah Bantry, he had loved her. Knowing her now he was confirmed in his love. He vowed to bear this secret lightly until Leah was prepared to receive it.

She wanted no more emotion in her life, Leah said. Not for a long time.

Zallman wondered: what did that mean? And did it mean what it meant, or was it simply a way of saying *Don't hurt me! Don't come near.*

He liked it that Leah encouraged Marissa to call him Uncle Mikal. This suggested he might be around for a while. So far, in Zallman's presence at least, Marissa did not call him anything at all.

Zallman saw the girl glance at him, sometimes. Quick covert shy glances he hesitated to acknowledge.

There was a tentative air about them. The three of them.

As if (after the media nightmare, this was quite natural) they were being observed, on camera.

Zallman felt like a tightrope walker. He was crossing a tightrope high above a gawking audience, and there was no safety net beneath. His arms were extended for balance. He was terrified of falling but he must go forward. If at this height your balance is not perfect, it will be lethal.

In the nature preserve in the bright warm autumnal sunshine the adults walked together at the edge of a pond. To circle the pond required approximately thirty minutes. There were other visitors to the preserve on this Sunday afternoon, families and couples.

The girl wandered ahead of the adults, though never far ahead. Her behavior was more that of a younger child than a child of eleven. Her movements were tentative, sometimes she paused as if she were out of breath. Her skin was pale and appeared translucent. Her eyes were deep-socketed, wary. Her pale blond hair shimmered in the sun. It had been cut short, feathery, falling to just below her delicate eggshell ears.

After her ordeal in April, Marissa had lost much of her beautiful long hair. She'd been hospitalized for several weeks. Slowly she had regained most of the weight she'd lost so abruptly. Still she was anemic, Leah was concerned that there had been lasting damage to Marissa's kidneys and liver. She suffered from occasional bouts of tachycardia, of varying degrees of severity. At such times, her mother held her tight, tight. At such times the child's runaway heartbeat and uncontrollable shivering seemed to the mother a demonic third presence, a being maddened by terror.

Both mother and daughter had difficulty sleeping. But Leah refused prescription drugs for either of them.

Each was seeing a therapist in Mahopac. And Marissa also saw Leah's therapist for a joint session with her mother, once a week.

Leah confided in Zallman, "It's a matter of time. Of healing. I have faith, Marissa will be all right."

Leah never used such terms as *normal*, *recovered*.

Mikal Zallman had been the one to write to Leah Bantry of course. He had felt the desperate need to communicate with her, even if she had not the slightest wish to communicate with him.

I feel that we have shared a nightmare. We will never understand it. I don't know what I can offer you other than sympathy, commiseration. During the worst of the nightmare I had almost come to think that I was responsible . . .

After Marissa was discharged from the hospital, Leah took her away from Skatskill. She could not bear living in that apartment another day, she could not bear all that reminded her of the nightmare. She was surrounded by well-intentioned neighbors, and through the ordeal she had made several friends; she had been offered work in the area. If she'd wished to return to work at the Nyack Clinic, very likely Davitt Stoop would have allowed her to return. He had reconciled with his wife, he was in a forgiving mood. But Leah had no wish to see the man again, ever. She had no wish to drive across the Tappan Zee Bridge again, ever.

Out of the ordeal had come an unexpected alliance with her sister Avril. While Marissa was in the hospital, Avril had continued to stay in Skatskill; one or the other of the two sisters was always in Marissa's hospital room. Avril had taken an unpaid leave from her job in Washington, she helped Leah find another job and to relocate in Mahopac, fifty miles north in hilly Putnam County.

Enough of Westchester County! Leah would never return.

She was so grateful for Avril's devotion, she found herself at a loss for words.

"Leah, come on! It's what any sister would do."

"No. It is not what any sister would do. It's what my sister would do. God damn I love you, Avril."

Leah burst into tears. Avril laughed at her. The sisters laughed together, they'd become ridiculous in their emotions. Volatile and unpredictable as ten-year-olds.

Leah vowed to Avril, she would never take anyone for granted again. Never anything. Not a single breath! Never again.

When they'd called her with the news: *Marissa is alive.*

That moment. Never would she forget that moment.

In their family only Avril knew: police had tracked Marissa's elusive father to Coos Bay, Oregon. There, he had apparently died in 1999 in a boating mishap. The medical examiner had ruled the cause of death "inconclusive." There had been speculation that he'd been murdered . . .

Leah hadn't been prepared for the shock she'd felt, and the loss.

Now, he would never love her again. He would never love his beautiful daughter again. He would never make things right between them.

She had never spoken his name aloud to Marissa. She would never speak it aloud. As a younger child Marissa used to ask Where is Daddy? When will Daddy come back? But now, never.

The death of Marissa's father in Coos Bay, Oregon, was a mystery, but it was a mystery Leah Bantry would not pursue. She was sick of mystery. She wanted only clarity, truth. She would surround herself with good decent truthful individuals for the remainder of her life.

Mikal Zallman agreed. No more mysteries!

You become exhausted, you simply don't care. You care about surviving. You care about the banalities of life: *closure, moving on.* Before the nightmare he'd have laughed at such TV talk-show jargon but now, no.

Of Leah Bantry and Mikal Zallman, an unlikely couple, Zallman was the more verbal, the more edgy. He was from a tribe of talkers, he told Leah. Lawyers, financiers, high-powered salesmen. A rabbi or two. For Zallman, just to wake up in the morning in Yonkers, and not in Skatskill, was a relief. And not in April, during that siege of nightmare. To lift his head from the pillow and not wince with pain as if broken glass were shifting inside his skull. To be able to open a newspaper, switch on TV news, without seeing his own craven likeness. To breathe freely, not-in-police-custody. Not the object of a mad girl's vengeance.

Mad girl was the term Zallman and Leah used, jointly. Never would they utter the name *Jude Trahern*.

Why had the mad girl abducted Marissa? Why, of all younger children she might have preyed upon, had she chosen Marissa? And why had she killed herself, why in such a gruesome way, self-immolation like a martyr? These questions would never be answered. The cowed girls who'd conspired with her in the abduction had not the slightest clue. Something about an Onigara Indian sacrifice! They could only repeat brainlessly that they hadn't thought the mad girl was serious. They had only just followed her direction, they had wanted to be her friend.

To say that the girl had been *mad* was only a word. But the word would suffice.

Zallman said in disgust, "To know all isn't to forgive all. To know all is to be sickened by what you know." He was thinking of the Holocaust, too: a cataclysm in history that defied all explanation.

Leah said, wiping at her eyes, "I would not forgive her, under any circumstances. She wasn't 'mad,' she was evil. She took pleasure in hurting others. She almost killed my daughter. I'm glad that she's dead, she's removed herself from us. But I don't want to talk about her, Mikal. Promise me."

Zallman was deeply moved. He kissed Leah Bantry then, for the first time. As if to seal an understanding.

Like Leah, Zallman could not bear to live in the Skatskill area any longer. Couldn't breathe!

Without exactly reinstating Zallman, the principal and board of trustees of Skatskill Day had invited him back to teach. Not immediately, but in the fall.

A substitute was taking his place at the school. It was believed to be most practical for the substitute to finish the spring term.

Zallman's presence, so soon after the ugly publicity, would be "distracting to students." Such young, impressionable students. And their anxious parents.

Zallman was offered a two-year renewable contract at his old salary. It was not a very tempting contract. His lawyer told him that the school feared a lawsuit, with justification. But Zallman said the hell with it. He'd lost interest in combat.

And he'd lost interest in computers, overnight.

Where he'd been fascinated by the technology, now he was bored. He craved something more substantial, of the earth and time. Computers were merely technique, like bodiless brains. He would take a temporary job teaching math in a public school, and he would apply to graduate schools to study history. A Ph.D. program in American studies. At Columbia, Yale, Princeton.

Zallman didn't tell Leah what revulsion he sometimes felt, waking before dawn and unable to return to sleep. Not for computers but for the Zallman who'd so adored them.

How arrogant he'd been, how self-absorbed! The lone wolf who had so prided himself on aloneness.

He'd had enough of that now. He yearned for companionship, someone to talk with, make love with. Someone to share certain memories that would otherwise fester in him like poison.

In late May, after Leah Bantry and her daughter Marissa had moved away from Skatskill—a departure excitedly noted in the local media—Zallman began to write to her. He'd learned that Leah had taken a position at a medical clinic in Mahopoc. He knew the area, to a degree: an hour's drive away. He wrote single-page, thoughtfully composed letter to her not expecting her to reply, though hoping that she might. *I feel so close to you! This ordeal that has so changed our lives.* He'd studied her photographs in the papers, the grieving mother's drawn, exhausted face. He knew that Leah Bantry was a few years older than he, that she was no longer in contact with Marissa's father. He sent her postcards of works of art: Van Gogh's sunflowers, Monet's water lilies, haunted landscapes of Caspar David Friedrich and gorgeous autumnal forests of Wolf Kahn. In this way Zallman courted Leah Bantry. He allowed this woman whom he had never met to know that he revered her. He would put no pressure on her to see him, not even to respond to him.

In time, Leah Bantry did respond.

They spoke on the phone. They made arrangements to meet. Zallman was nervously talkative, endearingly awkward. He seemed overwhelmed by Leah's physical presence. Leah was more wary, reticent. She was a beautiful woman who looked her age, she wore no makeup, no jewelry except a watch; her fair blond hair was threaded with silver. She smiled, but she did not speak much. She liked it that this man would do the talking, as men usually did not. Mikal Zallman was a personality of a type Leah knew, but at a distance. Very New York, very intense. Brainy, but naive. She guessed that his family had money, naturally Zallman scorned money. (But he'd been reconciled with his family, Zallman said, at the time of the ordeal. They had been outraged on his behalf and had insisted upon paying his lawyer's exorbitant fees.) During their conversation, Leah recalled how they'd first met at the Skatskill school, and how Zallman the computer expert had walked away from her. So arrogant! Leah would tease him about that, one day. When they became lovers perhaps.

Zallman's hair was thinning at the temples, there was a dented look to his cheeks. His eyes were those of a man older than thirty-one or -two. He'd begun to grow a beard, a goatee, to disguise his appearance, but you could see that it was a temporary experiment, it would not last. Yet Leah thought Mikal Zallman handsome, in his way rather romantic. A narrow hawkish face, brooding eyes. Quick to laugh at himself. She would allow him to adore her, possibly one day she would adore him. She was not prepared to be hurt by him.

Eventually she would tell him the not-quite-true *I never believed you were the one to take Marissa, Mikal. Never!*

The little family, as Zallman wished to think them, ate their picnic lunch, and what a delicious lunch it was, on a wooden table on the bank of a pond, beneath a willow tree so exquisitely proportioned it looked like a work of art in a children's storybook. He noted that Marissa still had trouble with food, ate slowly and with an air of caution, as if, with each mouthful, she was expecting to encounter broken glass. But she ate most of a sandwich, and half an apple Leah peeled for her, since "skins" made her queasy. And afterward tramping about the pond admiring snowy egrets and great blue herons and wild swans. Everywhere were lushly growing cattails, rushes, flaming sumac. There was a smell of moist damp earth and sunlight on water and in the underbrush red-winged blackbirds were flocking in a festive cacophony. Leah lamented, "But it's too soon! We're not ready for winter." She sounded genuinely hurt, aggrieved.

Zallman said, "But Leah, snow can be nice, too."

Marissa, who was walking ahead of her mother and Mr. Zallman, wanted to think this was so: *snow, nice*. She could not clearly remember snow. Last winter. Before April, and after April. She knew that she had lived for eleven years and yet her memory was a windowpane covered in cobwebs. Her therapists were kindly soft-spoken women who asked repeatedly about what had happened to her in the cellar of the old house, what the bad girls had done to her, for it was healthy to remember, and to speak of what she remembered, like draining an absess they said, and she should cry, too, and be angry; but it was difficult to have such emotions when she couldn't remember clearly. What are you feeling, Marissa, she was always being asked, and the answer was *I don't know* or *Nothing!* But that was not the right answer.

Sometimes in dreams she saw, but never with opened eyes.

With opened eyes, she felt blind. Sometimes.

The bad girl had fed her, she remembered. Spoon-fed. She'd been so hungry! So grateful.

All adults are gone. All our mothers.

Marissa knew: that was a lie. The bad girl had lied to her.

Still, the bad girl had fed her. Brushed her hair. Held her when she'd been so cold.

The sudden explosion, flames! The burning girl, terrible shrieks and screams—Marissa had thought at first it was herself, on fire and screaming. She was crawling upstairs but was too weak and she fainted and someone came noisy and shouting to lift her in his arms and it was three days later Mommy told her when she woke in the hospital, her head so heavy she could not lift it.

Mommy and Mr. Zallman. She was meant to call him "Uncle Mikal" but she could not.

Mr. Zallman had been her teacher in Skatskill. But he behaved as if he didn't remember any of that. Maybe Mr. Zallman had not remembered her, Marissa had not been one of the good students. He had only seemed to care for the good students, the others were invisible to him. He was not "Uncle Mikal" and it would be wrong to call him that.

At this new school everybody was very nice to her. The teachers knew who she was, and the therapists and doctors. Mommy said they had to know or they could not help her. One day, when she was older, she would move to a place where nobody knew Marissa Bantry. Away out in California.

Mommy would not wish her to leave. But Mommy would know why she had to leave.

At this new school, that was so much smaller than Skatskill Day, Marissa had a few friends. They were shy wary thin-faced girls like herself. They were girls who, if you only just glanced at them, you would think they were missing a limb; but then you would see, no they were not. They were *whole girls*.

Marissa liked her hair cut short. Her long silky hair the bad girls had brushed and fanned out about her head, it had fallen out in clumps in the hospital. Long hair made her nervous now. Through her fingers at school sometimes lost in a dream she watched girls with hair rippling down their backs like hers used to, she marveled they were oblivious to the danger.

They had never heard of the Corn Maiden! The words would mean nothing to them.

Marissa was a reader now. Marissa brought books everywhere with her, to hide inside. These were storybooks with illustrations. She read slowly, sometimes pushing her finger beneath the words. She was fearful of encountering words she didn't know, words she was supposed to know but did not know. Like a sudden fit of coughing. Like a spoon shoved into your mouth before you were ready. Mommy had said Marissa was safe now from the bad girls and from any bad people, Mommy would take care of her but Marissa knew from reading stories that this could not be so. You had only to turn the page, something would happen.

Today she had brought along two books from the school library: *Watching Birds!* and *The Family of Butterflies*. They were books for readers younger than eleven, Marissa knew. But they would not surprise her.

Marissa is carrying these books with her, wandering along the edge of the pond a short distance ahead of Mommy and Mr. Zallman. There are dragonflies in the cattails like floating glinting needles. There are tiny white moth-butterflies, and beautiful large orange monarchs with slow-pulsing wings. Behind Marissa, Mommy and Mr. Zallman are talking earnestly. Always they are talking, it seems.

Maybe they will be married and talk all the time and Marissa will not need to listen to them, she will be invisible.

A red-winged blackbird swaying on a cattail calls sharply to her. *In the Valley of the Shadow of Death I will protect you AMEN.*